A Game of Lies

ALSO BY REBECCA CANTRELL

A Trace of Smoke
A Night of Long Knives

REBECCA CANTRELL

A Game of Lies

A TOM DOHERTY ASSOCIATES BOOK
NEW YORK

This is a work of fiction. All of the characters, organizations, and events portrayed in this novel are either products of the author's imagination or are used fictitiously.

A GAME OF LIES

Copyright © 2011 by Rebecca Cantrell

A Forge Book
Published by Tom Doherty Associates, LLC
175 Fifth Avenue
New York, NY 10010

www.tor-forge.com

Forge® is a registered trademark of Tom Doherty Associates, LLC.

ISBN 978-0-7653-2733-8

First Edition: July 2011

Printed in the United States of America

0 9 8 7 6 5 4 3 2 1

To my husband, my son, and the athletes of the 1936 Olympics

Acknowledgments

Many people helped in the writing of this novel. My wonderful agents, Elizabeth Evans, Mary Alice Kier, and Anna Cottle, always contribute thoughtful edits and work so hard to help Hannah through her journeys. Kristin Sevick at Tor Forge works hard to keep Hannah and all her books on track. They work backstage, but the books would not be possible without them.

Many others selflessly and repeatedly contributed expertise: David Lang lent me his authentic 1936 Olympic album and I promise I washed my hands before opening it; Keely Costedoat shared information about her beloved teacher and 1936 Olympic gold medalist, Archie Williams; Dr. Horton McCurdy provided expertise that I can't list here because it would be a spoiler (if you go Google him, you are on your own); Robert Coleman at the U.S. Holocaust Memorial Museum recommended excellent reference material; Eugenia Ekhardt at the Gesellschaft zur Förderung und Sammlung aus Städtereinigung und Ensorgungswirtschaft sent me period photographs; Roland Drescher at the Berliner U-Bahn Museum provided historical subway maps; and Roger Heath and Richard Frajola answered my philatelic questions. If, in spite of all their efforts, I made mistakes, I have only myself to blame.

Thanks are also due to my wonderful writer companions, including the talented, tough, and transcendent members of Kona Ink: Karen Hollinger, Judith Heath, Kathryn Wadsworth, and David Deardorff.

The writer directors with their powerful visual sensibilities and supreme tact: Mischa Livingstone and Richard Gorey. Much gratitude must also flow to Joie Gavigan Hinden, my favorite hot chick, for injecting flamboyance and fun into my writing and my life.

Thanks to those friends who helped in a million ways big and small: Kelli Stanley, Tana Hall, Dan Mayer, and Peter Tuite. But the biggest thanks of all go to those who make it all happen and make it all matter: my mother, my tireless and supportive husband, and the most wonderful son in the world. Thank you.

A Game of Lies

1

The crowd pushed the three of us between the Marathon Towers toward the Berlin Olympic Stadium. The left tower displayed a simple clock. On the right, both politically and geographically, hung a twisted iron cross—the swastika. I understood the message: It was 1936, and the time of the Nazis had come.

Inside the stadium, I shied away from the enclosed white cabins that signaled press boxes. The journalists inside knew me as German crime reporter Hannah Vogel, wanted by the Gestapo for kidnapping the young son of the now-deceased Ernst Röhm. I nervously tilted my wide-brimmed hat to conceal my face and moved with the crowd down the stairs. Surely I would be difficult to notice among so many faces.

My current identity was Adelheid Zinsli, neutral Swiss reporter and, hopefully incognito, part-time spy for the British. I looked over at my contact, SS Hauptsturmführer Lars Lang, as we moved toward our seats in the stadium. Years of our deadly game made most trips feel routine, but this time I was frightened.

Lars and I pretended to be lovers, a fiction he enjoyed, and every few months, we switched off weekends in our home cities of Berlin and Zürich. But instead of a few days, my editor had insisted that this time I stay in Berlin for a full two weeks to cover the Olympic Games. To keep my job, I had agreed to attend events clogged with my old colleagues.

The crowd stopped and I bumped against Lars's friend, chemistry professor Andreas Huber. When he caught my arm, his sweaty hand lingered there.

I pulled my arm free. He let go reluctantly, and I shot him an inquisitive glance. Lars did not seem to notice. "Forgive me for running into you," I said.

"Of course." Andreas looked down at me with a crooked smile. "Quite a crowd."

"I believe that the German government expects one hundred thousand people for the opening ceremony." I quoted the statistic just to make conversation. I did not add that what the Nazis expected, they too often made happen.

"I hope it doesn't rain on them all." Andreas looked at the overcast sky.

"We will have to hope for sunlight," I said. "Even the Führer cannot control the weather—"

"There's a bar nearby," Lars interrupted. He pushed his black hair back. Longer now than he usually kept it, the new length made him look less militaristic. "We have time for another belt."

"I must stay in the stadium. For the paper." I hiked my leather satchel up on my shoulder. A drink sounded like just the thing to calm my nerves, but Lars did not need another one.

"So dedicated." Lars glared at me. "To your job."

"Not such a bad quality, dedication." Andreas took Lars's arm and led us down the nearest row to a seat at the end. A staunch party man, he understood the possible consequences of Lars's indiscretions. And his own responsibility to report them.

Lars sat, peeled off his dark brown suit jacket, clumsily folded it in half, and rolled up his wrinkled shirtsleeves. He caught me watching and blew me a sloppy kiss. If my life did not depend on the world thinking we were lovers, I would have left without a backward glance. Instead I put a warning hand on his bare arm.

Although he was not, he looked harmless in civilian garb. Ordinarily, he cleaved to his black SS uniform, but an order had come down, requesting all SS and SA members to refrain from wearing uniforms to the Games.

The German government had issued the order in response to criticism from the Winter Olympics in Garmisch-Partenkirchen the previous winter. Reporters had commented on the number of uniformed Germans in the crowds. This time we would have to guess how many men were trained for warfare.

Although I noted the new order, I would not write about it. If I did, I would not be able to move freely into Germany. Instead of exposing Nazi politics, any story I wrote would have to extol Nazi pageantry.

Indeed, it felt like a royal court with the peasants awaiting a thundering and massive coronation. I spotted a complete orchestra, several military bands with gleaming brass instruments, and a choir dressed in white that must have numbered a thousand. All calculated to impress German and international spectators. Nazis staged spectacles as cleverly as ancient Greeks.

My eleven-year-old adopted son, Anton, was far fonder than I of such events. He would have adored it. I wished I could take photographs for him, but foreign journalists were forbidden from taking pictures at the Games. I would tell Anton details when I got back home and retrieved him from Boris, my onetime lover, but for now I tried not to think of him. Superstitious, I knew, but I did not like to bring even thoughts of Anton into Germany these days.

As I searched for a pen, my fingers rolled over my perfume atomizer, a costly French gift from Boris. The tiny mother-of-pearl creation was called a Le Kid and evoked memories of the Charlie Chaplin movie and happy times together.

When this assignment came up, Boris had begged me to stay safe in Switzerland. After I refused, he ended our five-year relationship. It had been more than a month, but I still felt unmoored. I woke every night with my hand searching for him across empty sheets.

I dropped the atomizer and rooted around until I found my pen. I sketched the arc of the stadium first, then the crowd, the bands, the special booths, and the far-off oval of the field. I had often drawn pictures of courtroom scenes in my days as a crime reporter, and I enjoyed using the skills again. A shadow fell across the page and I looked up.

Overhead, the *Hindenburg* ponderously circled the stadium. A white Olympic flag, bigger than a house, flapped under her gondola. The familiar black swastika stood out on her tail. The Nazis owned even the skies.

Although Anton and I had traveled by zeppelin from South America to Germany a few years before, the giant silver shape made me nervous. One spark in the wrong location, and explosive hydrogen would ignite and shower a stadium of eager spectators, including me, with flaming debris.

Andreas followed my gaze. "They are very safe. All precautions have been taken to ensure it."

"Yet hydrogen is quite flammable, is it not?" I countered.

"Under the correct conditions, everything is explosive." Lars draped a heavy arm across my shoulders and I gave him an annoyed look. "And don't I always protect you?"

"So far, we have escaped fiery death," I said. "But that is no reason to let our guard down."

Andreas laughed.

"Must you always keep your guard up?" Lars leaned in close and mouthed the word *Hannah*.

If he said my real name aloud, fiery death might look like a good option, and he knew it. I turned the worry in my voice to anger. "It has served me well so far."

In the past, I had relied on his natural reserve and the caution he had cultivated during his years as a policeman to maintain enough discretion to keep us both out of trouble. But, as with everything else, those rules had changed. I had to figure out a strategy to deal with him before he got us both killed.

To spite me, he kissed me on the nose. I smelled Korn schnapps. "Back in a flash, Spatz."

I wanted to tell him that I was not his sparrow. Instead, I smiled so unconvincingly that he snorted out a laugh. He forced his way down the row and hastened up the stairs. I hoped his destination was the men's room and not the bar. I yearned to abandon everything and head back to Switzerland, but I worried about how I could support Anton without the newspaper job. We did not have Boris to rely on anymore.

I moved to the seat next to Andreas, leaving my satchel to hold Lars's seat from the crowds that thronged into the stadium. The smell of the antiseptic tar soap Andreas favored drifted to me. He and Lars seemed like an odd match. They had met back when Lars was still a policeman and Andreas often testified as an expert witness about the presence of poison in corpses. I wondered what they had in common, save an early interest in National Socialism. Perhaps they had grown close during those protracted and fevered meetings.

"How long has he been like this?" I asked in a low voice to prevent those nearby from overhearing. The noise of so many excited voices chattering made it unlikely, but you always had to be careful in Germany these days.

"Off and on for about two months. Worse in the past month."

My stomach sank. He had been drinking and perhaps indiscreet for over a month. "Do you know why?"

"Do you?" His brown eyes were curious and perhaps accusatory. What had Lars told him about our relationship? Did he know it was a sham?

"Should I?" I met his challenge with one of my own.

He spread his thin hands wide in a gesture of peace. "I am not trying to make problems. I fear you have enough of your own."

"Have I?" I struggled to appear calm while I wondered what he thought my problems were. Had Lars told him the true reason for my trips to Berlin?

"I apologize." Andreas kept voice low as well. "I did not intend to imply anything."

"What would there be to imply?"

"Indeed," he answered.

We sat in awkward silence until Lars slid in next to me, face shades paler. He gave me an apologetic look. "I might have a touch of stomach flu."

"I hope you feel better soon," I said, as if I believed that his trip to the men's room had more to do with flu than it did with alcohol. At least now he seemed fairly sober.

When the orchestra curtailed our conversation, I closed my eyes in relief, concentrating on the music and the weak sun on my arms. With my eyes shut, I did not see the swastikas, and I pretended that Germany was as free as it had been when I first escaped with Anton five years before.

But it was not, and that was why I was here. I had to do everything I could to keep the Nazis from taking over Europe as they had taken over Germany. The Nazi regime had killed many already, and I feared that many more would die before they were removed from power. Anything I could do to save those lives, I had to do, and not just because it was morally right, but also because I bore some blame. To save Anton, I had traded my chance to discredit Nazi leader Ernst Röhm by publishing his sexually explicit letters. Perhaps their publication would have made no difference, but perhaps my decision had helped the Nazis more than I dared to contemplate.

The music faded. Fanfare trumpeted from the fortresslike Marathon Towers. Hitler must have arrived. I opened my eyes and sighed. No more pretending.

Instead I pulled battered field glasses from my satchel and trained them on Hitler as he descended the stairs in a khaki suit and knee-high boots in front of two men in dark frock coats and top hats. Both wore the heavy gold chains of the International Olympic Committee around their necks. A larger group trailed behind.

Everyone rose to scream and clap. I stood, too. Tens of thousands of arms shot up in the Hitler salute, mine, regrettably, among them. I dared not stand out. I wished I knew how many in this forest of arms saluted out of fear, and how many out of patriotism. I quickly dropped my arm and picked up my field glasses again with both hands. Surely demonstrating a desire to see the Führer up close would excuse me from continuing the vile salute.

Hitler marched around the crimson cinder track while strains of Wagner, his favorite composer, rose above adoring screams. A girl in a cornflower blue sundress, blond braids pinned up in a wreath, ran to Hitler. She looked about five, the same age Anton had been when he showed up dirty and alone on my doorstep. I hated the way the little girl lent the proceedings an air of gentleness and innocence.

She dropped into a curtsy, bare knee pressed onto red cinders. Her upraised hands offered a bouquet of posies. Smiling indulgently, Hitler took the flowers and pulled her to her feet. He patted her head once before trotting to his loge of honor. The child scampered off the field and I lost sight of her in the crowd. Her sweet and simple gesture would be reported across the globe tomorrow. Another shrewd Nazi propaganda victory.

I glanced at Lars's wristwatch. I needed to sneak away soon to meet my erstwhile mentor, Peter Weill. Peter claimed to have uncovered something that would change the course of the war we were both certain would come. Thousands of lives were at stake, he had said.

I had a few minutes before my meeting with Peter, but I decided to leave while the men were distracted so I would not have to invent an excuse. I had not told Lars about my appointment and hoped to keep it from him. The less he knew about anything beyond our work together, the better, especially now that he seemed to be falling apart.

I stepped through standing crowds and lifted voices, hoping that Lars would not follow. I suspected that he trusted me no more than I trusted him, and he kept very close to me when I visited Berlin, but perhaps he was drunk and distracted enough by the spectacle to let me alone.

I hurried up the stone stairs. At the top, I turned and ducked behind one of the wide square pillars lining the corridor that circled the upper rim of the stadium. Spectators filled even the topmost row of seats, but the pillar hid me from their view. With all eyes on the spectacle, I felt blessedly alone. I breathed in the dusty smell of limestone.

Silence descended as the last notes of the German national anthem died away. The "Horst Wessel Song" followed. Written by a Nazi killed by a Communist in 1930, it had served as the accompaniment for more Nazi events than I cared to think about. A hundred voices sang it when a Nazi mob attacked Anton and me in front of Wertheim, a Jewish-owned department store, in 1931.

A hand grabbed my shoulder. I gasped.

"Shush," said a familiar rasping voice.

"Peter!" Rumpled navy suit, fedora tilted too far back on his head, grin as wide as ever. Peter Weill had mentored me at the *Berliner Tageblatt* and insisted that I take over his crime beat when he moved to Dresden to retire. I had not seen him in years, since before I fled, but it was his urgent message, more than anything else, that made me brave coming to the Games. Seeing him, I was glad I had.

His faded blue eyes sparkled with excitement when he pulled me into an embrace. Never large, now he felt like a bundle of sticks. I hugged him back with care, conscious of every one of his seventy-four years.

"Hannah!" I winced at the sound of my name. He gave me an appraising look. "It is good to see you again."

I stepped back and glanced up and down the empty corridor. "Likewise. But we are supposed to meet farther down. How did you find me here, and early?"

"Always so suspicious." He chuckled. "Made you the best Peter Weill."

"After you, of course." I had taken his name when I took over his beat at the newspaper; someone else used it now. "So, how did you find me?"

"I've been watching you for over an hour."

I imagined him dividing the stadium into sections and methodically sweeping each with binoculars, patient and thorough. And, like so many things he did, it had worked despite the odds. "Have you?"

"You and your SS consort. With your blond hair and blue eyes, you are quite the Aryan prize, I see."

"Why do you think he is SS?" I knew better than to lie to Peter directly.

Military music and applause swelled. Below, athletes marched in, starting with Greece.

"Did I teach you nothing? It's how they walk. How they stand. Their sense of entitlement." He ticked items off on his thumb and twiglike fingers. "They don't need uniforms anymore. It's under their skins."

Correct and dangerously astute, as always. I kept quiet.

"I could also see, even from across the stadium, that you are not pleased with the one who is pawing at you. Although he fancies you. I think Huber does, too."

"It is a very long, very private story." I paused. "How do you know Andreas's name?"

"Chemist. Used him as a source once." His blue eyes shifted left, away from mine.

I would follow up on how he knew Andreas later. For now I hugged him again, smelling pipe tobacco and whisky. "It has been far too long."

"Hasn't it, though? But I did not skulk around here to question your dubious taste in men. I'm here because I have news." His voice rose on the last word, as it had a thousand times before.

I smiled. News. Peter always had news.

He studied the empty hall. Then he stepped closer and lowered his voice as if to keep unseen watchers from hearing. "I've found out something horrible. Something that will show the world definitively that the Nazis are not peace seekers or peacekeepers, or whatever they call themselves these days."

Two huge Olympic bells, cast for the occasion, tolled homage to Hitler and the Games; softly at first, but steadily increasing in volume. "And you would tell me this, though you just saw me with the SS? Seems like bad judgment."

He grinned. "You're not one of them. Whatever you're doing over there, it has more to do with Bella than with them."

"Bella?" I cocked a curious eyebrow, knowing I would not fool him. My head throbbed with the peals of the bell.

"She gets things out, doesn't she? And I guess you work for her."

"Interesting guess." I did not work for well-connected socialite reporter Bella Fromm, but he was close enough. When Lars delivered me canisters of film containing pictures of top secret SS documents, I couriered them not to Bella, but to a British espionage contact provided by an old friend and journalist, Sefton Delmer.

"I want you to get information out. Information and something else." His faded eyes sharpened as he studied me.

He pulled a silver flask from his hip pocket: Peter's Famous Flask. He carried it everywhere and started drinking from it when events got well under way. He offered it to me, and I knew that the news was sure to come soon.

I took a small sip to be polite. Although Peter's expensive whisky tasted smooth as always, watching Lars today had soured any taste I had for alcohol. "And if I say I have no idea what you are talking about?"

Peter took the proffered flask and raised it in a mock toast. "Then I'd be proud of you."

"If you think Bella can get your information out, why not go to her directly?" As curious as I was to know Peter's news, something did not make sense.

His gnarled fingers lined up with geometric patterns engraved in his flask. "We don't move in the same circles."

A lie. But why? I knew that he and Bella were acquainted. The lie appeared pointless, and he did not believe in pointless lies. "When does the pfennig drop?"

His face crinkled in a smile. "There is a certain package that she can't deliver. But you can."

"Package?" Bella's network of sources and helpers was far more extensive than mine. I would have thought that she could deliver anything. A wave of heat ran through my body. I brought my hand to my forehead. I could not have a sudden fever. That made no sense.

Peter took a swig of whisky and coughed. He sniffed the flask.

"Peter?"

He wiped his trembling chin. "I don't feel well."

Tears coursed down his cheeks. Sweat broke out on his brow. Saliva dripped from both sides of his mouth. He reached up to wipe it off, knocking his fedora to the ground. I thought of picking it up, but took his arm instead.

"Are you in any pain? Chest pain?" His pulse raced under my fingertips. My own heartbeat sped up.

"No." His voice rasped.

"Perhaps you should sit?" We took a step toward a nearby bench.

"Hannah—" His face darkened to brick red. Not a sign of a heart attack. I listed conditions in my head, but none seemed to match his symptoms.

I wrapped my arm around his thin shoulders and dragged his trembling body another step toward the bench. Should I leave him and fetch a doctor? Did I dare leave him alone? Could I find one even if I did?

Before I decided what to do, Peter collapsed against my side, convulsing. Together we fell heavily to the concrete. My hip took the brunt of our weight, and the flask clattered to the floor.

"Peter!" I rolled off his too-light body. His pupils shrank to pinpoints.

His bowels let go. He twitched once, then lay quite still. I knew what to expect before I lay my cheek against his wet lips. "Please. Oh please."

No breath.

No need to check his pulse.

2

A pair of strong hands hauled me up by my shoulders and heaved me against the pillar. Peter lay dead near my shoes. I swallowed a mouthful of saliva. Had Peter been poisoned?

Anton's face flashed in my mind. His pale brows curved up on the inside edges, and his forehead was wrinkled. He looked worried. *Forgive me,* I told his face, but I knew he would not.

I tried to move back to Peter. My eyes streamed, everything blurred. "I must help him."

"He's beyond your help," a voice whispered.

"I must help him. He's my father." Talking was hard.

"He's not your father."

I struggled to pull free. "Friend. He's my friend."

Someone wrenched my hands behind my back as if to handcuff me. Pain knifed from my wrist. I blinked to clear my eyes.

"I'll break your arm to save your life, Spatz," he hissed, for the first time speaking above a whisper.

My eyes had not cleared enough for me to see him, but now I recognized his voice. Lars. "Let me go, damn you."

When I moved, he pushed against my wrist joint. I gritted my teeth, but my knees buckled from the pain. I was immobilized. Damn cop.

He yanked me off the pillar and marched me down the corridor away from Peter. I could not break free from his grasp. We walked in

view of the crowd, but their heads faced forward, watching the spectacle there.

We passed one column, two, three. My eyes were clearing. Perhaps
Peter was getting better, too.

Behind us, during a pause in the music, a woman's high-pitched
scream cut through the air. It sounded as if it came from where Peter
lay.

Lars quickened our pace. I struggled harder. I had to go back and
see Peter one more time. I wanted him to be alive, but the rational
part of me knew that he was dead, that he could not get better.

Loud voices carried down the corridor toward us. From the sounds
of it, the woman had been joined by at least two men.

Lars glanced over his shoulder and swore, a rarity.

I twisted my wrists to free my hands, but his grip held solid.

He spun me around. My back slammed against a nearby pillar that
hid us from those down the corridor, and he pinioned me against the
hard stone. I tried to knee him in the groin, but he had trapped my
legs, too. His chest pressed against mine. "God damn it," he said into
my ear. "Stop."

I smelled schnapps on his breath, but his behavior was cold sober.
He still held my hands behind me, pinned painfully between my back
and the pillar.

My wrists burned when I twisted them, but he did not let go. "Let
me go."

"Please." His quiet voice was desperate. I did not care. "Be still."

The music changed and the crowd applauded, backs of their heads
mere meters away. The band transitioned into another military march.
Not surprisingly, they had an endless supply.

Lars glanced back down the corridor, then leaned forward and covered my mouth with his. It was only the third time he had ever kissed
me, but unfathomably, this time I kissed him back. For a time, all else
disappeared.

"Excuse me," rapped out a rough voice behind Lars.

Lars pulled away reluctantly. I whimpered when his lips peeled off mine. His surprised dark eyes asked a question.

"No," I whispered, aghast. In a normal state, I would never have consented, but right now my lips tingled with desire to kiss him again. What was wrong with me?

A half smile played across Lars's lips. He knew full well that regardless of what my lips said now, they had done something quite different seconds before. My mind and my body had never been so far apart. That, most of all, shocked me into calm.

A finger tapped Lars's shoulder. "Excuse me, sir."

I looked past Lars. My eyes had finally cleared. A tall and broad policeman with a nose that tilted up like a hedgehog's stood there. He had a vaguely familiar air. I ducked my head behind Lars again.

Lars released my wrists and slowly pushed away. He paused, uncertain. I gave a small nod; I was back under control, at least marginally. He turned to the policeman. I kept behind Lars and wiped my eyes.

"Hauptsturmführer Lang." Lars's voice held the perfect note of anger and impatience.

The policeman took a step back and quickly saluted. "Heil Hitler! I remember you from the Alex, Hauptsturmführer. I'm Sergeant Bauer."

Lars returned the salute. "Yes, Sergeant?"

I pushed off the pillar and stroked the back of my hand across swollen lips. The floor took a step to the left, and I swayed against the pillar. My eyes felt better, but something was still very wrong with me. Without turning from Bauer, Lars put a hand on my shoulder to steady me. I gulped in a deep breath.

"Did you see anyone run past, Hauptsturmführer?"

"No."

"Are you certain?" Bauer sounded disbelieving.

"A battalion of tanks could have rolled by, and I would not have noticed. I was . . . occupied."

A blush traveled up my neck to the top of my head. I stared at my shoes. Why had I kissed him? A reaction to grief? Or danger? Or had it just been too long since I had been kissed and that Lars was, in fact, very good at it? I wished I knew.

"My apologies." Bauer lumbered down the corridor, presumably on the lookout for witnesses to Peter's death.

Lars's warm hands cupped my shoulders. "Spatz?"

"I want to see Peter again."

"You can't help him." His handkerchief brushed my cheeks as lightly as a butterfly's wings. "Look at you."

"But . . ." I pictured myself returning to Peter's body. If the police suspected, as I did, that he had been poisoned, at the very least I would be taken in for questioning. If they suspected I was involved in his death or whatever he investigated and the Gestapo became involved, a quick end would be the best I could hope for.

I closed my throbbing eyes. Lars was correct. I should not go back.

I had seen many men die. In the war and after. I could do nothing for Peter. It had been a foolish impulse. I had become too soft living most of the last two years as a housewife and mother. That had ended. Or at least the first half of it had. Boris was finished with me, but Anton was not. And he deserved a mother who did not take needless chances. One who would return to Switzerland alive.

I needed to don my old armor quickly. Germany under the Nazis was no place to show weakness. I sucked in a deep breath. My stomach had calmed, my eyes no longer burned, and my mouth was not full of saliva. If the whisky contained poison, the effects seemed to be wearing off. Or perhaps it had been an emotional response instead of a physical one all along.

When I opened my eyes, Lars's face hovered close. He stroked a strand of wet hair off my forehead. "Home?"

I shook my head. "I must go back down. To cover the opening for the paper."

His expression said that he wished to argue, but thought better of it, probably grateful that I had stopped insisting we return to Peter. "Very well."

I took a few ragged breaths. "I am ready."

He raised a skeptical eyebrow, but offered his arm.

To avoid Peter's body, we walked back toward our seats along a different route. My hip ached from the fall. Excited spectators squirmed on their seats, and chattering voices filled the air. Before I limped into open air, I paused. "Lars?"

He stopped and bent his head to mine.

"Thank you," I said.

He stared at my lips. "My pleasure."

I started walking again.

Below, the last group of athletes marched through the stadium to the tune of yet another military march. With much less grace than they, we stumbled to our seats.

Andreas stood to let us pass. A film of perspiration covered his forehead. He glanced at my doubtlessly bloodshot eyes and then at Lars. He probably thought we'd had a lovers' spat, a far better explanation than what had actually occurred.

Andreas also noticed that I winced when I sat. Lars kept a firm arm around my shoulder, as if he feared I might collapse or flee. Both felt like better alternatives than staying and pretending that nothing had happened. But that was what I must do.

"She is not feeling well, but she insisted on coming back." Irritation was plain in Lars's voice.

"Are you certain that is a good idea?" Andreas loosened his dark blue tie.

"Merely a touch of flu," Lars answered for me. "And I think my apartment is noisier than she is accustomed to."

Andreas's eyes widened. Before this visit, I had always stayed at a hotel when I visited Berlin, as befit a proper lady. "Indeed?" he said.

I shifted in my uncomfortable seat. "Lost hotel reservation."

I wondered if my reservation had been lost, or if Lars had canceled it. I suspected the latter, but either way, it had proved impossible to find another room in Berlin on the eve of the Games. Because I dared not expose my old friends to my double life, I was forced to stay with Lars, making it that much easier for him to watch me.

I closed my aching eyes to shut out the light and massaged the swollen lids with my fingertips. At least they were not streaming as they had been just after Peter's death.

"Is she well enough to stay?" Andreas asked in a low voice.

"There's nothing I can do with her," Lars answered quietly. "Ever."

"She might be ill, but she is not deaf." I opened my eyes to scowl at them, still dizzy.

Andreas had the grace to grin sheepishly, but Lars radiated anger. He worried for me. Let him. I had worried enough about his drunken behavior. It was his turn.

I shifted my gaze to the field. Separated by nation, groups of athletes stood at attention, shoes crushing the grass. Each blade had been watered, trimmed to the exact same height, and every enemy weed and pest poisoned so the field would look flawless when they stood on it. And it did.

I pulled out my new notebook. "Which nations performed the Nazi salute?"

I ignored Lars's warning glance.

"Afghanistan, Bermuda, Bolivia, Bulgaria, Italy, and Germany, of course. And Iceland." Andreas listed them off as if they were scientific facts, not political acts. With the rise of the Nazis, even scientific facts had become political, so he probably had ample practice at equating the two.

With a trembling hand, I made a note of it. "Which did not?"

"Great Britain, the United States, and others." His tone displayed the expected dose of outrage.

I wrote down the countries and doodled on the page. The International Olympic Committee awarded the Games to Berlin in 1931, before the Nazis came to power. While it could not undo that decision, the committee could have organized a boycott. A few months ago, it had seemed possible that the major nations of the world might send a clear message to Germany that its anti-Semitic and fascist policies were unacceptable. That reoccupying the Rhineland in direct violation of the Treaty of Versailles mere months before the Games might have unpleasant consequences. In the end, only Spain and Russia took that stand. The others had sent their athletes into the stadium to salute Hitler today.

I looked at the page and startled. My hand had sketched Peter's open eye. Peter. Dead. Snuffed out faster than a candle. Lars put his hand over mine and rubbed the back of my hand with his thumb.

The voice of the founder of the modern Olympics, Baron de Coubertin, boomed out of loudspeakers. My French had improved since the move to Switzerland, so I did not need to wait for the translation: "The important thing in the Olympic Games is not winning, but taking part; the essential thing in life is not conquering, but fighting well."

Exactly the honor code to which Anton subscribed, as did his hero, Winnetou the Apache brave from Karl May's books. A beautiful sentiment, and I admired Anton's moral certainty, but how practical was it here? Lars squeezed my hand. Doubtless, he thought our efforts to expose the Nazis to the British constituted fighting well, even if we had not yet conquered.

Lars had risked much when he decided to spy on his colleagues. Once an ardent Nazi, he said he had changed his beliefs after they came to power and their actions did not live up to his ideals of a proper rule of law. I tried to smile at him. He did his best, and I felt a pang of guilt that I dared not trust him more.

After another speech by Dr. Lewald, Hitler declared the Games open in one mercifully short sentence. I had not thought him capable of brevity in speech.

Steely clouds had threatened rain all day, but only scattered drops dared fall on the men in Prussian blue jackets who hoisted the Olympic flag in the arena and the flags of represented nations that ringed the stadium's rim.

Even though I expected it, I twitched when the artillery fired a salute. Andreas and Lars shook their heads at my reaction. I shrugged. I had no wish to become inured to gunfire.

A massive flock of white pigeons rose into the air on cue. Colored ribbons fluttered from pink legs as they flew over the stadium and disappeared into the city. I had heard that they were carrier pigeons and, like everything in this now well-ordered society, would not fly away free but rather return to their predetermined roosts.

Still, even I could not deny the spectacle's beauty. I wished I could write about the irony of pigeons as a symbol of peace, and the Nazis' real intent, but instead I noted the light on the ribbons and the reverent hush that fell over the crowd. All these things were real, but I knew which story I would prefer to bring to the world.

Like everyone else, I stood to watch the Olympic runner enter with the torch. As expected, he was tall, well muscled, with Aryan blond hair and features. I imagined a casting director from UFA had picked him out of a vast pool of eager hopefuls. He loped down the stairs and across the stadium, gait as fluid as a thoroughbred horse's. Blue smoke streamed off his handheld torch.

When he dipped the fire into the giant Olympic basin, nothing happened. The stadium fell silent. What would the Nazi authorities do if the torch failed to light? This moment was the culmination of a 3,075-kilometer run from Greece. Someone had been running with that torch since a lens and the Greek sun lit it on July 20, twelve days ago. So far, everything had been flawless, but what would be the fate of this last runner if it went out? Before I had finished imagining that unpleasant scenario, the torch flamed high.

I noted the position of Leni Riefenstahl's cameras, rolling on the flames and the sun peeking out of the clouds behind the torch. She would turn it into arresting cinema, something that would rival her well-received propaganda piece, *Triumph of the Will*. Would the talented dancer, actress, and director live to regret her close association with the party? Not yet, at any rate. She had all the access to Hitler her heart desired and all the resources that brought with it.

I sat again, light-headed. Was this grief over Peter's death? Aftereffects of drinking the whisky? Or was I on edge because I had kissed Lars? Not just kissed him, but enjoyed it.

I gripped my pen tightly and wrote whatever came into my head, knowing I must tear out the pages later and burn them.

Andreas took the seat next to me; Lars remained standing. I closed my notebook.

"Are you well?" Andreas asked. His eyes appraised mine almost clinically, and I was suddenly reminded that he had medical training.

"It will pass," I answered, as if I believed it. In truth, I was not so certain. Peter, after all, was dead.

"What happened to your hip?" I followed his nervous glance to Lars.

He claimed to be Lars's friend, but it was plain that he thought Lars had knocked me around. Why was that his first thought? I worried that I did not know Lars well enough to answer that question.

Even to clear Lars's name, I could not explain my injured hip without making things more awkward. With a silent apology to Lars, and with the knowledge that Andreas would not believe me, I said, "I misstepped."

Andreas recognized the lie at once and again glanced up at Lars, who stood with my binoculars aimed at the field, seemingly unaware. "Is everything in order with you?" He pitched his worried voice so that Lars would not hear.

"Fine," I lied. It was amazing how easily lies came to me these days. I had once prided myself on my honesty.

"If you are having troubles, I hope that you would consider me enough of a friend to confide in." Sympathy warmed his voice. "Perhaps somewhere more private?"

I bit my lip. I already had one Nazi in whom I dared not confide, and yet who knew enough to have me killed. I had no intention of collecting another. I raised my head to meet his anxious eyes and was as honest and polite as I dared. No point in making an outright enemy. "Thank you for your concern. But I am fine."

Cheers erupted from the crowd. Andreas touched my shoulder before standing. I could not believe he offered easy sympathy, but I

might be too cynical. I had seen him often on my Berlin trips to visit
Lars over the past two years, but I did not consider us close.

Lars muttered something in an undertone that sounded like
"Hahn" and handed Andreas the binoculars. Both men turned in the
same direction and shared worried expressions.

Once again, I retreated to my notebook, writing everything that
happened around me, if only to silence whatever happened within me.
By the time they started Handel's "Hallelujah" chorus, I felt calm
enough to stand with everyone else and watch the athletes parade off
the field.

After the ceremony, we waited for the mass of spectators to dis-
perse before heading to the subway station. Even with extra trains
running, it would take a good while to move so many people from the
stadium. Lars and Andreas watched the part of the field where they
had worriedly trained the binoculars earlier. Were they waiting for
this Hahn to leave?

I remained seated, grateful for the reprieve. My thoughts strayed
to Switzerland.

Anton and I rode through a Swiss park, he bareback on his favorite
horse, Arrow, and I on a saddle atop a disobedient chestnut gelding
named Comet. Leaves crackled under the horses' hooves as we can-
tered through a grove of bare elms. Autumn's cold bit at my cheeks,
and the day held unlimited possibilities. A long ride with hot cider
and pancakes at the end of it beckoned.

Boris's housekeeper, a plump and unattractive matron as unlike his
previous housekeeper as possible, was a wonderful cook. I had hired
her based on her sterling references and the extreme unlikelihood that
Boris would ever be attracted to her.

"Spatz?" Lars asked. "You look like you just bit into a lemon."

I pulled myself together. That ride had been ten months ago, when
life was much simpler. "I am fine."

"Shall we make the trek home?" He offered his arm.

I wobbled when I stood. My sense of balance had not fully returned. I grabbed Lars's bare forearm, ready to go home, even though I did not relish the thought of being alone with him while he questioned me about Peter. I wished that we, like Andreas, had purchased tickets to the opening play. That would buy me hours of time.

Andreas said his good-byes, holding my hand a second longer than necessary when he shook it. He walked away slowly, seemingly reluctant to leave me alone with Lars. If Lars noticed, he gave no sign.

"Should we go straight to the subway?" Lars asked. "You look peaked."

"First I must find a telephone and file my story." I wished I could use the telephones set aside for press at the stadium, but it was too likely I would meet someone there I knew.

"Are you certain?" Lars's brows drew together worriedly.

"I need to keep my job, Lars," I said. "And I feel fine."

That lie convinced neither of us, but Lars knew better than to argue. Together we looked for a public booth.

After some searching, I found one and stepped into the wood and glass structure, closing Lars outside. He clasped his hands behind his back and waited less than a meter away. Could he read lips? I would not be surprised.

The booth reeked of the last caller's cologne. I fed pfennigs into the slot and dictated my story to the eager young reporter on the other end, hoping that he could spell. I dwelled on the pageantry and scope, not letting slip any pro- or anti-Nazi statements. I did not mention who had performed the Nazi salute and who had not, deeming it too political. As I knew every other reporter would do, I described the scene with the little girl in the blue dress handing Hitler the flowers. If I neglected it, we would be scooped.

After I broke the connection, I dawdled in the telephone booth. I wished that I could call Boris and Anton in Switzerland. Anton would be delighted to hear from me. I could almost hear his high-pitched voice rattling on about his day. Today was Saturday. He had riding lessons, and he would have stories to tell.

Arrow was as young and high spirited as Anton, and the two often got up to mischief. Anton modeled his actions and his riding style after Winnetou. His habit of riding bareback whenever possible or hanging half off the horse while riding so that he could not be shot by imaginary cowboys frustrated his instructors. If my little brave had not been such a talented equestrian, I suspected that the riding academy would have dismissed him months before. I smiled to think of the scolding Boris had probably received from the instructor when he retrieved Anton from his lessons.

I wished I could hear about it, but to reach Anton, I would have to call Boris first, and Boris might respond badly. We had barely spoken since I moved out, only quick missives exchanged to coordinate Anton's regular visits. I was grateful that Boris loved Anton like a son and intended to stay close to him no matter how far he moved from me. Few men would have been so kind to a fatherless boy, and it was another reason I missed him.

Boris had not been home when I made the trip from my cramped apartment to his house yesterday. I regretted that I had not seen him to say good-bye. Instead, I left an angry and worried Anton with Boris's housekeeper and hurried on to Berlin.

Whether or not Boris might accept the call, I dared not make it. Like everyone else in Germany, I had to assume that the Gestapo monitored all telephones in Berlin. Assuming anything else was too dangerous. If they connected Adelheid Zinsli to Hannah Vogel, I would be arrested. If the Gestapo connected Hannah Vogel to Boris or Anton, so would they. The mask of kindness the Nazis had donned for the Games did not conceal their true intent.

Lars knocked peremptorily on the glass. I ignored him and ran my fingertips once down the warm side of the telephone box. I did not want to leave the booth and thoughts of Boris and Anton to face Lars. He would have questions about Peter that I would not answer, and questions that I could not answer. I sighed and opened the door. Best to get it over with.

The worst of the crush had dissipated; we fit on the next train. The

car was too full to sit and too loud to talk. My stomach had not settled since Peter's death, but I doggedly hung on to a leather strap and
wished I were home. Lars stood next to me, one hand protectively in
the small of my back, as if to keep me from falling.

All too quickly, Lars's front door closed and locked behind us. Nowhere to hide.

3

The familiar smell of lemon polish hung in his entryway. Lars kept an immaculate house. I placed my hat on the oak hat tree, hung my satchel on a hook next to it, and walked down the hall, through the living room, and into the kitchen.

I judged the kitchen to be the safest place to confront Lars, away from the alcohol in the living room. The interrogation would be easier if he remained sober. I opened the kitchen drawer and drew out a blue and white tea cozy. Lars waited silently while I walked back to the alcove in the hall that contained his telephone. While I fit the cozy over the telephone, I wondered if the fabric was thick enough to keep the Gestapo from hearing what went on in the apartment. If they were listening, we would have to hope so.

Back in the kitchen, I poured myself a tall glass of warm mineral water and took a roll from the bread box. Sitting on one of the sturdy oak chairs, I waited.

Lars spoke quietly from the kitchen doorway. "Who was the dead man?"

I took a bite of roll, chewed it thoroughly, and swallowed before answering. No matter what I said or did not say, he would find out through his own contacts. "The real Peter Weill."

He sucked in his breath, surprised. "From the newspaper?"

"The same." I took a sip of water. Carbonation scratched my throat.

"Were you close?" His voice rapped out the question.

"Very. Once." My voice quavered, and I took another drink of warm water.

He pulled the other chair next to mine. I moved sideways in my chair, away from him.

"I'm sorry, Spatz." He patted my knee.

He sought to help, but he also sought information. I shook off his hand. "Thank you for your sympathy."

He put his palm flat on the table. "Why were you meeting with him today?"

"It was a chance meeting." I followed the dark grain of the golden oak tabletop with one fingertip.

"A chance meeting?" He sounded skeptical, and he was correct to be so. It had been no chance meeting. But why Peter had asked me to come, I did not know.

A wave of exhaustion swept over me. "I can't do this now, Lars."

He lifted my chin so that I stared into his dark eyes. I could not read what I saw there. His gaze lingered on my lips. A blush traveled to the roots of my hair. I pulled my chin away.

He cleared his throat. "If I had not dragged you away, you would have put us both in prison."

Peter was known for his anti-Nazi views, but was standing next to his dead body really grounds for arrest, in these sunny Olympic days? "At least I would have been sober when I did."

Lars winced and a pang of guilt shot through me. But it was true. He needed to hear it.

"What did you two talk about?" He was nothing if not persistent. A trained interrogator, first with the police, now with the SS.

"Nothing. I said hello, asked how he was and . . . he died. . . ." I gulped.

Lars gripped my shoulder tightly. "What else?"

I dropped my gaze to the clean-scrubbed table. "Nothing else."

"Spatz," he said. "I know you are keeping something from me. But why don't you trust me? After everything we've been through these past two years?"

Beyond the scope of our work, I barely knew him. He could have me killed, as he had done to others. I did not dare trust him any more than I had to, though I sympathized with the pain in his voice. "There is nothing to trust you with," I lied. Until I knew what Peter had been working on, I trusted no one.

"You're lying, of course." He sounded as tired as I felt. "What about our work? Is this situation worth jeopardizing that?"

"I am not jeopardizing anything, Lars."

"You know this?" His voice rose. "We have risked our lives to bring out some important documents, and there are more to come. Are you engaged in some activity that will compromise us?"

"I hope not." I held his gaze for a moment. I did not know.

"I hope not, too," he said, "for both our sakes."

I folded my arms on the oak table and lay my head on them. I did not remember when I had felt so exhausted. Was it the poison? I closed my eyes. Perhaps Boris was right; perhaps I should give up and wait things out in Switzerland, abandon my crusade and my job and become a happy Swiss housewife.

Lars's chair creaked. "Oh, Spatz."

I took another deep breath and ignored him. I could not blame him for wanting answers, but I had no intention of giving them.

"Perhaps it is best for you to rest now," he said quietly.

I raised my head. "Thank you."

Once in bed, I watched shadows cast by headlights of cars outside flicker across Lars's smooth plaster ceiling. His neighbors argued on the other side of the wall, words indistinct but feelings clear. One was angry, one placating. And so the world went round.

Floorboards creaked in the living room. Probably Lars, drinking and trying to figure out what had been going on in the stadium between me and the dead man. What had I been doing? Listening, then watching him die.

I rested my cheek on my hands. I ached to be home in Boris's arms. But I was not, and I might never be again. I was here. Alone. Hot tears came, and I buried my face in Lars's pillow. I did not want him to hear.

Peter was gone. Forever.

Without his help, I would never have become a reporter. Who knew what indignities I would have been forced into during the inflation in the '20s to survive. Instead, for reasons I had never understood, Peter took an interest in one underfed poet and taught her a salable skill. I had enjoyed working the beat with him: days at the courthouse, afternoons talking to people and typing stories, evenings sitting around his sister's table, drinking with other reporters.

I pleated the wet pillowcase with my fingers, remembering Peter's laugh and his endless store of truisms. We had shared so many words and so many worlds. And it had disappeared in an instant. No more words for Peter.

The nausea I had fought since his death slowly subsided. In its wake came overpowering exhaustion. Even without Boris next to me, sleep quickly took me in.

Peter stood in front of me, smiling. His sparkling eyes offered a challenge.

I stared, uncertain.

He offered his silver flask, and I took it. The cool metal felt good against my palm. I traced the curlicues of the art nouveau design with my fingertips. I had always admired it. Laughing, I unscrewed the top. Before I drank, he knocked the flask from my hand. Crimson liquid exploded out.

Blood.

It spattered on my dress. On my cheeks. My eyes stung. I was blind. The metallic smell strangled me.

I sat up in bed, choking. My ragged breathing filled the room. I unclenched my fists, forced my breath to slow.

Peter's flask was wrong. His flask at the stadium had sported geometric patterns in the modern style that he hated. But the flask he usually carried featured an art nouveau design. Had someone switched flasks? Or had he simply purchased a new one?

As soon as I stopped shaking, I slipped out of bed, wincing when I put weight on my hip. I smoothed the sheets, tucked in the corners military fashion, fluffed the pillow, and centered it on the bed, positioned the black wool blanket on top, and flattened every wrinkle. There would be no more sleep for me tonight.

I tiptoed to the window and peered through filmy white curtains. The sun was barely up, so it must be around five thirty. Lars probably still slept. I performed my morning toilet, pulled on a yellow shift, and picked up my shoes with my left hand. Ready to go.

I crept out of Lars's bedroom and into the living room. He lay stretched across his black leather couch under a sheet. An empty schnapps glass rested on the nearby oval table.

Light fell through open curtains across his unguarded face. A lock of dark hair fell over his right eyelid. Seeing him relaxed underlined how rigid, how tense, he held himself while awake. He walked a difficult path of lies and deceit in Germany. At least I could return to the safety of Switzerland and, until recently, Boris. But Lars was trapped here. As far as I knew, alone.

I pushed the sudden thought of yesterday's kiss out of my mind before I slipped past. I lifted my broad-brimmed hat from its hook, hoisted my satchel over my shoulder, stepped over the creaky board in the entryway, and hurried down the hall.

Once out on the front steps, I pulled on my shoes, crossed the street, and sidestepped into the first empty doorway. Hidden from the street, I watched the front door of Lars's apartment building. Several minutes elapsed. He did not emerge. He had, indeed, been asleep.

Checking behind me one final time, I headed away from the leafy trees in the Tiergarten. My limp lessened the more I walked. To my right loomed the spires of Kaiser Wilhelm Memorial Church, where I had once received false news of Anton's death. That had led to a trip to Gestapo headquarters and my partnership with Lars two years ago. I looked away.

Although not the closest station, I made for Wittenbergplatz. I could catch a train there straight through to Hallesches Tor, my old neighborhood. Peter's sister also used to live there. Hopefully she did still.

My stomach rumbled. For the first time since Peter's death, I felt hungry. Not hungry, ravenous. I stopped at the first café I came to. Set back from the street, it had two round tables out front. One was free. At the other sat an Indian couple, the woman clad in a bright pink and gold sari, her companion in an orange kurta that hung to his knees. Visitors for the Games? I hoped that their dark skin would not cause them trouble. Official Nazi ideology stated that Indians were Indo-European and therefore acceptable, but I suspected that the average storm trooper thug might not appreciate such distinctions.

"Outside?" The stocky waitress straightened the starched white cap over her tight blond wave.

"Indoors, please." I did not want to be out on the street, in case Lars awoke and searched for me.

"It's a fine morning." She fiddled with the edges of her white apron.

"I prefer to dine indoors."

"Might be raining later."

"Do you have a table indoors or shall I dine elsewhere?" I gave her my most charming insincere smile.

She grunted and led me inside, where no one else sat in the gloom. Perfect.

I purchased one of each newspaper they stocked before I sat.

The waitress looked at me as if I were mad. "Why do you need more than one?"

"I collect them," I lied. No point in trying to explain. I ordered a tea and a full breakfast before turning to my papers. Headlines about the triumph of the Games' opening marched across each front page, little girl with the bouquet prominently featured, as I knew she would be. At least I had not been scooped.

I scanned the bylines for old friends and found only a few. Most of my old friends lost their jobs when the Nazis came to power; the bravest had ended up in concentration camps. What might have happened to me if I had never met Anton and had instead stayed in Berlin, trying to tell the truth?

The waitress dropped my plate unceremoniously on the table.

"Many thanks," I said.

I gobbled my roll, soft-boiled egg, and salty sausage.

She watched disapprovingly. Not only had I refused to sit outside, I had bolted my food. What would my mother think? I gave her another imitation smile, and she sauntered outside to attend to the tables of sensible patrons.

I sipped weak tea to which I had added a double portion of honey and read the articles I had previously skimmed. The anti-Semitic tone that had permeated all German newspapers since the rise of the Nazis was notably absent from the today's papers. Anxious to curry favor with the international community, Goebbels must have sent down an edict. The absence of racial slurs felt more ominous than had their presence, weeks before. It underlined the Nazis' control of the press, their ability to orchestrate reality's every detail.

I left enough coins on the tabletop to cover breakfast, checked that Lars was not in sight, then headed out to the street, where I tipped the folded newspapers I had purchased into a rubbish bin. Out of the corner of my eye, I watched the waitress shake her head. I kept walking.

A flower-seller peddled blooms from a battered wooden pushcart painted forest green. Matching metal vases held tulips, carnations, daisies, roses, lilies, and sunflowers. The fragrances made me smile. A traditionalist, Boris always bought me roses.

"Good morning!" said the wizened woman heartily. "Needin' a stalk or two to brighten your home or your heart?"

I thought of Lars's sterile apartment. "I fear it would take more than that. But I do need a few flowers."

"Something in a pink?" She pointed to a bunch of gerbera daisies.

"Not quite." My hand paused over a bunch of white lilies, the most

appropriate condolence flower. Instead I selected five bright sunflowers and a handful of foliage. The flower-seller's gnarled hands wrapped
them expertly in paper and passed them back.

I tilted the wet stems away from my dress and strolled to the subway
station. When I stepped into the brick building, I remembered other
times I had arrived here. One late night I chased a man dressed as a
harem girl to see if he had information about my brother's murder; another night I staked out the building for a hired thug missing an index
finger to see if he could help me to find Anton. Whatever happened on
this visit to Berlin, it would be preferable to the panic that had gripped
me during the days after the purge of the Night of the Long Knives,
when I had been unable to find Anton as the Nazis' body count grew.
Anton held my heart, and I was grateful that he was safe in Switzerland.

I shook off those memories. By day, the station was a friendly place.
Light warmed buttercup yellow tiles. People flocked through the building. Voices twittered in German, Dutch, and English, excited to be in
the big city during the big event.

Canny and eager to avoid international censure, the Nazis had taken
down display cases that usually held the latest edition of *Der Stürmer*,
the anti-Semitic rag published by Julius Streicher. Even though their
absence was only temporary, it made the station feel friendlier, more
like the old days. I felt cheerful. It was a treat to be in my home city free
of Lars. On my own.

I strode through the teeming station, down the stairs, and onto a
train. I laid the bouquet crossways on my lap for the six stops to
Hallesches Tor.

Once I arrived, I tarried on the busy platform, letting other passengers exit, then walked down Friedrichstrasse to Peter's old apartment.
Even in this usually grimy working class neighborhood, everything
now looked clean and groomed. Window boxes of red geraniums hung
from the sills. Bright Olympic flags flew from a forest of new flagpoles.
A few crimson swastika flags fluttered here and there, but not so many
as in Lars's neighborhood. Peter's district was once a Communist en-
clave; the Nazis would never own these workers' deepest hearts.

I paused at the end of the block to check my father's gold pocket watch. Although not quite seven, people streamed by, some sober and ready for church, others drunk and ready for bed. Anyone watching the entrance to Peter's sturdy red building had ample cover in the crowd. If there, a watcher would be difficult to spot. Still, I waited and watched.

People went about their business. No one but I loitered suspiciously. Seeing nothing out of the ordinary, but not convinced that it was absent, I gave up and mounted uneven front steps to the newly painted front door.

I rang the bell for WEILL. I had once come here so often that I had a key, but I returned it years before, when Peter left for Dresden and I took over his crime column.

I listened for footsteps on the stairs. Nothing. I rang again. I knew it was far too early to pay a social call, but Theresa had always been an early riser and I had to get to the fencing by nine. Lars was certain to catch up with me there, and I might not get another chance to slip away.

Just when I had given up hope, the door swung open.

"Come in," called a cracked voice from the dim entryway. Peter's sister, Theresa.

I stepped in and closed the door. A smudge of white hair and a pale housecoat ghosted in the darkness. No one had yet opened the curtains.

"Upstairs." She jerked her chin toward the steps and set off at a fast clip. Theresa never liked to waste time. I hurried after.

Inside her apartment, she closed and locked the front door before turning on the hall light. It fell on shabby furniture and floor-to-ceiling bookcases. The smell of books and Macallan's whisky took me back ten years in one inhalation. In spite of the circumstances, I smiled.

"He found you at the stadium." Her words were matter of fact. No emotion. My quick smiled faded.

"Barely." In the light, I took stock of her. She had changed remarkably little in the past decade. Thick white hair hung loose over her shoulders, celery green eyes still skeptical.

"Before his heart attack?" Her rough voice caught.

"Was it that?" We slipped into the familiar staccato I used with my most paranoid sources.

"I hope so."

"Oh, Theresa!" I embraced her. As always, she smelled of mothballs and taffy and stepped impatiently away.

"I've missed you," Theresa said. She pushed her loose hair behind her shoulders. "No need to get soppy."

"Apologies." I handed her the bouquet.

"Sunflowers." Her smile revealed toothless gums. "You remembered."

"With men, always remember the cigarettes they smoke. With women, the flowers they love." My quote came from Peter and we both nodded, recognizing it.

"Have you had breakfast?" she asked.

"On the way here."

"I as well, what I could eat."

"Theresa," I said. "I am sorry."

She wiped her eyes with the back of the hand holding the flowers. "Let me fix you some tea. And biscuits. I have a tin of Linzer biscuits. You love those."

"Wonderful." I followed her to the spare and clean kitchen. She never let us bring books or papers in here. She suffered us to enter her domain only if we followed her rules.

Theresa had nothing to do with journalism. Instead, she lived modestly on the proceeds of her gambling. She played only games she could win by reading other players, like poker. She never played against the house, and she never went broke. She always played at different places, never took too much at a time, and so escaped scrutiny. Those skills would serve her well under the Nazis.

Theresa put the sunflowers in a milky yellow vase and centered it on the blue and white checked tablecloth. It made for a striking arrangement. One hand lingered on the yellow petals before she turned to the cabinet. I was glad I had brought them.

She dealt biscuits like cards onto a chipped white plate. She had used this plate for at least as long as I had known her. I stared at the dish, imagining the many cookies Peter must have eaten from it.

Sighing, I nibbled. Shortbread with raspberry jam. Delicious.

"Eat all you want," she said. "You're always too thin by half. Although—" She paused next to the stove and scrutinized my figure. "You look well fed for a change."

"It has been a good few years." A good few years that were now over.

I snagged another Linzer, suddenly hungry again. She sat next to me and took her own. We chewed silently, two women in a small kitchen that felt empty, as if Peter would walk in at any moment, scoop up his own cookie, and tell us his latest news. I glanced at the dark doorway. "Why did Peter want to meet with me?"

"Figured you'd be there to cover news like that. Expected that he could find a secluded spot to meet among all those people."

She had answered the question, Why did Peter want to meet at the stadium? instead of the question I had asked. Interesting. "Were you there, too?"

"Too many people for an old woman. Too many salutes."

I nodded, grateful that I was not the only one repelled by the sight of so many arms raised to Hitler.

"And," she said. "I can never stand all the nationalistic screaming."

I thought of the Winter Olympics in Garmisch-Partenkirchen the previous February. The energy and enthusiasm and anger and joy that the citizens of each country poured into the achievements of their individual athletes frightened me. Nazis were not the only ones who elevated their athletes to iconic status.

"Did Peter go alone, then?" I asked.

She hesitated. "I think so."

"But you are not certain?"

"Tell me what happened." She squared her shoulders.

I paused, calculating risks, as always. "Peter met me in a corridor at the stadium."

"Alone?" She took another biscuit and spun it between her finger and thumb, scattering tiny crumbs on the immaculate tablecloth.

"So far as I know. Do you know something different?"

The cookie rotated like an empty roulette wheel. She fixed both eyes on it.

"He said he had news." How would I tell her? I sat and listened to the faraway murmur of traffic far below. "He sounded excited and happy, like a puppy with a new bone."

"What was his news?" The cookie stopped turning.

"He never told me. He just dropped. It was over quickly. One minute he was laughing and drinking out of his flask." I stopped to steady my voice. "The next he was gone."

"Heart attack?" Her voice held tears, but she did not surrender to them.

It had not looked like a heart attack. My reaction after had felt foreign, as if I had been poisoned and was not just reacting in grief and shock. But I had no proof, only intuition. "I do not know."

"Means no, if I know you."

I shrugged. "What news did he have?"

"Wouldn't tell me. You know how he could be. Secretive. Keeping his cards close to his vest, until he could slam them on a table with a flourish and listen to everyone gasp." She put down her cookie and stood to silence the whistling kettle.

She concealed more than she revealed. But why?

"That sounds like Peter," I said.

"Not only Peter." She gave me a look.

She busied herself with the tea, and I waited. After she sat, we stared at the old white teapot. The smell of jasmine tea wafted toward me. Again, I asked. "No guesses?"

"Dangerous times for guessing." Her eyes studied the checked tablecloth.

"Do you think someone killed him?" I asked.

"I think nothing either way. No percentage in it these days. I play the percentages." She picked a white hair off the table and dropped it in the rubbish.

"But the house always wins that way," I said.

"Rules are different now." She poured us each a cup of tea. Steam curlicued into the air and disappeared. "No chance to win some games. Those, it's best not to play. Waiting out games you can't win is a golden strategy."

I smiled at her familiar gambling analogies before I blew on the surface of the tea to cool it, then took a sip. It tasted like better times.

"I know you've been gone." She shook her head at my expression. "Don't let the clean and friendly streets fool you. It's a Potemkin village here now. On August seventeenth, the old rules apply."

August seventeenth, the day after the Olympics ended. "Today is only August second."

"You don't want to be dealt in, Hannah." She picked up her cookie and stared at it. "There's no winning. Peter knew better, too. But he was old. Grandiose."

"What was he on to?"

"You can't worm something out of me that I don't know."

I sipped too-hot tea and tried to think up a new tactic.

"He died how he wanted to, you know." She sniffed.

I reached out to take her hand, but she wrapped it around her white china cup.

"In the game." She took out a plain cotton handkerchief and blew her nose. "At the cusp of something big. Ready to poke his finger right in someone's eye. And plenty old." She smiled, wrinkles falling into familiar lines, like a map I had studied often.

"He did."

She cradled her teacup in her palms. "You're young. You have responsibilities, I imagine."

I thought of Anton. I had a responsibility to be his mother. But did I not also have one to show him what mattered? To make the world safer for him?

"Don't you go poking around in the same place as Peter," Theresa said.

"Why would I?"

"Lack of sense, I imagine." Her spoon clinked against the side of her cup.

"Not necessarily."

"Liar." She said it kindly. It still stung, though, because it was true. "Where do you live now?"

"Out of Germany." I stared at the inch of pale brown tea in the bottom of my cup. I dared not be more specific on my whereabouts.

"Alone? Peter thought you'd settled down. Some stolid thing. A banker?"

"How did Peter know that?" Worried, I turned over the possibilities in my head.

"He had his sources, same as you."

Perhaps, but I had told very few people in Germany about Boris.

"True, then? You're settled down all domestic?"

"I was. But about a month ago . . ." My throat closed.

She stirred another lump of sugar into her tea, waiting me out.

"We parted." It was a relief to tell someone, but I did not want to give details. The truth was that Boris had proposed marriage. But Boris offered marriage with conditions. He would give me his ring only if I promised to stop risking my life in Germany and instead settled down as a proper Swiss wife and mother. Boris hated the Nazis, too, but he did not wish me to die in what he called "a pointless campaign that has accomplished nothing." I had to concede him that point as well, as I had never heard anything from the British that indicated they put the intelligence we gathered to use. Certainly, their vaguely pro-Nazi stance had not changed since I started risking my life every three months. Boris had wearied of wakeful nights spent not knowing if I would return. I suspected he was also jealous of Lars and worried about the time I spent with another man, although he never said as much.

I could not blame him. But I could not abandon my courier responsibilities from Berlin if there was even a sliver of a chance that I might change one British mind. As much as it hurt, I stuck to the mission Boris had claimed he understood when we moved in together two years before. I had to bring out documents to warn the British about Hitler. I had to come when Peter called. I remembered the hurt in Boris's brown gold eyes when I told him, the resignation in his voice when he asked me to leave.

So, I came to Berlin. And now I had to stay. I could not let Peter's death be in vain.

"Hannah?" Theresa's voice came from far away. "Are you listening?"

"Yes." Had she been talking?

"You're not dealt many good men in life. Seems a shame to fold in the middle of a good hand." Her green eyes narrowed suspiciously.

"His choice," I lied. It had been as much my choice as his. And I missed him so much, I ached. But I did not regret my decision. I did not enjoy paying the cost, but if that was required of me, so be it. I clasped my hands tightly in my lap, trying not to think how things would have turned out had I said yes to his proposal.

"Entirely?" She shook her head, disbelief writ large on her countenance. "Hannah the innocent little maid?"

I unclasped my hands and toyed with a biscuit. "Sometimes you want different things." But had we?

"From the sound of your voice, sounds as if you might have wanted what he did."

"Perhaps." I stared at the chipped plate. "But I could not surrender what was needed to get it."

"Or did you just not want to?" Her voice was gentle.

I had not wanted to give up my independence, but I might have managed it. Perhaps. What I could not give up was any chance to bring down the Nazis before they started a war. But I could tell her none of that. I had not even told Boris that. If he did not understand it, I could not explain it. I cleared my throat. "What was Peter investigating?"

"Not your relationship with the banker. But that interests me more."

"Busybody." I took another bite of sweet shortbread. "Giving you gossip fodder is not why I came. Peter mentioned a package. Do you know what he was talking about?"

"I'll not help you get killed. You're out of it. Go home."

"I am home." I gestured around the kitchen, at every familiar pot and pan.

"Not by years." Her eyes met mine over the rim of her thick cup.

We finished our tea and spoke more about Peter, but she never budged. I would have to get my information somewhere else. But at least I knew where my next stop had to be.

When I reached her front door, I asked. "May I have one more biscuit, for the road?"

"I'll fetch one."

As soon as she was out of sight, I knelt on the wooden floor next to the umbrella stand. My fingers fumbled through open folds of an ancient umbrella, tapped across wooden ribs. I had almost given up hope when my fingertips brushed a package. I pulled it out and slid it into my satchel without examining it. I knew what it was.

Peter's notebook. He always hid it there, thinking his sister would not find it to snoop. I suspected she knew. She would also miss it after I left, but that could not be helped. I rose and dusted off my knees.

I stood, hopefully exuding innocence, when she returned with the Linzer biscuit. "Thank you," I said brightly.

She pulled me into an abrupt hug. When we separated, she pinched my cheek a little too hard. "And don't be a stranger. Come back for another visit before six years are up." She handed me a house key. "And come straight up. Don't want you skulking about on the steps."

"I promise." I rubbed my cheek and slipped the key into my satchel.

"Wish I could get more promises out of you."

"Most would be happy with one."

"Then give it to him." Her eyes were serious.

"I have no idea what you mean." Although, of course, I did. And I wondered if she was correct.

She snorted and opened the door. I had reached the top step when the lock clicked into place.

No one took special notice as I left, but I circled the block before heading to Hallesches Tor subway station. At the train's first stop, I dashed into the car behind mine. Only after making certain that no one had followed did I find an empty wooden seat and open the notebook, hoping a study of it would drive my thoughts from Boris and the life Anton and I might have had with him.

The snaky black lines appeared to be gibberish, but I was unworried. Peter used an unusual shorthand I had memorized years ago. I opened a page in my notebook and pulled out my jade-colored fountain pen, certain I could tease meaning from the page.

4

Even after several readings, I found no sense in his scribblings. But he had written a few words not in code. I made out the name *Schrader* and what I thought might be the word *leaf*. I doubted Peter's big story had to do with gardening.

The train stopped and people climbed on and off, but I paid them no mind.

I thumbed through pages with increasing frustration, tearing one. Had Peter left the notebook as a decoy, more to thwart followers than to help him remember? Perhaps that was why Theresa had let me steal it. She knew it was useless. Tempted to toss it across the car, I kept turning pages.

The last page contained a drawing of a stick figure with a square head holding what looked like a scythe in his left hand and a hammer in his right.

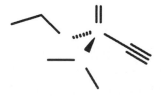

Hammer and sickle? A Communist symbol? Or a doodle?

Before we reached Wittenbergplatz, I stowed the notebook and realized that I had left my press pass in my suitcase in Lars's apartment.

I had not needed it at the opening, but I might need it at the morning fencing event. I berated myself for my carelessness.

I exited at Wittenbergplatz and headed to Lars's apartment. I circled the block and waited. Alone, I walked the final street. Fatigue dragged on my limbs. With luck, Lars would be gone.

I paused in front of his solid old building. A shadow moved across his living room curtains. He was home and awake. Exhaustion and worry washed over me. Since he tried to keep me in his sight every moment when I was in Berlin, he would be angry that I had slipped away, especially after I had dodged his questions about Peter's death yesterday.

Should I go to the Games without my press pass? No, it might prove awkward if I did need it. Avoiding Lars longer might well inflame him more and make it even worse the next time I saw him.

Better to confront him now. The time had come for him to learn that he was not to be my jailer for the next two weeks. I set my shoulders and marched up the front stairs. Fingers nervous in spite of my bravado, I fumbled to unlock the front door, then walked down the hall and moved my key toward Lars's lock.

Lars yanked the door open. He wore his full black SS uniform, except for the boots. An officer does not argue in pajamas. When I swept past, alcohol fumes hit me. I had not expected to find him drunk so early.

I had made a mistake.

I pivoted back toward the door, but he slammed it shut and stood in front, arms crossed.

"Where have you been?" His peevish voice sounded so much like my army officer father's that I winced.

I checked that the thick tea cozy covered the telephone and walked to the living room. Being in the middle of the apartment, it was where we were least likely to be overheard by neighbors. Our discussion might become loud. "I stepped out to get some air."

He stomped in behind. "Air?"

"Berlin is famous for it."

He glared. "What are you playing at?"

I thought of bolting to the bedroom, but the door did not lock, and the last place I wanted a drunken Lars was the bedroom. The walls there were the thinnest in the apartment, and it was also the place a sober Lars most wanted to end up. "I need to retrieve my press pass from my suitcase."

"You might sneak out the window instead." He moved closer. How much alcohol had he consumed? Unfortunately, not enough to incapacitate him. "I'd have to handcuff you to the bed."

My stomach tightened, and I knew fear showed on my face.

"Do you think I would do that to you?" He looked crestfallen.

The intelligent thing to do was to try to calm him down. To agree. Instead, I spoke the truth. "I do not know what you would do in this state. Do you?"

"State?" He drew himself up to his full height. He was not much taller than I, but he exuded menace.

"Drunk." I circled to put the oval coffee table between us.

"Whose fault is that?" He rested his hands on his hips.

"Yours?" I hated sounding like an aggrieved housewife, but it was worth it to keep the argument focused on his drinking and not on where I had been. If he knew that I was asking questions about Peter and why he might have been killed, Lars would pack me on the next train to Switzerland and I would have to avoid him, too, when I slipped off the train and returned to Berlin.

"What was I supposed to do when I found you gone? To know that you climbed out the window to escape from me."

"I did not climb out the window." Although impatience was clear in my voice, he ignored it.

"Wandering alone and unprotected."

"I thought Berlin's streets were safer now than ever before." I kept my hands loose at my sides, trying not to look threatening.

"Safe from criminals. Not safe from the police. Or the Gestapo. Especially not for you." He raked a hand through his dark hair. "Have you any idea how dangerous it is out there? Only yesterday I had to drag you away to keep you from being arrested."

"I had just watched a close friend die," I said. "I hope that such a thing will not happen again today."

"Spatz—"

"I am no child, Lars." I would not be coddled.

"No." He stepped around the table, voice deadly. "You invite adult trouble."

I stumbled back. My anger changed to fear. Just like that, he had turned dangerous. "I do not mean to."

"Really?" He closed the gap between us in one quick step, socks silent on the wood. "Have you ever wondered why you are always at the center of a deadly storm?"

"Bad weather forecasting?" I backstepped again. My spine flattened against the cold plaster wall.

He placed his right hand a centimeter from my left ear. "You're drawn to it."

I desperately wanted to dodge right and away, but he was too sober. If the action set him off, I would not make it two steps. "Am I?"

He stuck his left hand on the other side of my head, walling me in. "You have more storm in you than you admit."

"And you have more sunlight." I hoped.

He looked at my lips and smiled.

"No," I said quietly. "Not ever."

"Yesterday." He bent closer. "You rather seemed to enjoy it."

"I was trying to distract you." I lied, but he did not know that. I had no idea why I had kissed him, but I certainly did not intend to do it again now.

"I don't think so." His lips hovered centimeters from mine. His breath brushed hot against my mouth.

"Off." I sounded as if I yelled at a dog. He stopped. I pushed against his chest with both hands. "Now."

That last was too much, and I regretted it. He seized my arm with one hand and raised his other to strike. I flinched.

He froze, palm raised.

"Lars?" My voice shook.

He stepped back and buried his face in his hands.

I let out my breath. The balance had shifted. I recognized the moment from a childhood spent gauging my father's drunken rages.

I walked around him and picked up the nearly empty bottle of schnapps. He did not move when I went to the kitchen. I paused in the doorway, my frugal side pointing out how much money this liquor must have cost. I poured it down the sink and ran water after to rinse down the smell.

Lars tapped my shoulder and I jumped. The empty bottle clinked against the sink. I turned toward him, the neck of the bottle held tightly in my hand.

He held his hands palms out at shoulder height. "Forgive me."

"Please do not touch me." I enunciated each word carefully.

He retreated, hands in the air as if I had a gun trained on him.

I put the bottle in the sink and left him standing that way. In the bedroom, I opened the window and shoved the bed against the door. If I had misjudged him and he tried to come through, I stood a good chance of making it out the window before he managed to shift the bed out of the way.

I collapsed on the neatly made bed. Lars had never come close to striking me before. I had worried what he might do if drunk, but it had never crossed my mind that he would hit me. I felt like a fool.

The man was a trained SS interrogator. I had spent only days with him over the past two years. I knew him very little. Andreas seemed to think him quite capable of hurting me. What exactly had I expected?

I had grown soft living with Boris. I had forgotten how dangerous men could be. I touched bruises forming on my arm. My dress did not cover them.

I pressed my ear to the door. Silence. What was he doing? If he had left, I would have heard the front door. I gathered up my press pass, but stopped with my hand on the knob, afraid to go through. I thought of climbing out the window to escape him.

The telephone rang, the metallic sound muffled by the tea cozy. Lars barked his side of a short, hot argument. Then the receiver crashed down. Less than a minute elapsed before the front door slammed. Off to work on a Sunday?

I pushed the bed away from my door, glad that he lived on the ground floor. I would hate to explain to a downstairs neighbor why I moved the furniture. A quick walk through the apartment revealed that it was empty. I read a note on the kitchen table.

I was called away to work. If I can get away, I will try to meet you at the evening fencing. My deepest, deepest apologies. My behavior was inexcusable.

Lars

I left the note exactly as I found it.

He had been to the bakery before I arrived, and a spread of pastries covered a ceramic plate. A full kettle rested on the stove; dry leaves sat in the bottom of the teapot. Every item in the kitchen spoke of how long he had been awake, waiting for me. Worried.

I tried to decide what to do. I could stick to the original plan, stay in Berlin, cover the Games for the paper, pick up the film Lars had secreted in a locker somewhere, and then go back to Switzerland and meet my British contact. The Games lasted only two more weeks, and I might keep him sober until the end of it. But if I could not, how much was I at risk from him? If he chose to, he could hurt me quite badly, or kill me, without having to fear the consequences.

I tore out the pages I had written to calm myself at the stadium after Peter's death. I found a match and lit them in the sink. The smell of burning paper stung my eyes. Once the paper blackened to ashes, I rinsed them down the drain and washed up the breakfast things.

I could go straight home. Even if I lost my job, Switzerland presented the safest alternative. Lars was wrong about many things, among them that I did not understand the dangers of Germany under the Nazis. I did. If caught, I would end up beaten to death in a Gestapo cell or condemned to a slower death in a concentration camp.

Anton would be raised without a mother, perhaps never knowing what had happened to me. I ran that risk every time I came, but this time it felt more immediate.

I pictured Anton waiting in Boris's front room, eyes glued to the path that led to the door. I remembered the last time I saw him.

Anton stood at the end of Boris's path, one hand on the gate. I had to leave soon or I would miss my train to Berlin.

"Boris explained it," he said. "What you are going away to do."

I waited. If I missed the next train, I could catch a night train. "He did?"

"It's about a treaty." His face was grave. "Both sides must follow the rules they agreed on before the peace pipe was smoked. You are sneaking into the enemy encampment to make sure that they do."

I set down my suitcase. Anton only reverted to his Indian metaphors when very excited or upset. I wished again that I had not left Boris a month before, that I was not leaving Anton right now. I played along with him. "It is a secret mission."

"Boris told me that, too." Anton swung the gate back and forth a few centimeters. "It is dangerous, but it is more important than the life of a single warrior. Even you."

"I have done this many times," I said. "And I have always returned alive."

I felt Anton's arms around my waist. I leaned down to kiss his short blond hair.

Then I took my leave. All the way to the train station, I thought about missing the train and going back. I could have undone it all.

A part of me knew that I was wrong to have left him in the first place, and doubly wrong to stay. But I was here now, and I had work to do, work that would benefit Anton in the future.

Despite our uneasy partnership, I owed Lars, too. If I left him in Berlin, and he kept drinking, he would eventually be indiscreet, and they would kill him. He had gone to work at SS headquarters this morning drunk and angry. I bore some responsibility for that. I, too, could have left a note. Now, who knew what he said or did?

I could not forget that, at great personal risk, he had saved my life. Countless times, including yesterday. I did not love him, but I cared for him. Over the past two years, I had been forced to trust him with my life. So far as I knew, he had never betrayed me. I had come to admire his courage and his resourcefulness as we worked together to undermine the Nazi regime. Every risk I ran, he ran one hundredfold.

But that gave him no right to threaten to hit me.

I packed my things and left the apartment with my heavy suitcase and satchel, unsure if I would return. Perhaps a hotel room would open up, and I would not have to spend another night locked in the apartment of a drunken SS officer. Spy or no, Lars's position in the Gestapo still frightened me, and with the amount he was drinking, he was bound to make a mistake. I thought of leaving a note, but I did not know what to write.

Outside, streets and buildings boasted fresh-scrubbed surfaces. Red, white, and black swastika flags alternated with white Olympic ones in perfect rhythm. I wondered if the government had issued them or forced the buildings' occupants to buy them.

At Wittenbergplatz, I sat on the painted iron bench and let the rush of hot air from incoming trains pass over me several times before I felt reasonably certain that no one in the station watched, then hopped a train toward Ruhleben. Even if the government had loosened its restrictions on everyday citizens for the Games, it was still watching, and the Nazis had long memories.

I rested my forehead against the side of the car and closed my eyes. As always, the famous Berlin air streaming through the window smelled like cinders, tar, concrete, cigarette smoke, and crushed rock. At least the Nazis had not defiled that. Yet.

I opened my eyes and studied Peter's notebook, but made no more of it than before. I suspected that the word breaks were not correct.

Too many short words. My mind ran over random characters in Peter's journal again and again, but they never made sense.

I disembarked at the station newly renamed to Reichssportfeld, although why they had not left it as Stadium was beyond me. Not Nazi enough, I supposed. I angled through the throng to present my ticket at the door of the Cupola Room, sparing a quick glance through floor-to-ceiling windows at the pines and birches waving in the outside breeze. Peaceful and pastoral, as the Nazis had intended.

Fencers already stretched near the raised wooden strips they would fight on. Around the strips, the oak floor gleamed. Spectators chattered on seats above the athletes while officials in civilian suits milled about the floor.

I wished the Olympics had been held somewhere else, and I could have watched the fencing with Anton. He enjoyed watching, but was an indifferent fencer. He did not like to humiliate other students by winning, nor did he like to throw a match and lose. Still, he was forced to do it. The Swiss valued the old martial tradition of the aristocracy as much as the Germans. Fencing, like the javelin throw, was based directly on an activity designed to kill. I had no doubt that the German athletes would excel at both.

I missed Anton, and I missed the person I could be when I was with him.

Searching for the least exposed seat, I dragged my suitcase into the bowl-like Cupola Room. Unfortunately, the seats were arranged in a circle, no seat more or less visible than another. Thwarted by clever architectural design, I tilted my hat forward as if I believed it would help.

More men in coal black Nazi uniforms attended this event than the opening. Once again, I failed to make a note of it. The room was only half full. Too early in the day for those who had stayed up for the opening-night festivities? I checked my gold pocket watch. It was almost nine, time for the fencing to start.

White-suited men fidgeted in folding chairs lining the edge of the competition area, awaiting their turn. Each team consisted of four young men. They joked together and put on and took off their jackets. The moment they had trained for all their lives had come. What moment had I waited for all my life? I wondered if it had passed unnoticed.

Two fencers faced off on the strip, rectangular slips of paper with their competitor numbers affixed to their backs, helmets on, and ready to begin. Four judges in civilian suits watched intently.

I concentrated on the white-suited fencers in front of me as their foils clashed together again and again. Fierce and lightning fast, they would have cut me to ribbons in an instant. Fauconnet, the first Swiss fencer, lost, and his three waiting teammates stirred anxiously. The fencers possessed great skill, but I found myself watching the aroused spectators instead. Ordinarily stolid Swiss burghers yelled from their seats and men in traditional Greek costume gesticulated back. Their fervent enthusiasm reminded me too much of Nazi rallies. I shifted uncomfortably on my seat and turned my attention back to the athletes. In the end, the Swiss men's team squeaked a victory out over Greece, although the number of matches won and point totals were tied. Victory was decided on hits given and hits received. When the Swiss victory was announced, I heard fierce yelling in what I assumed to be Greek.

In the next set of matches, Greece also lost to Belgium, so the Swiss advanced to the second round in the evening without having to fight another team, and I found myself unexpectedly free at ten thirty.

I sneaked out before results were posted, thereby avoiding the crowd and any other reporters. I hurried a few blocks to the phone booth I had used yesterday, regretting not leaving my suitcase at Lars's apartment, and called in the story. Duty done until the evening fencing, I set off to investigate the mystery of the notebook.

5

I hopped a subway toward Alexanderplatz, hoping to find my friend Paul: the one person who might know if Peter had invented a new code instead of changing the old one. Hopefully he had not moved and was at home.

At Alexanderplatz, tall wooden poles twined with evergreens lined the street, like the famous Christmas market in Nuremberg, a city now more known for last year's anti-Jewish Nuremberg Laws than for its charming Christmas festivities. Patriotic flags smothered faces of buildings, making the fragmentary glimpses of the underlying stone seem too insubstantial to support them.

I stood in front of the massive brick-clad police headquarters, undecided. Fritz Waldheim, a policeman and close friend, worked only meters away. With a well-placed question or two, I might discover how Peter Weill had died. But Hannah Vogel was supposed to be out of the country. I dared not show my face at the police station, in case someone recognized me from my days as a crime reporter and then remembered that I was still wanted in connection with the kidnapping of Ernst Röhm's son. Still, it was tempting.

Instead I hurried up Hirtenstrasse into the Jewish quarter. Parallel to the street, metal flagpoles stuck out of the top floors of the buildings. Only Olympic flags hung down these buildings. If a Jew, even one who had been a German citizen until the Nuremberg Laws stole his citizenship last summer, flew the German flag, the punishment was a year in prison.

People clustered in small knots around doorways, ready to flee inside at the first sign of hostility. They watched me pass in silence. When I smiled reassuringly, they lowered their gazes to newly swept sidewalks.

They would accept no reassurance from me.

The buildings had been cleansed of Nazi graffiti, every pane of glass in the windows whole and polished. If it had not been for the frightened looks of people in the street and the absence of big red flags, I would not have known that I traveled in the Jewish quarter.

I glanced at Herr Klein's old shop as I passed. I had been relieved to hear that the jeweler had left soon after I did, in 1931, for New York. In his last letter, he told me that his business flourished, he and his wife always had a spare room for me, and his cough had cleared up now, so he would make a quieter housemate. His Berlin storefront currently sold kosher meats, but iron bars still protected the broad plate glass windows, and I was sure they still had the same strong bolts barring the thick wooden door.

I walked aimlessly, making certain that no one dogged my footsteps. My caution seemed excessive, but I did not want to lead anyone here. Any connection between me and my friends, especially the Jewish ones, must remain buried. Satisfied that I was alone, I circled back.

I stopped in front of my friend Sarah's former apartment. She wisely fled Berlin before I did, borrowing my identity to do so. The stone building had been cleansed of soot. Its pale gray sides now appeared newer than it did when I first saw it as a grieving nineteen-year-old who had lost her intended husband. With water and brushes, the Nazis had removed its venerable patina. How much time would it take for them to wash away the history of those who occupied it?

I pressed the bell for BERNSTEIN, pleased to see that Sarah's metal name plaque remained. In her letters, she had told me that she gave her apartment to our friend, Paul Keller. For years, Paul and I had worked together at the *Berliner Tageblatt*. Like all Jews, he was fired from the paper in October 1933, with the passage of the Editor's Law.

Although I had been back in Berlin a few times since I moved away, I had not dared visit Paul. Maintaining the façade of my relationship with Lars monopolized the handful of days I spent in Berlin each year. To shield my real friends from my contacts at the SS, I kept them completely separated.

Today I did not intend to waste my hours of freedom. Paul had known Peter Weill even longer than I. If they had kept in contact, he might know Peter's mysterious news or at least how to decipher his code.

An old friend of Sarah's, Herr Greenblatt, came out the front door. A retired soldier, seventy years if a day, he still carried himself as if he marched on a parade ground.

"Good morning, Herr Greenblatt," I said.

"My word, but it's little Hannah," he said in a delighted voice. "We haven't seen you for ages."

He held the door open politely, and I stepped inside. After we exchanged pleasantries, he clicked his heels and bowed a farewell, like all soldiers of his generation. I felt heartened that he had not viewed me with more suspicion.

I clomped up the stairs. My suitcase grew heavier with each step, and my satchel strap cut into my shoulder. When I reached Sarah's front door, the bronze mezuzah was the same. I set down my suitcase and touched the patterned metal with one fingertip, remembering the day she had hung it.

A woman dressed in black answered the door before I knocked. Her heart-shaped face looked squashed flat, like a Persian cat's, her expression just as pleasant. "Yes?"

"I am a friend of Paul's," I said, taken aback. "From the paper."

Her accent sounded foreign, but Paul's family had lived in Berlin for generations. A wife, perhaps? Sarah had not mentioned it in her letters, but gossip from Germany was hard to come by.

The woman rubbed her hugely pregnant stomach and eyed my suitcase suspiciously. "So?"

"May I see him?" I raised my voice, hoping Paul would hear.

"No." Her coffee brown eyes gave nothing away. She pushed the door closed, but I wedged my suitcase in it. Did she understand a word I had said?

"Is Paul here?" I spoke loudly, hoping that he would hear if he still lived there. Perhaps he had given the apartment to others and fled Germany. My heart lightened at the thought.

"Who is at the door?" I recognized the voice, and my heart sank again. Paul had not yet escaped Germany. He peered over the woman's shoulder. Stubble dotted his chin, and his shirt was unbuttoned. It reminded me of the mornings when he used to leave my Berlin apartment, years before.

"Hannah? Why are you here?" He eyed me for a few seconds from the doorway.

"Hello, Paul," I said. I used my neutral reporter voice, the one that projected calm interest but nothing more. "May I come in?"

I watched him weigh the consequences of letting me into the apartment versus leaving me in the hall. Years ago, when he had asked me to become his wife, we trusted each other with everything. I forged on. "Or would you rather discuss things in the hall? Or perhaps I could send you a telegram?"

He glanced up and down the hall to see if anyone might overhear us. I watched him decide that it was better to let me in than have me make a scene in the hall. He nodded to the cat-faced woman. Reluctantly, she stepped out of the doorframe. He ran one hand comfortingly along her shoulder before picking up my suitcase and bringing it inside.

The odor of boiled cabbage rolled into the hall. I gritted my teeth and stepped into the smell.

"Miriam, this is Hannah, an old colleague from the paper," he said stiffly. A colleague? We had been close friends for years after our romantic relationship ended. I did not know why, but I had obviously been demoted. I smiled pleasantly and wondered if Miriam understood what he said. I wondered if I did.

"Hannah, this is Miriam, my wife."

"Best wishes on your marriage." I held out my hand for Miriam to shake. She did not take it. I glanced at Paul, who shrugged. He did not shake my hand either. I lowered it. Not quite the welcome our almost twenty years of friendship had led me to expect.

We entered the living room. Sarah's aubergine horsehair sofa still stood next to the graceful coffee table, and her lace curtains hung in the windows, but nothing else was the same. Dark rectangles on the walls showed where her pictures had once hung, among them one of myself and my murdered brother, Ernst. Her personal things were gone. Shipped to her, or sold?

I walked behind the sofa and slid my hand across the smooth fabric, remembering hours spent here laughing with Sarah and Paul.

Miriam asked Paul a quick, angry question in a Slavic language. Polish? Whatever the language, it sounded like a challenge.

"Would you be more comfortable in the kitchen?" A note of defiance peppered his words. What waited in the kitchen?

"Whatever you prefer," I said.

Miriam glowered. I was not to feel comfortable in any room in this apartment; that was clear.

Paul led us to the kitchen. Miriam took care to keep herself between Paul and me, as if to protect him.

Ceramic crunched under my shoe when I stepped across the threshold. Shards of broken crockery littered the floor. Someone had thrown a dish against the wall. I guessed it had once been a plate.

I glanced at Paul. He shook his head fractionally. I stepped around fragments and sat at the table. He could keep his secrets. I certainly would keep mine.

I took in the well-scrubbed surfaces. Of that, Sarah would approve. A knife rested on a wooden board next to a loaf of bread.

"I have not been here in ages," I said, reminded of my last visit. Perhaps it was even the same knife. "Not since—"

"Since you almost skewered me?" Paul asked. In 1931, before I left Germany, Anton and I had been hiding in this apartment after someone ransacked mine. When Paul stopped by unannounced, I nearly stabbed him.

"You must accept the consequences if you enter someone's house without knocking." I tilted my head toward the broken plate. "Sometimes even if you do."

He gave me a tight smile. Suspicion clouded Miriam's eyes as her head swiveled between us, uncomprehending. She understood little German. Curious.

He said something in an undertone. So, he had learned Polish. She shook her head, a mutinous set to her jaw.

I breathed through my mouth to keep from smelling cabbage. "Would it be easier if we met elsewhere?"

"That would be more complicated." His eyes flicked anxiously to his wife. She crossed her hands above her stomach.

"Should I leave? I have no wish to cause trouble." Not entirely true, as I was angry about the treatment I had received from both of them. Whatever their personal fight, I had nothing to do with it. I just wanted to ask about Peter Weill.

"You didn't cause it." His chair creaked when he shifted to stretch his leg out to the side. I wondered if the wound in his leg from the Great War still bothered him. He caught me watching, stood abruptly, and filled a battered black teakettle.

Miriam clanged the lid off the pot of cabbage.

Paul busied himself putting the kettle on. She stepped past and sprinkled dark green leaves into the teapot. It did not look like tea.

Paul handed me a glass of warm water that tasted like metal.

"What brings you here?" he asked. "I haven't seen you since I left you in that hospital bed."

Five years before, he had sneaked in to see me when I lay in hospital after being shot. He had brought me the passport I needed to escape and enough money to get myself away. "Thank you for your help, and the money." I opened my satchel. "I wish to pay you back."

He waved his hand impatiently. "I don't want your money. I am glad it helped."

Miriam said something, and he answered sharply. Although I did not understand the words, I understood the argument. I pressed a fifty-mark bill into her sweaty palm.

He turned to me. "I just said—"

"For the baby," I answered.

"Thank you," she said in heavily accented German. He threw up his hands in defeat.

Her sharp brown eyes darted to my suitcase.

"Also, please tell her that I am not asking to stay. I only wish to repay you and ask a few questions. Nothing more."

He translated that, too. Her shoulders did not relax.

"And why are you carrying a suitcase?" he asked.

"You never know when you might need a change of clothes."

Paul shook his head. "Same old Hannah."

"Just older." The weight of the last five years pressed on me. "Today, much older."

When she poured tea, the bitter grassy scent of nettles stung my nostrils. "Thank you," I said, although I hated stinging nettle tea. I wondered if they had gathered it themselves.

I picked up my hot cup to blow on the tea. Miriam took it out of my hands and tipped a dollop into the saucer to cool. My mother would have been appalled, as would Paul's. "Thank you," I said again, wishing I knew how to say it in Polish.

Paul unwrapped his long, elegant fingers from his cup before she poured some into his saucer as well.

"Tell me what you have been doing," I said. "Since I left."

Paul paused, and I knew he was deciding what he could safely tell. I waited, saddened that he felt he had to be so cautious.

"As you probably know, all Jews were forbidden to work for newspapers in 1933. The Editor's Law."

"I do." I sipped tea from my saucer. Every bit as vile as I remembered, like grass, spinach, and a hint of cabbage.

"I was German enough to fight for my country in the Great War. German enough to carry shrapnel in my leg for the rest of my life."

His hand brushed across his leg where the wound was. I remembered the days I had worked with him as a nurse, helping him to regain its use and learn to walk on it.

"I know, Paul. I was there."

He talked over me. "And even for all that, I was only half Jewish. I had never even been to temple."

Miriam put a comforting hand on his arm. When she moved, a finely wrought gold locket on an insubstantial chain swung free of her dress. The locket was round, like a pocket watch, with a design of leaves around the edge and a small circle in the center from which rays extended to the sides. It had once belonged to Paul's mother. He gave it to me many years ago, and I had returned it to him when I turned down his marriage proposal.

Paul took a deep breath, but his voice was still full of anger and bitterness when he continued. "So I became the Jew they had condemned me to be. I studied the Torah. I learned about the heritage that I was forced to claim. I am Jewish now, in a way I was not before they drove me to it. For that, I am grateful."

He did not sound grateful. "I see," I said, although I was not sure that I did.

"I am not German anymore," Paul said.

"Yet you are here." I gagged down another sip of fetid tea.

"We cannot get papers to leave." His voice rose. "The quotas for Jewish immigrants have always been low, but now most countries, like the United States, are not even admitting their usual quotas."

"I know. But I know someone who—"

"There will be no more assimilation."

"But—"

He again talked over me as if he had not heard, and I suspected he had not. "The choice is to blindly wait for our fate while kowtowing to our German masters or to repudiate them and seek solace inside ourselves."

I must have looked unconvinced. "Perhaps there is a third choice. Leaving—"

"You do not understand. You cannot understand. You are one of them." The bitterness in his voice stung.

"Them?" I shot back. I set my saucer on the table with a chink.

"Aryans." He directed the venom in his voice at me.

I stood. I had done much and risked more to expose the Nazis. "I see."

Paul sighed impatiently. "I did not mean it so, Hannah."

"You meant it just so." I carried my dishes to the sink. I set them inside gently, because I wanted to smash them. Enough had been broken here today.

"You do not know what we've been through," he said. An effort to placate, but I did not care.

"No one knows what another goes through, Paul." I turned to face them. "How many times did you tell me that yourself?"

We stared at each other until the doorbell rang. Miriam shot me an accusatory glance, and Paul's expression shifted to anger. "Are you expecting anyone?"

"I do not live here," I pointed out. "It is more likely that you are expecting someone."

"Excuse me while I see who it is." He hurried out.

Peter was an Aryan, too, by Paul's definition. I could not imagine that they would have shared secrets. I picked up my suitcase and took one last glance around the room, thinking of Sarah. Nothing remained for me here.

Paul stepped into the kitchen with Bella Fromm, former society reporter for the *Vossische Zeitung*. She wore a tailored linen dress and a pert straw hat, dressed for the Games. Jewish, like Paul, Bella was also aristocracy with strong ties to the international diplomatic community. The Nazis had to treat her with care.

"Bella!" I said, grateful to see her. I set my suitcase down.

"Hannah!" She crossed the kitchen, and we embraced stiffly. With her connections, I suspected that Bella knew of my work for the British government. We had never been close friends, but as staunch anti-Nazis in a growing Nazi world, we had developed a grudging respect for each other.

"I am sorry Gonny will not be competing," I said. Bella's daughter Gonny was a talented swimmer. But as a Jew, she could not compete in the Olympics for Germany.

Bella turned eyes on me as brown and deceptively soft as the center of a pansy petal. "How kind that you remembered."

She sounded so touched that I was taken aback.

"I cannot stay." Bella held up a gloved hand to stop Miriam from pouring tea for her. She knew how to deal with servants. Miriam nodded and stepped back.

We remained standing.

"Peter Weill," she began, "had a heart attack at the stadium yesterday."

"Another tragedy." Paul shook his head. "Thank you for bringing us the news."

I clenched my hands together, remembering how Peter always said the word *news*.

"This morning, his sister, Theresa, was found dead." Bella's voice was sad.

My knees swayed. I leaned against Sarah's sturdy wooden table.

"She committed suicide," Bella finished.

6

"She did not." I spoke too loudly.

All three swiveled their heads to stare at me. Bella seemed sad but resigned. Paul seemed unaffected by the news and my reaction. Still, I suppose Peter and Theresa were another couple of Aryans to him, as was I.

"How did she die?" I asked.

"She hanged herself," Bella said, putting a hand on my arm. "According to my source from the coroner's office."

"No," I said more angrily than I intended. She moved her hand away.

"You may not be aware of it, Hannah, but suicide rates are high in Berlin these days," Paul said, as if talking to a small child. "We lose people nearly every day."

"I saw her early this morning." I rounded on him, fists clenched by my sides. "She was upset about Peter's death. But she was not suicidal. Not one bit."

"Why were you there?" He sounded accusatory.

"A condolence call, for Peter." I drew the back of my suddenly cold hand over the cheek Theresa had pinched this morning.

"Peter died yesterday evening." Bella twisted one of her expensive rings. "How did you know he was dead?"

"I have sources, too." I met her gaze angrily.

Paul broke the silence. "Good ones, I guess."

"How long are you in Berlin?" Bella asked me. "Where are you staying?"

"It is rather complicated." I still had no idea where I would sleep that night, but even if I had, I would not have told her. Paul's reactions had reminded me that I could not trust even my oldest friends in the Germany newly wrought by the Nazis.

"Thank you for coming to tell us, Bella," Paul said. "I am isolated these days."

"Then spend more time gathering news and less in seclusion," Bella said sharply. "Even if the news won't be published."

"It's not so easy." Paul rubbed his fingers across his unshaven chin, looking suddenly self-conscious.

"I know," she answered. "Because I do it."

She added something in Yiddish. I did not understand it, but Paul and Miriam clearly did. Both looked sheepish.

"I must leave." Bella straightened her straw hat. "I am attending the Olympic fencing this evening and must see to a few matters before then."

"As must I," I said, eager to go. "May I accompany you?"

"Naturally."

We trooped through Sarah's living room and into the hall, Miriam bringing up the rear.

"I'd like to speak with Hannah alone for a moment, Bella. Can you wait for her downstairs?" Paul asked as we stepped into the empty hall.

Bella sniffed. She hated waiting for anyone, but her good breeding showed through. "If she hurries."

Paul shut the door, closing an agitated-looking Miriam inside. I watched his worried face until Bella's light footsteps faded, then spoke. "Paul?"

"I know what you are thinking. You want to find out who killed them, if they were killed." He stepped in close. "Don't."

I did not bother to deny my goal. "Why not?"

"It's not like it was when you left. People disappear every day. Peter and Theresa were old. They could very well have died from a natural cause and suicide."

"Then it should be easy to confirm and involve little risk." I glanced up at him, suddenly aware of how much weight he had lost. Always thin, now his face was gaunt.

"Even if they didn't, what purpose can it serve for you to know? You cannot bring their killers, assuming there are killers, to justice. There is no justice anymore."

"What if they died to unearth someone's secret? And I can bring that secret to light?" I felt the weight of the satchel's strap on my shoulder and thought of the notebook inside. And I thought of Anton, home in Switzerland waiting for me, blue eyes as anxious as they had been when we said good-bye, jaw set bravely but still trembling. What world would he grow up in if I turned away from my work here?

"You don't know how it is." Paul leaned against the banister, angling his long legs away from me. "No one can be trusted."

"I trust Bella." I was unsure if I did, since Peter had not seemed to, but I had to have something to say.

"Bella." Paul waved his elegant hand dismissively. "If she disappears, the embassies will be in an uproar. She has strong protectors. You don't."

"Why, Paul." I fluttered my eyelashes like a starlet. "Don't I have you?" My tone was sarcastic, because we both knew that I did not. In Germany these days, I had no one. In fact, it seemed as though no one had anyone.

"This is no joke, Hannah." His voice rose.

"Friends died, Paul. I cannot walk away." I took a deep breath. "Not until I know why. And you of all people should appreciate that."

"Do you think this is unique? I've had dozens of friends murdered. If I tried to find all the culprits, I'd have no life left, even assuming I weren't killed for my troubles."

He had suffered more than I. He, too, had lost friends. "But, Paul, I cannot—"

"You can. You should." He spoke in a level tone, but his voice shook with anger. "Do you think they would have wanted you to die for them?"

"If they were prepared to die for something, I imagine they thought it important." I gripped the smooth handle of my suitcase tightly.

He shook his head in disappointment. "It's not like you think it is, Hannah. And it hasn't been for a very long time."

Sarah's front door opened. Miriam beckoned to him. He gave me a final helpless look before turning toward her. He had made his choices, and he kept to them. Who was I to judge?

I reached past him and stroked my index finger along the mezuzah's warm metal surface. "*Auf Wiedersehen*, Paul."

I headed downstairs and out the front door, where Bella waited in the backseat of a gleaming Mercedes with a uniformed chauffeur in the front. I had forgotten that she had a car and a driver. She was protected. I was not. Paul was correct; I must always bear that in mind.

The driver hurried to open the rear door. His white gloves held the edge of the door while I seated myself in the backseat; then he closed the door gently, careful that a loud noise not disturb us. Bella had a reputation for having the best servants.

He disappeared behind us, depositing my suitcase in the boot with a discreet thump.

"Could you take me to Friedrichstrasse instead of the Games?" I asked her.

She cocked her head to one side. Violet berries quivered on her hatband. "Theresa's?"

Before I answered, the chauffeur got in front. I watched the back of his black cap and did not answer. He pulled smoothly into traffic, apparently oblivious of our conversation.

"He's quite trustworthy," she said.

We rounded a horse and wagon and picked up speed. "I would rather speak with just your ears listening."

She studied me for a split second. "Karl, please turn on the radio."

He leaned forward, clicked a dial, and seconds later, an excited voice chanting Olympic statistics filled the car. I had never ridden in an automobile with a radio before. The sound quality was uneven, but at least it was loud.

She leaned in close, blanketing me in the scent of Chanel No. 5. "Is that acceptable?"

"Yes." The powerful car quickly left the white Olympic flags of the Jewish quarter behind, and the red, white, and black Nazi flags reappeared.

"Where should we drop you?" She pulled a jet black square compact from her purse, checked her raspberry-colored lipstick, and reapplied it.

"A block from Theresa Weill's. I want to circle around to be certain that I was not followed."

"My driver is trained to look for such things. We won't be." Her voice told me how she disapproved of the idea.

"Humor me."

She chuckled.

The driver stopped at the streetlight and a troop of boys in Hitler Youth uniforms marched across the street. They were no older than Anton, but they already marched in perfect formation. The determination in their faces was eerie. I compared their military formation to the casual packs in which the boys in Switzerland traveled, grateful Anton had that freedom. I turned my gaze back to the inside of the car. Bella's dark eyes watched the boys, too.

The boys reached the sidewalk, and our car started forward again. I shook myself. "The address is—"

"I know it." She gave the driver a cross street on Friedrichstrasse a block from Theresa's apartment and he immediately turned right. How did she know the location? If he and Bella were friends, why had Peter wanted me to smuggle out his story? Why had he not gone to her directly? It hung on the package he had mentioned. But how?

"When were you last at Theresa's?" I asked. Afternoon sun glinted off the windshields of the oncoming cars.

"A few weeks ago. The last years have made for strange bedfellows." She patted ivory-colored powder on her nose. "Peter was one of us."

Peter had been "one of us" to me since before the Nazis came to power. I bit my lower lip. Class distinctions had given way to political ones. This was no time to be angry at Bella for being a snob. Politically, she was my most trusted ally for hundreds of kilometers. I trusted her more than Paul.

"Tell me the things you wouldn't tell Paul." She clicked her compact shut and returned it to her bag, then folded her gloved hands expectantly in her lap. "I imagine that's quite a lot."

I weighed the situation for only a second. I did not fully trust her, but I needed her, so I quickly outlined my last meetings with Peter and Theresa. I struggled to stay analytical and matter of fact. Something kept me from mentioning Peter's notebook or the package. If he had not told her about them, neither should I.

"Do you know what he was working on?" I asked when I finished. Perhaps Bella could solve this and I would be free to go home to Anton. I felt like a child hoping that the adults would solve my problems, but even as a child, I had known better.

She stared out the window, carefully outlined lips pursed. "This puts a different light on everything. I must consult my sources. See what I can unearth. While keeping your involvement secret, of course."

"Where can I reach you?" If she found something, I wanted to know. If she resolved it, I could take the next train to Switzerland. As Anton's mother, I would not risk my life a second longer than I needed to. Even if I lost my job over it, at least I would still be alive.

She handed me an engraved card with her name and telephone number. I memorized the number and handed it back. No links.

"Is there anywhere that I can reach you?" she asked.

"No," I said without hesitation. Lars and Bella must be kept separate.

The driver pulled up near the cross street. Same red brick buildings and flags as this morning. He opened the door and offered Bella

his hand, then helped her out as if she stepped from a coach. I struggled not to smile at the absurdity as he handed me out as well.

He left to fetch my suitcase from the boot.

"One more thing," I whispered while he was gone.

"Isn't there always?" She waved the driver away when he walked
up. He set the suitcase near my feet, touched his cap, and returned to
the front seat. He faced forward, away from us. "What do you need?"
Bella asked in the resigned tone of someone besieged for favors.

I bristled. "Only to let you know that I am covering the Games
under a false identity."

"You are attending events crawling with press under an assumed
name?" Her voice rang with disbelief. "Most Berlin reporters know you."

"I had no choice," I said. "I managed to get through the Winter
Olympics in Garmisch. I keep far from the press box. But should I
run into you at the Games, my name is Adelheid Zinsli. I am a Swiss
widow, so you can introduce me as Frau Zinsli."

Her look told me how foolish she thought I was. "I will help if I
can, but I can't very well introduce you as Adelheid Zinsli if there is
anyone around who already knows you as Hannah Vogel."

"Do what you can. I expect no miracles." Behind her head I noted
the cars that passed so I would recognize them if they reappeared soon.

She embraced me, a genuine hug this time, and I again inhaled the
scent of Chanel No. 5. "Bless you, Hannah, for all that you do."

"What do I do?" Bella did far more than I.

She tapped my cheek with her gloved index finger. "Good. You are
doing good. And there are so few of us left."

She climbed in, the driver closed her door, and they pulled away. I
watched until their automobile turned the corner, waited to see if another car followed them. When none did, I picked up my suitcase and
circled the block, noting the vehicles in the street to see if anyone had
stayed to follow me. I noticed no one.

While I walked past the tall brick apartment buildings, I thought
about the events at Paul's. I deeply regretted losing my temper with

him. He clearly lived hand to mouth and probably feared for the world into which he was bringing a child. Paul was no Bella Fromm. If he disappeared, no one in authority would care. His life was hard, and instead of sympathizing, I had taken offense and fled. Coming from a safe and well-fed Swiss life made it too easy for me to judge him.

I stopped in front of Theresa's building and fished the familiar metal key out of my satchel. I slotted it in, suppressing the thought that the woman who had handed it to me, only hours before, lay dead on a slab at the morgue.

7

I took the uneven stairs more slowly than this morning. Of course, this time I carried a suitcase, my satchel, and twice as much grief. Afternoon sunlight revealed dirt-smudged walls and stair treads worn by too many feet. Nothing appeared out of the ordinary, but I stopped at the landing and scrutinized the entryway from above. Still nothing.

I paused before Theresa's door and ran my fingertips along the glossy white-painted doorframe. The surface was unblemished, the lock unscratched. No one had forced it open. Either the killer had a key, as I did, or Theresa let him in. Or her.

I unlocked the door and stepped into the too-familiar scent of Peter's tobacco and whisky. I drew in a shaky breath of good-bye. I doubted I would ever stand here and smell it again.

As Theresa had done this morning, I hurried inside and flicked on the light. I expected her to come through the hall scolding me, but the apartment stayed stubbornly silent.

I put down my suitcase on the bare wooden floor with a thump and turned slowly in one spot, scrutinizing my surroundings. Coatrack with winter coats that had probably hung untouched for months. Clean-swept floor. Umbrella stand. I paused. I had found the umbrella, and left it, unfastened. Someone had refastened the strap around the end of the ribs.

But who? Who else knew that Peter hid his notebook there? Had Theresa opened the umbrella to see if I had thieved it? Had the killer?

I froze, listening. Had the intruder returned? My ears strained for the slightest sound. A car horn tooted on the street below and I jumped. This was an unacceptable situation. I could not stand here forever.

I opened the front door again, so that any commotion that might happen inside would be heard on the landing, and to provide me with a quick exit. I hurried through the rooms. Once certain I was alone, I closed and locked the door, fitting the chain into place.

I combed the living room, checking inside books, searching under the table and the rug. I wished I had Anton's facility for spotting the incongruous, and his ability to make a joke about it. But I was here alone, and humor was far away.

I sat in Peter's reading chair to think. On the table near my right hand rested a leather-bound collection of poetry by Goethe. My index finger traced the gilded letters on the spine. Probably the last book Peter ever read. As I paged through, a piece of folded paper fell out.

I unfolded it with careful fingers. Spidery letters in Peter's familiar old code crawled across the page. Hurriedly I deciphered it. It was a list of flowers: Chicory, Violet, Stepmother Flower, Gooseflower, Thistle, Rose, Lily, Tulip, and Bird-Of-Paradise. *Thistle* was struck through. *Bird-of-Paradise* had a question mark next to it. Why encode a list of flowers?

I searched for a pattern. Chicory and thistles were weeds, not something he would purchase from the florist, unlike lilies, roses, and gooseflowers. Stepmother flowers, or pansies, were common garden flowers. Bird-of-Paradise was the only tropical flower in the list. No connections yet.

Peter kept track of the favorite flowers of his female sources. Whose favorite flower was the thistle? Anton's. He liked it because it was in the coat of arms for Scotland. The chicory? Perhaps the flowers represented something else, or the letters served as an anagram. I folded the paper in half and tucked it into my notebook. I would try to figure it out later.

I walked into the kitchen and paused. Everything tidied away, as always. The sunflowers I had brought clustered in a milky yellow vase on the orange tablecloth. Atop the tablecloth sat an ordinary cardboard box.

A box that had not been there when I left.

I opened it. I drew out Peter's gray fedora and caressed the felt brim, remembering the jaunty way it used to sit on his head, and the way it had fallen off just before he died.

The police must have returned his personal effects to Theresa. Had that been enough to tip her over the edge into despair? I shook my head. Not Theresa.

I pulled out the neatly folded yet still wrinkled suit jacket that yesterday surrounded arms that had embraced me. I stroked my palms over the navy wool, remembering how it felt with Peter inside, his frail body warm with life, the way his voice rose when he said that he had news.

"What news did you have for me, old friend?" I asked the empty room.

I rifled through Peter's pockets for clues. His left pocket held a poker chip, and his other pockets contained crumpled bits of paper, a sack of tobacco, a pipe, a pair of reading glasses, and a ticket to the opening of the Olympic Games. I dropped them into my satchel and peered into the box. I pulled out an inventory of the contents, which listed everything I had removed, plus, "Flask, silver, engraved with the initials PW and geometric patterns."

Where was his flask? I felt around the inside of the box. The flask did not magically appear. If it had been there, I could have had it tested to see if he was poisoned. But it was missing. Had someone stolen it at the police station before they delivered the box? Had Theresa hidden it or thrown it away? Or had the killer taken it?

I stared at the box neatly centered on the orange tablecloth. "Perspective," Peter had once said. "Change it, and you change everything. You're an artist. You should know that."

With my back against the wall, I scooted down and sat on the smooth linoleum floor. Theresa had not been as thorough at sweeping as I had thought from the chair. I got on all fours and examined the dirt under the cabinet. Something glittered. I ripped an empty page from my notebook and folded it in half. Using it as a dustpan, I swept everything from underneath the cabinet onto the paper.

I rose, careful not to spill, and set the paper on the tablecloth. A miniature golden hinge rested in the center, back bent as if it whatever it had been attached to had been smashed. What would use such a tiny hinge? A very small box? Jewelry?

I sorted through the rest of the detritus, which contained a shard of glass and a single dark splinter. Any of them might have been under the cabinet for years, or they might have been swept there this morning.

I found a yellowed envelope on Theresa's desk and sealed the scraps in it, just in case.

I had found nothing that resembled the package Peter had mentioned. What kind of package could I carry out, but Bella could not? It made no sense.

I returned to the kitchen and picked up Peter's suit jacket to put away. It stood out in sharp contrast to the orange tablecloth. I folded the jacket and neatly returned everything to the box, including the list.

The tablecloth hung crooked. I reached to straighten it. And stopped.

The cloth had been blue and white checked this morning, but now it was solid orange.

I took everything off the table, including the cloth. The wooden surface revealed no secrets. Perhaps the secrets rested in the old cloth.

I went to Theresa's laundry basket, but it contained no tablecloth. I searched every centimeter of the apartment. Not so much as a thread remained. I saw no evidence that the police had done any kind of investigation. Besides, if they had taken the tablecloth, they would have left the table bare.

Had Theresa or someone else used it as the noose? Bella's friend at the coroner's office might know.

I rearranged the sunflowers and set them back in the center of the tablecloth next to the box of personal effects. Bright yellow petals, still fresh, shone. What if I had stayed after I gave them to her instead of going back to Lars's? If it was suicide, I could have prevented it. If murder, perhaps I could have prevented that, too. Or been killed as well.

The front door slammed against the chain.

I looked wildly around the kitchen. Nowhere to hide. The only exit was the front door, and I had tarried too long.

I drew a carving knife from the drawer and waited.

"Hallo!" called a man's voice.

I exhaled and put the knife away. "Panzer!"

I hurried toward the front door. Peter's son, Panzer, got his nickname when he served in a tank commando in the Great War. With his barrel chest and too-small head, he even resembled a tank.

I pulled the chain back and opened the door. His appearance was much the same as always, except his face was a bit paler than usual, and his clothes were unkempt. Usually a natty dresser, he had lost his father and his devoted aunt in the last two days. It had taken a toll on both of us.

He stepped across the threshold and swept me into a rib-crushing hug. "Sisterlein!"

I hugged him back. His aunt and father once hoped that we would marry, and we had dated for a few months, but no chemistry existed on either side. I viewed him as the big brother I had never had, and for his part, he seemed happy to have a little sister.

Once I struggled out of his grasp, I studied his tired face. "My condolences on your losses, Brüderchen."

"You heard?" He fidgeted with dark buttons on his suit.

"From a colleague." Technically true. I had also heard the news from Bella.

"It's quite a thing, isn't it? Both so close together." A button came off in his hand and clattered to the floor.

"I am so sorry."

He covered his mouth and coughed once, as he always did when he suppressed emotion. I bent and retrieved his button, dropping it into his pocket.

He grasped my hand in both of his strong ones. "I am so glad you are here. But what are you doing?"

I had no ready answer. "I . . . I . . . wanted to sit here for a while. I had my old key, so I let myself in. I hope you do not mind."

"Of course I don't mind." He squeezed my hand. "I came here for that reason myself. I haven't been here since I found out, but now that I am, I know it's true. It doesn't feel real anywhere else."

"I can leave," I said. "If you want to be alone."

"Not yet. Please." He dropped my hand and looked around the apartment uncertainly, as if he, too, expected Theresa to appear and scold us for tarrying here.

I tugged on his hands and led him into the tidy kitchen.

He released my hand to straighten the vase of sunflowers before pulling out a chair for me.

Instead of sitting, I shook my head. "Shall I make tea?"

"Something stronger." He disappeared into the living room, returning a moment later with a nearly full bottle of Macallan whisky. He poured us each a shot, the familiar smell of Peter's whisky drifting up.

We clinked our glasses together and drank, as we had many times before. As soon as I swallowed, I regretted it. Had someone poisoned the whisky? Too late. We had already drunk. I held my breath.

Panzer laid a heavy hand on my shoulder. "Hannah? Are you all right?"

I thought of telling him my worries about the whisky, but if it contained poison, it was already too late for us both. Peter had showed signs by this point. I let out my breath. "Just a bad memory."

Panzer gave me a sharp look. "About whisky?"

"Whisky has caused me more than one bad memory," I said. So, if Peter was poisoned, someone tampered with the flask after he left Theresa's. I remembered her evasive answer when I asked if he had gone to the Games alone.

"I doubt that, darling Sisterlein. The one Father loved best."

"He loved you very much," I said, swallowing another sip of smoky whisky. "He was so proud when you got the math professorship."

"I didn't say he didn't love me. Just that he loved you more. You were always his secret-keeper."

I thought of the secret Peter had failed to impart before he died. I had not turned out to be an adequate secret-keeper in the end. "The Reporter Code."

"More than that, little Hannah." Panzer reached over and tousled my hair. I gave him a mock angry look. No one had had the effrontery to tousle my hair in years.

"Don't be upset." He drained his glass. "I have missed you."

"I moved from Berlin a few years ago." I hesitated, uncertain how much to disclose.

He poured himself another drink and topped mine off as well. "I know. Without a word to anyone."

"It was complicated." I stared into the amber liquid.

He clinked his glass against mine and downed the contents. "Of that I am certain."

"I would have told you if I could have." Whisky warmed my throat as I took a cautious sip.

"Always secrets with you." He turned his empty glass in his fingers, as his aunt had spun the cookie that morning. "Did you see my father recently, before he died? Or Theresa?"

I did not have the heart to lie. I would have to tell him details, if he asked. "I watched your father die . . . at the stadium."

His bullet-shaped head recoiled in shock. "How?"

I repeated what I had told Theresa, leaving out any mention of Peter's news and his mysterious package.

"So, he didn't suffer?" His green eyes, so much like his aunt's, met mine.

I held his gaze. "I think not. Or at least not long."

"Why were you with him at the stadium?" His voice sounded as suspicious as Paul's.

"To see the opening ceremony. We ran into each other in the corridor. He spotted me in the crowd and came to say hello." A lie, but a believable one. Panzer did not need to know the background.

"What did he say?"

"His last words?" I thought back. "He said he was working on a story; then he said he was not feeling well."

"That's all?"

"Yes. It was—" I gulped. "—a short meeting."

Panzer dropped a beefy arm around my shoulder and pulled me in to his side. We sat in silence. He cleared his throat. "I'm glad you were with him, at the end. It must have mattered to him."

I swallowed a lump in my throat, and he coughed again. He dropped his arm from my shoulders and sloshed another round into our glasses.

"I have to go," I said. "I am covering the Olympics for a Swiss paper."

He drained his glass and pulled mine toward him. "I think I'll sit here for a while. With the ghosts."

We sat for a few minutes, staring into space and holding hands like a married couple that had long since fallen out of love.

"Should I stay?" I asked, finally taking my hand back. Panzer could be a maudlin drunk. Sometimes, an angry one.

"I would rather be alone." He tousled my hair again, a little more roughly this time. "But that doesn't mean I don't want to see you. Where are you staying?"

Twice in one day I had been asked that question. I still had no answer. "I am not certain."

"You are welcome to stay here." He refilled his glass. "It's paid up through the end of the month, if I know Aunt Theresa."

"Are you at the old place?" He had a fashionable apartment off Unter den Linden, not far from Friedrich Wilhelm University, the university from which the Nazis stole twenty thousand volumes to burn in May of 1933. How had Panzer dealt with the new administration? Math seemed a neutral subject, but nothing was truly neutral anymore.

He raised his glass. "Still there. Off and on."

I stood to go.

Panzer rose automatically. "The Requiem Mass for my father is Tuesday. At Saint Hedwig's. At eleven."

Saint Hedwig's was a Catholic church. Peter would not have wanted a church service, and most especially, not a Catholic one. He had renounced his support of the Catholic Church years before. I held my tongue. Funerals were for the living. "If I can, I will be there, Panzer."

"Thanks." He set his glass on the orange tablecloth. "I'd hate to do this without my Sisterlein."

He pulled me into another hard hug and I hugged him back. We were the chief mourners of Peter's death, and all we had left of him were our memories.

When Panzer released me, I asked, "What about your aunt's funeral?"

"Don't know yet. She was a suicide, so the Church won't do a service, or bury her in consecrated ground."

I winced. That, too. "I am sorry, Panzer."

He coughed. "I'll tell you Tuesday."

We walked hand in hand to the door. Should I leave him alone and drinking? Even if I stayed, I could do little to stop him. "Watch yourself," I said from the doorframe.

He handed me my heavy suitcase. "You, too, Sisterlein."

I was halfway down the stairs before I realized that he had not locked the door behind me. Unlike Theresa, he did not feel at risk in the apartment.

I walked once around the block, looking for followers. I was so intent on looking behind me that my suitcase banged into the driver's side of a wine red Opel Olympia parked half on the sidewalk. Opel had announced them in early 1935 and named them after the Games. I had seen many of them since my arrival.

I glanced in the back at a pile of blue composition books and smiled, remembering school days when I had written in such blue books myself for every examination. Life was simpler then. I studied the teacher's gleaming zeppelin hood ornament introduced by Opel for the Olympia. I could not seem to escape zeppelins. In my day, teachers did not make enough money to drive such automobiles.

I walked two blocks before I circled back to the subway station, cursing my suitcase. It was heavy and out of place. Except for at the train station, tourists in Berlin were settled by now.

I set the suitcase next to my feet on the train, grateful for the rest. When I rummaged through my satchel for a handkerchief, my fingertips chanced on the round ridged poker chip I had pilfered from Peter's jacket pocket. I pulled it out. Black, with eight gold crowns stamped around the edges. In the middle, a golden lion roared in profile. The chip did not list the amount, nor did it list the establishment where it would be honored.

I knew someone who would know the chip's provenance, and perhaps how it came into Peter's possession. I guessed that it belonged to Theresa, but she herself had said that these times were too dangerous for guessing.

8

I left the subway at Reichssportfeld station again. I did not bother to check to see if I had been followed. Any fool could hide in a crowd this size. Hopefully even I.

Instead I lugged my suitcase up the steep stairs and walked the long way to the Cupola Room, past Marathon Towers and down a walkway to the House of German Sport. I was winded and my arms ached by the time I arrived. A line stretched in front of me. If I waited with the other spectators, I would be late.

I pulled out my press pass and let myself be shuttled to the press line, bypassing at least thirty others, who glared at me. I held up the pass and shrugged, feeling guilty and hoping that the other reporters had already gone through. I would hate to meet them in line.

Luckily, I was alone in the press line. I heaved a sigh of relief. While the official examined my papers, I scanned the room, searching for Area Two, where the Swiss team should be hard at it against the USA team.

I spotted Lars and Andreas seated together near the Swiss, and recognized Lars's sacrifice. The German team fought the British in Area One, so for him to be sitting watching the Swiss instead, he must have been truly remorseful.

Andreas sat next to him with his arms crossed and a resigned expression on his face, head craned to watch the German team. Lars waved. I nodded back.

"What's the suitcase for?" the officious guard asked. I hesitated. I hated to answer questions, especially when the answers could cause trouble. I scanned the sunny room to see if anyone noticed. So far, no one appeared to care about me.

"I beg your pardon?" I asked.

"The suitcase. Why do you have it?"

"Just in," I lied.

"Where are you staying?"

Not his concern, but if I pointed that out, I would be here for hours. Still, I felt a rush of irritation that he dared question me. I tamped it down. It was far too dangerous to start a pointless fight. "I am staying with a . . . friend."

I gave Lars's address. It was all I had.

"The name of your friend?" His close-set eyes glared down his narrow nose at me.

"Lars Lang." I did not mention his title. It might serve to help me, but it might also cause trouble for Lars.

His disapproving sniff conveyed his opinion of loose women like me. I tried not to wince when he wrote the name on a pad of paper. I had created another potential problem for Lars.

Across the row of seats, he stood. I shook my head. Best to get through this on my own. If a former colleague noticed me at the door, I did not want them to see me rescued by a man they might recognize as SS, uniform or no.

The guard opened my suitcase and moved aside dresses with the end of his pen.

Likely he would have pulled out my underthings and laid them on the table, but behind me, two rowdy young men shouted at the other guard. They had lost their tickets, but felt strongly that they should be admitted.

The bureaucrat closed my suitcase, leaving the blue corner of a dress poking through the crack, and handed it to me. He found two angry young men more interesting than a woman of dubious morals. I almost felt insulted. "Move along, Frau Zinsli."

I slunk into the room, hoping that the strident yells behind me attracted the attention of anyone glancing toward the door.

The Swiss and USA match ended to scattered applause. Who won? I could procure that information at the press station, but dared not. Obviously not my best option, I would have to ask Lars. It was still early. This was men's team foil, so more matches would follow that I could observe and report in detail. I would need details to keep my editor happy.

Lars hurried over. When he automatically took the suitcase, I hesitated before letting him.

We stopped before we reached Andreas. Lars whispered, "O hour of my muse: why do you leave me?" Rilke.

New fencers stepped into position on their strips and raised their weapons. I pulled my hat down as low as I dared and quoted from further down the poem, thinking of Theresa and Peter, "I have no home."

Lars looked pained. "I am sorry for what happened this morning."

I remembered his expression of rage when he raised his hand to strike me. "As am I."

The fencers started and I glanced over Lars's shoulder when the first foils whipped through the air. I needed to see the match, I needed to be somewhere less conspicuous, and I needed to make a decision about Lars.

"I—I promise not to touch another drop while you are here." Lars set my suitcase on the highly polished floor. "Not a drop."

I let my skepticism show. "The Games run for two more weeks."

"Please stay." He put a hesitant hand on my arm. "Please. Let me try."

He had asked for something only once, years ago, before we had started working together. Right after he risked his life to rescue me from a Gestapo interrogation, he had asked me to listen to what turned out to be a request to help him spy. He looked every bit as terrified now as he had then.

I owed him, and I hoped I was not going to pay with my life. "For now."

"Thank you." He gave my arm a quick squeeze and led me to their seats, near the back and well away from those reserved for press. Every newspaper would have sent a representative. I held my breath the whole way.

We made it to the seats without my being recognized. I groaned inwardly when Andreas's eyes flicked to my suitcase. He would ask questions about that as soon as he got a good chance. "Feeling better today?"

"Much." I cast about for a different subject. "How are things at the university?"

Andreas once specialized in the detection of foreign elements in human blood. I did not know what he did now, besides teaching.

"I have my own division," he said proudly. "Since the Jewish chemists lost their places, there is increased opportunity for the Aryans who remain."

I kept my expression neutral and tried not to think what must have happened to those Jewish chemists, out of work in Hitler's Germany. "What are you working on?"

"Pesticides." Andreas lifted up his right hand as if it held a piece of chalk and he was ready to write on the blackboard.

"Fascinating," I lied. I did not try to sound interested.

Lars chuckled.

Andreas smiled. "It is, actually. Proper pesticides can increase crop yields tremendously, which in turn can lead to greater population loads for the Fatherland."

I was unsure if I wanted the Fatherland to increase its population load. "Are pesticides not poisonous to both pests and humans?"

"That is why they must be tested rigorously. Not every poison that kills an insect is carried into human blood."

"Indeed," I said. I turned my attention to the strip when another match began. Both fencers were so blindingly fast that I could barely follow their foils. At a match with real swords, they would cut each other to ribbons.

Lars and Andreas watched, transfixed. They must have fenced in officer school during the Great War. Even I had fenced in school, although I did not have the reach to be good at it.

My brother, Ernst, had been a gifted fencer. My father was proud of him for it. Ernst once told me, "Father would burst into flames in his grave if he knew how my skill with a blade parallels my more personal pursuits." I smiled at the memory.

Lars tilted his head enquiringly, but I shook my head. It was too complicated and too personal to explain.

During a break between matches, Lars left me alone with Andreas. Was he off to snag a quick drink? Worried, I watched him disappear into the crowd.

"Why do you have your suitcase?" Andreas asked as soon as Lars was out of hearing.

I fixed my eyes on the men in white dancing and parrying on a strip across the room. "To carry things."

He laughed, but persisted. "Why do you need to carry your things around with you?"

I shrugged. I had no obligation to explain it to him, not here or ever. And I did not like that he asked so many familiar questions.

He spoke again, his voice so low and intense that I leaned in to hear. "I've seen him drink, Adelheid."

He had guessed the reason for my suitcase so quickly that I wondered what Andreas had seen Lars do. I thought of relaying Lars's promise to stop drinking, but that felt like a betrayal. "Have you?"

Sweat beaded on his brow. I watched him struggle to decide whether to continue. He did. "I know what he does at work."

"What does he do at work?" Lars never shared details, and I never asked for them. Anything I did not know could not be tortured out of me, so I tried to stay as incurious as possible. But perhaps the time had come to open those doors into Lars's life before they slammed on me.

Andreas froze. I would receive no answer to that question. But why not? I tried to meet his eyes, but he would not let me. "Andreas?"

"Do you need a place to stay?" he blurted out. He sat back in his seat, clearly relieved that he had forced out the question.

I paused, taken aback. Andreas was supposed to be Lars's best friend. I never would have expected him to betray his own friend like this. He must be very worried for my safety. "I—"

"I suggest nothing improper," he interrupted. "But if you needed a place to stay . . . with distance from Lars . . . quite understandable . . ."

I waited for him to wind down to silence, my mind racing. "That is very thoughtful, Andreas, and I appreciate the gesture very much. But I can sort out my own arrangements."

Lars reappeared, seeming quite sober. He gave Andreas a barely perceptible nod.

I longed to ask what that meant, but knew they would not tell me. I scribbled, forming a story in my mind, but I had more interest in Andreas's remarks. What, indeed, did Lars do at work? Why was his friend so frightened for me?

I tried to turn my attention back to the matches, but instead my mind wandered to Anton. If he were here, we would be watching the equestrian events. He much preferred riding to fencing, where winning depended on him and the horse. I smiled, remembering his last lesson.

Anton galloped out of the stable, riding Arrow bareback. Together they tore down the manicured field. Anton issued a fearsome-sounding war whoop. He had removed his shirt, and as best as I could make out from my position near the stable door, he had also adorned himself with black and red greasepaint.

Four instructors rode to surround him. Even with their considerable skill at coordinated riding, it took them twenty minutes to catch him. Anton and Arrow were a nimble team. I bit my twitching lips to keep from laughing.

Anton's friend Christoph trotted out of the stable. His horse was saddled, but he, too, had no shirt and a greasepaint design on his face and chest. I shook my head, imagining the dressing down we would receive when the boys were finally apprehended.

The apoplectic head of the school called us into his office for a good shouting at. I nodded at all the correct junctures. I knew he would have sent us packing on the spot had they not had a competition with a rival school scheduled in three weeks. For all my son's unruly antics, Anton and Arrow were the team's best hope of winning. Unfortunately for them, Anton knew it.

Outside the office, I gave Anton a stern lecture about following rules. Once we were off school property, I stopped. I had seen enough blind obedience in Germany to take him out for an ice cream after. I wanted to teach him to think more than I wanted to teach him to obey.

The matches ended. The USA team trounced the Swiss, thirteen wins to three. If the Swiss lost against the next team, they would be out of the running in the 1936 Olympics.

Sadly, the Swiss were paired with the Italians, who had a very strong team, and to them they lost even worse than they had to the Americans. They eked out only one win to the Italians' fifteen. It would be challenging to write a story that did not make their showing sound pathetic. Perhaps something about fighting bravely to the end, in spite of overwhelming odds.

I pretended to take notes while the hall emptied. Before standing, I checked that my fellow journalists had left.

"Shall we eat before the semifinals?" Lars asked.

The semifinals started at eight. I might as well cover it, even if the Swiss team did not advance. After that, I had a bit of time before the individual events began. Fencing was the most rigorous event to watch in the Games, with matches from early morning until late at night. That was why it was the only sport I was covering. My editor had received a detailed schedule early and assigned us all enough sports to keep us busy night and day. As the only reporter with a single event, I was one of the lucky ones.

We milled out. A hand gripped my elbow. Startled, I turned.

The strong young man holding my arm was Wilhelm Lehmann, an ex-boyfriend of my brother's. He knew me only as Hannah Vogel, crime reporter wanted by the Gestapo. The last time we spoke, in 1934, I had persuaded him to steal files from Lars's office and then to procure Lars's home address so I could break into his apartment.

I thrust my hand out immediately. "Adelheid Zinsli."

Wilhelm's blue eyes widened. I held my breath. Would he play along? Once a kind boy, he had been close to my brother. But now he was SS, and the Nazis had changed everything.

He took my hand. "Wilhelm Lehmann. My apologies, I mistook you for someone else."

I relaxed fractionally.

He turned to Lars. "Heil Hitler, Herr Hauptsturmführer."

Lars returned the salute, face impassive. Hewing to the order, he wore civilian clothes, not his SS uniform. He had to wonder how Wilhelm knew his rank.

I wiped my sweaty palm on my dress, in case more handshakes were in order.

"We met in 1931," Wilhelm filled in. "After the death of my father."

"Of course." Lars spared me a worried glance. He clearly remembered, and understood that Wilhelm could expose us both. Wilhelm not only knew my real identity, but he was aware that Lars must know it, too.

"I wish to present my wife." Wilhelm gestured to a blond woman with a swollen stomach who had rushed to stand next to him. "Frieda Lehmann."

Another pregnant and unexpected wife. This one less pregnant but more unexpected than the last. Wilhelm had never shown interest in women before. But now a good Aryan bride meant the difference between life and death.

"Delighted." Lars bowed. "This is my fiancée—Adelheid Zinsli."

Wilhelm's expression of surprise was so comical that I wanted to poke him. He had shown up with a pregnant wife, and I kept a straight face; surely he could extend me the same courtesy when I showed up with an equally ridiculous fiancé.

Lars kept talking. "Also my friend, Herr Professor Andreas Huber."

He and Andreas shook hands all around. When I held out my hand to shake Frieda's, my dress sleeve rode up. Andreas's eyes lingered on the bruises. He knew that they had not been there yesterday.

Frieda did not seem to notice the bruises, but she still eyed me suspiciously. Not my day to meet wives. First Miriam and now Frieda.

"How do you do," I said.

Her nod was frosty, and her sharp glance to Wilhelm said she suspected something was amiss. Lars, too. And Andreas, as well. A trifecta of suspicion. I shifted nervously in place, fighting down an irrational urge to run.

"Exciting matches," Wilhelm said heartily. "They are so extraordinarily quick."

"In a real match," I rejoined, "speed means the difference between life and death."

"They don't dare let down their guard, not for a second," Wilhelm answered.

I nodded, relieved. We would both keep our guards up.

"With all that padding and ugly headgear, they can't feel a thing!" Frieda protested.

Clearly she had never been hit by a foil, even in full gear.

"It's more painful than it looks, dear," said Wilhelm.

"Lars." I put my hand on his shoulder. "I feel most unwell."

"My apologies," he said. "I must get Adelheid settled."

After a quick exchange of polite farewells, we headed toward the door, Andreas in tow.

I leaned heavily on Lars, acting ill and keeping my eyes on the floor. With my hat low and my head lowered, I hoped that no one else would recognize me. My stomach twitched. Nerves at almost being exposed by Wilhelm?

"Adelheid should be home in bed." Andreas took my suitcase from Lars.

I did yearn for my home and the broad feather bed I shared with Boris, but both were far away. "It comes and goes. I felt fine when I entered the stadium."

"You do not look fine now," Lars said.

"Thank you," I snapped.

"I did not mean to imply—" He looked so confused that both Andreas and I laughed.

"I know," I said.

Andreas deposited us and my suitcase next to an empty telephone booth. He left with a worried backward glance. I kept my face neutral, but his fear for me was contagious.

I phoned in the story of the Swiss defeat while Lars paced on the busy sidewalk outside. Boris might read the story aloud to Anton, and then they would know that I was all right. So far.

But what if Wilhelm had called my name before I stopped him?

"Let us find a restaurant," I said after I finished my call. I wanted to minimize the time I spent with Lars alone in his apartment.

We walked down the cobblestone sidewalk, searching for a place with an empty table. I let Lars lead while I thought of Switzerland. I called the paper's home office in Zürich daily, but could never call Boris, even if I could assume he wished to hear from me. Again, I yearned to make an unstaged phone call from Berlin. But I dared not underestimate the Gestapo's reach.

What was Boris thinking this very minute? Despite our parting, I suspected that he worried about me. I knew that he had loved me. Our years together had been happy, except for the times when I ventured back into Germany. Every parting had been bitter. He had always shut down the night before I left, eyes shuttering, body turning away from mine. As much as it hurt, I knew that he was simply preparing himself for the chance that I would not return.

Perhaps he did not miss me at all. He had certainly eschewed all contact since we parted. He took pains to be absent when I dropped off Anton on weekends. It had been almost a month, and I well knew that Boris never lacked for offers of female company. Perhaps he had found someone else. Perhaps he had even found someone else before my departure.

After much walking, Lars and I found a beer garden with solid wooden benches facing square tables like pews to an altar. The sky was still light, but someone had illuminated the strings of colored bulbs and closed the navy and goldenrod umbrellas. It looked quite festive, and eerily similar to the beer garden Lars took me to on our first official date after my Gestapo interrogation in 1934.

I read a slate board listing the menu in yellow chalk. They served three kinds of wurst with sauerkraut. Simple but nourishing.

Lars led us to a bench in the corner. We sat on the uncompromising wood. He slid an arm around my shoulder and leaned to whisper in my ear. "What about this Lehmann?"

His breath in my ear annoyed me. I twitched my head. "I trust Wilhelm Lehmann not to give me away."

"Do you trust him with your life?" His dark eyes probed into mine.

"I have in the past." I raised my chin, glad that I could be honest.

We sat without speaking. Excited babble filled the room, reviewing every step of the fencing in different languages. Lighthearted conversation about sports. How I longed to be having one.

We ordered wurst with sauerkraut and apple juice from a harried waitress in a sweat-stained dirndl. I felt relieved that, so far, Lars had kept his word not to drink.

"These Games have become more dangerous for you than I expected," Lars said in a peevish voice. "We didn't have these troubles at the Winter Games in Garmisch."

"I was bundled up like a ball against the cold. Those Games were far from Berlin. No one knows me in the wilds of Bavaria." Except the Röhms, and luckily, I had not encountered them.

"I suppose."

"I had near misses there as well," I said soothingly. "But it came out fine."

The muscular waitress slung two beers onto our table then swept her blond braids behind her shoulders. She looked like a heroine straight out of a Wagner opera.

"Apple juice," Lars reminded her.

She shook her head in disbelief, picked up the steins, and took them away.

He stared at me without speaking. "Lars?"

He did not answer, eyes far away. "Lars?"

He snapped back to alertness. "Let's put you on a train to Switzerland tonight. I'll tell everyone that you were ill and returned home. We can pick up your film canisters on the way to the station."

"But—"

"Then we will break off our engagement, and you can stay there, safe and sound." He folded his hands on the table as if the decision were made.

I was surprised at how quickly my heart rose at the thought of leaving, but I could not go yet, as much as I wanted to. For Lars to suggest such a thing was unheard of. He had never before suggested that we stop our work. "Why now?"

His eyes shifted right, over my shoulder. "It feels dangerous."

"A hunch?" I asked to needle him. He was not the type to act rashly based on intuition.

"Not a hunch." His voice had an edge. "Let's examine the facts. Yesterday your friend from the paper dies in front of you. I barely drag you away before the police arrive to ask why you are standing over the body of a known anti-Nazi activist. Tonight another old friend shows up who could expose us both."

"And?" Wilhelm had not exposed us, and I did not think he would.

"And I don't know what you do when I am not around to watch you—"

"Watch me?" I crossed my arms over my chest. "You make me sound like an invalid!"

He talked over me. "But I imagine your other activities are not safe either."

I bit back a retort because the waitress was right behind him. She deposited our wurst, sauerkraut, and apple juice with hearty efficiency before sailing off, shaking her blond braids. Adults not drinking beer with dinner. Hard to imagine such a thing.

"Such faith in me." I took a sip of the sweet apple juice, wishing it were beer.

"I say that because I do have faith in you. Faith that you will throw yourself straight into danger."

I toyed with my bratwurst. Of course I was in danger, perhaps more than ever before, but I had to find out what Peter had died for. I had to collect the package he had left for me. Peter had said thousands of lives depended on it. So, I lied to Lars. "I have seen nothing that seems more dangerous than any other time I came to Berlin."

"Don't pretend to be naïve. This time is very different. You usually come for only a weekend, and we stay away from areas where you might meet friends. I pack you off on a train with your film, and no one is the wiser." He dipped a bit of wurst in mustard. "I saw how tense you were this evening when we walked near the press rows."

"But—"

"I could throw you on a train to Switzerland." His eyes narrowed.

"You could." I dropped my fork. "Remember when you put me on a train to Switzerland in 1934?"

He gave me an exasperated look. "You got off again."

"There you are." No one ordered me around. If I had not allowed Boris to do so, and had lost any chance of happiness I had with him because of it, I certainly would not allow Lars.

9

Much later, Lars steered me into his apartment. I deliberately stepped on the creaky board. Even though I saw that he was angry, he laughed.

"I know you can step over that quietly. So I assume you are telling me that you can be quiet, or you can make noise. And I should not forget that."

"Perhaps I merely misstepped." He knew me far too well.

He snorted and led us into the living room. I sat on the black leather club chair. On the coffee table rested a picture of his parents, next to a framed picture of me. Years ago, he stole it from my ransacked apartment. Lars had spent years trampling through the ruins of my life.

He dropped my suitcase in the bedroom, then took the sofa across from me and crossed his ankle over his knee. Ordinarily we would have a drink. I waited and wondered if the tea cozy was in place.

"Mineral water?" he asked.

"Please."

He stood, peeled off his gray overcoat, and draped it on the sofa back. He headed for the kitchen, stopping near the telephone, probably to make sure that it was covered.

I dropped my face into my hands and massaged my temples. On top of everything else, I had a pounding headache.

Lars returned, knelt next to me, and put a hand on my knee. "Are you all right?"

I opened my eyes and took a warm glass of water from his other hand. "Tired."

"I have headache tablets."

"I am fine," I snapped, annoyed that he had seen my pain.

He retreated to the sofa and drank his water in one gulp, clearly wishing for something stronger. "I found out some things for you today."

"You did?" Why would Lars investigate anything for me? Guilt over his behavior this morning?

"I am very sorry to tell you this." He rolled his empty water glass between his palms.

"And?" I clenched my hands in my lap. It certainly did not sound like good news.

"When I was looking into . . . I discovered . . ." His voice trailed off. He stared at the wall behind my ear, the wall where he had almost struck me that morning.

I did not turn my head to follow his gaze, not wanting to remember. "Please tell me, Lars."

He gave me a worried look. "Your friend's sister, Theresa Weill, is dead."

I stared at him, astonished. "How do you know?"

He reached into his briefcase and pulled out two gray folders. "I have proof here. You do not have to look at it."

I thought of telling him that I already knew of Theresa's death, but decided to hold my tongue. Still surprised that he had taken them for me, I quickly held out my hand for the folders.

His fingers brushed mine when he gave me one. The other he kept. He stood behind my chair and read over my shoulder. Irritating.

I opened Peter's first. The SS had begun a file on him years ago, before they came to power. In my work as a crime reporter, I had read police files daily. After I read the one for my brother, I never viewed them the same way again. This would not be so different.

"You don't have to read it," he said. "I can summarize its contents."

"I do." I shifted back in my chair, obscuring his view. "But thank you."

I started to read. *Peter Weill: Communist and potential agitator.* His fierce anti-Nazi stance had been noted. Nothing that I had not expected, but I felt a rush of pride.

They suspected him of investigating Project Zephyr. My heart sped up. Had Peter found something big? I pointed to the word *zephyr.* "Do you know what this is?"

Lars leaned around me to see. "I found nothing on a Project Zephyr. It's not an SS project, I suspect."

"Or perhaps top secret, even from you?"

He looked affronted. "Always a possibility."

I went back to reading the file. It said that Peter possessed modest means, but that he owned a valuable postage stamp, a gift from a Jewish financier whom he had helped to flee. Experts described it as a two-cent Hawaiian missionary stamp and listed the value as *high.* Hopefully it would make Panzer wealthy indeed. A handwritten note in the file indicated Hauptmann Harold Bosch as an interested buyer for the stamp and had requested that its whereabouts be tracked.

I thought of the small golden hinge in the envelope in my satchel. Had the stamp been stored in a little wooden box in Theresa's unassuming apartment?

Perhaps this Bosch already knew the stamp's whereabouts. "Do you know Hauptmann Bosch?"

"I've met him a few times," Lars said. It did not sound like he had enjoyed the experience.

"The file states that he wants Peter's stamp." I pointed to the words.

"His acquisitive nature is well known." Lars lingered over the word *acquisitive.*

"Meaning?"

He hesitated before speaking again, more slowly than before. "At least one Jewish collector claimed that Bosch stole his stamp. After the accusation was made, the collector vanished."

An icy shudder traveled down my back. "Do you think he—?"

"Perhaps. Like any valuable item, stamps can be worth killing for."

I hated to think that Peter had been killed for the sake of a gummed square of paper. I tapped my fingers on Bosch's name. Peter would not have called me back to Germany to discuss a stamp. There must be something more.

I finished reading the file, but nothing else gave a clue as to what his package might have been, or his news.

I turned to the last page, the account of Peter's death. It listed the cause of death as *heart attack, owing to subject's advanced age and the heat.* My hand shook when I stared at his death photo, taken on the floor of the corridor at the Olympic Stadium. I remembered how it felt when he had collapsed against me, and my hip throbbed. Those seconds on the floor had been the last seconds of his life.

Lars took the photo from my hand, returned it to the folder, and closed it. "I'm sorry, Spatz."

My hand lingered in the air, as if I still held the photograph. Peter's blue eyes flashed in my mind, pupils contracted in death.

Lars stepped to the front of my chair and pulled my hand down to my lap, resting his warm hands on top of my cold ones. I felt grateful not to be alone with the secrets of Peter's death.

"What." I cleared my throat and moved my hands out from under his. "What do you have to say about the file?"

He moved to the couch, dark eyes narrowed as they always were when he was thinking. When he spoke, words came slowly. "Nothing in that file indicates that his death was anything other than the natural end to a long and successful life."

"So, you think the file is correct?"

He paused again before answering. "He was seventy-four."

"The other file." I shook my head stubbornly. "Please."

He slowly handed me the second folder.

I read through Theresa's secrets, knowing how she would have hated it had she known. The Nazis found her politically neutral but suspect because of her brother. Information about her gambling took up more space than her political affiliations. She would have been proud of that. I ran my index finger down the list of clubs and casinos. She spent a great deal of time at one of Jack Ford's establishments.

I pointed to Jack Ford's name. "Is he still operating in Berlin?"

Lars read the name upside down. "So far as I know. I haven't had dealings with him in years." He smiled grimly. "I suppose you know him, too."

"After a fashion."

He made an exasperated sound, but I ignored him. I returned to the file. It noted that her entire income came from gambling. No debts listed. Was that accurate? Or did her murder and perhaps also Peter's have something to do with her gambling?

I turned to the page that dealt with her death. According to the report, she hanged herself approximately two hours after I left. A neighbor found her body fairly quickly because the front door stood open. The neighbor noticed it, checked the apartment, and saw her. Why was the front door open? I heard the lock click when she locked it behind me after I left.

I took a deep breath before pulling out her black-and-white death photo, trying not to see her distorted face. A checked cloth cut into the darkened flesh of her neck. My stomach flipped. The missing tablecloth.

Think, I told myself. *What does it mean?* Why would she replace the tablecloth with a new one before hanging herself? She would not do such a thing. And if she had not, someone murdered her. Someone sneaked through her front door after I left and killed her. They strangled her with the tablecloth, then spread a new one over the table. I had suspected it ever since Bella told me, but now I knew. I ran one fingertip over the tablecloth in the picture. Who would do such a thing to an old woman?

"Spatz?"

"I am fine," I lied. I stood and pushed the folder into his hands. "Thank you again for bringing these to my attention."

The formal phrase sounded ridiculous.

I strode into the kitchen and tried to pour myself another glass of water. More water splashed on the counter than into the glass. I gripped the metal edge of the sink with both hands and drew in deep breaths. The information in the files was not news to me. It should not affect me so.

Lars stood behind me. Gently, he set his hands atop my shoulders as if I might float away.

I grabbed a linen cloth and wiped down the counter, stepping away, pushing down an irrational urge to turn around into his arms. I wanted a door between us. "I am going to bed."

"I must excuse myself, then. I have matters to attend to."

"You are leaving?" Quite late for that. Odd.

"I must return these files, among other things."

"Good night." I folded the cloth and hung it over the edge of the sink.

"Spatz?"

His term of endearment grated, but it was practical, since either one of my names might be the wrong one to utter at a given moment. "Yes?"

His words came in a rush. "We are invited to a formal party to celebrate the Games tomorrow. I must attend. I can make your excuses, but . . ." He shifted from side to side.

"But?" I wanted to be alone. Tonight and tomorrow.

"But I have made excuses for you so many times that some of my colleagues doubt your existence." He grimaced.

I took a deep breath. I forced a smile. "An imaginary playmate?"

"I had one as a child." Lars's voice softened. "A bunny named Hasenpfeffer."

I imagined him talking to an invisible rabbit. "What happened to Hasenpfeffer?"

"I grew up. And he went back to his rabbit hole." He laughed. "You can smile about it. I realize how ridiculous it sounds."

"More endearing than ridiculous." The words slipped out before I had time to think.

"About the party?" he asked.

"Will there be anyone there who knows me, from before?" I knew the illogic of my question. He did not know whom I knew.

"Doubtful. No press, except you. No policemen, except me. No criminals, except high-ranking Nazis. That summarizes your friends, does it not?" He gave me his familiar half smile.

I did not respond to the list of my friends, as I could only have conceded its accuracy.

"If it is important to you, of course I will attend." I tried to sound sincere, but I dreaded the thought of an evening spent pretending to be a Nazi to Gestapo men and their fanatical wives.

"Thank you. Please be here at six."

"I shall." Did I have an appropriate dress? I had a simple black frock that might suit the occasion. It would blend in with the black SS uniforms. As Anton would say, "A brave understands the value of camouflage." Perhaps no one would notice me.

Lars gathered the files and his overcoat from the sofa, although the night was warm, and left me alone.

10

I took a bath and thought of Theresa, Peter, and Panzer. Panzer had lost his mother to the Spanish influenza epidemic in 1918, but he'd had a doting aunt in Theresa. She had been gruff but loving.

As far as I knew, Panzer had never married. So he was alone. I sympathized. I, too, had been alone for a long time before I found a family. My only living blood relative was my detestable sister, Ursula. But I had my foster son, Anton, and until recently, I had Boris. Could I have him if I met his conditions? As much as I missed him, the stubborn part of me knew that I could not relent. Some things were worth risk. If he did not understand that, perhaps I was better off alone.

Brave words, but did I believe them?

I slapped the surface of the water. I did. Even Lars understood the importance of our work. He had risked his own life every day for two years to gather documents because he believed in it, too. Yet Boris could not even sit around worried for two weeks.

A door slammed. I started. Water slopped over the sides of the tub.

I pushed wet hair out of my eyes and listened. Voices argued next door. The neighbors had arrived. Where was Lars? When would he return? Speaking of Lars, why had he shown me the folders? If he truly wanted me to leave Berlin, he would have known better than to give me potential clues to the Weills' killer.

I stepped out, drained the water, and rinsed the porcelain. After donning my cotton nightdress, I tumbled into bed. Like yesterday, I was asleep instantly. I awoke only once, my hand searching for Boris.

When I arose the next morning, I felt better rested than I had for days. Insistent light pushed through the curtains. Even this early, it promised to be another warm day. I pulled on a pale blue dress and searched the apartment. No Lars. He had not returned last night. Was he in trouble?

Perhaps he had a lover. I reminded myself that I was not his fiancée, regardless of our playacting. As long as he did nothing that endangered our lives, it was none of my concern. But what if he *did*?

A hard knot of worry settled in my stomach. Probably Lars had felt like this when I slipped away. Well, if he could stand it, then so could I.

I took out the day's schedule. Luckily, no fencing today. That room held the most danger in Berlin for me, outside of a Gestapo cell. The Swiss had not made it to the finals of men's team foil, so I did not need to cover it. Instead I decided to interview the Swiss fencing team at the Olympic Village. I had worked with them before they left Switzerland, so I should have no trouble gaining access. If I avoided running into German reporters on the way in and out, I should be perfectly safe. If.

I downed a roll and cup of strong tea. The best way to avoid local reporters was to arrive early. I gathered my belongings and strolled down the sunlit street, where I purchased some newspapers from a stand near the subway station, leaving a few extra pfennigs for the seller. Seeing his stump of a left arm reminded me of Schmidt, the legless news seller near my old apartment. For years he had sold me my daily papers. How had he fared under the new regime?

I pushed through the throng of Monday-morning commuters to the train. No point in looking for followers in this crowd. I settled into the last seat on the subway and pulled out the first paper. A Negro athlete named Cornelius Johnson had won a gold medal in the high jump yesterday, with another Negro American, Dave Albritton, taking silver. Hitler and Goebbels must be apoplectic. I smiled. It was lovely to see the non-Aryan athletes making a fool of Nazi racism.

Passengers streamed into the car but I ignored them and turned to the page announcing the art medals. The Germans had done quite well there, with Werner and Walter March taking gold for Municipal Planning around the construction of the Reich Sport Field; a gold for lyric works and a silver for epic works in the literature category. In music, they received a gold, silver, and bronze for Solo and Chorus and gold for Orchestra. I scanned down the results. A Swiss gold! I felt a rush of pride, even though I was not even Swiss, happy to see that Swiss artist Alex Diggelmann had won the commercial art category.

Deciding to stop reading while I was still cheered, I closed the paper and puzzled over Peter's notebook, no closer to understanding it than the first night. I wished I knew someone fluent in codes, but I did not. I certainly could expect no help from Paul. And what did the list of flowers mean, if anything? I closed the notebook and left the subway at the Stadium stop. I hurried through crowds and caught a cream-colored bus bound for the Olympic Village.

As I suspected, no reporters rode on the first bus of the day. My colleagues had never been early risers. I settled into a seat near the back, taking notes for my planned interviews. A straightforward article about Swiss athletes and fencing, it need have no mention of Nazism in it.

I doodled on my paper, thinking.

Boris and I fidgeted on hard wooden chairs in the headmaster's office. I had never been called into the office as a pupil, but Anton could not make that claim.

Boris slid an arm around my shoulder. "You look like it's a firing squad."

"What do you suppose he has done?"

"Nothing ordinary," Boris said. "Of that we can be certain."

I thought of the other infractions we had been called in to discuss: climbing a tree and refusing to come down unless asked in Apache and convincing the other children to paint their faces with mud and perform whooping Indian dances.

The headmaster entered and handed me an examination booklet. He stared down his narrow nose at me while I read it. It contained an essay on Swiss history. Nothing inflammatory. In the left margin an Indian on a horse shot an arrow through the words at an American cavalryman in the right margin.

"And?" Boris asked.

"The handwriting—" The headmaster flared his nostrils. "—is atrocious."

I stared at it. It was far from tidy, but it was readable. This meeting must be about more than handwriting.

"And?" Boris asked again. His voice held the anger of a banker called out of work in the middle of the day to discuss poor penmanship.

"If he has time to produce these . . . doodles." The headmaster pointed his index finger at the Indian. "He has time to form the letters properly."

"We will speak to him," I said.

"Perhaps next time my wife could come alone?"

"So Frau Zinsli is your wife?" The headmaster's icy tone lingered on the word *wife*.

Boris stood so quickly, his chair clattered to the ground behind him. The headmaster flinched but stood his ground, his mouth pinched in disdain. Worried that Boris might strike him, I grabbed Boris's arm and pulled him out of the office. He did not speak a word on the drive home.

A month later, Boris issued me his ultimatum: Stop spying and marry him, or move out. The bus lurched to stop and my pen slid across the page, leaving a ragged blue line that ran from my doodle of a fencer, his blade leveled toward his opponent's heart. I packed up my notebook and hurried off. I had reached the Olympic Village.

The guard in the lobby examined my press pass and my Zinsli passport before sending me on my way with detailed directions to the Swiss barracks. I did not imagine I would need them until I exited through the rear door and appreciated the scale of the Village. I knew it covered half a square kilometer, but had not comprehended the implications. I stood on the edge, gazing across at the almost 150 buildings. The Swiss resided, predictably, in the far corner.

I turned left and strolled past whitewashed buildings with terra-cotta roofs, newly updated for the occasion. I cut across the rolling meadow, passing a large black stork that stared at me incuriously.

The cabins for Luxembourg and Denmark stood on my right, France and Holland on my left. I was headed in the right direction. I strolled across a verdant lawn, past more white buildings for Afghani-stan and Italy, turned left toward Peru, lost hope as I passed Greece and England, but found Switzerland as promised behind Liechten-stein, backing onto a stand of birches. I felt like Nellie Bly. But I had circumnavigated the world in minutes.

The interviews went well, even though the team had lost. Some members, those fencing in individual competitions, acted upbeat about their chances there. Those who had come only to compete in the team event were hungover, but quietly polite. A few hoped to keep training and do better in the 1940 Tokyo Olympics.

"It is beautiful here," said Gustav, the athlete who had lost the first bout. "The Germans outdid themselves with the Olympic Village."

The Nazis, not the Germans, I silently corrected. "Do you have much contact with the other athletes?"

"But yes!" Gustav's head nodded with enthusiasm. "In the dining hall and at the events. Just today I was talking to an American Negro. He said that at home he must use a different bathroom from the white people. He said the Germans are more tolerant."

Perhaps that is why the Americans did not boycott the games. They did not want to draw attention to their own racist policies. "Tol-erant?" I asked, surprised.

"I know," he said. "I know. But what I have seen here is not like what I expected. Everyone has been kind and generous to all the athletes."

"I am happy to hear that," I said. The Nazi propaganda machine was functioning efficiently, as was to be expected.

I used the telephone booth in the Swiss barracks to call in a story to the paper so I would not meet any reporters in the main hall, not wanting Adelheid to find more trouble. I dictated the story to a curious young man on the other end and broke the connection. Barely noon and my job finished for the day.

I headed back toward the bus stop, nervous. Other reporters might be up and about by now. They might arrive on the bus that I would take to leave. If I got through this safely, I promised myself a good lunch.

Afterwards, I could meet Agnes, an old contact at Jack Ford's. Together we might sort out the mystery of the poker chip in Peter's personal effects. Perhaps that would solve his murder. She was bound to know if Jack Ford's men had killed Peter.

I rounded the New Zealand cabin and spotted Wilhelm loping toward me clad in a tan suit instead of his uniform. It made him look younger.

But why was he here? Worried, I hefted my satchel up on my shoulder. He had seen me, too, so I must face him. I hoped he would not give me away. I stopped by Brazil to wait.

On the grassy meadow, I watched several Negro athletes stretching in athletic pants and shirts with USA on the front. I recognized gold medal winner Cornelius Johnson, runner Archibald Williams, and the runner on whom the Americans had pinned many hopes—Jesse Owens. Owens laughed at something one of his teammates said, throwing his head back. They looked so young to me that I supposed I must be aging faster than I wanted to admit. I silently wished them well in the Games and back home with their segregated bathrooms.

"Adelheid!" Wilhelm had arrived. I stood and he gave me a quick embrace. "Imagine running into you here."

"Imagine," I said dryly.

He studied the dark-colored men on the lawn before saying, "There's a fairly private corner of the lake near Yugoslavia."

Did he think that the American athletes might inform on us? "The last time we went into a private corner, you came out buttoning your pants and humiliated me in front of a room full of men." I referred to our last meeting at a gay cabaret turned into a Nazi building. Wilhelm had pretended we had been intimate in a private office so that no one would suspect we had been discussing how to illegally procure SS files.

Wilhelm grinned, his face happy and open. "I feel quite nostalgic for those days."

I had to smile back. "They were simpler."

He walked toward the lake. I fell into step, hurrying to keep pace with his long-legged stride. "What are you doing here?"

"Looking for you." We nodded to a Japanese athlete with round-framed glasses. At his side walked a woman in a kimono with demurely downcast eyes.

"How did you find me?" I asked.

"Called the Village and asked if a reporter named Adelheid Zinsli had checked in. I figured Switzerland was out of the fencing, and you'd have nothing better to do."

I felt like a fool. Even Wilhelm had tracked me down. Perhaps Lars was correct; I should be on a train home. We cut right to avoid two dark-haired men talking animatedly in Spanish. Spain had boycotted the Olympics, so they must be from South America. I had lived in Argentina for a time and had decided they were probably Bolivians before they passed us.

I continued my conversation with Wilhelm. "Being seen with me is not the best idea."

"I doubt that anyone else here knows either of us," he said.

I did not point out that the Swiss athletes and the man I had checked in with knew quite a bit about me. We reached the lake and skirted the edge. I admired the magnificent and aloof swans. When the ducks swam over eagerly, I regretted that I had no bread. At home, Boris, Anton, and I had fed the ducks in the park every Sunday. Monday mornings I emptied crumbs out of pockets before I did laundry. Yesterday Anton and Boris had fed the ducks without me.

"What are you doing with Lars Lang?" Wilhelm smiled politely, as if we talked about the weather.

"How is that your concern?" I smiled back, not so politely.

"Given your political tendencies, I find it odd that you would marry an SS Hauptsturmführer, even under an assumed name. Especially one you were investigating not so long ago."

We both stopped talking as a dark-haired man with a French flag on his shirt jogged past. He flashed a set of white teeth in a smile before increasing speed away from us.

"Perhaps he swept me off my feet." Boris had, once upon a time. It was possible, at least in theory.

Wilhelm laughed. "That seems unlikely."

I stifled a grin. "You have more experience with men sweeping you off your feet than I."

"Careful, careful." He scanned the lakeshore. A group of what I assumed to be Indians in turbans were the only other people to be seen. "No experience of that type lately, sadly."

"I hear that the government has reopened the bars for the Games."

"Only an idiot would go," he said. "In two weeks, they will be closed and life will be back to normal."

A white stork landed in front of us with a splash. The Village setting felt so much like a fairy tale that my uneasiness grew with each passing moment. Fairy tales always had monsters.

"Your wife is lovely." She had all the necessary attributes for Aryan beauty. Wilhelm was lucky to have married her.

He grimaced. "The wife is a necessary evil."

"What wife does not wish to be referred to in such loving terms?" I reprimanded him.

He shrugged.

"Does she know about you?"

His eyes widened. "Of course not."

Poor jealous blond Frieda. I was the least of her worries. "Do you love her?"

"I don't think she loves me either, if that makes you feel better. The marriage solved different problems for both of us. Urgent problems."

I thought about her swollen belly and did not press him further. At least Frieda received some benefit from the marriage. "What are you doing these days?"

"Pilot. Luftwaffe."

"Congratulations," I lied. "Spain?" It was the most likely posting. The German government had sent planes to Spain to help the Fascist dictator, Franco. Also, I suspected, to train the pilots for another war.

"*Sí.*"

"Do you know a Gerhard Adler?" Boris's daughter, Trudi, had married a Nazi pilot by that name. It had become too dangerous for Boris and Trudi to send letters, and I knew they missed each other desperately.

He shook his head. "Why?"

"Friend of a friend." No news to carry back to Boris.

We reached a wrought iron bench and sat. He asked, "What have you been doing since I last saw you?"

"Yesterday?"

He laughed and dropped his arm to the back of the bench. "Before that."

Not counting last night, I had not seen him for two years. He had helped search for my son after Anton was kidnapped by Ernst Röhm's men during the purge now known as the Night of the Long Knives. Wilhelm and I had left a cowboy bar together: he to return home, I to break into Lars's apartment in search of files that might help me find my son. In fact, reading those files had saved Boris's life. "I found Anton."

"Will you bring him to Berlin to live after you are married?" His voice told me he knew the answer to that question. Across the lake, the Japanese athlete and his wife watched the swans.

"Perhaps." What an abhorrent thought. Anton would stay safe in

Switzerland as long as I could manage it, or longer. Boris, I knew, would keep him if something happened to me. We had discussed it during one of our fights about my trips to Berlin.

Wilhelm pitched a stone into the lake. The ripples subsided before he spoke. "About your Hauptsturmführer."

"Yes?" I hated to lie to him. He had told me his marriage was a sham, and I wished that I could tell him that my engagement was one as well. But the confidence was not mine to reveal. My desire to be honest to a friend could not put Lars's life in danger.

Wilhelm glanced around again. We seemed quite alone.

"Yes?" I asked again, in a quieter voice.

"I don't know what you are up to. But I must caution you. I am worried that he might harm you."

"You are a fine one to be giving romantic advice."

He squirmed as he and my brother used to as a teenagers in my kitchen admitting to unfinished homework. "Nevertheless."

The ducks gave us up as a bad job and paddled away, quacking angrily.

He squared his shoulders, decision made. "Lars Lang is under investigation by the SS."

Wind ruffled the birches. I could not breathe. If Lars was in danger, I was as well. Had our activities together endangered him? "Are you certain?"

"I know a man in records. I had him look up Lang after I saw you two together."

"Why?"

"I knew you were up to something, and I wanted to know if anyone else did."

"Do they? Am I involved?" This time I glanced nervously around the lake. My stomach twisted.

"It has nothing to do with you, near as I can tell. For the past few weeks, he's been trying to transfer out of interrogations, although he is quite good at it, and his new superior, Sturmbannführer Hahn, wants to know why. He suspects him of unpatriotic motives." Wilhelm said the last two words as if they indicated the worst offense imaginable. With effort, I kept myself from glaring at him. Wilhelm had always been an unapologetic Nazi, but he had still done much to help me.

Why had Lars not told me of his desire to transfer? Did he plan to end our espionage efforts, or was he involved in something else? "Where does he wish to transfer to?"

"Anywhere, I think. He tried transferring back to the police force, training as a pilot to go to Spain, even as a tank commander."

"Tank commander?" I had never asked Lars what he had done in the War, although I had always thought it was something to do with sharpshooting, as I had once seen schoolboy medals for shooting in his apartment.

"With his exemplary war experience, and his medals, he would be a prime candidate, if they'd let him go."

"Wartime medals?" I had no idea Lars had received any medals. He kept much from me, as I did from him.

"Iron Cross first class, among others. How can you know so little about the man who swept you off your feet? Your future husband?"

I ignored his sarcasm. "Why won't they let him go?"

"He's the best interrogator they have. Especially with women. Especially lately."

"What does that mean?" My voice came out sharper than I intended.

He gave me a calculating look. "If you want details, ask him."

I stared at the sun-spangled lake. What did Lars do so well at work that neither Wilhelm nor Andreas would tell me? Why was he trying so desperately to leave?

Wilhelm pitched in another stone. "Stay away from him, Hannah. He's a dangerous man in his own right, and once he's suspected of something, they will eventually hang him, guilty or innocent. They would be quite happy to catch you, too."

"Catch me doing what?"

"Just leave him. I have no idea what you are doing. And I want none."

I was grateful that he would not try to push me for information. "Thank you, Wilhelm."

"You are a welcome break to the routine." He leaned in close. "As always."

"Have you heard of a Project Zephyr?" I asked.

His eyes shuttered and he sat back up.

"Wilhelm?"

"I know little." He tossed a flat gray stone from one hand to the other.

"But what little do you know?"

"Sturmbannführer Hahn is associated with it."

Then Lars should know about it. Perhaps he had shown me the file that mentioned it to watch my reaction. Or perhaps he was telling the truth and he did not know about Project Zephyr. "What else do you know?" I asked Wilhelm.

"It's top secret. I shouldn't even know that. Why do you wish to know?"

"To lead a well-rounded life," I said.

"I suspect your life is too well rounded already." He curled strong fingers around the stone. "It sounds like it might be Luftwaffe, doesn't it? A zephyr is a kind of breeze."

"If you hear of any details, will you tell me?"

"Perhaps. How may I reach you?"

We exchanged telephone numbers.

"Leave a message with Lars inviting us to your house for dinner," I said. "We can find a chance to talk there."

He crossed his muscular legs. "Frieda will be less than delighted to see you."

"I am sorry," I said, contrite. "Do you have a better plan?"

He shook his head. "It's a good thing. If she's jealous of women, it keeps her eyes pointed in the best direction."

Poor Frieda. "Could I trouble you for one more favor?"

He rolled his eyes. "How many laws must I break?"

"None, I hope. How did you get here?"

"Took my car," he said. "Little Hanomag, but it beats the bus."

"Could you give me a lift to the city? I would prefer to avoid the Olympic bus."

"But, of course."

He pulled out a coffee brown sandwich and offered me half. Liverwurst on pumpernickel. While we ate, we listed our mutual friends who had ended up in camps, fled, or married.

When we talked about Frieda's baby, Wilhelm bubbled with enthusiasm. He hoped for a boy. I remembered the care he had taken with Anton when they pretended to be a soldier and his medic after I pushed Anton down to keep him safe, and he skinned his knee. Wilhelm had carried him upstairs, bound his knee, and told him Winnetou stories until he fell asleep. He would make a good father. At least Frieda would get that much.

The trip back took only minutes. Not surprisingly, Wilhelm was a reckless driver. My foot was tired from pressing an imaginary brake on my side of the car by the time I climbed out in front of a recently cleaned office building on the fashionable Kufürstendamm. I barely noticed the Olympic and Nazi flags, habituated to the air of nationalism coating everything like soot.

I pulled open a brass and glass art nouveau–style door and stepped from the noisy street into a silent lobby. Time had stopped here. With the exception of a picture of Hitler on one wall and a wooden flagpole with a limp red flag that must have a swastika on it, it looked much the same as it had a decade before, when I came here for the first time.

I gave the receptionist behind the cramped desk a number to call. She handed me the telephone.

"Ford's," said the musical voice on the other end. Agnes sounded the same as always.

"Peter." She knew me as Peter Weill, since that was the pseudonym I had written under at the *Tageblatt* for years.

"Why so it is," she said. "Ages have passed, darling."

We had not spoken since the summer of 1934. "I will see you in a minute."

"Of course." She broke the connection at once. One did not keep Jack Ford's line engaged for a second more than necessary.

I pressed the elevator button and watched the street behind me in the mirror, alert for suspicious characters. I deemed it unlikely that I would see one, and I did not. But it rattled me that Wilhelm had found me so easily.

If the liveried elevator operator remembered my previous visits, he gave no sign. "Your floor?"

"Four," I answered, noting how he stood straighter after I said it.

We rode in silence, but I caught him sneaking a peek in my direction. He probably wondered if I was a prostitute or a client. I gave him what I hoped was an enigmatic smile, causing him to blush and stare at the floor. That certainly was not the intended effect. I checked that my dress was properly buttoned. It was.

I stepped out of the elevator. "Thank you."

He nodded and pulled the metal gate closed with a white-gloved hand, not meeting my eyes.

I hurried down the hall to the single door at the end and rapped on the oak with my knuckles. Three taps, a pause, then another tap. Peter Weill's knock, since before my time.

Agnes's starlet voice carried through the door. "Please, come in."

The lock buzzed. I pushed the door open and stepped in. I did not know if she had intentionally betrayed me in 1934. I had asked her if I could speak to a certain man, and when she sent him to me, he threatened to kill me. The question remained: Had Agnes known that he wanted to kill me when she sent him? I could not be certain. Even so, she was the best hope I had.

The room remained unchanged, not so Agnes. She was still dressed in the height of fashion, but her small face was haggard. A dwarf, she had always been tiny, barely over a meter tall, but she had never been so rod thin.

She stood and held out her arms. "Peter!"

I crossed quickly to her desk and hugged her. The familiar smell of spicy French perfume made me smile. Some things stayed the same.

"Once again, it has been years," she said.

"My apologies. How have you been?"

She shook her head once. She did not intend to discuss that. "You look well."

"Thank you."

"Where do you live these days?" She perched on her custom-made stool behind the gleaming glass desk.

"Out of Germany."

"Wise choice. Yet here you are."

I pulled the black poker chip out of my satchel and handed it to her. "One of Jack's?"

She gave it back after only a cursory glance. "Hardly seems worthwhile to charge for that information."

"A charge is not required."

Her perfectly painted lips smiled. "But it is."

I pulled a bill out of my satchel and pushed it across the table.

"Last time you had Swiss francs."

I retrieved the bill and rummaged in my satchel. I pulled out a gold Swiss coin and pressed it into her waiting palm. "Better?"

"Better if it had a friend."

I found a second one. The price was too high, and we both knew it. I held the coin, watching her. She must have her reasons. She looked so frail.

I gave her the second coin.

She tucked both into her purse before speaking. "It is one of ours. From the Monte Carlo, just down the road."

"It belongs to a friend."

"Lucky friend. It's worth a hundred Reichsmarks."

"Unlucky friend," I answered, wondering why Peter had been gambling for such high stakes. He did not play games of chance, at least not formalized ones. But perhaps Theresa had given it to him. "Dead."

No emotion made it to Agnes's flat copper-colored eyes. "Condolences."

"I am curious as to the accounts for this particular friend." I took care not to mention my friend's gender.

"Are you the executor for the will?" she said lightly.

I stifled a smile when she raised a perfectly plucked eyebrow. Agnes and my brother, Ernst, had shared the same beautician because they admired her work on eyebrows. "Perhaps."

"And what do you wish from me?"

"May I see the accounts?"

The telephone burred. She answered it and repeated back the customer's order. Someone wanted three prostitutes, but they had to be true blondes. I did not speculate how their hair color would be established. From the directions, it sounded as if they were being delivered to a barrack in the Olympic Village. Which country's cabin would they be visiting? I wondered if it would improve international relations or strain them further.

While she wrote details about required costumes, I fidgeted and studied the black-tiled walls. Modern in the '20s, they now felt dated.

She finished her conversation and hung up. "I might be able to arrange a brief viewing, tomorrow night."

"The cost?"

"A name." She folded her stubby hands in her lap.

I stared at her, startled. She had only ever desired cash before.

"A name?" She knew far more people than I. Agnes was the one everyone else sought out for names.

"The man who did your passport."

"At the passport office?" I wanted to be perfectly clear. I did not like surprises, especially not from someone who commanded Agnes's resources.

She clucked her tongue. "Your other passport."

Herr Silbert, my forger contact. "Why?"

"I require his services." Her deep voice sped up. I suspected she was irritated at my questions.

I kept asking them. Agnes must have her own contacts. Why use mine? "For yourself?"

Her amber eyes held my gaze for several seconds. "Yes."

I had not spoken to Herr Silbert since he had procured Swiss passports for Anton and me. They had held up beautifully for the last five years. I would not give out his name if I could avoid it. "If you give me your photo and details, I will try to find him and deliver them."

"How soon?"

"Why not use your own people?" I wanted details before I delivered a package to Herr Silbert, assuming I found him.

She sighed impatiently. "Very well. I would like to be out of Germany before the end of the Games. And I don't want there to be a chance that I am traced."

"Jack will not let you go?"

"He might." She shrugged her petite shoulders. "But then again, he might not."

"Why do you need to leave?" Agnes had a firm position in the criminal underworld. Her contacts had taken a lifetime to develop, and I could not imagine her leaving them.

"It's the Law for the Prevention of Hereditarily Diseased Offspring." Her hands twisted in her lap. "The Nazis are sterilizing everyone they consider to have an inheritable physical or mental condition. Or asocials. And I've heard from a reliable source that they are considering starting on dwarves next."

I stared at her, aghast.

"I don't intend to ever have children, of course," she went on. "But I won't let some Nazi butcher stir around my insides with a knife."

I tried to pull myself together.

She put one hand on the table between us. "I've never seen you so shocked, Peter."

"I am sorry," I said.

"I don't need sentiment." She tapped her nails against the glass table. "I need documentation."

"Of course."

"In exchange, I will give you the items you require at the casino tomorrow. Say nine?" She tilted her head expectantly.

"Monte Carlo. Nine."

"Remember that silver dress you always used to wear?"

"Yes," I said. I had left it in Berlin five years before. "But I—"

"Don't wear that. Unless you want everyone to know that you can't afford to gamble." Her rich laugh echoed through the room.

"What would you suggest?"

"I have just the thing in the back." She studied me from head to toe, and I was suddenly conscious that she was a madam. "Schiaparelli."

I had no idea what Schiaparelli meant. "That is?"

Agnes laughed again. "She's a designer whom you would have heard of if you paid proper attention. Regardless, it's your size and will look smashing on you. But you must return it clean. There is, of course, the matter of price."

With Agnes, everything came with a price. We haggled until we agreed on it; then she returned with a sea green, floor-length satin gown. The shoulders had straps the width of a ribbon but were otherwise bare, and the neckline fell lower than I had ever worn. I eyed it skeptically.

"It's no whore dress," she said, judging my expression accurately. "It's respectable."

I gave her a dubious look.

"Don't be such a matron. I have more fashion sense in my little finger than you do in your whole body." She held up her pinkie to show me. "And you see how tiny my finger is."

We both laughed.

She packed the dress in a long white box. "I assume you have no matching shoes or gloves?"

"Why would I?"

"Because you are a woman, and most women do," Agnes said tartly.

"I am Peter Weill," I said. "I do not trifle with such things."

"You don't have a decent suit either." She pulled a pair of matching green shoes and satin gloves from under her desk. After I tried them on and she pronounced them suitable, she added them to the box, shockingly, for no extra charge.

"And for God's sake, Peter, bring a man. Or you will end up leaving with one."

"I—"

"Shall I rent you one?"

"I will find an escort," I said quickly, although I wondered how I would. Panzer, perhaps? He might be a game companion for a trip to the casino.

She took in my expression and shook her head. "Call if you change your mind. I can find someone up to the last minute."

"Thank you," I said in a frosty tone that made us both smile.

11

Late afternoon slanted through the tall buildings by the time I stood again on the sidewalk in front of Agnes's office. I tucked the box carefully under one arm before heading for the Zoo subway station. I shuddered to imagine what she would charge if I damaged or stained the dress.

I had a little time left before Lars's party, and I decided to treat myself. Without him shadowing me, I could visit my childhood friend Bettina.

I took the subway to her house and knocked on her door. It had been two years. The door was freshly painted a glossy white, the brass knocker polished to a high gleam. Overhead a Nazi flag flew. Had she hung it or the owner of the apartment building? A flame of worry ignited in my heart.

"Hannah!" She flung open the door and swept me into a soft vanilla-scented hug. "Years. I've waited years to see you, and you just turn up."

"You can't get rid of a weed." Her husband, Fritz, appeared behind her. He gave me a more subdued embrace and herded us off the street and into the house. A policeman, he had once been my primary contact at Alexanderplatz.

As she always did, she asked, "Are you hungry?" Bettina always tried to fatten me up.

"Not a bit."

"I have strüdel fresh from the oven," she said, wiping her hands on her blindingly white apron.

"I am fine," I said, although I knew she would not let it alone until she had fed me. "And I have little time for a visit."

She put her hands on her rounded hips. "A quick piece, then."

I let myself be towed inside, Fritz carrying my dress box. When we passed through the hall of family portraits, I noticed that the lone picture of Bettina and me as schoolgirls was gone.

Bettina's shiny copper pots glowed with warm afternoon light. As always, her kitchen smelled heavenly. Today it smelled like baked apples and cinnamon.

"Did you just arrive?" She pulled a strüdel from the oven and cut me a large piece. "Are you here to cover the Games? Are you still writing in Switzerland? Do you still have that little boy?"

"I have not put him out in the street quite yet." He was not so little anymore. When he showed up on my doorstep, he had been very small for his age. He had lived with an abusive prostitute for his first five years and never ate regularly. I left Germany to keep him away from the Nazi father who had let that happen. Although it had been difficult, I never regretted it. Now that Anton lived a more ordinary life, he had sprouted up and was one of the tallest boys in his school year.

"He'd just come back. That's what children do." She giggled.

"How are Sophia and the boys? Are they home?"

"The boys are off doing guard duty with the Hitler Youth."

I clenched my teeth. I remembered how she had fought to keep them out of the Hitler Youth two years before. She had purchased a garden plot to give them an excuse to be too busy for meetings, and had even considered sending them to Switzerland. Back then, she had worried that her children might denounce her for her anti-Nazi beliefs. Now she spoke so casually of sending them off to be indoctrinated. Would I have become so inured to the Nazis that I would have sent Anton marching off in a brown uniform so easily had we stayed? I could not imagine it. "Are they?"

"Don't look like that. They're outdoors and with friends. It's not at all like I thought." She turned big eyes to Fritz.

"Indeed?" I asked, struggling to keep anger from my voice. "You consider the Hitler Youth a wholesome activity?"

Fritz put a solid hand on her shoulder. "Things are different now."

I bit my tongue. These were my friends. I might not see them again for years. It was not a time for arguments. Instead I asked about their daughter. "How is Sophia?"

"She has a meeting with the League of Young Girls. Some of them are over at the Frisian House, helping the women athletes. Running errands and such."

"And how are you two?" I searched for a neutral topic of conversation, not wanting to think about how all their children were engaged in pro-Nazi activities. And that Bettina and Fritz did not seem to mind.

"Wonderful," she said.

"We're all going to the Games tomorrow," Fritz said.

Bettina's hazelnut brown eyes danced. "Fritz heard that you were caught in a compromising position with former Kommissar Lang, you naughty girl."

"Who told you that, Fritz?" My stomach clenched, anger at their pro-Nazi stances turning to fear for my safety.

"Sergeant Bauer. Used to work traffic in your day, I believe."

I remembered him now. That was why his hedgehog nose had felt so familiar in the corridor at the Olympic Stadium. And he had recognized me, too.

This changed everything.

"What did you say when you heard?"

"I gave him a dressing down for spreading scurrilous rumors." Fritz's baritone voice rang with indignation. "I told him that I would see him disciplined if he told anyone else. And I told him that Hauptsturmführer Lang's women all look the same."

"All?" I asked, surprised. "How many are there?"

"A fair few," he said. "And for years now, they have looked like you."

"So I just fit his pattern?" I felt angry and then ridiculous for being angry.

"Or you set the standard," Bettina said.

I ignored her statement. "Did you say anything further, Fritz?"

"That you'd left the country, so it could not have been you. Guess I'll have to . . . revise that opinion."

"Please do not revise it. I might as well be gone already." I should leave immediately, even if it cost me my job at the paper and Weill's death remained unsolved. But I knew I would stay.

He shook his head disapprovingly, but said nothing. He knew what I meant.

"How many people did he tell?" My hands shook so that I feared to pick up my fork to eat my strüdel.

"I hope I was the first, but I don't know." Fritz clucked his tongue at me. "You shouldn't swan around the Olympic Stadium if you don't want to be talked about."

Bettina elbowed him. "It's nice to hear that you got into an embarrassing situation with a man. Finally. And Lang would be a good match, if it's true."

She would never give up matchmaking. "Still trying to marry me off?"

"Marriage is not such a bad thing." Her eyes twinkled at Fritz, who smiled back. I thought of my life with Boris. Marriage might not have been such a bad thing. But we had shut that door.

She poured us all tea from a half-empty pot. "And Lang is a Hauptsturmführer in the SS. Quite an influential position."

"I have heard that." Instead of saying more, I took a bite of strüdel. Tart and firm. Bettina's baking had not suffered under the Nazi regime either.

"Still, he's always been a quiet sort. Wily interrogator. Not sure if he'd be the best match for you," Fritz said. "Are you certain you've made the best decision?"

"If Hannah is swanning in the Olympic Stadium with him, they must be a good pair, Fritz!" Bettina admonished. She turned back to me. "Are you moving home again? It's not as bad as the foreign newspapers say."

Back? Not while the Nazis were in charge. I took a sip of tea before answering, "I thought that reading foreign newspapers was illegal."

"You know what I am trying to say." She wagged her index finger. "Things are much more stable in Berlin now, as they were before the Great War, when we were children. It's safe to walk around unaccompanied."

"Assuming one is Aryan." Anger crowded out my fear.

"You would get in real trouble if you stayed here, talking like that," Fritz said.

"Even to you?"

"Even to us," Bettina answered firmly for both of them. Always a united force, marriage suited them. And now they were united behind the Nazis. Our whole conversation led to this single point.

My head spun to think of it. I had never thought they would fall prey to Nazi propaganda, even though it had been poured into their ears for two years. Theresa had been correct: I was years away from home. Home was gone. The Nazis had invaded even the friends of my childhood.

"Hitler is not some demon." Bettina poked Fritz in the ribs. "Tell her."

"Hitler is not some demon," he parroted. I could not imagine Boris so obedient, even if we were married.

"He is known across the world for his humanitarian actions," I said sarcastically. "Especially toward Communists and Jews."

"The world came out to see him at the opening, though, didn't they?" Fritz's gray eyes regarded me coolly. "Television of the events was broadcast everywhere, for the first time ever."

I took an angry sip of tea, hoping it would calm me down. It did not. I did not like to think about the Nazis exploiting the new technology of television for their propaganda purposes. They were already too effective with radio and film.

Bettina continued for Fritz. "And reporters from all over the world. Athletes from everywhere saluting Hitler."

I shrugged. To that, I had nothing to say. Unfortunately, they were correct.

"And he has brought law and order." She pointed her sticky teaspoon at me. "Something you might not appreciate since you're never here."

No, I did not appreciate strong-arm law and a new order that penned my friends in ghettos or concentration camps. "Oh," was all I said.

"How dare you come here and judge us?" Bettina's brown eyes narrowed angrily. "You sit in some mansion in Switzerland and think you know what it's like here. You don't."

I set down my fork. "I do not sit in some Swiss mansion. But I do read the foreign papers and perhaps I know things you do not, since all my news sources are not censored by Joseph Goebbels."

Bettina drew in a deep breath. I knew from experience that a tirade was to follow.

So did Fritz. He put up a warning hand. "Don't let's fight. Who knows when we will see you again?"

Neither one looked upset by the prospect of not seeing me again anytime soon. Well, neither was I.

I said my farewells as soon as I gracefully could and hopped a subway back to Wittenbergplatz. I could not believe that I had lost Bettina and Fritz to the Nazis. It stung like a personal betrayal. They were good people, decent people. We had been friends for more than two decades. Bettina and I had shared girlhood hopes and dreams. Yet she had deliberately closed her eyes to the evils of the Nazis. Would Fritz inform on me? If he did, would Bettina support him? I wished desperately that I had stayed away from them, that I could cherish my illusions about them. I stared blindly at the subway's window.

I remembered riding this very same subway with Bettina soon after my husband-to-be had died and she had married Fritz. We both wore new dresses, mine black for mourning, hers pale pink. She had insisted on paying for my lunch, feeding me already, and we had chattered about men and fashion and the Danish film *Himmelskibet* about a journey

to Mars. It was hard to believe that we had ever been those girls. Mars
felt closer than those days.

I opened Peter's notebook to distract myself, but arrived no closer
to an answer than ever. Perhaps it was gibberish intended only to pun-
ish anyone foolish enough to steal it.

I strolled down Lars's empty hall with half an hour to spare, but he
was already home. He opened the door in full SS dress uniform. Several medals that I had never seen were pinned to his chest, including
an Iron Cross First Class. He would hold his own in the sea of Nazi
medal bearers into which we would soon be swept.

Should I tell him about Bauer? I thought back to my conversation
with Wilhelm about the investigation and Project Zephyr and held
my tongue. I would have to be very careful and not just of Lars. If
Bauer had told enough people at the police station, someone might be
searching for me. Would he be there tonight? It seemed unlikely that
a police sergeant would attend the kind of party Lars had described.

Lars gestured to the box under my arm. "Shopping?"

"A dress. I rented it."

"For tonight?"

I balked at the thought of wearing such a revealing dress in a room
full of Nazi officials. "Not for tonight."

I marched into the bedroom instead of explaining.

Before I hung the dress in his wardrobe, I sniffed it. It smelled like
expensive French perfume of the type Agnes always used. I stared at
light glinting off the silk, trying to decide whether to hang it next to
Lars's suits and make him spend the next week smelling like a French
woman of distinction.

In the end, I hung it in his bathroom. He had enough worries.

My simple black dress felt dowdy as I slipped it over my head. I
smoothed it down in front, grateful that it covered more than the
green one or gowns from the '20s. The event would be easier to en-
dure with as little exposed as possible.

I ran a wet comb through my hair and applied Chinese red lipstick, a shade redder than what I used for every day, straightened the black seams on the back of my stockings, and stroked my hand down the silk. I sprayed myself with my purse-sized perfume atomizer, the gift from Boris. The fragrance inside was Joy by Jean Patou. The scent instantly brought back parties and hotel rooms and time spent in Boris's arms, Anton off with friends and the two of us able to explore each other's bodies as thoroughly and noisily as we wanted. I pushed the thoughts out of my mind and surveyed myself in the mirror on the front of Lars's wardrobe.

I looked presentable, if slightly nervous. How could I get through an evening of Nazi luminaries? If Theodor Eicke or Hans Frank attended, it was unlikely that they might recollect me from my visits to Stadelheim Prison to see Röhm before his execution two years before, but I hated to bet my life on it.

I stepped into the living room, thinking about pleading illness so that we could leave early.

"Spatz," Lars said. "You look wonderful."

"You sound perhaps too surprised."

"Not at all," he said hastily. "You are always beautiful, of course, but I have never seen you dressed formally before. I shall be the envy of every man there."

Not wanting to prolong that discussion, I walked to the door as quickly as I could, strides shortened by the dress, which was cut tight across my thighs.

We left the building in silence, and Lars led me to a black Opel Olympia parked in front, silver zeppelin gleaming on the hood. Did everyone have one these days?

"Is that a permissible parking space?" I asked.

"I only brought it around while you were dressing." He opened my door, sounding peeved.

I did not try to explain that I was teasing.

Lars closed my door and got into the driver's seat. He straightened his perfectly straight hat before pulling into the street. So, he felt nervous, too.

I'd had little contact with Nazis before I left, and surely no one would connect the sweat-stained woman in a wide-brimmed hat on the steps of Stadelheim Prison with the Swiss woman in velvet I had become. Or, perhaps, they would.

"Have you anything to drink?"

He pointed to the glove box. I drew out a metal flask. Remembering Peter, I held it in a toast and sipped. Korn schnapps. It burned my throat and did nothing to settle my stomach. "Not a drop?" I said, reminding Lars of his promise. I finished it.

"I did not drink any. You did."

I put the empty flask back and stared nervously out the window. I wanted to warn him that he was under investigation, but I hated to expose the existence of a source within the SS before I knew why he was trying to quit his job. If he intended to double-cross me, it was best if he thought that I suspected nothing. I fiddled glumly with the black gloves Agnes had rented me. Second-guessing everything was exhausting. But I dared not trust Lars.

He gave a crooked smile. "Don't paint everything gray quite yet."

From someone more pessimistic than I, this came as a surprise. "Indeed?"

"You might enjoy the evening."

I raised my eyebrows, but held my peace.

When we arrived at the party, yellow light fell from every window onto the front lawn and onto the familiar thicket of huge Nazi flags interspersed with Olympic ones. I wondered to whom the house belonged.

A white-gloved valet in a black suit took my gloved hand and helped me out of the automobile. I felt as if I traveled with Bella. Lars handed his keys to a chauffeur, effectively preventing us from making a quick escape.

I faced the wide manicured lawn. Black-uniformed SS swarmed across it like ants, most accompanied by blond women in various fine dresses. My dress was barely fashionable enough and too severe. I would have looked less conspicuous if I had toughed it out in Agnes's daring silk number.

Lars took my elbow. "You look lovely."

"Thank you," I answered, eyes on the crowd. "When can we go?"

He laughed. "Considering your usual haunts, this is probably the safest place in Berlin."

Not the best time to contradict him. I took one more look around the lawn. Among the blackshirts were important foreign visitors. I saw a Japanese man in an elegant evening suit and gleaming round glasses, what could only be an American in an expensive yet rumpled tuxedo, and an Indian with a burgundy turban.

We proceeded to the open front door. Once inside, I tried not to stare. The entrance hall was so large, I wondered if we would be issued bicycles. We hiked across its black marble floor to the ballroom, where about a hundred Nazis sipped drinks and chattered, almost drowning out the musician diligently playing a full-sized grand piano. It looked like a toy in the huge space. Atop the piano an oak tree sat in a pot. Tomorrow it would be given to a medal winner with the laurel.

Lars introduced a round, pudgy man with sweaty hands as Obersturmbannführer Richter.

"He has been keeping you all to himself for far too long," Richter said, not releasing my hands. He squinted at me as if nearsighted. "I have wanted to meet you for two years."

Lars must have told him about me shortly after we started working together. But why? "Delighted to finally meet you," I said.

Richter patted my hands. "The pleasure is all mine."

I forced a smile before pulling my hands away from his.

We spent the next hour in a whirlwind of introductions. Lars knew most of the top rank of the SS. If they ever discovered our activities, we would have a slow and painful death indeed for having fooled them. He had to face these people every day and lie and hope for the best. If he could fool them, he could fool me. Should I trust him more? I squeezed his arm, and he glanced over in surprise, "Spatz?"

"Thank you." I leaned against him.

He gave me a puzzled smile. "For what?"

"For all you do." Impulsively, I hugged him.

He pulled me close. "You are most welcome," he whispered into my hair.

Blushing, I stepped back.

Lars smiled. "I believe I see someone else to introduce you to."

He introduced me to another official, but I was too flustered to mark the name. We chatted and smiled through the ballroom until we came to the buffet off a side door. Joints of meat, rolls, and fruits and vegetables from all over Europe were piled high on tables. Enough to impress even the most particular foreign guests. Too nervous, I ate little and drank less. True to his word, Lars drank only water.

I spotted Leni Riefenstahl in an elegant French gown. She posed perfectly, head up and shoulders back like the dancer and actress she had once been. She stroked one hand absently down the dove gray silk while she talked. From her regal pose, she conversed animatedly with a man wearing a gold chain that signified him as a member of the International Olympic Committee. The room was bursting with Nazi and Olympic elite.

"Do you see the man over there?" Lars pointed to an army captain standing alone in the corner with a half-empty champagne glass.

"Popular-looking fellow."

"That's Bosch," he said. "From the file."

I examined Bosch with more interest. He was tall and spindly, with fine blond hair and jerky movements. "I want to meet him."

"Don't tell him about the stamp."

"How big a fool do you think me?"

Lars raised his eyebrows instead of answering, but led me to Bosch and introduced us.

"How do you do?" I transferred my empty champagne flute to my left hand.

Bosch took my gloved hand. "Delighted to meet you, my dear."

His voice came out scratchy and breathy, like Peter Lorre's. I recoiled from the sound. To me, that voice would always belong to Hans Beckert, child killer in *M*.

"Adelheid's nephew collects stamps," Lars said. "Allow me to freshen your glass."

He took my glass and disappeared. Did he assume I would fare better with Bosch on my own?

"Such a fascinating hobby," Bosch said, patting his thin blond hair. "What does your nephew specialize in?"

"He asked me to get him some Olympic stamps. What do you recommend?"

"Oh, buy the full sheet. There are special editions for the Games. Two sheets of four each. I believe you can purchase them quite easily at the stadium. There are at least forty stamp salesmen walking the crowd at any given time. Stamp collecting is becoming more popular each year."

"I bought him some when I was on the Graf Zeppelin a few years ago." That trip was in Adelheid Zinsli's SS file, so I saw no reason to conceal it. "He would love some from the South Seas. He's mad about Kästner's book, *The Thirty-fifth of May: or, Conrad's Ride to the South Seas*."

"Lovely stamps come from the South Seas. You can find everything from quite inexpensive to some of the most expensive stamps in the world." He talked more quickly now, voice breathier.

"Are those the kind you collect, then, South Seas stamps?"

He bowed his head awkwardly. "I have a varied collection. But I do have a keen interest in island stamps."

"What is your favorite?" I tried to modulate my voice so I sounded more polite than curious.

His eyes gleamed. He probably rarely got a willing audience. "The most famous island stamp is the two-cent Hawaiian missionary."

"Missionary?" He had arrived rather quickly where I wanted him, suspiciously so. I tried to look bored.

"It's from the days when the missionaries arrived in Hawaii. The stamps are not as old as some. They started making them in 1851, my grandfather's time."

"Surely there must be hundreds," I said dismissively. "They're so recent."

He shook his head sternly, as if offended by my naïveté. "Fewer than twenty, I believe. You must remember that stamp collecting was only a schoolboy's hobby back in those days."

"My nephew is a schoolboy." I smiled in what I hoped was an amused fashion, but sounding annoyed that he had denigrated my imaginary nephew. In front of us, couples waltzed.

"I mean no disrespect. I collected stamps as a schoolboy, too, but now I've moved on to more serious collecting." He puffed out his skinny chest.

"You have this Hawaiian stamp in your collection?"

"Not yet." His spiderlike fingers twitched his champagne glass nervously. "I would love to add it. Who wouldn't? It's one of the most valuable stamps in the world."

"How much could a scrap of paper and paste from Hawaii possibly be worth?" I watched the twirling dancers, as if more interested in their finery than in my present conversation. They reminded me, bizarrely, of the Olympic fencers.

"Thousands of marks." He leaned down and spoke in a whisper. "Men have killed to possess that stamp."

A chill went down my back. Had Lars set me up? "Have they?"

"Indeed they have." He stepped closer. I resisted the urge to step back and instead looked up into his eyes. He was a great deal taller than I.

"In 1892," he finished.

I relaxed. "Tell me."

"A wealthy man named Gaston Leroux was found murdered in his home. It baffled the gendarmes. Baffled them." He shook his balding head as if he, too, were baffled and drained his glass.

"Indeed?" I scanned the dance floor as if I wanted to be rescued from his boring story.

He hurried on. "His valuables were untouched: gold, cash, jewelry all safely tucked away. He had no known enemies. So why was he killed?"

"How did they determine the stamp was missing?"

"One detective was a philatelist, a stamp collector," he said proudly. "He discovered that the two-cent Hawaiian blue was missing."

"Was it ever found?"

"It was!" His breathy voice sped up. "They searched all the stamp stores of Paris to no avail, but the detective understood about philatelists and investigated the dead man's friends. His friend Hector Giroux had an unexplained Hawaiian blue. He confessed and was hanged for his crime."

"So he did not try to sell it?" I asked. "He wanted only the stamp, not the money?"

"Of course, Frau Zinsli. Stamps are worth much more than the petty monetary amounts arbitrarily set on them by collectors." He gripped his empty champagne flute so tightly in his excitement that I worried it might break.

"What a wonderful story," I said. "Unless you were Monsieur Leroux."

"A man with such a treasure must choose his friends carefully." His breathy voice held certainty.

"I hope we all choose our friends carefully."

As if on cue, Lars appeared at my side, holding a full glass of champagne. "Your champagne, Spatz."

"Thank you," I said. I appreciated both the champagne and the rescue. Bosch made me uncomfortable, and I thought it was more than just his eerie voice.

"Ready for a quick turn around the floor?" Lars asked.

We had danced only once—after my Gestapo interrogation in 1934 and just before we started working together. He had stomped so soundly on my toes that time, that I did not relish a repeat performance. "Certainly."

"Would you care for a new glass?" I asked, handing it to Bosch.

"Excuse us," Lars said.

Bosch nodded graciously, taking the full glass of champagne, but I could tell that he had not run out of stamp stories.

I took Lars's hand with trepidation when we reached the dance floor. I hoped that my toes would survive the song. But I need not have worried. This time he was the perfect partner, graceful and assured. I relaxed and enjoyed the dance, grateful for a moment's peace.

When the waltz ended, I looked into his eyes in surprise. They were so dark, like ink. "Have you been taking lessons?"

The music started again. "Why would you say that?"

I bit my lip and danced without meeting his gaze.

He let me stew before smiling. "I was not at my best that night in the beer garden."

"So I see." We danced a few beats in silence.

"I've never seen Hauptmann Bosch so animated. I believe you have made another conquest."

"I believe he was grateful to have an audience. Nothing more."

Lars raised his eyebrows skeptically. "What were you discussing so intently?"

"Stamps," I said. "My advice is not to bring up the subject unless you have a great deal of time to spend."

"Did you find out more about your friend's stamp?"

Before I answered, a tall, muscular man with what looked to be a dueling scar on his left cheek tapped Lars on the shoulder. I wondered what fencing club he had attended to procure his scar, such an aristocratic symbol. "May I cut in?"

Lars's hand tightened painfully on mine, but his expression did not change. "Certainly."

I looked between the two, awaiting an introduction. I counted the silver pips on his uniform, four to Lars's three. He outranked Lars.

Lars bowed and relinquished me to the stranger. "Frau Zinsli, please meet Sturmbannführer Hahn."

"Delighted to meet you," I said. So here was the man Wilhelm had told me was involved with Project Zephyr. He was also Lars's superior.

"Likewise, I'm sure." Hahn kissed my hand. Fury flashed across Lars's face.

I drew my hand back very slowly, keeping Hahn's eyes turned toward me until Lars got himself under control. He was usually circumspect. Why did Hahn anger him so?

"Excuse me." Lars gave a small bow and marched off the dance floor, shoulders set straight.

Hahn put one hand on my lower back and with the other took firm hold of my gloved fingers. I settled one hand on his black-clad shoulder, and we stepped into the waltz. He was an agile and accomplished dancer. With his grace and timing, he must have been an accomplished fencer. He reminded me of a panther, claws barely sheathed.

Lars watched from the edge of the floor with a wooden expression. I fought down panic and gave Hahn a charming false smile, on guard. He turned us so that I no longer saw Lars. Intentionally, I was certain.

"That is quite a luscious scent you are wearing." His hand on my lower back pulled me closer. I gritted my teeth, repulsed. "And you are a most graceful dancer."

"You, too, are quite adept." I spotted Andreas in the corner, holding a plate of grapes with a lost air.

I had not expected to see him here. Ordinarily, a simple college professor would not be invited to this kind of event. Perhaps he, too, had secrets. Regardless, he was more pleasant than Hahn. As soon as this song ended, I would head over to him, feign illness, and when Lars reappeared, I would convince him to leave. It was a plan, anyway.

"Thank you." Hahn inclined his head slightly. "Charming as well. Hauptsturmführer Lang certainly has the golden touch with women."

"Has he?" I tried not to sound startled.

"Best in his field. As I imagine you know?" We glided across the floor, each movement melting into the next. He was by far the best partner I had ever danced with, but I hoped for the song to end quickly so I could escape him. For reasons I could not yet analyze, he terrified me.

"He is a man of many talents," I said, unsure where the conversation might lead.

"Indeed?" His gaze lingered on my lips and traced down my neck to my breasts. I was grateful that I had not worn the low-cut silk dress.

"What is it that you do?" I hoped to draw his eyes higher. I had a strong urge to yank my hand out of his and quit the dance floor.

"This and that." His thumb caressed my back.

I leaned forward quickly, shifting his hand. "Is that challenging work?"

"How did you meet your dear Lars?" His thumb came to rest back where it had been.

"During a Gestapo interrogation," I said. "Much like this one. Except without music."

He threw back his head and laughed, yellowed teeth glittering. "When, again?"

Everything was recorded in my file, so I had to hew closely to our agreed-upon story. "Two years ago."

"Ah, so it was a straightforward interrogation?"

What did that mean? "A case of mistaken identity."

"Whom were you mistaken for?"

"I do not know," I lied. In fact, I had been mistaken for myself—Hannah Vogel. Only Lars's intervention and quick thinking had saved my life.

"I loved your pieces on classical sculpture," he said. "Quite clever."

My stomach dropped to my knees. Why had he read my articles as Adelheid Zinsli? "Thank you," I answered.

"As clever as you are—" His hand tightened painfully on mine. "—don't you think you should leave reporting to the men?"

"Whatever for?" I smiled vapidly.

"It is time for you and Lars to finally marry. Two years is a long time."

"I believe that is a matter between Lars and myself." Behind his head, I found Lars again. He stood next to Richter, talking animatedly, gesturing to Hahn and me. Was he asking Richter to cut in or ostentatiously ignoring us?

"Are you aware that being unmarried is deleterious to his career?"

Another item that Lars had failed to mention. I missed a step. Hahn immediately caught me up.

"A woman does not involve herself in a man's affairs," I said. Standard Nazi propaganda, and it chafed me to spout it.

"Surely you want the best for him?"

"Always." I smiled. "I believe he has no complaints."

"I cannot see how he would." Hahn's eyes traveled over my body again. "You seem like the kind of woman who could have any man she wanted."

His palm slid lower on my back. A hand's-breadth and it would be on my bottom. I twitched my back and lied. "And I do."

"Lars Lang?" His hand dropped a centimeter. "Surely you can do better than that."

I did not like his questions, and I did not like his groping.

"He is an extraordinary man," I said hotly, "and I'll thank you not to insult him in my presence."

"I said nothing untoward." His thumb started again.

"But you implied a great deal." I reached behind me and took his hand off my bottom, then pulled my other hand free. I had a vision of my hand reaching to slap him, but I did not dare to indulge it. "Good evening."

I turned and stalked away as well as I could in my too-tight dress. Lars was nowhere to be seen, so I headed toward Andreas. I felt Hahn's eyes on me all the way.

Andreas, too, watched with his mouth slightly open in shock. On the one hand, I should not have let Hahn bait me. I might have gained valuable information. On the other, I had at least ended the encounter before I revealed too much.

I stopped in front of Andreas. "How lovely to see you at this illustrious Olympic party," I said.

"He is right behind you," Andreas said. "I advise you not to anger him."

"Too late for that, I expect." I turned to face Hahn, shoulders back and false smile plastered on my face.

"My apologies." He bowed. "I believe I may have overstepped."

"Indeed you did, Sturmbannführer Hahn." I could hardly perform a reversal. Next to me, Andreas looked ready to collapse. Who was Hahn that he frightened him so?

"Dirk. Please," said Hahn. "I think that we could become very fast friends."

I had no intention of calling him by his first name. I held my tongue, not knowing how to proceed. Andreas's reaction confused me.

"The Swiss are such a stolid race. I had no idea that their women could be so—" Hahn lowered his voice. "—excitable."

"Everyone is excitable when properly roused." The prudent move would be to flirt, but I could not bring myself to do so. I twisted my hands and wished that Andreas would say something to distract Hahn from me. Andreas stood as silent as a tree.

Lars's arrival saved me. He held a glass of champagne for me and what looked like a glass of water for himself.

"Have you been toying with her, Sturmbannführer?" Lars looked between us. "She'll not countenance that."

"I see that now." Hahn chuckled. "You've chosen well, Lang. She's quite the firebrand."

"I do not enjoy when people speak about me as if I were not here." I sipped champagne and scowled at both. Andreas had regained some color, but still looked upset. I wondered if he would ever regain the power of speech.

"I don't know how you do it, Lars, you old dog." Hahn clapped him on the shoulder and strode toward the bar.

"Who was that?" I tossed back more champagne than prudent.

"He pretends to work in interrogations, and lately he has been becoming more . . . hands-on with his questioning. I believe his actual function is to investigate other SS officers," Lars said. "I report to him."

"She almost slapped him." Andreas found his voice. "Hahn."

"He needed slapping." It was too late to apologize.

"He would have enjoyed it if you had, if that helps to stay your hand next time," Lars said.

Andreas blushed.

"May we leave?" I said. "I feel quite ill."

"You don't look ill," Lars said.

"I am skilled at concealing it."

Lars and I glared at each other while Andreas squirmed. Lars dropped his gaze first. "Very well. I suppose I have showed you off enough."

We headed for the door. Lars leaned down close, warm hand resting lightly on the small of my back. "What happened between you and Hahn?"

I gave him a quick summary. "I should not have lost my temper, so spare me the lecture."

He had an expression in his eyes I had never seen before. "No," he said softly. "You should have behaved exactly as you did."

Before I could ask what he meant, I spotted Bauer, the police officer who had seen Lars and me at the Olympic Stadium, plowing into the room like a draft horse. If he caught us here together, our lives were forfeit.

12

I dived for a side room, frustrated by the tight cut of my dress. I could take only short steps. Tables stacked with food filled the space. I ignored the temptation to duck under a table and instead minced through the swinging door into the kitchen. I neither knew nor cared if Lars followed. Without me next to him, Bauer could not prove that he was associating with a known traitor who was using an assumed name.

The chef and his white-suited helpers gaped.

"You have entered the kitchen, Fräulein," the chef said in a surprisingly high-pitched voice. "The festivities are behind you."

"Apologies." I walked past him to the back door and into the night.

I leaned against the outside wall and took an uneven breath. A shaft of light pierced the darkness. Lars's silhouette paused in the door before he stepped into the yard.

"Spatz?" he called softly.

"Here."

He crossed the wet grass between us in two steps. "Bauer?"

So he had seen Bauer, too, and guessed the reason for my flight.

"Yes." The stone wall felt cold against my back. "I am leaving now."

"Bauer is my problem, too."

"Without me to identify as Hannah Vogel, it is only your word against his." I thought of all the dignitaries he had introduced me to. "And your word appears to be sterling."

He stepped in front of me. It reminded me of how he had pinned me against the pillar at the Olympic Stadium. "Not everything is as it seems," he said.

Perhaps he did know of the investigation Wilhelm had mentioned. "I will return to your apartment to pick up my things," I said.

"And then?"

"I will go into hiding until I leave." I stepped away from the wall. I still had Peter's death to investigate.

"Which is?"

"When I am ready, Lars."

When I walked across the dew-damp lawn, he did not follow. A shout of laughter drifted through the opened windows. Here and there, couples had retreated to the privacy of the back lawn, but they were too absorbed in each other to notice me. I hoped.

I made it to the sidewalk and hurried to the subway station, trying not to glance over my shoulder every other step. Bauer. I did not think that he had seen me. But if he had, and let my name slip as Lars's companion, anyone in that room would investigate it further. Especially Hahn. I was grateful that I had not slapped him after all. I had already drawn more than enough attention to myself.

I took the train to Wittenbergplatz and tried not to think about Bauer, because each time I did, I began to shake. Instead I wrote a note for Lars, telling him that he was under investigation for unpatriotic motives because he tried to transfer out of his current job. After meeting Hahn, I did not blame him.

When I arrived at his apartment, Lars was just inside the door, holding my white dress box. Two suitcases stood next to the door. Mine. And his?

"I will drive you to the train station," he said.

"I have no intention of getting on a train. Do you?"

"You have no damn idea what you are dealing with," he said.

I stared at him, surprised. He did not often swear. "Then tell me."

He gathered our suitcases. I took the box.

"Not here," he said. "If Bauer talked to Hahn, we must disappear."

We went down the hall and into the Olympia without another word.

After he got clear of traffic, he drove too fast, straight ahead into the Tiergarten. Black pines towered on both sides of the empty lane. With no moon, the only illumination came from Lars's headlights.

He yanked the wheel to the right, and we left the pavement, bumping across cobblestones before he stopped and turned off the engine. We sat on the edge of a grassy meadow. Blades of grass shone in the headlights until he turned them off. Then we sat in total darkness.

"I do not think this is a permissible parking space either," I said, trying for a smile.

His gaze never moved from the windscreen. "You knew Bauer from before." Not a question. An accusation.

"Barely."

Leather in his gloves creaked when he tightened his grip on the steering wheel. He took one deep breath after another. I had never seen him so angry, not even when he almost hit me.

I stepped out and walked toward the front of the automobile. The scent of crushed grass drifted up. Behind me his door slammed.

"Spatz," he ordered. "Talk."

Even though I disliked orders, I told him how Bauer had directed traffic near my apartment in 1931, and I told him what I had heard that afternoon from Fritz concerning Bauer's gossip about Lars and me. Lars could pay the price for my activities, and keeping them private only endangered him more.

"Why did you not tell me earlier?" His voice was brisk, clipped.

"I knew you would insist I go back to Switzerland." So, to further my own ends, I had risked his life without telling him. Guilt wormed in my stomach.

"Send you to Switzerland rather than see you dead? Yes, I would."

"If I stay away from Bauer—"

"You must go." His words sounded urgent, and afraid.

"No." I gave my automatic response to being told what to do. But what if he was correct? I knew that Peter's secret was important, if only I could unearth it. But could I manage it before the Nazis caught me? They certainly had the odds in their favor. Thinking of that gave me enough anger to consider staying.

The cooling engine ticked loudly.

He leaned against the driver's side fender and patted the metal next to him.

Not sure what else to do, I leaned against the car, too. The diagonal vents felt as warm on my skin as a living creature. "I have a few things that I must—"

He chuckled. I stared at him. "Lars?"

He bent over double, laughing. Was he hysterical? What could I do with an out-of-control SS officer in the middle of the woods at night? I waited, glad he'd had no alcohol.

After several minutes, he pulled himself together, mopping his eyes on his black sleeve. "Do you see what this means?" He hiccupped. "It is quite over, Spatz, for both of us."

"It is not. If Bauer spread the story, wouldn't we be caught already?"

"Perhaps." He sounded serious again.

"Then we are probably in the clear. Of course, we cannot know for certain—"

"But I do know for certain what will happen to you if you end up in Gestapo headquarters."

"It has not come to that yet. And it might not." Besides, I did not add, how were we to flee if the situation was so dire? I had only two sets of papers: Adelheid Zinsli and Hannah Vogel. If Bauer's talk had started an investigation, both were useless. I would have to procure new papers for myself in order to escape. And I must obtain some for Agnes as well. I had given her my word.

"Every day . . ." His voice trailed off. I watched indifferent white stars and waited. When he spoke again, I had to strain to hear it. "Every day I see people brought in and beaten. You cannot know what it's like."

"I am sorry. It must—"

"Did you know that beautiful women are most sought after to break?"

"Then I should be safe," I said, hoping to lighten the conversation.

He twitched his head impatiently.

I spoke again. "Nothing happened when I came to the Winter Olympics in Garmisch. This will be no different."

"It's gotten worse since then. Much worse."

Wind blew through the leaves. A peaceful sound, but a finger of dread traced down my spine.

He stared straight ahead, face tightened into a tense mask. "Two months ago, Hahn changed the rules."

We sat in darkness. Crickets chirped. I sensed that Lars had something important he wanted to say, but I feared that the slightest action might spook him. I waited. Wind sighed through the trees again.

"Now, if a woman is Aryan"—he spoke barely above a whisper— "you are encouraged to . . . to take her by force. As many times as you want."

I inhaled sharply. "Do you—?"

"No." He drew in a slow breath and let it out before continuing. "I go in after. I'm the good one. The one who cleans them up, dresses their wounds, gives them water. I gain their trust. Get their information."

"My god, Lars." My voice cracked.

"Not your god or mine. He doesn't come into those rooms." Lars hunched down as if to make himself disappear.

I moved in front of him. He had pulled his arms against his stomach, and he rocked ever so slightly from side to side. It had cost him dearly to tell me.

"Lars." I pulled him into my arms. At first he stiffened, but he did not pull away. I tightened my arms around him.

He collapsed so suddenly, I almost dropped him. Then he wept. Each sob sounded wrenched out of him. I held him silently. I had no words of comfort.

When he stopped, I loosened my grip to relieve my aching arms. I moved one hand in a circle on his back and felt him slowly relax.

Much later, he pulled away and wiped his eyes with his fists, as Anton always did. "I have made a mess all over your dress."

"It will all wash out."

"It won't." His voice caught.

I eased back to my former position leaning against the fender, moving carefully so as not to startle him.

He took a deep, shuddering breath. "Thank you."

"Of course."

He leaned next to me. We listened to the crickets.

"Why do you stay?"

He smothered a groan in his throat. It was the most painful sound I had ever heard. "Someone has to show those women kindness. Even for a moment."

Something hooted. We both jumped. It hooted again. Only an owl, I told myself and forced my shoulders to relax.

"What if you leave and never come back?" I asked quietly.

"Not many countries accepting SS officers." His voice sounded calm again.

"Come to Switzerland." I took his cold hand. "To start."

"Then you and I and the banker could set up house together? Wouldn't that be charming?" His harsh voice silenced the crickets.

"I am not living with Boris anymore."

Lars cocked his head, surprised.

I winced inwardly. I had not meant to tell him that. I hurried on. "But that is not why I am inviting you. You must leave."

"As must you." He squeezed my hand. "Bauer can cause us both trouble. If no one has put the pieces together, you can probably get out as Adelheid Zinsli, but you must go tonight."

I had known that the Gestapo was dangerous each time I came to

Germany. Adelheid Zinsli and Hannah Vogel would have to disappear, but I could stay. Peter and Theresa were still dead. Someone had still murdered them. No one would ever know for what they died if I gave up. I could not run away now. "I must stay a bit yet, Lars, but you must go."

He released my hand. "Why?"

"You are under investigation by the SS, did you know?"

He stood still in the darkness for several seconds before speaking. "I did not, but it does not surprise me. Unpatriotic motives?"

"Yes."

He ran his palms down his face. "Because I've been trying to transfer out?"

"I think so. I did not actually read the file."

"How did you find out about it?"

"The usual way, breaking into SS headquarters and snatching it."

He sucked his breath in. "Really?"

"No," I said. We both laughed. "But you know I will give you no other details, so let us assume that is the truth."

"How many variations of the truth can you believe at once, Spatz?" He sounded as if he expected me to have an answer.

"We should go." I shifted. "We cannot sleep in the park."

Where would we stay? Hotels were out. Berlin was bursting at the seams with visitors. Perhaps I could bribe my way into some of the dives with night clerks that I had once used as sources. Perhaps, not. It had been years since I'd had contact with any of them. Now they were likely as not to turn me in to the police.

If I was truly in danger, I could not go to Paul's or Bettina's either. Theresa's? But perhaps her murderer had her apartment staked out.

"If we separate, do you have anywhere to go tonight?" he asked, echoing my thoughts.

"I can find something," I lied.

"Why not return to Switzerland?"

That was not his business. "I have something that needs doing, Lars."

"Your friend from the paper is dead," he said. "Your death won't bring him back."

"Perhaps it has nothing to do with him." But of course it had everything to do with him. Lars reached over and put his arm around my shoulder. I let him. I felt ready to tip over.

At that moment, a voice boomed out of the darkness. "What are you doing here?"

13

I put up my hand to shield my face from the light of an electric torch. My eyes dazzled and I was reminded of how they felt in the stadium after Peter's death.

A policeman stood in front of us, glaring suspiciously. "You kids should be at home."

Caught in the dark like a couple of necking teens. As ridiculous as it was, I blushed.

Lars pushed off the still-warm fender. "Hauptsturmführer Lang." His voice brooked no argument.

The beam traveled down to his uniform. The light switched off.

"I b-beg your pardon," the policeman stuttered.

"As you should," Lars said.

The policeman bobbed his head up and down. I could not help but think that Lars enjoyed the power he wielded.

"I'm doing extra sweeps to keep the parks safe during the Games," the policeman said. "I apologize for disturbing you. I did not know who you were; otherwise, I would never have—"

Lars snapped his hand up into a Hitler salute, and the policeman stopped talking at once. They exchanged Heil Hitlers and he hurried off.

"That is the second time we have been caught by a policeman in a compromising position," I said.

"We are affianced." I heard the smile in Lars's voice. "A little mis-behavior is to be expected."

"Perhaps I should gather the tatters of my reputation and push off."

He opened my door, and I sat in the front seat, watching him walk around to the boot, back rigid as ever.

He stopped and drew his suitcase out of the boot.

I swiveled in the seat to watch him. He pulled out a civilian shirt and jacket and changed out of his SS uniform. He looked less con-spicuous now.

He closed the suitcase back in the boot and got into the front seat. "Where to?"

Too late to call Bella. She was my best hope. I hesitated.

"I know a place with rooms." He put the car into gear.

"Even during the Games? I do not want them turning in my pass-port information."

Lars shook his head. "They won't. And they should have a room free. They rent by the hour."

"Sounds luxurious." I rested my head against the back of the leather seat and closed my eyes.

The hotel's district was exactly as I expected. Even the Nazis had not bothered to clean this street. Half the streetlights were out, and a clutch of prostitutes huddled on a dark corner, shivering in the chilly night air. What diseases and pests might I catch from the sheets?

Lars saw my expression. "It's the best I can think of."

"It is fine," I said. "Tomorrow I will be somewhere else."

"Switzerland?"

I got out of the car. He pulled our two suitcases from the boot.

"I will take mine." I reached for it.

"I will check you in," he said. "I know the proprietor."

"Really?"

"I used to be a policeman, remember?"

I hesitated, wondering if his contacts were better than mine. Even if they were not, a man and woman checking into a seedy hotel late at night wishing anonymity were far less likely to attract attention than a woman alone. I followed him to a peeling black door with a small light burning next to it. The feeble glow barely lit the dingy HOTEL sign. He opened the door and gestured for me to precede him into the lobby.

I stepped over the threshold into a dimly lit room with no chairs. If you wished to meet someone, plainly it should be done in a private room for a fee.

"Herr Lang," said the man behind the counter in an oily voice. I noticed that he used neither Lars's SS rank nor his police one. His one eye sized me up, his other hidden behind an eye patch. Whom did Lars usually bring here? "We have not seen you here for some time."

"Good evening, Herr Grafton. I require lodging for the night," Lars said, rather formally considering the situation.

The man's eye traveled over me, and I had the desire to take a bath. I was grateful again for the high-necked black dress.

"The entire night?" he asked.

Did Lars usually rent rooms here for only a few hours at a time? I lent him a questioning glance. He shook his head, then tilted his head to one side.

I was to leave them alone. I stepped back, assuming he wished to bribe the man without my presence. Or perhaps they had other confidences to share that I should not overhear. I examined spotted wallpaper, trying not to breathe so deeply I might accidentally smell something. I tried not to imagine the expression on Boris's face if he could see me here with another man. He would think all his suspicions about my trips to Berlin confirmed. But now, I supposed, he would not care.

Minutes later, Lars retrieved me from the corner. "This way."

He led me to the third floor, near the back. Moans seeped from behind more than one door. Prostitution ran brisk trade here tonight. Part of the extra revenue promised by the government for the Games, no doubt.

He unlocked the door and held up a hand for me to wait. He disappeared inside, a light went on, and he returned a few seconds later. "It's empty."

"You certainly know your way around," I said.

He blushed. I had never seen him blush before and stared, astonished. "My, my."

"Best to get in the room quickly." He picked up our suitcases.

I stepped inside. The room was better than I had feared. It smelled of stale cigarette smoke, a blessing considering how it could have smelled. What I saw of the dark-colored bedspread looked clean. This must be their best room.

He deposited my suitcase on a spindly-looking wooden chair, the only piece of furniture besides the bed. I stepped onto a threadbare rug spread over the dusty wooden floor.

"Where is your room?" I asked.

"Here. I'm not leaving you in this room alone."

"It is perfectly safe," I said. Immediately, a loud crash sounded against the wall. I jumped.

"I'll sleep on the floor." He stripped the gray bedspread off the bed, folded it twice, and spread it out near the door.

I sat on the bed, trying to decide whether to argue. Rhythmic moans issued from the wall opposite the one with the crash. I dropped my face into my hands. In truth, I did not wish to be left alone here either.

Lars sat next to me. "We could try for someplace else."

"I think this is as good as we can expect."

The situation was completely absurd. The woman next door let out a frenzied wail, and in spite of my best efforts, I laughed. Once I started, I could not stop. Lars joined in, and we collapsed on the bed, giggling like children.

"Long night," I said finally, wiping tears of laughter from my eyes.

He coughed. "I expect he will finish soon."

"I suspect she will find another."

I scooted back to the wall, ran my hand down the peeling wallpaper to verify that it was clean and dry, and rested my back against it. He leaned next to me.

"Mint?" He took a packet from his pocket.

After first checking that it was not the kind embossed with a swastika, I popped one in my mouth.

"I have been thinking about your reporter friend's death," he said.

"Why?"

"Because you are involved. If you are involved, I will be eventually as well."

"Not if I can prevent it," I said quickly.

"And, dearest Spatz, you cannot prevent everything, no matter how hard you try."

I ignored that. "What do you think?"

Something thudded into the wall behind us.

"What are they doing?" I asked. I sucked on the strong mint.

"Probably best not to dwell on it." He smiled mischievously. He looked younger than I had ever seen him. I could not help smiling back.

I looked around the bare room. "If it is like this room, all they have in there is a chair."

"And each other," he pointed out. "Limitless possibilities."

I swallowed. "Back to Peter Weill. Do you think he had a heart attack?"

"Perhaps," he said. "I am no doctor. You aren't, either."

I paused long enough for the woman next door to fall silent. How much would I tell him? Were we truly in this together?

He took off his suit jacket and hung it over the back of the chair. In his braces and shirt, he could have been an ordinary man with ordinary problems.

He sat next to me again and waited.

"Silence as a technique," I said. "Often effective."

"Is it this time?"

"I do not believe it was a heart attack. His sister's death was no suicide either."

"By all accounts, they were close."

I swallowed the hard remains of the mint. "They were. But she did not take her own life. I spoke to her only hours before."

He let out an exasperated sigh. "As usual, at the center of the storm."

"She was not suicidal." I drew my knees up to my chest. "She said that he was investigating something."

He shifted when something slammed against the wall behind his back. "If I promise to investigate, will you leave Germany?"

"No." I rested my chin on my hard knees. I wanted to fall asleep.

"I was a policeman once, you may recall. I have my old connections, plus more I've cultivated with the SS."

"I thought you intended to leave?"

"I've been thinking about that. Without you, it's Bauer's word against mine. I think I can hold off a bit. You, on the other hand, are a danger to both of us."

The man next door started a second round, if the sounds were any indication. "Will they never go to sleep?" I said.

"They did not come here to sleep," he said. "We're the only ones who came here to pay by the hour to sleep."

I grimaced and sat back up.

"The second the Weills' deaths are resolved, will you take that train to Switzerland?" he asked.

"Once I know who killed them, and why—"

"You'll go?"

I hesitated. "Will you come with me?"

He smiled. "Perhaps."

I had not meant it as a proposition. "Forgive me, but—"

"I know." His smile faded. "It still means a great deal to me."

The thumping against the wall stopped.

"I have—" I hesitated. In for a penny, in for a pound, as my English journalist and spy friend Sefton Delmer always said. "—I have a notebook from Peter."

"When did you get it? Before he died?"

"Not exactly."

"I know you didn't take it from him after."

"Let's drop the questions about where I got it," I said, angry. It had been difficult enough to tell him about it.

Lars bowed his head. "May I see it?"

I fished it out of my satchel and handed it to him. "Peter uses a kind of code."

He flipped through it. I had never noticed how strong his hands were. "Do you know it?"

"I used to. But he changed it."

Lars tapped a finger on the last page. "May I try to decipher it?"

I stopped looking at his hands. "Of course."

He ran his index finger under the last line, gaze far away and face unguarded. He must have looked so before he joined the army and the police force and waded through death daily. Innocent and open.

I pushed myself to the edge of the bed and stood abruptly. "I am going to try to sleep before the noise starts again."

He climbed off the bed. I changed into my nightdress under the sheet, folded my dress, and laid it across my ear. Perhaps it might filter out the noise when the woman on the other side of the wall returned with her next customer.

I thought of Anton asleep in his comfortable bed at Boris's house. The sheets, I knew, would be freshly laundered and ironed. He would miss me, but he would also be very happy to be in the home where he had spent most of the last two years with the man he had come to love as a father.

When Boris and I told him that I would be moving into an apartment in the city, he had at first said nothing.

Anton still wore his school uniform; his square schoolbag dangled in his hand. He stood in the kitchen, where he had expected to find a quick snack on coming home from school.

"I am coming with you?" he asked me in his bravest voice. He bit his lip while he waited for the answer.

"Yes." I fought to keep my voice level.

"But you will come back here for weekends with me." Boris's face was grim. A muscle twitched in his jaw.

"I see." Anton's schoolbag clunked to the polished oak floor. He dropped next to it and pulled his knees into his chest. "And the brave has no voice in this council?"

Anton rarely referred to himself as a brave anymore. He had grown out of it over a year ago. For him to use it now showed how upset he was.

I sat on the floor next to him, and Boris sat on his other side. We each put a hand on Anton's shoulder. This was what my decision to keep spying meant. Anton would lose the only father he had ever known.

"It is not your decision," Boris said gently. "Your mother and I—"

"Don't love each other?" Anton cut in.

I looked helplessly at Boris. I still loved him, and I could not lie to Anton about it.

"It is more complicated than that." Boris ran one hand through his thick hair. "I will always love you. And your mother and I will always be dear friends. But we won't be living in the same house."

"Will another woman move in here?" Anton glared at Boris.

Boris shook his head. "Not for a long time, if ever."

Anton's angry eyes met mine. "You will be moving a new man into the new apartment?"

"No," I said. "It will be just you and I."

"The brave cannot understand it," Anton said.

I had not been able to explain it to him.

The door slammed next door. I opened my eyes. My decisions had brought me here. I, too, could have been sleeping in safety on fresh sheets. Instead, I was stranded in the heart of Germany. I did not even dare attend the events I needed to report on, so even if I got out with my life, I had no idea how I could make a living and support myself and Anton. I stared at the mottled ceiling until I fell asleep.

14

I woke to Lars thrashing on the dirty floor like a fish newly heaved into a boat. I stood and circled his body. My bare feet picked up grit. "Lars?"

I feared to touch him. He moaned and stopped moving.

I knelt, knees cushioned by the twisted bedspread. "Lars?" I said more loudly. I shook his shoulder.

His eyelids snapped open, dark eyes wild in the light from the streetlamp.

"It's Hannah." I watched him, ready to jump away if he made a threatening move. "You were having a nightmare."

He sat up immediately, shaking violently.

"It's gone," I said in the calmest voice I could muster.

"It's never gone." He did not stop shaking.

I sat and stroked one hand down his back. Sweat soaked his undershirt.

"I see them," he said. "They always ask why I do it. Why I take part." He drew in a ragged breath. "I never have a good answer. Not one time."

I winced. "Oh, Lars."

He rubbed his palms together. "I feel their blood on my hands, like when they're in the room."

I moved my hand in circles on his damp back, trying not to think about blood on his hands, or the rooms where he bloodied them.

"They're not here, are they?" His voice rose in panic.

"It is only you and I. Just us." I stroked his back. I had no idea what to say. Shadows cast by the curtains flickered against the wall.

He slowly stopped trembling, only to suddenly shake like a dog, as if coming fully awake. "Forgive me for troubling you."

"It is a small thing to sit here with you."

He took my hand. "It matters."

"Does this happen every night?"

"Only if I fail to drink enough."

Guilt flashed through me for making him promise not to drink without understanding the cost.

"At home, I can't have the neighbors hearing." He gestured around the nearly empty room. "No one cares in a place such as this." He flicked a sheepish glance at me. "But where the neighbors know my name . . ."

I shivered.

He wrapped his arm around my shoulder. "Are you cold?"

I was cold, but more from life than from the room's temperature. "Where did you sleep last night?"

"In my car. I prefer not to, as I worry I'll be rousted by the police. Last night I figured I could tell them I had a fight with my wife."

"I am sorry." Three completely inadequate words.

"It is late." He stood and helped me to my feet. "You should get back to bed."

"And you?"

"I'll be awake for a good while, I expect." His voice strained with the effort he put into keeping it even.

I reached out and embraced him. He held me so tightly, it hurt.

Eventually he released me and stepped back.

"Bed for you," he said in an unsteady voice.

I slid quickly between the rough sheets.

He put my suitcase on the floor, pulled the chair to the window, took out Peter's notebook, and stared at it for what must have been hours. I woke periodically to the scrape of a pen nib across paper, before returning to fitful sleep.

The next morning, sun shone through the streaked window. Still early. Lars sat on the floor, chest draped over the chair, seemingly asleep. I held still so as not to wake him.

"I know you're awake." He sat up. "Your breathing changed."

I did not like thinking about him listening to my breathing all night. "Is there a bathroom in the hotel?"

"Down the hall, third door on the right."

I pulled my father's gold pocket watch from my satchel. He had left it to my brother, who gave it to me. I had always hoped to bequeath it to Anton. First, I had to get it and myself out of Germany. It was already eight. I had slept later than usual, but I had hours before Peter's funeral.

Not wanting to walk on the hall floor with unprotected feet, I put on shoes. I got up, gathered together my toiletries and my black velvet dress from the night before. Too formal for breakfast, yet it was the only dress I had suitable for a funeral.

I peeked out the door. The corridor was empty and luckily I encountered no one. I had no desire to meet the woman from next door or her last customer. Perhaps everyone else had done their business and gone home.

After I locked the bathroom door, I looked at the filthy tub and could not bring myself to touch it. The sink was little better. My stomach already felt queasy, and I had not yet eaten. I cupped my hands and caught water to wash my face, keeping centimeters of space between my hands and the porcelain. I glanced at the towel. Who knew what complicated history it had. I dried my hands on my nightdress.

When I returned to the room, Lars was shaved and dressed in a civilian suit. He beamed like a man who'd had a full night's sleep. I resented it, like a woman who had not. Yet he'd had less sleep than I.

"Good morning, again. You look quite charming." He grinned inanely. I stared at him, perplexed. He was in a better humor than I had ever seen him. He positively radiated good cheer. In contrast, I felt exhausted and irritable. I resisted the urge to slap him.

"Where did you shave?" I thought I was in the only bathroom.

"There is a bathroom on each floor."

"Is there?" I asked. He was obviously familiar with protocol here.

"Stop smirking," he said.

"I have no idea to what you are referring."

"I see that."

When we walked past the proprietor, he winked at Lars. I supposed that was the reaction to expect when one left such a hotel in the morning with a man, wearing the same dress one had worn the night before, but my face flushed with anger when Lars winked back. I shot him a poisonous look.

He shrugged with mock innocence. "There is a café around the corner. Passable food."

We strolled through early-morning sunshine. Olympic and Nazi flags hung listlessly above windless streets. I purchased several different newspapers from a recently spruced-up newsstand.

Headlines shouted about a gold medal for the American athlete Jesse Owens for the hundred-meter sprint. Today he was competing in the long jump and tomorrow the two-hundred-meter sprint. The reporters' enthusiasm bubbled through the articles. I smiled to think that perhaps the hero of the Aryan Olympics might turn out to be an American and a Negro. The propaganda ministry must have been up all night trying to figure out how to counter it.

We sat outside at a round table under a faded yellow umbrella. I ordered tea and rolls with marmalade.

"Will that be enough?" Lars asked.

"Yes," I said, "Mother."

"I am always in trouble when you call me Mother."

I ignored him and snapped open the first paper. I inhaled the scent of fresh ink, but before I began reading, Lars spoke.

"In case you're curious," he said, "I figured out Weill's code."

The paper slipped from my fingers. Lars caught it before it hit the floor. I stared at his smug smile.

"The word breaks are random, but the rest—well, it's simple when you think about it."

How had he done it? Did he have cipher training? If so, why had he never told me? "What does it say?"

"I copied out the last few pages."

I held out my hand. "Thank you."

He shook his head. "No."

"Why—?" The waiter came with my tea and Lars's coffee.

After he left, I asked again. "Why not?"

"I would like to define the conditions of our working relationship first."

"Conditions? Working relationship?" I said, bristling.

"So far, it's been rather one way, wouldn't you say?"

"I would not say." I took a sip of my tea. It tasted stronger than I liked. I swallowed it anyway.

"Which brings me to my first point: If I give you this, then you must keep me apprised of everything you uncover. And I mean everything." He stirred his coffee, completely at ease. I had never seen him so relaxed and cheerful. I was not certain I liked it.

"But—"

"I know how you hold things in, Spatz. I've watched you do it for years." He set his spoon on the edge of his saucer with a clink. "I won't work with you on this unless you are completely honest with me."

"I have no desire to work with you on this. I thought I made that clear."

"And I figured out the notebook. I thought I made that clear as well."

"B-b-but," I sputtered.

The waiter returned with rolls with marmalade for me, herring and eggs for Lars.

"I am not saying I accede to your first point, but please list your second."

He suppressed a smile and held up his thumb and forefinger. "That once this is resolved, one way or the other, you leave—or by August sixteenth. Whichever comes first."

Today was August 4. It might not be enough time. "I do not make compromises."

"Pity." He cut the egg yolk. Yellow oozed across his plate. I turned my eyes back to my own meal. "The notebook was fascinating reading."

I needed that information. And he knew it.

He ate, looking entirely too self-satisfied.

"If I make a deal," I said, "how do you know I will honor it?"

"Because you always do," he said. "It's one of your weaknesses."

"What are my other weaknesses?" I asked, between clenched teeth.

"Private," he said. "But endearing."

I resisted the urge to fling tea in his lap. "How many conditions do you have?"

He held up his thumb and two fingers. "The final one is that we work this together. Partners."

"It is most likely not political. Why do you want to bother with it?"

He put down his fork in exactly the three o'clock position on his plate and started counting on his fingers again. I should think he could count without them, but apparently not. "First: I want to keep you alive. Your life is more precious to me than it clearly is to you. Second: Project Zephyr sounds political. Third: I would like to be a policeman again, if only for a few weeks."

His counting fingers returned to his fork, and he went back to his eggs. I felt guilty for being so uncharitable. I nursed my tea while he finished his breakfast in silence, points made.

I hated the idea of working with Lars any more than I must. We already shared enough dangerous secrets without adding more. It was not a matter of trust. I did trust him with this, but sorting out Peter's secret was my responsibility, and I did not want Lars to risk his life, too. Still, he had information I needed—information I did not have the time, resources, or opportunity to find. What we might uncover was too important to let my pride or protectiveness stand in the way.

I knew it. He knew I knew it. What was the point in delaying? I sipped the last dregs of tea, delaying.

Out of rationalizations to sort through, I put down my empty cup. "I agree."

He set down his knife and fork, three o'clock again. "Share everything? Leave by August sixteenth? Work as partners?"

"All three."

"Splendid!" He held out his hand and, grudgingly, I shook it.

"The pages?" I turned my outstretched hand palm up.

He pulled two neatly folded pages from the inside pocket of his suit jacket.

I brushed stray crumbs off the tablecloth before unfolding the crisp paper and spreading it in front of me. Lars's cramped but precise writing filled both pages, front and back. He had indeed accomplished much while I slept.

I flipped to the last page. The back listed appointments, including mine. Lars tapped it with his finger. "Stadium? Four o'clock? PW? That's you."

I read, hoping he would lose interest.

"And yet I believe you told me it was a chance meeting." He tapped the page again.

"It was chance that I met him before four."

"Did he contact you before you came to Berlin, or after?"

I folded my arms across my chest.

"Partners, remember?"

I groaned inwardly. "Before."

"How?"

"Through friends. I cannot tell you their names, partner."

He ignored the heavy sarcasm in my voice. "So you came here to meet him?"

"And to report on the Games. Also to take out your film, as always."

"What did he tell you?"

I took a deep breath, trying not to think of Peter dead on the floor. "Only that he had news and a package that I was to bring out of

Germany. And, before you ask, I still do not know what the news was, nor have I found the package."

He studied me before nodding.

"May I return to the pages for which I have paid so dearly?" I asked.

He gestured toward them. "Please do."

I scanned the back page again. Peter had missed several meetings since his death, but what had he expected to do today? He was to meet a TR at 4 P.M. at the corner of Hermann-Göring-Strasse and Unter den Linden. I hated to ask. "What street have they renamed after Hermann Göring?"

"Probably plenty," Lars said. "What's the cross street?"

"Unter den Linden."

"That used to be Friedrich-Ebert-Strasse. Before 1925, it was called Budapester Strasse."

Every regime renamed the streets, not only the Nazis, but it bothered me more that they had. "By the Brandenburg Gate?"

He nodded, and I returned to the pages. *Almost fatal to GS.*

Below that was a list of initials and the words *Berlin → Saratova.*

"What are the Nazis doing in Russia?" I asked.

"Training Luftwaffe pilots," he said.

"Is that Project Zephyr?" I thought of Wilhelm's supposition that it was a Luftwaffe project, and also that Hahn was associated with it.

"Perhaps. But, as far as I know, that's not in Saratova. It's in Lipetsk." He took a sip of coffee. "We've sent documents to Britain about Luftwaffe training ourselves."

"Have we?" It rankled that I did not know what we had passed along.

He sat his cup back on the table so suddenly, liquid slopped over the side. "Don't you read them?"

"No," I said. "I have to hand off the film undeveloped."

"So you have no idea what we've been passing out all this time?" He blotted his fingers on his napkin.

"I deemed it safer."

"It is safer." He folded his stained napkin and placed it next to his plate. "But I never imagined self-preservation would overcome your natural curiosity."

Irritated, I started to read the pages again. "Perhaps my survival instinct is stronger than my curiosity."

"I've seen no evidence of that." Out of the corner of my eye, I watched him smile. He certainly was chipper this morning.

"And I also do not have access to a secure darkroom," I admitted. Lars chuckled.

I tried to ignore him and reread the appointment page. I would keep Peter's appointment this afternoon. After all, I was Peter Weill, too. But what was the meeting about? Almost fatal? Perhaps a poison? I wished I trusted Andreas more. He might know.

"What are you planning?" Lars asked.

"Why would you ask?"

"Experience," he said. "Remember the first condition?"

"I can see this will be a wonderful partnership."

"And?"

I hesitated. But I had given him my word. "I intend to keep Peter's four o'clock appointment."

"I will go, too." He spoke in the firm tone of someone who expected obedience.

"No, you will not." That would not do. My tone was equally firm.

"Partners, remember?"

"That does not mean that you follow me everywhere like a puppy." I crossed my arms again.

"Perhaps guard dog would be a more appealing metaphor," he said. "If that's the direction we must go."

"Look, Lars. If this source is as skittish as I suspect, he will bolt if two people show up." I paused, deciding whether or not to spare his feelings. I decided not to. "Especially if one is you. You exude policeman from your pores."

"Not all the time," he said indignantly.

"Every moment." I thought of his military posture, his unconscious air of authority, and the way he never stopped noticing things.

"Four o'clock is late." He pushed his plate back. "What else do you plan to do?"

I pulled out my gold pocket watch. "In about an hour, I will attend Peter Weill's funeral as Hannah Vogel." I took a deep breath. "Alone."

"Why not shoot yourself and have done with it?"

"I beg your pardon?"

"Is it perhaps not the wisest choice to attend a funeral crawling with reporters who routinely speak with the police? And as Hannah Vogel, a reporter who disappeared in 1931 because she was wanted by the police for murder and the top ranks of the Nazi party for kidnapping? The same Hannah Vogel who resurfaced in 1934 long enough to be linked to Ernst Röhm before he was killed in the purge?"

My mouth dropped open. He had a point, but I would attend the funeral regardless. It was for Peter, and I had promised Panzer. My sense of loyalty was stronger than my survival instinct.

"Well?" he asked.

"I do not imagine that most of the attendees are working as reporters anymore," I started. It sounded weak. "And I hardly think that I am newsworthy."

Lars cocked his head skeptically.

"Even if I were," I continued, thinking fast, "by the time they would tell anyone, Hannah would have gone back under cover. More important, most of the attendees are probably anti-Nazi, too."

"That is your entire defense of this preposterous idea?"

"That and the fact that I am going, no matter what you do or say."

We glared at each other. I dropped my gaze first.

"Lars," I said. "I will keep out of sight, and far from the church, but it is Peter's funeral. I must go."

"I doubt he would want you to risk your life to attend it. For the record, if the situation ever arises, I would not want you to risk your life to come to mine." He covered my hand with his, dark eyes concerned. "I understand why you want to go, Spatz. But please, don't."

"Unless you plan on handcuffing me somewhere, that decision is made."

He encircled one wrist with his thumb and forefinger, as if measuring me for handcuffs. My wrist tingled.

I took my hand back. "Partners must trust each other's judgment, correct?"

He looked unconvinced. "Then let me go with you."

"The only thing worse than Hannah Vogel being caught at that funeral would be Hannah Vogel caught with Lars Lang." I rubbed my wrist under the table.

"Promise me that Hannah Vogel disappears after the funeral until you are safely in Switzerland?"

"Probably."

"Probably?" he asked.

"Unless I need to use that identity."

"You are not very gifted at compromise," he said.

I shrugged.

"It is still a terrible idea," he said.

"What are your plans?" I hoped that they were equally foolhardy.

"First, I have to convince my superior that I am too ill to attend work for the next few days. Then, I will procure innocuous number plates for the car and follow up on the Berlin–Saratova connection. I think Project Zephyr is connected to that." He raised his finger to signal the waiter, who bustled over with the check.

I twisted my hands together in my lap. This evening I was to meet Agnes at the Monte Carlo. If I must avoid my friends as much as possible, I had no one whom I could invite. I could ask her to provide me a paid escort, or I could ask Lars.

"Is everything in order? You look . . ." His voice trailed off.

"I—well—tonight—there is this—at the casino—" I felt like a schoolgirl but stuttered through.

He leaned forward in concern. "Spatz?"

I felt myself blushing. This marked the first occasion where I had ever asked him to go somewhere with me, but it should not be so difficult. "At nine o'clock tonight. At the Monte Carlo. I have an appointment."

"And?" He waited, a small smile playing across his face. He did not know what was so awkward, but he clearly enjoyed seeing me flustered.

My anger at that drove me through the next sentence. "I am meeting a friend. She suggested I bring a gentleman with me as apparently I should not arrive unaccompanied."

"Are you extending me an invitation?" He leaned back in his seat, unsuccessfully smothering a grin. He did not look like he tried particularly hard to do so either.

"Yes," I snapped. "I would think it would be obvious to someone with your abilities as a detective."

"Even experienced detectives can be caught off guard when something completely unexpected occurs," Lars said. "But I would love to come."

"You will need a tuxedo."

"I shall procure one." He put down a bill for the waiter. "Is that what the green dress is for?"

"Could you meet me at Kempinski's Haus Vaterland at eight? The Türkische Café. We can have dinner, and I can change there."

"It's a date," he said.

I thought of correcting him, but it did have all the characteristics of a date. I felt uneasy thinking of it in those terms. And I was not certain that I looked forward to spending the evening with the new jaunty Lars Lang.

15

On the subway to Hausvogteiplatz, I began to dread the funeral. Peter would have protested against a burial by the Catholic Church, as Panzer well knew. Should I have argued with him about not respecting his father's wishes? But Peter was dead, and Panzer was not.

I had procured a hat with a thick veil that rendered my face unrecognizable, but I did not trust myself to go near the church. If I watched from afar, I would not be able to comfort Panzer, but I might be able to get through the funeral alive and unnoticed.

I stepped into a doorway on the far side of the square, admiring Saint Hedwig's Cathedral. Atop the circular church sat a lovely dome, patterned after the Pantheon in Rome, albeit much smaller. My brother, Ernst, always called it "the Catholic breast."

Safe in my perch, I watched a crowd gather in front of the grand arches. Even from here, Panzer looked drunk. Two attractive women who looked to be in their early twenties propped him up. A redhead stood with her arm encircling his waist, and a blonde draped over his other shoulder.

A sharp-faced older woman glowered at Panzer. Her black dress did not hide her angular figure. She had scraped her hair back in such a tight bun that my scalp ached at the sight. Was she Frau Professor

Müller, Panzer's long-time girlfriend? Peter had thought her a good match for Panzer, but it did not appear to be going well.

Once a noted chemist, if I remembered correctly, she had lost her teaching position because she argued that science was international and should not be based on racial ideology. There was no more pure science now, only German science. Perhaps Peter had used her as a source as well. I wondered what Andreas had made of her arguments. Since both were in the chemistry department, he must be familiar with her and the issues around her dismissal.

I recognized Ulli Herzog, a former colleague from the *Munich Post*. A staunch anti-Nazi, he, too, had lost his job when they came to power. He cut a particularly dashing figure in black, as he probably well knew. He seemed to be watching Panzer's attractive companions. Probably choosing the weakest to cull from the herd. He ran his fingers through his thick blond hair and turned to scan the crowd. Even though I was across the square, I stepped farther back into my doorway. My black dress and veil would make it hard for him to identify me unless he came over, something he might do.

I felt cheered that Ulli was still alive and had come to Berlin for the funeral. Ulli had helped me procure the address of Ernst Röhm's mother after the Night of the Long Knives. At the time, I had hoped she might have Anton. I fingered the ribs that I had broken just before I met Ulli that summer. Healed, but the memory remained.

Panzer stepped forward to shake a hand, forcing the women to relinquish their holds on him. Ulli darted to take his place. He had a brief conversation with the redhead and handed her something that I suspected was his card. I stifled a grin. He was a man who got things done and knew how to use those trademark eyes to full advantage.

Ulli had violet-colored eyes. One of the names on the list I had found in Peter's apartment was Violet. Another was Bird-of-Paradise. My last name, Vogel, meant "bird." Was that intended to be me? Was Peter part of a larger group? Had he planned on recruiting me, hence the question mark next to the word *Paradise*? I ran over the list in my head. Long ago, I had teased Peter that his eyes were the same color as chicory flowers, so he might be Chicory. An interesting theory, but I had no proof of it. Perhaps the list simply referred to paint colors or items he needed to get at the nursery.

My and Peter's newspaper colleagues clustered at the base of the church's front stairs, all of them missing the Olympics and potentially lucrative sportswriting assignments to pay their respects to Peter. I glanced from one to another, wondering if any of them were on Peter's flower list. I had once spent every day with them, and I had not realized how much I missed them. If they knew of Peter's anti-Nazi activities, and I suspected most must, then they knew that attending the funeral presented risks to them, yet they had come. I felt cowardly hiding across the square, but was not foolish enough to join them.

Paul and Miriam stood apart from the others, next to Bella Fromm. Miriam looked too hot in her thick black dress. Her head jerked when Maria, Paul's former lover, joined the crowd. Miriam need not have worried. Under the Nuremberg Laws, any resumption of Maria's relationship with Paul would be punished by imprisonment or hard labor, and I doubted Maria would expose herself to such a risk.

Maria worked her way through the crowd toward Paul and Miriam. The fashionable cut of her black dress showed how well she fared under the new regime. I tried to stifle such a petty thought and be more impressed that she had come at all. Of course, she had been writing under Peter Weill's name since my dismissal.

A resigned set to her shoulders, Bella turned toward Maria. Maria had nearly made it to them when the church bell tolled. An image flashed through my mind of a living Peter standing in the corridor with the Olympic bell tolling. The procession carrying Peter's coffin crossed the stone tiles. No more time for conversation. The men stood with hats in hand. I straightened my veil and waited.

A priest dressed in full black regalia stepped out of the arch behind the crowd. He intoned a psalm in Latin. Peter would have hopped out of the coffin if he could have. I almost saw the reproachful look on his face, that it could end so. Bella gave the tiniest shake of her head. She, too, must know how Peter felt about religion.

I wished I could have joined them and said a proper farewell to Peter. It hurt to watch from afar. Too much of my life happened from afar these days. I sighed. Nothing to be done about it. If Peter were alive, he would chastise me for self-pity. And rightfully so.

I walked away. I had seen enough. I took the subway to Unter den Linden and strolled down the street. I paused in front of the pair of massive Grecian-style statues installed for the Games. I stood next to one that depicted two muscular nude men, one running to hand the other a laurel wreath. Their Aryan features were well defined, their size an indication of how the Aryans and their athletes towered above the rest of the world.

I treated myself to an early lunch at the "Grand Hotel" Adlon, near Panzer's apartment. I had visited the hotel often in the 1920s, but my last visit in 1934 had ended with me wounded in their wine cellar. Now, flags of coats of arms and Olympic rings decorated the building's façade. I noted the absence of swastika flags. Hotel Adlon was sometimes referred to as Little Switzerland, because more foreigners patronized it than Nazis. I would feel more relaxed there, even though the presence of all those foreigners ensured an equal number of Gestapo agents.

I ordered tea and fruit. I had a wait ahead, but they did not mind if you sat a long time at the Hotel Adlon. They catered to those with an excess of money and time. While I waited, I puzzled over Lars's translations. Perhaps he would find a link to Saratova today or my meeting would pan out. Otherwise, I did not know how to proceed. Maybe if we met with dead ends, I would hop a train back to Switzerland after all and escape with my life if not my job.

When enough time had elapsed for the funeral to be complete and Panzer to be home for the wake, I hurried to the immaculate telephone booths in the lobby. The interior smelled of beeswax furniture polish, and the telephones gleamed. I requested Panzer's number, wondering if he had returned home from the funeral yet.

An unfamiliar female voice answered. "Hello?"

"May I please speak to Panzer?"

"Why?" asked the voice suspiciously. I suspected it came from Frau Professor Müller.

"To offer my condolences."

She paused, probably unwilling to give Panzer the phone with an unidentified female caller on the line. "Who are you?"

"Tell him it is his Sisterlein. He will know."

"That's all? Sisterlein?" Her voice rose in disbelief. "Panzer is an only child."

An SS officer's black uniform walked down the hall and I turned my back to him, hoping he was not someone who might recognize me.

On the telephone line, a deep voice asked a question, and a few moments later Panzer's baritone sounded in my ear. "Sisterlein?"

"Hello," I said. "I wish I could have come into the church with you."

"Trouble?" he slurred.

"Busy," I lied. He would know it was trouble. The SS uniform kept walking.

"You were always too busy, while I was always too idle."

"You are not that idle," I protested. "Your father—"

"I was never the son he wanted." I heard tears in Panzer's voice.

"You were the son he had. He always loved you."

"You were the son he wanted." Panzer sounded angry now.

I hated to argue. "I was not—"

"You've been gone a long time, Sisterlein."

"No amount of time would change how your father felt toward you." Peter had never been demonstrative, but he had loved his son deeply.

"Actions could." I heard Panzer swallow something, probably whisky. "Actions did."

"Nothing you could have done—"

"I know you are trying to comfort me," he interrupted. "It is kind of you. But don't speak of things you don't understand. You took my father from me years ago."

And he broke the connection. I stood in the small wooden booth and stared at the telephone receiver. I wanted to call back, to explain, but Panzer was correct about one thing: I knew nothing.

Instead I walked toward his apartment. I stopped a few blocks away. Bella's car would come this way after the wake, I hoped.

I did not have many minutes to wait before I spied a familiar black Mercedes.

I flagged it down, and her driver helped me into the backseat.

Bella did not look surprised. She nodded once to the driver, who switched on the radio. Olympics statistics crackled into the car.

"Where to?" she asked.

"Just around."

She raised her voice. "Drive around for a bit."

The chauffeur gave a single nod and turned toward Unter den Linden.

"A lovely Catholic ceremony," Bella said. "You were wise to miss it."

"Exactly the kind Peter would have hated," I answered. "I wish I could have seen it."

"I counted at least two Gestapo informers, and it's always the one you don't see that causes the problem."

"Things have become awkward for me," I said. We drove past the university where Panzer taught. His father had been so proud of his appointment there. Had they really drifted so far apart?

"Perhaps you should stop reporting as a Swiss meters away from colleagues who know you are not."

"I have stopped," I said. "Although I hate to let the identity go. Not to mention the job."

I needed the money. Without it, I did not know how I would support Anton.

"Fine," she snapped. "I'm attending the fencing through to the end. If you call in the evenings, I can give you stories."

"Bella." I was quite overcome. "How can I—?"

"Thank you would be enough." She patted her black hair into place with one elegant gesture. "I do not want you to be fired for dereliction of duty. And I like to keep my hand in reporting, even under someone else's byline."

"Thank you," I said.

She handed me a sheaf of paper. "Here are the results for the women's individual foils this morning. I wrote it down during the chanting."

I smiled. Trust Bella to accomplish something useful while everyone else complied with ritual. I skimmed it.

"Call late tonight," she said. "And I will tell you who advances to the finals. The matches start at eight. None of your Swiss athletes made it to the semifinals. But Helene Mayer did."

"Did she?" Helene Mayer was a world-class fencer. She won the gold medal for Germany in the 1928 Olympics in Amsterdam and the world championship in 1929 and 1931. With her wheat blond hair and green eyes, she had the picture perfect Aryan appearance, but she was half Jewish. In fact, she was the only athlete with any known Jewish ancestry competing in the Olympics for Germany, the token selected by the German government to placate the International Olympic Committee.

"She lives in California now, of course, but I still would have thought she would know better than to compete for the Nazis." Bella's lips pursed in annoyance.

"Perhaps she intends to win and show them a thing or two," I said.

We drove past an advertising column sporting a giant Olympic poster. The bronze man depicted sported laurel leaves in his hair and a resolute look on his lantern-jawed Aryan face. In front of him, the dark gray horses of the Brandenburg Gate pulled a chariot with a German eagle, presumably to victory.

"Jesse Owens won a gold medal yesterday, and he is clearly no Aryan. But has it caused anyone to change their ideology? His victory changed nothing."

"Perhaps indirectly."

She clucked her tongue. "It's not like you to be so optimistic on that subject."

I scanned her notes again. "Wish I could have seen the matches."

"If you think it was too dangerous to do so, I imagine you were more than correct. Your tolerance for acceptable risk is foolishly high."

I folded her notes and stuck them into my satchel. "Panzer mentioned that he and his father were estranged. Do you know about that?"

She took out her compact and examined her lips critically. "My lips look positively naked without lipstick."

"Bella?" Outside our windows, more flag-bedecked shops slid by.

"Peter and I never discussed personal relationships." She rummaged in her purse and pulled out a silver tube of lipstick.

"What did you discuss?" I itched to snatch the tube out of her hands and force her to concentrate on what I said, but I folded my hands in my lap instead.

"Politics. How to get people out and stay alive." Her brown eyes were guarded.

"Was Peter part of a resistance group?" I asked. The driver turned off Unter den Linden onto a shadier side street.

She settled back in the seat. "Why would you think so?"

"Something with you, perhaps Ulli?"

"If we were, do you imagine I would blurt that out here?"

"But perhaps Peter intended to recruit me?"

She applied her lipstick and blotted it on a tissue before answering. "Peter's decisions were his own."

Her eyes were brown, like the brown smudges on the yellow petals of stepmother flowers, also known as pansies. "Pansy?" I asked.

Her face remained impassive. No reaction.

"Anything else?" she asked.

I doubted I would learn more from her on that topic, but I found her lack of response to such an odd query telling. She had not asked why I called her Pansy. Perhaps she already knew. If she was Pansy, Ulli was Violet, Peter had been Chicory, and I was Bird-of-Paradise. Who were Lily, Rose, Tulip, and Daisy? And who had been Thistle?

The chauffeur stopped to let a woman push a pram across the street.

"Have you heard of the two-cent Hawaiian missionary stamp?" I asked.

She groaned. "You leave no stone unturned, do you?"

On our left stood a horse and wagon, on our right a sidewalk full of Japanese visitors, complete with kimonos, probably in town for the Games.

"Did Peter have the stamp?" I asked.

She tilted her head to one side, like a bird. "I believe that he did, but I never saw it. He asked me to find him a buyer a few weeks ago. Discreetly."

"Did he sell it?" My neck jerked when the car lurched forward.

"I don't know, but if he managed it as privately as he hoped, I wouldn't, would I?" She snapped her compact closed and stowed everything away in her purse.

"What did he plan to do with the money?" How would a retired newspaperman conceal, much less spend, that much money?

"We did not discuss personal matters, but I sensed he had an urgent use for it."

"What do you think he might have used it for?"

"I have not the palest inkling, Hannah, no matter how many times you rephrase the question." Bella adjusted her gloves.

She would have been wonderful on a witness stand. I tried a different tack. "Do you know where he kept the stamp?"

"Did Panzer ask you to find that out?" An undercurrent of anger ran through her words.

I lost my train of thought, startled. "Panzer and I never discussed the stamp. Did he know his father had it?"

She shrugged her slim shoulders. "I have no idea."

"It is his now, I imagine. If it can be found."

"Was there a will leaving it to him?" Her words were icy.

"Do you think Peter might have disinherited him?" That was not the Peter I remembered, but I thought back to Panzer's words. "Did they have a falling out?"

"We did not discuss personal issues, as I believe I mentioned." She sat straighter. "But where such a large sum of money is concerned, I'd wish to see legal documentation before making assumptions."

A pat answer. But Bella must know more.

The radio switched from Olympic statistics to a Hitler speech. The driver quickly changed the station. "Where could Peter's will be found?"

"I imagine his lawyers have contacted Panzer about it." She glanced out the window, overly interested in a young man walking a poodle. He doffed his hat to a young woman walking a dachshund. She inclined her head toward him, but we pulled away before I saw his reaction.

"I met a Hauptmann Bosch at a party last night," I said, returning my gaze to the inside of the car. "He was quite interested in the stamp."

Her face fell into an expressionless mask.

"Do you know him?" I asked.

"Did you tell Bosch that Peter had the stamp? Or that Panzer might have it?"

"No." I remembered Bosch's unnatural excitement when he talked about the stamp. "But I saw in Peter's SS file that Bosch was interested in the stamp, and that he knew Peter had it."

"How did you come across Peter's SS file?"

"We all have sources, Bella."

"We do not all have sources who can deliver SS files." Her eyes met mine, but I only smiled back.

More Olympic news poured from the radio, the announcer's voice rich with exuberance.

"One more thing." She handed me a stiff calling card.

"Who is this from?"

"I think it is a lawyer." She eyed me for a second. "He passed them out at the funeral to Panzer and me. He also asked if we knew of your location. Both Panzer and I took an extra card to give to you, should you turn up."

I turned it over in my hand. "Thank you."

"Of course," Bella said.

"Please let me out by a subway station," I said. "I can find my way."

"Where are you staying?" she asked. "I can drop you there."

I saw no reason to lie. "I am staying at a different place every night. Things have become rather complicated for me in Berlin."

"Do you need help?" Her tone was matter of fact. Bella expected a request she had become accustomed to fielding.

"Not yet," I said. "But I might soon."

16

After she dropped me near a subway station, I called in Bella's story. I happily recited details about Helene Mayer's match. The only Jewish athlete representing Germany advancing to the semifinals was big news.

I felt guilty not giving Bella attribution, but doing so was unsafe for us both. I broke the connection and moved to another phone booth before calling the number on the card given to me by Bella. I did not want Adelheid Zinsli and Hannah Vogel to make calls from the same telephone with the same voice, just seconds apart.

"Offices of von Stein and von Eulenhaus," answered a mellifluous voice.

Lawyers. "A Herr von Eulenhaus requested I call him. My name is . . . Hannah Vogel."

"Fräulein Vogel," he said. "Herr Doktor von Eulenhaus was expecting your call. He asked me to tell you to be at our office at three o'clock on Thursday."

The day after tomorrow. "Why?"

"For the reading of Herr Weill's will."

"I am in Herr Weill's will?"

"You must be mentioned in it, of course, to have received a special invitation." He bit off each word, as if I were a slow and annoying child.

I turned his card over in my hand and read the address, thinking. I could not imagine that Peter had left me money, but perhaps he had left his package there or a way to find out more about the secret news he might have been killed for. I had only to stay alive two days to find out. Maybe by then I would have to cut my losses and go home. Bella would help me pretend that I was here reporting on the fencing, so I did not need to stay. I had responsibilities at home, and the time had come to act on them, too. Anton needed a mother more than I needed to follow up dead ends. If I did not discover something soon, I would leave.

On the corner of Unter den Linden and Hermann-Göring-Strasse, I checked my watch. Almost four o'clock. Mere paces away was a bar where Peter and I had often met sources. The crotchety bartender knew us as Peter and Petra Weill. I wondered if he still worked there. I had not visited in more than five years.

I thought about waiting inside, assuming that was where I was to meet the source, but the notebook had specified only the street corner, not the bar. As Theresa had said, times were too dangerous for guesses.

Two large draft horses pulling a wooden garbage truck clopped up. I crinkled my nose at the fetid smell of sour milk and rotted vegetables. The horses stopped in front of me: one bay and one dun. Nobody cared if garbage teams matched, unlike the grand teams that pulled carriages when I was a girl. The horses flicked their docked tails, but even with long ones, they would not stand a chance against so many flies.

The driver jumped from his wooden seat. I stepped out of his path, assuming he needed to collect cans from the bar, although none had been put onto the street. He caressed the smooth nose of each horse. A second later, I heard a crunching sound. He'd given them a treat. He touched his cap to me and hurried into the bar.

His partner held the reins loosely, cigar clamped in the corner of his mouth, cap pushed back on his head so that his grimy white fore-head shone in the sun. He adjusted the ragged wool blanket padding his seat.

The nearest horse whickered. I stepped forward. "May I touch him?"

"Suit yourself. Buckskin don't bite."

I reached out and stroked the dun's soft nose. Anton would have been thrilled. He never passed a horse that he did not stop to pet. Blinking, the horse leaned his warm head against my chest. I shooed flies from his eyes, but they alighted again immediately.

"Don't waste your time." The driver scratched his neck, pushing aside his dark shirt. "Flies don't bother him anymore."

I shooed the flies again. Both horses were surprisingly well cared for. Dust coated their backs, and they'd worked hard today, but it looked as if they were brushed regularly and their hooves cleaned. With working horses, the stables sometimes took poor care of their charges. The driver of this team must be insistent that they received their due.

The door to the bar opened, and the other garbage man strode out. He walked to me and stuck his hands on his hips.

I stepped away from the horse. "Your colleague said that I could pet the horse."

"Weill?" he asked.

I blinked twice, surprised. Peter was meeting with a garbage man? "Petra." I held out my hand for him to shake.

He wiped his palm on his thick pants, then took my hand in his callused one and shook it without giving his name.

"Eddie," he called to his friend. "Get in the back."

Eddie cast me an interested look but climbed off the seat and onto the running board on the sidewalk side.

My source looked nervously up and down the street. He cracked his knuckles, then sighed. "Climb up."

"On the truck?" I ran one hand down my velvet dress. After wearing it to Peter's funeral, I never wanted to wear it again, but that did not mean I wanted to drag it through garbage. Dun horsehairs covered the front already. I brushed at them.

"Yes. And hurry." He cast another glance down the street.

I placed a foot on the square iron step, grabbed the hot metal seat bracket, and swung myself up. I settled on the hard wooden planks. The garbage smelled stronger, yet I smiled. It had been too many months since I had sat behind horses.

He clambered next to me, cracked the whip over the horses' backs, and guided them into traffic. From up here, the automobiles and motorcycles traveled far too quickly.

"I thought you were a man." He glowered at me.

"I am not." I did not try to explain.

"See that. Could you cover up with the blanket?"

"Why?"

"I don't often give ladies in velvet rides." His eyes darted from side to side.

"Do you often give ladies in blankets rides?" I would look even more ridiculous up here wrapped in a blanket like a mummy on a sunny summer afternoon.

He grunted. "S'pose not."

We clomped past more huge stone statues of Aryan athletes and Greek gods. I wondered what Eddie could hear over the rush of automobiles, the clopping of horses, the creak of harness, and the banging of a can against its moorings in the back. Likely more than I wanted him to.

"Bartender says you're all right." He sounded as if he tried to convince himself.

"I like him, too."

A car swerved in front of the horses. They pulled up sharply. The garbage man swore. He yanked the brake lever next to his seat. I braced my feet and grabbed the wooden seat back, realizing how far I was from the street and how little protected me from the automobiles.

"Where are we headed?" I hoped it was close. Automobiles and horses formed an unsafe combination.

"About a block up this street." He flicked the reins to start the horses again. "Velvet Lady."

"So." No time for a circuitous line of questioning. "You have something for me?"

"Depends on what you have for me." He pulled his dark cap lower on his head.

Money, I suspected, but I took nothing for granted. "What do you need?"

"Promise you keep me strictly out of it. I wouldn't have told, but it's wrong. Whatever is going on, it's wrong." His fervent voice rose.

"I will keep you out of it." I lowered my voice, hoping he would do the same. Whatever he knew, I did not want him screaming it across the street.

"But can I trust you?" His voice had quieted, but he seemed to be asking the horses' backs more than me.

"Where is this thing going on?" I did not have a single specific detail.

"Friedrich Wilhelm University." He cleared his throat and hawked over the side. "Chemistry building."

"And?" The wagon shook as we hit a bump. I kept my hand on the back of the seat this time.

"Don't know. Go there tomorrow morning. You'll know all I do. We pick up early. Be there before eight."

He pulled over. We had hardly traveled a block.

"Wait—"

"I think that's enough, Petra." He sized me up again and shook his head. "I don't know why you wore a party dress to the meeting, but you look wrong up here."

"You have told me almost nothing."

"Remember that in case you're asked. Now get down." Another minute and he would likely shove me off.

"How do I contact you?" I asked quickly.

"You don't. Same as before. I contact you."

I had no idea how he contacted Peter. If I let him drive off, I would never see him again. "But what if I need more information quickly?"

"You won't. Tomorrow morning you'll see all I know. And you can decide how to stop it."

"But—"

He clambered down and held out his rough hand. I took it and let him help me onto the sidewalk. "Do you have a package for me?" Unlikely, but I did not think I would see him again.

He released my hand and jerked his head in surprise. "No."

"Thank you." I did not explain about the package.

Eddie waved from the front. Peter's informant leaped back onto the seat next to Eddie without answering. They pulled away before I realized that I had given him no money for the information. And, come to think of it, he had not asked for any.

Lost in thought, I walked slowly up Unter den Linden, toward Hotel Adlon and Friedrich Wilhelm University. What had put the garbage man so on edge? Something in a garbage bin that was only blocks away. I had plenty of time before I had to meet Lars.

I crossed the busy street, narrowly avoiding being struck by a double-decker number nine bus bound for Wilmsersdorf. The advertisement for Bullrich's Indigestion Salt passed mere centimeters in front of my nose. Safe on the cobblestone sidewalk, I walked facing oncoming traffic, which would make it difficult for a car to follow me. The sidewalk was nearly empty, which would make it harder for someone to trail me on foot unobserved.

What could chemistry professors be throwing out? Plans? Papers? No, that could not be. I did not imagine that the garbage man had time to read papers discarded in his bins, and he seemed certain that it would be in the bins again tomorrow morning.

I walked past more stone statues but I barely noticed them. Cars, motorcycles, and bicycles jockeyed for position on the busy street. I felt relieved that I was not in a horse-drawn wagon. It felt much safer on the cobbled sidewalk.

A flash of reflected light caught my eye as a car swerved out of traffic. I froze. A dark automobile leaped onto the curb and headed straight for me.

I jumped to the side. The front fender slammed into my thigh while I was still in the air. I flew onto the hood. My head struck the windscreen, and the world went out of focus.

17

Cars flashed by in a blur. I pushed with my arms. My satchel caught on something then pulled free. I rolled off the side of the fender and landed hard on the stone sidewalk. Beside me, two women in matching navy blue skirts screamed.

I heard the engine moving away.

Shaking, I pulled myself to a sitting position and hefted my satchel back up on my shoulder. A metal object fell onto the cobblestones with a clunk. I picked it up. A zeppelin? I always knew I would be in a zeppelin crash. I turned it over in my hands—it was a hood ornament from an Opel Olympia.

Women in navy knelt on either side, like bookends. Otherwise, the sidewalk was empty.

"Her head!" screeched one.

I reached up and felt wetness. Blood ran down the side of my face. Too much blood. But still, I felt no pain.

Who had driven the automobile? Someone big. In a hat. I grimaced. A useless description. I did not know if it was a man or woman. Some crime reporter I was.

A police whistle shrilled in the distance. I grabbed a nearby signpost and heaved myself upright. I looked up and read the black letters on the street sign: Friedrichstrasse. High on the buildings Olympic and Nazi flags snapped in the wind.

"Don't stand," said one woman. "You don't know how badly you're hurt."

The bright street spun and I retched into the gutter. Concussion? I tried to remember symptoms from my nursing days, but my brain did not help. My lack of recall was not reassuring.

The older woman put a strong arm around me. "Sit down, ducks."

Slowly, the spinning stopped. That had to be a good sign.

I wrenched free of the kindly woman and stumbled toward the street to flag down a taxi. One stopped immediately. I blessed my good fortune, as usually they were not there when you needed them.

I fell into the backseat, satchel banging painfully against my hip. The women in navy skirts stared as if I had taken leave of my senses. A distinct possibility. I waved. One raised her hand uncertainly and waved back.

"Hospital?" the driver asked. He handed me a brown cloth of indeterminate cleanliness. "Don't bleed on my seat."

"Agreed." I held the fabric to my wound.

"Hospital?" He pulled in front of another taxi. It honked.

I dared not go to hospital. There would be paperwork. Police would be called. "I have a doctor friend who is closer," I said. I did.

"Where?"

I stared at him.

"Where?" he repeated. "Your doctor friend?"

I gave him the names of two streets.

"That's in the Jewish quarter, isn't it?" He eyed me suspiciously.

"It's on the edge." As if that mattered.

He headed in what I hoped was the correct direction. I slumped against the seat. The cloth grew damp under my fingers.

I closed my eyes and did a quick inventory of my body. The adrenaline had worn off. My leg hurt where the hood struck me, but nothing felt broken. My hands hurt from my attempt to brace my fall. I avoided thinking about the damage that might have been done to my head. As if to remind me, it throbbed.

I opened my eyes and examined my palms. Blood covered the right

one. I must have landed on it. Lucky I had not broken my arm. I took
the rag off my head to wipe my hand clean.

I tried to think of a single identifying detail about the driver.
Nothing. A fedora, perhaps? The quick flash of reflected sunlight that
had warned me had also obscured my vision.

The driver pulled over at the cross streets I had specified. "Will
you make it on your own, Fräulein?"

"Yes." I hoped it was true.

He opened the door and helped me out. I pressed his fare into his
hands. "There's extra," I said. "Can you say you let me off at the hospital?"

He counted the money carefully before answering. "I can."

I watched his black car with its checkered stripe down the side pull
away. I did not move until it disappeared, supporting myself on a tree
trunk with my uninjured hand. When I took a few deep breaths, it
did not hurt too badly. I knew from bitter experience that meant no
broken ribs.

Once the driver left, I walked through a nearby building, across
the courtyard, and out the back. No red Nazi flags hung here. I must
be in the Jewish quarter. But what were the white flags with the rings?
Olympics, I reminded myself. Olympics.

I turned left and hobbled a few extra doors, grateful that I had not
told the driver to stop still farther from where I needed to go.

Then, for no reason at all, the ground rushed up and hit me. I lay
on the cobblestones, waiting for them to hold still.

"What do we do with her?" asked a child's voice from a hundred
kilometers above my head. A little girl, I thought.

I pulled on my eyelids, but they stubbornly remained closed.

"Leave her," said another voice. "She looks Aryan. That means
trouble for us."

Sometimes, I thought, *being Aryan in Nazi Germany is no help at
all.* This struck me as funny.

"She might bleed to death," said the girl's voice.

"That'll cause trouble," said the other voice, perhaps her father.

"We can't just let her die!"

I was flattered that the little girl felt outrage at the thought of leaving me bleeding there. Would Bettina's daughter, Sophie, be so kind to a Jewish woman lying on the street?

The father sighed. "We won't."

I pried my eyelids open. Sun beat down strong. Two shadows fell across my face. They were cast by a young girl in a sundress and a tall reedy man with forelocks standing next to her.

"Could you please help me up?" I asked.

The girl extended a hand down, but her father batted it away. Sighing as if he knew he would come to regret this, he offered me his hand.

I took his hand with my left, the one that was not slippery with blood, and he heaved me to my feet. This time the cobblestones stayed put on the ground. I wiped dirt off the side of my face. The man held my hand until I finished, then dropped it like a slimy fish. He picked my satchel off the ground and gave it to me.

"Thank you," I said. "Does Frau Doktor Spiegel still have a practice nearby?"

The little girl nodded. Her father glared at her and she dropped her gaze to the street.

Blood continued to run down the side of my face. I swabbed at it with the taxi driver's cloth.

The man took the little girl's hand in his. He tilted his head toward a door a few meters away from where I had fallen, and then dragged the little girl quickly down the street.

I stumbled to the door and rang the bell. A woman in her late fifties came out to meet me. "I am sorry," she said. "My practice is not—Fräulein Vogel?"

"Frau Doktor Spiegel." I would have inclined my head but worried that I might fall over.

"Bella did not say that you were in town." She took my arm and led me inside. In a few steps, we crossed her comfortable sitting room. She propelled me into the bathroom and sat me on a metal-framed chair in front of a graceful sink.

"Bella?" I tried to remember if I knew any Bellas, suddenly irritated.

She tilted my head from side to side and peered intently into my eyes. "Did you lose consciousness?"

"I do not think so." I struggled to remember. Walking on the sidewalk thinking. A flash of light. A huge dark blur. A zeppelin. Standing supported by a woman in navy blue. Vomiting.

She pulled aside the cloth, ran her fingertips gently along my scalp, checked my ears. "What happened?"

"A car hit me."

"Where?"

"Unter den Linden, by the university."

"No." She shook her head. "Where on your body did the car hit?"

I pointed to my thigh. "I rolled off the side of the hood after."

Her fingers slid over my injured leg. I winced.

"Just bruised, I think. Although I imagine it feels most unpleasant." She took my wrists and turned my hands over. "A bit of dirt in the right one."

"How bad is it?"

"You do not appear to have a concussion. Did you throw up?"

"Just a little."

She sat back on her haunches. "Why didn't you go to hospital?"

"Not safe." My teeth chattered. Although the bathroom was warm, I shook.

She pulled a glass bottle from behind the toilet. "Drink." She hid it there because her husband was a drinker. I felt proud of myself for remembering something.

I took a quick swallow. Sweet and smoky. Brandy. It warmed my throat and stomach. I drank another slug.

"Was it an accident?" She pulled a towel off the rack and wrapped it around my shoulders like a hairdresser.

"I did not intend to get hit," I said indignantly. "I was walking on the sidewalk."

"Do you think the driver meant to hit you?" She poured iodine in the wound and I yelped.

"It only stings a little," she said in an irritated voice.

"Maybe it only stings your head a little, but it hurt mine like hell," I shot back, although I had given such advice myself many times.

She laughed. "You have changed very little."

"Nor have you." Frau Doktor Spiegel was one of a handful of female doctors during the Great War. She had managed to complete her training before the universities stopped training women doctors. She had overseen my nurse's training. Brisk and efficient, she had little patience for complaints.

"Wait here." Her knees creaked when she rose. But she was not so old, only about ten years older than I.

She returned with a needle and thread.

"Is it sterile?" I gritted my teeth.

"That is the first sensible question you have asked," she said. "And yes."

I twitched the first time she put the needle in, but held still for the next two stitches. I was not going to listen to another comment about how it did not hurt.

She wiped the incision down one final time and stared at it critically.

"So," she said. "Did the driver mean to hit you?"

"I do not know," I lied. I must have been seen on the garbage truck. By someone who circled around the block and tried to kill me. I wished I knew how to get in touch with the garbage man. I should warn him.

The seam of my dress had split from hem to waist. I stroked my uninjured left palm down it. Still soft.

"You can't go out in that dress," she said. "But I think it can be fixed."

"I do not want it."

"It's quite nice." She caressed the velvet. "Almost new. It can be mended."

"Keep it. Give it to someone."

She held my palm under water.

"I just wore it to a funeral," I told her. "Then I was hit by a car. It is no lucky garment for me."

She scrubbed my palm, and I sucked in a quick breath.

After she bandaged my hand, I stood. Pain radiated from my thigh and my head. I gasped and sat back down.

"Hurts?"

"Yes."

She shook a white pill into my uninjured palm. "Opium. No more alcohol."

"Why did you save this until after you finished your stitching and scrubbing?" I asked.

"I wanted to make certain that you had come back to your senses first. I cannot do that once you are under the influence of opium."

I raised my eyebrows and took the pill with warm water, but I missed the brandy.

Once it took effect, the pill made my leg feel warm. The pain vanished and my head grew light. Even though I had no reason to be so, I felt happy and relaxed.

Frau Doktor Spiegel insisted I take a bath. I washed blood carefully out of my hair. She gave me a clean cotton dress to replace the torn velvet. It hung loosely, but was certainly better than running around naked.

"Presentable?" I asked.

"Sit at the table," she said. "I will heat some soup."

I sat. "Frau Doktor Spiegel, if you wanted to poison someone quickly, how would you do it?"

"Nervous about the soup?" She stirred the pan with a wooden spoon. "You are full of problems."

"You could have poisoned me with the pill, so I imagine the soup is safe."

She laughed. "Such a suspicious nature you have."

I gestured to my injured leg. "Not suspicious enough. But suppose you did want to poison someone with something that would dissolve in whisky. What would you use?"

"Cyanide, I suppose. It's easy to come by and takes effect quickly."

"I think I might have seen someone die of poison," I said.

"You think?" She brought the spoon to her mouth and took a taste. "Too cold."

"I saw an old man drink from a flask and minutes later he was dead. His pulse became rapid, he collapsed, had convulsions, and his face reddened."

"Could be cyanide," she said. "The red face does not sound like a heart attack."

I thought so. "I drank a little, too."

She eyed me sharply. "How did you feel?"

"My eyes hurt in the sun and watered quite a bit. I was nauseated and my mouth filled with saliva."

She tapped the spoon against the side of the pot. "That does not sound like cyanide. Are you certain you were not just crying because you were upset?"

I thought back. It was not easy to remember it through the fog of the opium. "It felt different than that."

She spooned the soup into a bowl, dropping in a dumpling. "I cannot say, then. Eat this."

I took a spoonful. Heavenly. "Have you really closed your practice?"

"Where did you hear that?" She dished out her own bowl. "I still practice, but who knows for how long."

"Why?"

She sat across from me. "The Nazis have already stopped Jewish physicians from practicing in Munich. It is only a matter of time before they stop them here. It is much worse here than the Olympic's façade makes it appear."

I took another spoon of the savory soup. "Have you tried to leave?"

She chuckled. "I have tried little else. It is not easy. I am on a list, waiting, with thousands of other Jews."

I finished the soup. My stomach felt full and calm.

"I have to go," I told her, after looking at my watch. "I have an appointment at eight. He will panic if I do not show. I am already late."

"You should be in bed," she said.

"It is a very important appointment. At Kempinski's Haus Vaterland," I added. I had not been there since I waited for Wilhelm in the Wild West Bar. He had given me Lars's address so I could break in, and now I was meeting Lars for a date there. I giggled.

"More important than taking care of yourself?" She scowled disapprovingly.

"It is urgent," I said, although nothing felt urgent. "Life and death."

"You should be careful tonight. Do you have someone you can rely on to take care of you?" She picked up my bowl and brought it to her sink.

I wanted Boris with his strong arms and citrus cedar smell. He was an excellent caretaker and would know just what to do with a bed rest order. I sighed. All I had was Lars. "Yes. I think."

"I will write down instructions for your caregiver. You must get to bed as soon as you can. And you will need someone who can wake you every few hours to make certain that you are not disoriented. Do you need to come back here for that?" She covered the pot with a thick lid.

"No." I tried to imagine spending the night in that seedy hotel again, feeling as I did. "I have a man who I think will help me."

"Really?" She smiled, pulling a piece of paper out of her desk. "Is he handsome?"

"In a certain light, sometimes," I said. "But he is very reliable in every light so far."

"Isn't that a description every man hopes for?" She wrote quickly.

"There are worse things. Ugly and unreliable. That's quite a stigma."

"I suppose." Her hand moved across the paper. She did not look up as she spoke.

"But I do not quite trust him," I said. "His past is . . . complicated. His present, too."

"That can be said of many."

"How can he live with what he does? It's worse now, of course, but he has done horrible things for many years." I turned my palm over and tugged at the gauze. "He has always been upstanding to me. To his colleagues he seems upstanding, too, I imagine. Yet there he is not."

"Are you certain you wish to tell me all this?" she asked.

"He lies to so many people. How can I be certain that he is honest with me?"

She stopped writing to look at me. "Hannah—"

"I know." I held up a hand. "I have to lie, too. So I want to trust him. I do."

She pinched the bridge of her nose. "I cannot speak to your current situation, Hannah, but I have never known you to trust a man, not fully. Perhaps you expect too much from them. From him."

I thought of Boris, and my unwillingness to change to suit his needs for me. Before that there had been Paul, whom I also had refused to marry. And Walter, who had been killed before our wedding. Had I trusted any of them fully?

But no one had warned me against them, and many had warned me against Lars: Sefton, Wilhelm, and even his own friend Andreas worried that Lars would harm me, and Lars had almost struck me a few days ago.

She cleared her throat. "I will take you to your appointment."

"How charming!" I said. "We have not been out together for years."

"Do not make such advances, you saucy girl," she said. "I am an old married woman."

I laughed.

She finished a rather long note and placed it in a paper bag with pills, gauze, and a bottle of iodine. I insisted on paying her twice what she wanted, even though I could barely concentrate well enough to sustain a good argument.

We found a telephone booth a few blocks outside of the Jewish quarter, where I called a taxi. I did not want to bounce around in a subway car.

We took the taxi straight to the round front of Haus Vaterland. No extra walking tonight. Plus, as I discovered when I checked my pocket watch, I was shamefully late. The giant statues posted along the curve of the roof looked ready to topple on us both, but the neon lights were spectacular. The light haloed around them in a most amazing way. Frau Doktor Spiegel followed my gaze, snorted, and dragged me through the front door.

The huge building teemed with people come to eat at the themed restaurants and attend the theater. What was playing? Perhaps later I could trip over and see. But for now Frau Doktor Spiegel kept a firm grip on my elbow and navigated us straight to the Türkische Café as if she did not even notice the lovely colors and noises.

When we entered the dining room, Lars was already there. The punctual man had even secured a table. I pointed to him, sitting behind the octagonal table on a low stool with a gold and red checked silk cushion. "He's right there."

He stood and started toward us. He looked rather dashing in his tuxedo.

"He is handsomer than you led me to believe. Perhaps it's not the light."

"Politically he used to be quite unattractive. But he's shifted," I said.

"Has he?"

"I hope so. Would you care to meet him? Ensure that he is up to your caretaking standards?"

"No," she said. "I meet no one I don't have to these days. It keeps me out of trouble. Something you would be wise to emulate."

I embraced her. "Thank you, Frau Doktor."

"Rest," she said. "And be more careful."

Then she was gone.

18

I turned back to the dining room. Lars suddenly stood next to me. Was he moving quickly, or was I seeing slowly?

He took my elbow. "Spatz?"

I realized how my shabby cotton dress must contrast with his tuxedo.

"Shall we sit?" he asked.

I took a tentative step. The floor remained wonderfully stable. I could see this through. "Yes."

We passed under the magnificent Moorish arches painted with elaborate geometric patterns. One could stare at them almost indefinitely. I stumbled and grabbed a smooth red pillar to catch my balance. A dark-skinned couple next to me spoke English with a queer accent. Were they from New Zealand? New Zealand was in the summer Games, although it had not attended the winter ones.

Lars made sure I was firmly seated on the stool before crossing to seat himself. Behind his shoulder, water plinked into a four-tiered fountain. He had a bruise on his jaw that had not been there this morning. Perhaps he had been hit by a smaller car than I. I stifled a laugh.

"That is a different dress than you wore when you left the restaurant this morning," he said.

"I never liked the other one." True, but as I watched the other diners, I realized how underdressed I was in this simple cotton shift. Not only in comparison to Lars. Everyone dressed so smartly.

He leaned close. "You are late, and you smell like iodine."

"Touché, Herr Kommissar." I pulled my damp hair back to show him the laceration that ran along my hairline. "It only took three stitches for the doctor to close it. I find that astonishing, considering the amount of blood that poured out. Head wounds produce so much blood."

His face hardened.

I let my hair fall forward again and dropped my bandaged hand to my lap. "Your tuxedo looks quite smart."

"What happened to your head? And also your hand?"

"I fell down," I said, lifting my hand up and staring at the palm as if I could see through the bandage. "Cut them open."

"How did you fall?"

I picked up my wineglass and held it to the light, turning it to and fro. Rays of light reflecting from it dazzled. "Amazing!"

"How much pain medication did the doctor give you?"

"More than enough, I would say. I feel wonderful."

"I see that."

The dining room was huge, the largest dining room I had ever seen. Colors glowed deeply, like jewels. Golds, reds, and blacks twined in intricate geometric patterns on the walls and ceiling.

"Lars," I said, standing. "Let's dance. You are a wonderful dancer! Such a shame to miss an opportunity."

He gently pulled me back down onto my stool. "There is no music."

Astonished, I stared at him. "You do not always need music to dance."

"Perhaps later." He took the paper bag out of my hand. "What is in here?"

The brown paper crackled in the most delightful way.

"Spatz," he said. "What's in the bag?"

"Instructions for you."

"From the doctor?"

"I think so. She wrote them."

He pulled out the paper and began to read.

"Perhaps we should go to Switzerland," I said. "The chocolate there is divine."

He smiled with half his mouth, gaze moving down the paper. "I can only imagine what you would do to me once your drugs wear off."

"Me?" I sipped at a glass of water that had magically appeared on the table, as if conjured there. It tasted like a fresh mountain spring. "I thought I saw someone smoking a hookah pipe. A Turkish man with a drooping mustache. Probably here for the Games. They have fielded a fencing team, at least for men, but wrestling is where they are expected to medal. He might be a wrestler. He had the shoulders. Do you think we can get a hookah pipe, too?"

I craned my neck back the way we had come, but the smoker must have been behind one of the arches.

"I think you have ingested quite enough foreign substances for one evening," Lars said. "Perhaps we should be late to your meeting?"

"No," I said. "She insists on punctuality. Very strict. Like a school-marm."

"Are you sober enough?"

"Judgment is the first thing to go, is it not?" I giggled.

"I suggest we find a place to sleep and try again tomorrow," he said. "Bed rest is what your doctor recommended."

"One hour," I said. "Then I will follow her instructions to the letter."

"You must be quite impaired," he said. "All this talk of you following instructions is completely out of character."

I stood, steadied myself against the table, and picked up the white box. "Is my dress in here?"

"Shall I escort you?"

"Only if I fall down." I turned slowly and glided to the restroom. I felt sturdy on my feet.

The young bathroom attendant squealed when I unwrapped the dress. I sniffed. Lars had it cleaned, which made me laugh.

"Lovely." She slid a tentative finger down the smooth fabric.

"Quite." I felt like a little girl playing dress-up.

Her nimble fingers helped pull the dress over my head. I was grateful that my slip covered my thigh. When I was in the stall, I found that a darkening bruise ran from the top of my hip to my knee. After the pain medication wore off, it promised to be excruciating.

She stood behind me and zipped the dress closed. "You look gorgeous, ma'am."

I stole a glimpse of myself and retreated a step in shock. The woman in the mirror appeared completely foreign. Wide, dark eyes stared at me, surprised. My skin was so pale, it glowed. The dress fit like a second skin. Sumptuous and silk, something Marlene Dietrich might strut around in. I imagined how proud my brother, Ernst, would have been to see me dressed in such finery. Or the look on Boris's face if he could see me now. It would be bound to lead to something quite pleasant. I smiled.

I seated the glove carefully over my bandaged palm and slipped into my rented shoes. Then I transferred my money and toiletry items into the small beaded bag Agnes had also tucked into the box. My costume was complete. The attendant folded my old dress neatly and packed it in the box. Far away, a thrill of panic shot through my stomach at the thought of walking into the dining room wearing the dress, but it was so small, I paid it no heed.

I overtipped the attendant before heading for the dining room. Heads turned as I passed. Conversation stopped. Without any real concern, I wondered if the men gawking recognized the dress from its former occupant, Agnes's prostitute.

Lars leaped to his feet and pulled out my stool. I slid in.

He took his seat across from me, looking dazed.

"Thank you for having the dress cleaned."

He nodded dumbly.

I forged on. "Is the dress that awful?"

He hesitated. "It is not what I would have chosen to go undercover."

"I do not think it would look the same on you."

He laughed.

"Does it look—" I hesitated, searching for the correct word. "—improper?"

"Not at all," he said quickly. "You look stunning. Every man in the room noticed you in that dress. You look quite . . . memorable."

"They will remember the dress, then, not the woman in it."

"That I doubt very much." He stood and offered his arm. "Let us leave before you create more of a stir."

"I created no stir," I said. "It was the dress."

He paid for the wine one-handed. He kept my arm tucked firmly under his elbow, probably worried that I would waltz around the room if left to my own devices.

We dropped everything in his car, then strolled down to the Monte Carlo. Lars kept sneaking peeks at the dress, presumably when he thought I was distracted. But I noticed, and I did not mind.

Cool air chased over my skin like caressing fingertips. I shivered.

"Are you cold?"

"Nicely so."

He shot me a skeptical look. "I think perhaps we should abandon this plan."

"I need to do this to get myself out of Germany," I said, "and we both want that."

"Alive," Lars said. "I'd like you to get out of Germany alive."

"You are fussy," I said, pulling him down the street.

"On matters I believe to be important, I can be quite . . . fussy."

I shook my head and looked ahead.

"There it is!" I pointed to the brightly lit façade of the Monte Carlo.

We stepped past the burly doorman and inside. The main room of the Monte Carlo was larger than the Türkische Café. Ceilings soared away to infinity. Crystal chandeliers glittered and cast rainbows throughout the room. Everyone wore the latest fashion—men in tuxedos, women in long silky dresses like mine. Here, too, I spotted dark-skinned foreigners in the crowd. The Olympics was broadening the pool of gamblers.

I pulled loose from Lars and twirled around once in the main room, staring at the largest chandelier. "It's fabulous!"

I hummed "It's Only a Paper Moon." How did the song start? "Say it's only a paper moon—," I began.

Lars took my elbow, above the end of my glove, and pulled me to the side of the room. "If this must be done, let's get it over with quickly. Where is your friend?"

"The back, I imagine. Probably bent over an account book. She has no small talent for numbers." I stared at rainbows, hypnotized. Anton would have loved it! Colors everywhere. Rainbows without storm clouds.

"Spatz," Lars said. "We should go home."

"We have no home, remember? We are orphans. You cannot send us out into the snow to sell matches."

"No snow. No matches." He steered me toward the door.

I stamped my foot. "No!"

Several heads turned. He stopped.

"One hour," I said. "Sixty minutes. Remember?"

I pulled my arm free of his and proceeded up the stairs to the cashier's cage. Following the money would lead to Agnes. The cashier wore a white jacket, a tie, and a guarded smile. Lars followed closely. He looked as if he had just swallowed a bug.

"Agnes Johansson said you were the one to see." I leaned forward and gripped the cashier's arm through the grate. "She is waiting for me. Weill is my name."

"Weill?" he asked. "I will check my lists."

Lars peeled my hand off the cashier's arm. "This is most unwise," he hissed.

"You sound like a snake."

"You are in no condition to talk to anyone. Much less someone at a casino. Much less in that dress."

The cashier emerged from a clever door to the right of his grate. It was quite invisible until he opened it. "She says I am to take you to her."

Lars nodded.

"Alone." The cashier stood between us and the door to the back. "She was very specific."

I shook off Lars's hand. "Back soon. Play a game. That is what the casino is here for, you know."

He pressed his lips into a thin line again. Meddlesome, as usual.

"Sixty minutes. You promised," I said.

"Did I?"

I stepped through the door before he answered. Darker than in the room with the chandeliers, the hall stretched ahead long and empty. Anything might happen here. No one would know. Too late now.

19

I trailed my hands on the wallpaper, striped in gold like an Olympic medal, while the cashier and I walked down the hall. Nothing covered the wooden floor; wainscoting clad the wall to waist height. It was quiet back here, as if the noisy and bright world of the casino had vanished. I had an urge to return the way I had come to make sure that everything was as I had left it.

The cashier rapped once on a plain wooden door. Agnes herself opened it. "Why, hello, Herr Weill." She shooed away my attendant.

The room was so dark, I could not see the walls. Trolls could be lurking there. My heels knocked against the hard floor when I entered.

"It is a cave in here." I stepped into the puddle of golden light next to a desk stacked high with papers. A tall stool sat in front of the desk so that Agnes could reach it. "Do you grow mushrooms?"

"Peter," she said, "are you high?"

"Doctor's orders." I lifted my dress and slip to show her my bruised leg.

She pulled my dress back down. "Don't do that out front."

I gave her an old-fashioned salute, the kind popular before Hitler came to power.

She studied me with a practiced eye. "I was correct. That dress becomes you."

"The previous occupant must have been very popular," I said. "Men react to it quite favorably."

"Especially if you keep showing off your leg."

"You are the only audience treated to that show. So far."

"Lucky me." Her forehead wrinkled in thought. "I will write down what you need to know. Probably the best policy considering your . . . state. But no names."

"No names," I repeated. "Anonymous. Or pseudonymous, like Peter Weill."

She sat me on a hard wooden chair, climbed onto her stool, and pulled over a heavy ledger. I stroked its burgundy spine, then bent and sniffed the leather.

"Peter," she said sharply. She opened the ledger and ran her tiny index finger down a list of red figures. They danced on the page. I reached out to touch one, to keep it still.

She yanked the ledger away. "Your Peter Weill has sizable debts."

"Peter?"

She wrote a number on a sheet of paper. "I am surprised Jack Ford let him get into that kind of debt. He must have considerable assets, but they're not listed."

The stamp. "But he was never a gambler before."

"That is not what the books show." She tapped a figure with far too many zeros to make any sense. "And the books never lie."

"Do you think Jack would have had him killed for it?" The ease with which I said it surprised me. This morning I would have cried about it, but tonight it seemed casual and far away.

"How was he killed?"

"Poisoned, I think. The police say heart attack."

She tapped a pencil against her teeth. "That's not Jack's style."

"Style? Jack has a killing style? Like a fashion style, but darker?"

"When you kill someone for gambling debts, it is not supposed to look like an accident." As I had told Lars, she sounded like a school-marm. "You'll never get the money back from a dead man, so his only use to you is as an example. Making it look like a heart attack doesn't provide you a useful example."

"Oh." I stared at the lovely leather spine. Perhaps I should write bound books. Something lasting and significant, instead of newspaper columns that probably ended up lining birdcages.

The pencil tapped on. "He is not listed as deceased. Are you certain he is dead?"

With surprising detachment, I remembered Peter's red cheeks next to mine on the floor of the corridor. "Very."

"We will have to get a death certificate for him." She sighed irritably. More work for her. Agnes slipped a rubber band off a small dog-eared notebook, made a note in it, and put the rubber band back. I reached over to twang it, but she put it away.

"So if Jack did not kill him, who did?"

"You assume it was murder. It might actually have been a heart attack. People do still die of natural causes." She closed the ledger with a thump. "But if not . . . if your friend owes Jack . . . he probably owes others."

"What about Theresa Weill?"

She put down her pencil. "I checked on her. No debts."

"Free as . . . as a homing pigeon," I said, and added, "So not free at all."

"You should go home."

I stood and slid a bit with my first step. "I have no home. No home has me."

"They rent rooms here."

"Pesky bureaucratic questions when you check in?"

"Not Jack's style either. Collect your escort, and I will reserve you both a room. I don't think you are safe on the streets in your state."

She opened my beaded purse. It matched the dress, and I told myself to remember to return it. Inside she placed an envelope. "Here is the information you need to pay my fee. Come by the office on Kufürstendamm when it's complete."

"A new identity," I said, plopping back into my chair. "Cunningly fashioned."

She pressed the purse into my hand. I smelled her lovely French perfume.

"Go directly to your escort." Her starlet voice enunciated each word carefully, as though I were deaf. "Take him to the balcony. I will send someone to bring you to your room. Wait there until I do. After that, stay in the room until your drugs wear off."

"But we are not sleeping together." I thought about last night. "Or at least not like you think."

"I have no thoughts on the matter. Except that you need a minder. Can he keep you out of trouble?"

I shrugged, but felt a little sick. "Can anyone?"

"Can he at least keep you out of sight?"

I thought of Lars's irritated expression. "I think that is what he would prefer to do most."

"Let's go find him." She clambered off her stool. Her heels clicked across the floor to the door.

I lurched to my feet and saluted her again. She frowned sourly.

She led me down the hall and back through the hidden door to the main room. She watched from the cashier's area until I reached Lars's side, but she was not the only one who stared. The dress created quite an impression.

Lars sat at a card table with a large pile of chips in front of him. I touched his jacket sleeve. Wool, high quality. Where had he found it on such short notice?

"Hello, card shark," I said. "Are you taking their money?"

"There you are, Spatz." He rose to take my arm. "You know I could be quite good at this."

I tried to count the chips in front of him but lost interest. "Did you win?"

"A bit." He leaned over and whispered in my ear. "I didn't try to win every time. It didn't seem the wisest course. But I could have, if I'd wanted to."

His breath in my ear sent shivers down my spine, and I leaned against him.

Across the room, Agnes pointed one imperious finger toward the open doors to the balcony.

"May we go for a walk?" I asked.

Lars blinked. "A walk?"

Agnes glared and shook her finger. I was to hurry. Very well.

"Now?" I patted his high-quality wool arm, admiring the thread count.

He scooped up his winnings. We crossed to the cashier's cage and exchanged them for an impressive pile of cash. Eyeing me worriedly, Agnes counted out the money herself. When I blew her a kiss, she rolled her eyes. It reminded me of the first day of the Games, when a drunken Lars kissed me on the nose. It was much funnier from this side.

Lars put a restraining hand on my arm. "Spatz, please."

He and Agnes exchanged a sympathetic glance. Clearly, both knew the hardships and perils of dealing with me. I smiled at each in turn. Agnes shook her head.

When Agnes pointed to the door to the balcony, Lars nodded. In cahoots already.

I took his hand and led him onto the balcony. Piano music drifted out. Jazz. I listened for a few beats before closing the door. We were alone. That should suit them.

I walked to the edge of the balcony and wrapped my hands around the iron railing. It was unpleasantly cold even through gloves. The drug must be wearing off. Earlier I would not have cared how cold or warm the metal felt.

"How much did you start with?" I asked Lars.

"Considerably less." He put one hand around my shoulders, as if afraid that I might spring into the street below. "What did you find?"

"Debts aplenty for my old friend, nothing for his sister. But Agnes does not think he was killed for them."

"It did not appear to be that kind of killing."

"That is what she said." I shivered. Now the cold did not feel wonderful, only cold.

He draped his warmed tuxedo jacket over my shoulders like a cape. "Wise woman, your friend Agnes."

"She also said that I am to speak to no one else until I am more myself." Unfortunately, I suspected that would be soon. "Except for you. I am always speaking to you."

"So, is it back to our luxury hotel from yesterday?" he asked.

"They rent rooms here," I said. "Also no questions asked. Agnes will send someone to fetch us."

"Is it safe?"

"Safety in numbers, they say."

Lars sighed. "Spatz, do you think it is safe to stay here?"

I slid my arms into the sleeves of his tuxedo jacket and pulled the front closed. My leg throbbed. "I do."

"You trust this Agnes?"

"Not completely," I said. "But she needs me to do something for her. Something very important. Something I cannot do if I am dead. And I will not do it if you are dead either."

"I am touched." Lars studied my face, probably trying to decide whether I was in any condition to make that kind of judgment. "I suppose dragging you around elsewhere has its own risks."

The original cashier came out onto the balcony and gestured to Lars. They murmured in the corner while I watched traffic below. From up here, it was hard to believe that a car was big enough to hurt me. The streets were full for a Monday night. So many were here on vacation to watch the Games. I started counting the familiar white flags with their interlocking rings but kept losing track. Clearly the drug had not worn off completely.

Lars put his arm around my shoulders and turned me from the street. "Time to go."

"Yes, sir."

We marched through the rainbow-spangled main room. The dress caressed my legs and floated around me. Perhaps I ought to buy one like it. One without a prostitute past.

Lars steered me down a carpeted hall that expanded the farther we walked. After the ballroom, the gilt wall sconces threw little light. It felt like a magical tunnel, something out of Ali Baba. Someone got rich and someone ended up cut into four pieces in that story. I looked over at Lars. He had won tonight, so did that mean I would be quartered?

"Spatz?" he asked. "Are you all right?"

I nodded and put one foot in front of the other. My exhaustion mounted with each step. My left leg ached but not enough to limp. Something told me it would soon get much worse.

Just when I had decided to lie down on the floor to rest, he stopped in front of a white-painted door. He unlocked it, reached inside, and turned on the light.

"Hallelujah," he said. "There's a sofa."

I laughed. "You might be the first man ever to utter that sentence here."

"Wait in the hall." He disappeared into the room. I leaned against the wall. My leg told me not to put weight on it. I obeyed.

He reappeared.

"Where did you go?" I asked.

"Checking out the room. Empty. One door with a solid lock. Just as expected."

I repeated his question from the stadium. "Must you always keep your guard up?"

He gave me a knowing look. "It has served me well so far, Spatz."

The room was large and smelled a little of smoke and a little of furniture polish. It held a double bed, a wardrobe, a white sofa with a curved back, a coffee table, and a door that I hoped led to a bathroom. If nothing else, my hotel fortunes had improved. Boris would approve of the room, if not the company.

I stepped out of my shoes and headed for the bathroom door. I needed to get out of the dress and into bed before I fell down.

The tub, sink, and toilet gleamed in the overhead light. They looked clean enough to eat on. A large oval mirror hung above the sink. I stood in front of the mirror, both arms working behind my back, struggling to unzip my dress.

No matter how I strained, I could not reach the top. My arms cramped from reaching. *Stop,* I told myself, *you might tear the silk.* Who knew what Agnes would charge for that?

I met my tired eyes in the mirror. I knew how women got out of this kind of dress. The same way I got into it. With help.

My gaze strayed to the closed door. I hated to ask Lars for help undressing, but no ladies' maid came with the room.

As if he read my thoughts, a light tap sounded on the door. "Everything in order?"

I sighed. I could not sleep in the dress, I could not get it off alone, and I did not think I could stand much more on my leg. Inescapable.

"I need a bit of help with a zipper."

He opened the door. He had loosened his tie and rolled up his sleeves. He, too, looked tired.

Lars stepped in close. His warm thumb glided down my spine as he slowly undid my zipper. I shivered and closed my eyes. He left his palm resting gently on the small of my back.

I stood there for a moment before opening my eyes. Our gaze met in the mirror. I looked away first.

"Why not?" he whispered, mouth centimeters from my ear. I tried to ignore the path his thumb had traced down my skin.

"I love Boris," I said. But was it still true?

"Then why aren't you in Switzerland?" He leaned forward. I felt the warmth of his body against my back. I should step away.

"I have w-work to do here," I stuttered. It had seemed like a good answer for the same question when Boris left, but this time I was not so confident.

His eyes met mine again in the mirror. "Then why are you two no longer together?"

I reached behind and took his hand from the small of my back. A spot, the shape of his hand, cooled. "That does not concern you."

"On the contrary. It concerns me greatly."

I stepped around him, unable to meet his eyes, and limped into the bedroom. With my back to him, I slipped the dress off my shoulders and draped it over the edge of the bed. I should have hung it up but had no intention of parading in front of Lars in my slip any more than necessary. I flopped into bed and pulled the covers over myself. My leg throbbed.

Under the sheet, I moved my hand lightly over my bruise and realized that I had gone to bed in gloves. I peeled them off and the bandage stayed inside. I had torn open a large scab on my right palm. I hoped there was no blood inside the glove. Agnes would charge for that.

I stared at blood dripping off my hand. I would have to get up to fetch a handkerchief, but the thought of standing made me want to groan. I had no wish to walk around in my slip again, either.

"Spatz." Lars knelt next to the bed. "Why are you limping?"

"That is where the car hit me." I turned my hand palm up and cupped it to keep blood from dripping onto the sheet.

"A car hit you?" His voice rose. "When?"

"This afternoon. On Unter den Linden. I told you. Could you—?"

He interrupted me angrily before I could ask for a handkerchief. "You told me that you fell!"

"I did. After the car hit me."

His jaw tightened, but he sounded calm when he said, "Please show me your leg."

I flipped up the blanket and hiked up my slip to show the bottom of the bruise. Blood dripped from my palm. Lovely. Agnes would tack on an extra cleaning fee for the sheets, too.

He stared at the blood droplets for several seconds, transfixed. Emotions I did not understand played across his face.

"Lars?"

He took his eyes off the blood and straightened. With mechanical motions, he removed the gauze from Frau Doktor Spiegel's paper bag and gently bound up my hand. When he reached over and ran his fingertips across my bruised thigh, gently and professionally, as she had done, my breath caught in my throat.

"I saw a doctor." I took his hand off my thigh. "Remember? She gave you those instructions."

"Of course you did, darling." His voice sounded uncharacteristically warm and solicitous. And he had never called me darling.

"Lars?" I asked, worried.

He pulled my hair back gently and ran his index finger below my stitches. "Excellent work. You won't even have a scar on that beautiful face."

I stared at him. Something was wrong.

"Now, tell me what happened. From the beginning. Leave nothing out. You cannot always be the best judge of what's important." He took my uninjured hand in his. "Let's start."

I pried my hand free gently. I did not want to startle him. "I will tell you everything, of course."

"I know." He gave me a conspiratorial look. My uneasiness grew. "But remember that we have little time."

My stomach lurched.

This was his bedside manner.

This was how he acted with tortured women he interrogated. They came to him bloody and damaged, and this is what he did. His eyes stared patiently into mine, warm, sympathetic. And false.

Fear chased down my spine. The Lars I knew was gone. He believed I was one of those women, and he was ready to interrogate me. In the hospital, I had seen shell-shocked soldiers go into a state like this. Usually they were harmless, but not always.

I had to change the situation to make him recognize where he was. I flipped the blanket over my leg, smoothed my hair over my stitches, and hoisted myself backwards until I leaned against the headboard, not allowing myself to wince when I did so. I slipped my bandaged hand under the covers, hiding the blood that had triggered his reaction.

My mind raced. I was much more terrified than I had been when I thought he would hit me. He was someone else. Who knew what he might do? I thought of trying to get past him, but flight would likely set him off.

"Now, let's start. What do you think you need to tell me?" His voice sounded concerned, calm, and wrong.

How could I reach him? What would happen if I did not?

"Lars—"

"Do you need water? Medication?"

"No, but—"

"Then let's begin." He crossed his legs and leaned forward as if about to take notes. "The sooner we start, the sooner we can finish, and I know we both want that, don't we?"

I did not want to know what would happen after he decided we were finished. "Lars—"

"Enough of that." A note of steel underlay his tone. He did not intend to be trifled with anymore. "Start."

I searched his eyes for recognition. I saw none.

I had to bring him out of this state. I leaned forward and did the one thing I had promised myself that I would never do.

I kissed him.

20

The kiss was tentative at first, but it changed. I kissed him harder. Lars moaned. I buried my hands in his hair and pulled him closer. His arms tightened as he eased from chair to bed.

I did not want to stop kissing him, but eventually I did.

When I pulled back, we both breathed hard. "I am not them, Lars."

"I know, Hannah. God, I know." He leaned forward and kissed me again.

No pretending that my body did not want his. He ran his hands hard down my sides. I arched against him.

He stroked his hand along my bruised thigh. I groaned. We both froze. I blinked as if I had just awoken.

"Forgive me." He moved his hand up to my side, and a current of electricity went with it.

I trembled and took his hand in both of mine.

He leaned forward again.

"No." I shook from head to toe, and I did not want to say the words I knew I had to. Was it because of Boris? Or because I dared not trust Lars? Or myself? "I can't."

His hair was mussed from my hands, his breathing uneven. His dark eyes stared into mine, stunned and hurt.

"I am so, so sorry," I said.

He took back his hand.

I wanted to crawl under the blankets and hide. I contented myself with pulling them up to my chin.

He stood and buttoned his shirt. I had unbuttoned it. My face burned. "I just—"

"Spare me," he said. "Please."

We stared at each other for an eternity.

"I very much wish to leave." His voice shook. "But I can't. Doctor's orders. I have to wake you every few hours to ensure that you are not acting erratically."

"Like just now?"

A muscle twitched in his jaw. "I will be back in an hour to check on you."

"I can ask Agnes to send—"

"I don't trust your friend Agnes."

He crossed the room in a few strides.

"And I don't trust you." He slammed the door.

I punched the pillow. My leg hurt, my head hurt, but mostly my feelings hurt. What had I done?

Much later, I took an opium tablet to sleep.

The next morning, I woke feeling terrible. Per doctor's instructions, Lars woke me every few hours all night to ask inane questions. I understood that he needed to check that I did not have a concussion. I even appreciated his diligence, but I was exhausted. My left leg throbbed before I got out of bed. When I put it on the floor, it buckled. Clearly my leg had had enough of this nonsense. I hopped to the bathroom without waking Lars.

He had moved a chair next to the sink and set my suitcase on it, probably foreseeing the problems I would have walking this morning. His solicitousness made me feel worse.

I washed and dressed slowly. I could take an opium tablet, and the pain and worry would vanish. I did not. Instead I kept up a steady stream of encouraging talk inside my head as I moved. My body needed a great deal of reassurance this morning.

When I made it back into the room, Lars sat awake on the sofa, looking much the worse for wear.

"Good morning," I said. "Thank you for taking care of me last night."

"Spatz." He shifted on the sofa, not meeting my eyes. "I—I—I am sorry about what happened just before I left the room last night."

I gaped at him. If ever there was a misplaced apology.

He soldiered on, staring at the rug. "You were in shock, under the influence of drugs. I should not have presumed."

I could not let him shoulder the blame. "I knew what I was do-ing."

"The entire time?"

My leg protested. I leaned against the wall. "I do not deny that I was . . . surprised by how things played out, but I do not blame you."

"Does blame have to enter into it?"

"No." I pushed off the wall. "But—"

"Let's leave it there, shall we?"

I took a step forward, one hand on the smooth wallpaper. I wanted to ask him if he had known what he was doing before I kissed him, but I was afraid of the answer and knew that he likely would not re-member the event. If I pushed him, I might even trigger another epi-sode. This was not the time or place. But I needed to stay on my guard.

"May I help you to walk?" he asked.

I did not want him to touch me. I had no idea what might happen. At this point, I did not trust myself, a position I had never occupied before. I gritted my teeth and took another step. "Thank you, but I can manage."

"So I see."

The Monte Carlo did not serve breakfast so early. I left the box hold-ing the dress and accessories for Agnes with a doorman who looked as if he had slept well, eaten well, and could take on an army of war ele-phants.

I limped back to Lars's car. We stowed the suitcases in the boot. Sweepers cleaned up the messes left by last night's revelers. The Nazis must have hired extra street cleaners for duration of the Games.

At Kempinski's, I ordered tea and some of their famous pastry. Perhaps something there would give me strength for the day. Luckily I had only two activities planned, and neither required much walking.

Lars turned into the policeman he had been when we first met. I summarized the funeral, my meeting with the garbage men, and the attack by automobile. He questioned me with the cool efficiency that I had grown accustomed to. But even he could extract no more details than my vague impressions: large, probably wearing a fedora, driving erratically.

I pulled out the hood ornament and set it on the table. Lars picked it up and turned it over. "Hard to believe it came off so easily. There must have been a flaw in the metal."

"I told you zeppelins were dangerous."

"This is not a humorous matter," he said.

I stared at the chrome zeppelin.

"It's from an Opel," he said. "An Opel Olympia."

"That's no help at all, then," I said. "They seem to be everywhere."

He handed it back and I stuffed it in my satchel.

"How about you?" I asked. The sweet, flaky pastries tasted sumptuous. "What did you do yesterday?"

"I spent a great deal of time at freight companies, pretending to be a railway inspector. For the record, no one tried to kill me."

"Perhaps you were not applying yourself," I said.

He smiled with half his mouth. "Or, you were applying yourself too vigorously."

"What did you uncover?"

He sipped his coffee, eyes far off. I suspected he was organizing his thoughts before presenting his report.

"Lars?"

He put down his cup and realigned his spoon on his saucer. He raised his thumb. "First, there has been a twenty percent increase in passenger traffic between Berlin and Saratova. They travel over various train stations, and through various connecting stations, but I think it's still significant."

He raised his index finger, and I stifled a smile. Counting points on his hands again. "Second, there is an increase in freight. It's difficult to determine what's going there, and that in itself alarms me."

I found it hard to concentrate. I remembered the feel of his lips against mine last night, the weight of his body on top of mine. He might chalk it up to shock and opium, although I was not entirely certain that he did, but I knew better.

"I'd like to go Saratova and scout it out. I suspect—" He stopped midsentence. "Spatz? Are you paying attention?"

I swallowed a sip of tea sideways and choked. When I finished coughing, I said. "Of course I am."

He burst out laughing. "I see that. You are even attentive in your drinking of tea."

I wiped my mouth with as much dignity as I could muster. I held up one thumb. "First, unexpected numbers of passengers going to Saratova. Freight as well, but concealed enough to make it more suspicious."

I did not point out that I had summed it up using only my thumb. It felt petty. Amusing, but petty. "What happened to your jaw?"

He touched the back of his fingers to the bruise. "I fell."

"On your face?"

"Against a bench," he said. "What are your plans for today? Nothing that involves a footrace, I hope?"

I had never seen him fall, even drunk, but I kept my peace. "I am going to the university to check their rubbish bins."

"What do you expect to find?"

I pushed my chair back. "The answer to a hunch."

He dropped coins on the table and rose. "I shall accompany you."

"But—"

"The last time you wandered off on your own, you fell under a car."

"He swerved onto the sidewalk! He was trying to kill me."

"You are not aiding your case." Lars took my elbow and helped me to my feet. I let him. "Remember the terms of the agreement? Partners?"

Hot pain shot up my leg when I put weight on it. I drew in a quick breath. I did not want to pass the scene of the accident alone, nor did I want to consider the number of stairs I would have to climb to take the subway. "A car and driver would be quite useful."

"If those are the terms, I accept," he said.

I concentrated on getting myself to the door without falling down. My leg gradually felt stronger. As painful as it was, walking helped.

I paused in front of a nearby hat store to give my leg a rest. A row of marble busts, installed for the Games, modeled hats. The Grecian faces looked incongruous in women's hats tilted at a rakish angle to cover one eyebrow and modern men's fedoras set straight. I imagined Caesar wearing a straw fedora to shade his face against the Grecian sun.

I hobbled to Lars's car. "You drive an Opel Olympia."

"Would you like to check it for dents?"

I touched the zeppelin, then ran my hand across the smooth hood. "I landed here." I pointed to the windscreen. "And somewhere around here is where I cut my head."

Lars opened my door. "Do you remember the color?"

"A dark color," I said. "But I do not think it was black like this one."

"Then I'm in the clear?"

"So far." I climbed in and he shut the door firmly.

He insisted on stopping near the scene of my accident. "Stay in the car, please."

If I never saw that stretch of cobblestones again, it would be too soon. "Fine."

I leaned my head against the seat and fell asleep. I woke with a start when the driver's door slammed. "Did you find anything?"

"Such an event always leaves a mark on the surrounding environment."

So officious. "And?"

He drew in a deep breath.

"Partners, remember?" I reminded him. "Share everything?"

"I don't recall that I agreed to that. Only that you did."

"Lars," I said in a warning tone.

"Very well. I found a—" He cleared his throat. "—a scrape of rubber where the wheels hit the curb, a chip of dark red paint on the streetlamp he sideswiped . . ." His voice trailed off.

Nausea climbed my throat. "What does that tell you?"

"He made no attempt to brake. He intended to hit you, run you down, and keep going."

"Lovely."

He spoke in a mild voice, but a slight quaver betrayed him. "I also found a splash of your blood with a few strands of blond hair next to a storefront, in case it interests you."

"Not much."

"Spatz," he said. "You are very lucky you survived."

"Luckier would have been not to be hit."

"Perhaps we could skip the garbage and go on to Switzerland?" he asked hopefully.

"What could happen to me? I have a guard dog, remember?"

"I am not joking." He glared at me.

"Nor am I." I checked my gold pocket watch. "We have to leave now, so we can arrive before the garbage man."

We would barely make it on time, as slowly as I had to walk.

He heaved a sigh and started the car. Driving past the rows of giant stone statues on Unter den Linden felt like driving through a museum. We did not speak in the few blocks it took to reach the university. Relief rushed through me when we found a nearby parking space.

I limped to the back of the grand buildings that housed the chemistry department, Lars patient beside me. I thought of sending him ahead, but I wanted to see whatever it was first.

Waist-high rubbish bins lined the curb. The square containers were made of scrap metal riveted together in uneven patterns, like quilts. Lars lifted the small metal handle on top and opened the first hinged lid.

I gagged at the stench of rotten banana and fish. I peered inside.

The bin contained food scraps, smeared paper, and broken glass. Nothing seemed remarkable. Why would someone want to hit me with a car to keep me from looking into these? We moved from bin to bin.

When we reached the last bin, my leg ached so much, I could barely stand. I pushed hair out of my eyes and leaned on the side of the bin. Nothing of note in it either.

"Spatz?" He had one hand behind my back. I sensed he was worried I might topple over. As was I. "What are we searching for?"

"Not the faintest idea. I hoped I would realize when I saw it."

"Did you?"

I shook my head. My leg throbbed, my head ached, and I knew I had missed something.

"What if you sit before you do yourself more damage?"

As I turned from the bins, I noticed a hedge. I hobbled over, Lars in tow. Perhaps whatever was supposed to be in the bins had blown out.

Nothing interesting clung to the branches of the hedge. I pushed myself through a spindly section, scratching my arms. The hedge fronted an empty lot. Nettles straggled here and there, along with bits of paper and small crosses sticking out of the dirt. Crosses?

With a ridiculous amount of effort, I knelt on the edge of the field. Each cross was made of two twigs tied together by twine. I pulled one from the dirt. "It looks like a grave marker."

"So small?"

I dug my hands into the dry soil, not sure if I wanted to find anything. Lars knelt next to me and took over digging. He unearthed a furry carcass and pulled it out of the hole. I wrinkled my nose at the smell. I thought of my erstwhile pet, Mitzi. "Cat?"

He turned the corpse over with the tip of his finger and pointed to its long ears. "Rabbit."

I struggled to my feet and stared at the crosses. "Do you think all the crosses mark rabbit graves?"

Two children ran toward us, hands clenched into fists. Lars stood and stepped between us.

"Grave robbers!" yelled the first. His short blond hair stuck up in front. He looked no more than five. His passionate response reminded me of Anton, and I smiled.

"You put it back!" The second child resembled the first closely enough to be his sister. I put her age at nine, close to Anton's eleven.

Lars dropped to his knees and obligingly buried the animal.

"Did you make all these?" I asked.

"Why?" The boy stuck out his chin pugnaciously.

"It's a wonderful tribute," Lars broke in. "Like a soldier's graveyard."

A chill went down my back, but the boy stared at him with interest. "Really?"

Lars dusted off his hands, but remained kneeling, eye level with the children. "They have fields of crosses like this in France, for soldiers who died in the War."

"How do you know?" asked the sister.

"I fought there," Lars said. "Many men in my company are buried there."

I had never heard him talk about the War. I stared, as curious as the children.

"So, what is under these crosses?" he asked.

"Bunnies," said the boy. "All bunnies. We pick one to bury each week."

Had he stolen the bodies from a poor man's dinner table, or were they from somewhere more sinister?

"Where did you find them?" Lars asked.

I followed the boy's pointing finger to the rubbish bins we had examined. "Wednesdays. Early. But not today."

"Maybe it's the Olympics," the girl chimed in. "Maybe the bunnies are at the stadium. Or perhaps the garbage man came early."

I stared at the rubbish bins, speechless. Someone was killing rabbits on purpose. I looked up at the chemistry building. The rubbish bins contained their rubbish. I thought of Andreas's work on pesticides. Were they testing a poison on the rabbits? Was that the link to Peter? Had this same poison killed him?

Lars patted down the mound of dirt over the rabbit we had unearthed.

"How do you think the rabbits died?" I kept my voice light and curious.

The children shrugged.

"What—" I paused dramatically. "—what if they were poisoned?"

Lars looked at me sharply.

"Touching them might be dangerous," I said. "Perhaps it would be wisest not to disturb them."

"Unburied?" The girl shook her head disbelievingly. Her hair whipped from side to side. "They belong in a graveyard, not a rubbish bin. And we take only one and the bins have many."

Lars stood and looked down at the children. "But you could wash your hands after, just in case?"

"We always do," she said, with a haughty dignity that led me to believe that perhaps they did.

A woman's voice called from tall apartment buildings on the other side of the vacant lot. The children snapped to attention. "Breakfast," said the boy. "Can't be late or Frank will eat it all."

They pelted away.

I brushed dirt off my dress. "Bunnies."

That was what the garbage man meant for me to find. I knew from the way he took care of his horses that he loved animals. Finding so many dead rabbits in his rubbish bins week after week would have upset him. It upset me.

"You found what you were looking for?" Lars asked.

"It seems likely."

He took my elbow. We walked back toward the chemistry building. It felt so different from our first walk, in the Hall of the Unnamed Dead, where I worried that the police officer and SS man at my side might discover my secrets. Now he knew them.

He caught me looking. "Yes?"

"It has been a good long time since our first walk together."

"I knew you lied then, by the way." He tightened his grip. "And I was concerned for you."

"Now I am telling the truth, and you are more concerned."

"You are a little ode to progress, aren't you?" He smiled. I remembered tracing his cheekbones with my fingertips the night before and blushed.

"Lars!" called a voice.

We both jumped. We were supposed to be incognito, in case Bauer had started an investigation. We turned to see Andreas hurrying toward us, probably on his way to work.

Lars relaxed, but I did not. I thought of the field of dead rabbits behind the chemistry building, and Andreas a chemist. What if Project Zephyr was about a deadly pesticide tested on rabbits? If so, Andreas must know about it, and his arrival also meant we could not sneak into the chemistry building unobserved.

"What are you doing out here so early?" Andreas asked.

"Strolling. Adelheid wanted to take pictures before the light changed." Lars sounded appropriately long-suffering.

"Light is the most important element in a photograph," I said tartly.

Andreas's eyes took in the dirt on my dress and Lars's trouser knees. "Don't forget the subject of the photo."

"No," I studied him. "I will not."

A puzzled expression crossed his face. "Where are you off to next?"

He looked ready to accompany us, but I feared to walk in front of him. My limp would arouse his suspicions, and I had no ready explanation.

Lars was not thinking along those lines. He took a step toward the street, with me on his arm. I limped beside him.

"What happened to you, Adelheid?" Andreas asked, shocked.

"I . . ." If I said that a car hit me and he told anyone, they might think to dig up the report.

"She fell off a bicycle," Lars lied. "Although she's embarrassed to admit it."

I held up my bandaged palm. "Clumsy."

Andreas drew his eyebrows together, but good breeding made him hold his tongue. "Are you attending today's fencing?"

I paused, torn. I had told him that I was covering mainly the fencing for the newspaper, but I hated to expose myself to more danger. "Of course."

Lars pulled me closer to his side. He did not approve. I did not like it either.

"I'd love to join you, if you don't mind a third," Andreas said.

"Not a bit," said Lars smoothly. "You are always welcome."

We walked as quickly as my leg could manage across the campus to Unter den Linden. Lars kept up a light conversation, even as I leaned on him heavily. I ached to sit down.

At the curb, he dropped my arm to hurry forward and open my door. His keys clanked against a grate on the curb. They had fallen through, and he crouched to fish them out.

I shifted my weight onto my good leg. A gust of wind blew my dress up on the left, exposing the bottom of my bruise.

Andreas gasped. "My God, Adelheid. Did he—?"

"It is none of your concern, Andreas." Too late, I smoothed my skirt back down. I hoped that Lars could not hear our conversation with his head in the grate and traffic rumbling by. "And I would thank you not to discuss it with me."

"But—"

"It is not what you think, but even if it were, it is none of your affair. He is my husband-to-be." I had to start an argument with him to keep him from getting into the car, but I hated doing it. He had always been kind. I drew in a deep breath. "You are supposed to be his friend. Not someone who is making advances on his fiancée."

"I have made no such—" He stepped back and crossed his arms.

"Is that so?" I made my voice icy. In truth, he had offered only sympathy, but we both knew that he wanted more. Peter had seen it from across the stadium. I had known for months, but I had also known that his honor code would keep him from ever acting on his feelings, particularly if I avoided spending time alone with him. So far, it had worked.

He stared, openmouthed.

"Perhaps it would be best if you left us alone." I lifted my chin to look into his eyes, wishing I were taller.

His eyes narrowed angrily. I had succeeded, but I took no joy in it.

Lars finally opened the passenger door and gestured. "Come along, you two!"

I limped over. Andreas followed.

"I have work to do today." Andreas spat out each word, clearly furious and lying. "I am afraid I cannot go with you after all."

Lars's eyes widened. "If you are certain—"

"Very much so."

I slid into the front seat without a backward glance or farewell to Andreas.

"Enjoy the fencing, Adelheid," he called. "Wear your protective gear."

21

Lars got in after me and shut the driver's door. "What did you say to him?"

Cars streamed by outside.

"Well?" he asked more quietly.

I remembered my promise to tell him the truth. "He thinks you are beating me. I told him it was untrue, and none of his affair."

Lars blanched. "He thinks . . ."

"I look worse each time I see him." I smoothed my dress over my knees, toying with the hem. "If all I am doing is covering the fencing and spending time with you, what else could he think?"

"I see." He stared out the window, jaw muscles tense. "Where to?"

I gave him an address in Kreuzberg.

"What's there?"

"A way out," I said. "Perhaps."

We drove between the tall athletic statues, past patriotic flags, and down unusually busy streets.

In Kreuzberg, I climbed out before Lars made it to my door. I struggled to stand on my good leg. Perhaps Frau Doktor Spiegel had missed a more serious injury.

I steadied myself with one hand on the warm car roof and examined the front of the building. SILBERT AND SONS—STATIONERY AND

SUPPLIES. Thinking of the supplies that the son sold, I smiled at the innocuous wording.

The store had a prosperous air. Freshly painted gold letters stood out against the cobalt blue background. The front windows gleamed. Here, too, the window display was Olympic themed. A black Grecian urn with a terra-cotta-colored scribe holding a stylus sat in the middle of the window, surrounded by a few replica styli and several fountain pens in black and rich reds and dark yellows. I paused before going in. Once I took Lars in to meet Herr Silbert, there was no going back. Perhaps I should purchase something, send Lars away, and come back on my own. I looked from the store to Lars's questioning face.

"You need to purchase paper?" he asked.

"I need to procure a few items." I limped toward the store, decision made.

A bell tinkled when we opened the door. I looked up. Affixed over the frame, as always, was a polished brass bell.

I paused inside the threshold and took a deep breath. The shop smelled of leather and ink. Two of my favorite scents.

"Spatz?"

"It smells wonderful," I said.

"Did you take your medicine this morning?"

I gave him an exasperated look and limped to the glass-topped counter. Costly fountain pens in the display case glittered like jewels.

The man behind the counter sat with his back to us, hands busy. "A moment only."

My heart lifted. I had expected to find the father; instead I had found the son, the man I sought. "Do take as long as you need, Herr Silbert. I hate to disturb an artist at work."

The object clattered onto the desk. His chair swiveled. "Hello!" He paused, probably uncertain of which of my names to use. He wore a fine linen shirt of the type he favored, well ironed and with the sleeves carefully rolled up to protect them from ink. His thinning brown hair had been expensively barbered. Every strand was in place. He was back in his element.

I smiled. "You are looking much more prosperous than when last we met." In Tegel Prison.

"As are you. When I did not hear from you after our last transaction, I feared the worst." He wiped his clever fingers delicately on a scrap of gray flannel and held out his hand to shake.

I took it. He held it a second longer than protocol dictated. Lars cleared his throat.

"I would like to present Herr Lang," I said. "Lars, this is Herr Silbert, an old friend."

Both glowered at each other. Had Lars once arrested him?

Lars shook Herr Silbert's hand. "I am also her fiancé."

I thought of correcting him. His engagement was with Adelheid Zinsli, not Hannah Vogel. But I found no easy way to explain that, so I let it be.

"Our lovely Fräulein has been single far too long." Herr Silbert smiled thinly. "Many would love to stand in your shoes."

"I would not say many," I protested.

Herr Silbert said, "You underestimate yourself."

"I have need of your services again, I fear."

"A pen?" he asked. "Or a custom notebook for your work?"

"I wish to purchase an item similar to the last one. Three items."

He peered down his nose at Lars, not an easy task, since Herr Silbert was even shorter than I. "Let us talk in the back."

"I trust Herr Lang completely." Did I?

"How fortunate for you. I, however, do not." His tea brown eyes allowed no room for compromise.

Lars did not release my elbow. "I prefer to keep you in sight."

"A jealous man?" Herr Silbert steepled his ink-stained fingers.

"A worried one," Lars countered.

"You have won the hand of the lovely Fräulein. What could possibly worry you?"

"The hand of the lovely Fräulein."

"Lars." I whispered in his ear. "I have known him for many years. I must speak to him. Please trust my judgment."

I hoped Lars listened. I hated to make a scene, but I would. I suspected he saw that, because, reluctantly, he released my arm. "I will be right here, should you need me."

I did not pat him on the head and tell him he was a loyal but overly protective guard dog. But I did hold the thought in my mind.

Herr Silbert led us through a locked door into the back of the store. Tall metal shelves ranged from floor to ceiling, most filled with brown cardboard boxes.

He sat me down on a tall metal stool. "Fräulein Vogel, how long have you known that man?"

"Five years," I said. "He has had my life in his hands many times. So far, I am still alive. He has no love of the Nazis. He will not betray you."

He studied me before sitting on the stool next to mine. "Very well. What do you wish of me?"

I pulled out paperwork that Agnes had given me the night before. "I have need of three false passports. This is one. The other two are for myself and Herr Lang."

He took Agnes's papers and photo. He pulled silver-framed reading glasses from his breast pocket and donned them. "When?"

"Soon. Today if possible."

He contemplated me over the tops of his glasses. "Times for me are much busier than ever before."

"Business is good, then?" I wondered what the boxes contained. Herr Silbert liked to keep his money in portable form, like collectible coins and stamps, instead of cash. And he did not believe in banks.

"Since the Nazis came to power, I have more work than I can handle. Mostly Jewish, of course, but they are not the only ones trying to change their identity these days. Many are hoping to slip out with the visitors from the Games." He tapped the paperwork in front of him. "Prices have risen since 1931."

"I have Swiss francs."

"One must love the Swiss."

"From whom do you get the names?" I had always wondered.

"After my trade secrets, too, my dear?"

"I would feel more comfortable if I knew whom I was impersonat-
ing."

"Cemeteries," he said. I thought of the rabbit crosses. "I travel
around various cities to find children born at the correct year who
died before their first birthday. There are a sobering amount of them.
One merely has to search for the lambs. Fortunately, I made an extensive list some time ago, as I have no time for it now. Certainly not
with arthritis in my knees."

Anton and I had stolen the identity of two dead children to get out
of Germany. I felt nauseated.

"Have you source material for me?" he asked.

I handed him the Adelheid Zinsli passport he had made five years
before. In Switzerland, I lived as Hannah Vogel. If Bauer had started
an investigation, both were useless here.

He studied the photograph. "Rather an old picture."

"Have I changed so much in the past five years?" I asked, startled.

"As a gentleman, I must deny it." He bowed his head like the gentleman his father had always hoped he would become. Then he raised
his head and gave me the rapscallion smile that had thwarted his father's well-laid plans. "But as a businessman, I think a new photo is in
order."

"I had a difficult night." I felt defensive.

"Did you?" He raised his eyebrows.

"How much?" I certainly was not going to discuss last night's tra-
vails with him.

We haggled about the price, more because I knew that he loved to
do so than because I was unable to pay it.

Price settled, I asked him about the Hawaiian missionary stamp.

"I have not heard of it," he said. "But I can bring you a stamp book
to look it up in while you wait."

"First, let's retrieve Herr Lang. I think he has waited enough."

"Always keep them waiting, my dear. It heightens their appreciation."

I chuckled and followed him to the front of the store. Lars looked relieved to see me. Herr Silbert hurried to the window and flipped over the OPEN sign.

"Follow me," he told us.

"Both of us?" Lars asked coolly.

Once in the back, Herr Silbert took our pictures, our particulars as to age, height, eye and hair color. While I recited my vital statistics, I remembered the rubbish bins at the university. They, too, had been numbered.

Herr Silbert ushered us into a claustrophobic room behind the storeroom. This one had a sofa, a reading light, and a bookshelf. "Now, you must wait here. I have blanks ready for someone else, but I can use them for you instead. It may take a few hours." He closed the door.

I sat on the sofa. My leg still pained me and exhaustion washed over me. My body felt the effects of the sleep it had missed last night.

Lars sat next to me. "Thank you for the chance of a new start with a new name. I know it cannot have been easy for you to trust me enough to bring me here."

I wanted to say that I had trusted him with far more. "You are not easy to shed."

I tipped my head back and immediately fell asleep.

I awoke to the sound of Herr Silbert clearing his throat. I had drawn my legs up onto the sofa, and my head rested on Lars's lap. Face burning, I sat and rubbed my eyes.

Herr Silbert sat next to me. "I found the book you requested."

I stared at him blankly for a second. "Ah, the stamp."

Herr Silbert opened a thick book with yellowed pages and pointed to an entry.

"The Hawaiian Missionary stamps," I read aloud for Lars's benefit. "Are known as the Missionary Issue and are comprised of three values: 2 cents, 5 cents, and 13 cents. All were printed by letterpress at the Government Printing office. They were first sold on October 1, 1851 at the Honolulu and Lahaina post offices."

I stumbled over the exotic names. It was odd to imagine that a tiny piece of paper had found its way through seventy years of time and thousands of kilometers into Peter's possession.

Lars read over my shoulder. "A set of stamps, known as the Grinnell Missionaries were discovered in 1920 and judged to be forgeries in 1922."

I thought of Bosch's Frenchman, the one who had killed his friend to steal his stamp. The Missionary stamps had enticed many to crime.

"Your ink must be dry." Herr Silbert bustled out and returned carrying three passports.

"Here you go!" Herr Silbert presented me two passports with a flourish, one Swiss and one German. "You, Fräulein Vogel, are a Swiss citizen named Hannah Schmidt. You were born in Poland in 1900. I took a year off your age, Women love that."

I opened the top passport. Agnes's. I opened the other. Mine.

"Your parents moved here when you were quite young, in case you do not speak Polish."

I thought of the conversations between Paul and Miriam that I had missed. "Indeed I do not."

He handed Lars his passport. When he opened it, two gold rings fell out.

"You are Lars Schmidt. Also a Swiss citizen. Born in—"

My eyes skimmed my passport. "We are married?"

Lars stifled a smile. "Do not sound quite so dismayed. I will make a fine husband."

"But—"

Herr Silbert tilted his head to one side. "Since you are already engaged, it seemed simpler. Less scrutiny than if you were to apply for a marriage license."

Lars slid one ring onto his finger. "No conditions."

He took my hand and slid the other ring onto mine, his touch gentle. His eyes were serious as he said, "With this ring, I thee wed."

I pulled my hand free. "But, wait—"

Herr Silbert handed him a plain brown envelope. "Your marriage license is in there as well."

I stared at him, dismayed.

"Is something amiss?" Herr Silbert asked.

"I think Hannah is disappointed to have missed her own wedding." Lars's voice revealed that he struggled not to laugh.

I looked from one to the other, one amused, the other confused. I shot Lars such an angry look that he leaned back, but it was illogical to be angry. Even if Hannah Schmidt had married Lars Schmidt, Hannah Vogel had not. Hannah Vogel was who I would be the moment I got to Switzerland. None of this should matter. But it did.

A muffled thudding sounded from the front of the store.

"A customer!" Herr Silbert said. "I must bid you farewell. Exit through the back."

He hustled us out the back door and into a small alley paved with cobblestones, too narrow for any but the smallest automobiles.

I stared at Lars, dazed. The ring felt uncomfortable on my finger. I twisted it with my other hand.

"Spatz, I see you find it odious to be married against your will. And to me, of all people." Hurt was plain in his voice.

"I . . ." My voice trailed off. I had no idea what to say. Again, this was not his fault.

"Once we get out of Germany, assuming you wish to keep your Hannah Schmidt passport, you do not need to be concerned. I give you my word that I will grant you a divorce immediately, under whatever terms you desire."

"Thank you," I said. "It is not that I do not—"

"There is not much to be gained by continuing this discussion. And much to be lost." He took my elbow again. "Where to next?"

I struggled to switch to a new topic. "I—I would like to go back to the university."

"Why?"

"Those bins were numbered. Two fourteen to two twenty, I believe. If that corresponds to room numbers, perhaps we can see where the rabbits originated."

An automobile on the street tooted its horn. We both jumped. I bit my lip when I settled back on my leg. The rest had helped, but it still ached. A young woman on the opposite side of the street waved to the driver. She looked as if it never occurred to her that the car might jump onto the sidewalk and strike her. Lucky woman.

We drove back to the university, parked farther from the chemistry building than I would have liked, and found rooms 214 to 220. Most were offices. One had HERR PROFESSOR ANDREAS HUBER stenciled on the door in black letters. If I had not picked a fight with him, perhaps I could have asked him what the rubbish bins contained. As it was, I relaxed when I saw his office was empty. I did not recognize the names on the other offices. I wondered which office had once belonged to Frau Professor Müller. Room 220 was the most interesting. From the hall, it looked much larger than the offices. A classroom? A laboratory, perhaps? I tried the door handle. Locked.

"A dead end." I wanted to groan in frustration.

Lars looked down the empty corridor. "Let me know at once if you see someone."

He knelt, drew two thin pieces of metal from his pocket, and inserted them into the lock. I had not expected him to be able to pick locks.

"That is illegal, Herr Kommissar," I said.

"Compared to all the laws you've broken, I find this one rather trivial."

I kept lookout, nervous. Since my brother's death, I was the one causing trouble, not acting as guard dog. "Which laws have I broken?"

"I hate to list them. It makes me feel inadequate as a policeman."

The lock opened with a click, and he turned the handle.

A rectangular slate-topped table dominated the center of the room. Over the middle of the table hung a large glass box that led to a duct, presumably to exhaust the air. An unlit Bunsen burner stood next to the glass box. I glanced at glass-fronted cabinets full of various carefully labeled chemicals and beakers.

I hurried to the desk. Underneath the lamp rested a piece of paper. I pulled it out and eyed the drawing it contained:

"It is the diagram from the notebook!" I copied it down. This time with letters filled in. "A chemical formula. Is this the poison that killed Peter? The poison that filled the rabbit graveyard outside? What do you think, Lars?"

He did not answer.

I turned.

He knelt next to the glass box. His hands worked at a locked drawer.

I hurried over as he unlocked it. "You are very skilled at that, Herr Kommissar."

He pulled the drawer open carefully, as if whatever was inside might explode. It contained only a tiny tightly stoppered glass flask with a brownish liquid in the bottom.

I took it out and held it to the light. I glanced over at the exhaust duct. My blood turned to ice. The exhaust duct could be used to exhaust poisons. I remembered how light-headed I had been and how my eyes had streamed after I was close to Peter while he lay dying. Perhaps the flask contained a poison that worked in liquid and gas form. The German army had shown itself willing to use poison gas in the Great War. Had it developed something even more potent here?

"Take care." Lars put a hand on my arm. "Remember the rabbits."

The door swung open. I slid the flask gently into my dress pocket, hoping that the stopper was as tight as it looked.

Andreas stepped into the laboratory. "Lars? Adelheid? What are you doing here?"

Lars jumped back as if he had been scalded. "I—we—"

Andreas and I stared at him. I hoped Lars had a good lie ready.

"We were in search of a place with—privacy—just for a few moments."

I realized what he intended and flushed scarlet, as he had probably hoped I would.

"The door was open and we—well—we." He reached down with one hand and straightened the front of his pants. Subtle.

I smoothed my dress and came around the table. "I think that may be enough explanation, Lars."

"Or too much." Andreas sounded unconvinced. "What are you doing in the chemistry building at all?"

"I came to apologize. For this morning." I limped toward the door. First we needed to get out of the lab before anyone else caught us. "What I said was inexcusable."

Andreas stepped out of the doorframe. Together we three entered the hall.

After the door closed, Andreas locked it and turned to me. "You broke into that room. Are you with Peter Weill?"

Stunned, I took a stumbling step back. I grabbed for the wall, but it was farther away than I expected. I lost my balance completely and fell.

Glass crunched under my leg. The flask. I pushed myself into a sitting position with a groan. Lars knelt beside me.

Shards of the flask were embedded in my bruise. I lifted my skirt and pulled one out. Blood welled up. I hoped Lars would not revert to his interrogation persona.

"Did you steal something from the laboratory?" asked Andreas.

Then it hit.

Light scalded my eyes. Tears poured out. Saliva filled my mouth. I tried to wipe it off my lips, but my hands shook too much. I vomited.

"Adhelheid?" The voice echoed from far away.

"What did she take?"

"I don't know!" Lars sounded panicked.

"Don't touch her!" Andreas shouted.

Lars held my hands.

Uncontrollable shaking took me. My eyes and nose streamed. What had happened to Peter was happening to me. I was dying. Poor Anton. The path to Boris's door would always be empty. He would wait for months. An Apache brave does not abandon his friends, even when all seems lost.

Lars wiped tears off my face. "Andreas! Do something."

Everything whitened to painful light. Then, mercifully, all went dark.

22

I opened my eyes. My head pounded. The room spun when I tried to sit. I retched.

A nurse stood beside me, a bowl in her hand. "Nice to see you awake. My name is Sister Matilda."

She held a glass of warm water to my lips. The water tasted like steel.

"Your husband will be so pleased. He's been so worried. You are lucky to have him. He's so devoted."

I had no husband. I stared at her, trying to make sense of her words. Lars? Boris? Where was I? I tried to look around, but light stabbed my eyes. I closed them again. How long had I been unconscious? My body ached.

"He hasn't left your side, not even to eat," the nurse prattled on. "We nurses have been sneaking him meals or else he'd probably starve."

"Where?" I croaked.

"Where is he? The doctor insisted he leave this morning for at least an hour." She fiddled with a swastika pinned to her dress.

Swastika. I must be in Germany. I tried to reconstruct my last days. The Olympics. I remembered attending the opening with Lars and Andreas.

"Doctor," I said. "Headache."

"I'll go fetch one. You lie still. You've been through quite a bit."

"What?"

But she flicked open the curtains and left the room without answering.

I struggled upright and headed for the door, hoping to find a bathroom. I wore a diaper. I tried not to think about what that meant.

My side plastered to the wall, I crept forward. My muscles ached as if someone had beaten me all over with a stick. I remembered that I'd had an injured leg before. In comparison to everything else, it felt fine.

I made it to the bathroom, went, and washed. A face the yellow color of old newsprint stared back with bloodshot eyes. What had happened to me?

I began the trek back to bed, sliding along the wall to keep my balance. My head threatened to float off my body.

I had gone barely two steps when someone lifted me off my feet from behind. Lars. I had not thought him strong enough, but I kept that to myself. He was not as pale as I, but he, too, was much paler than usual. Dark circles shadowed his eyes. He did not look as if he had slept in far too long, but he had clearly just bathed, changed clothes, and shaved. His dark hair was still wet.

I relaxed against him.

He set me gently on the bed. "Are you supposed to be walking?"

"Probably not." I reached for the blankets. My arm trembled with exhaustion.

He pulled the blankets over me, tucking them over my arms. "Your name is Hannah Schmidt. Mine is Lars Schmidt. We have been married for twelve years."

"Why?" I tried to concentrate on his words, but they sounded flat, like a voice from a radio turned too low.

"I thought it safest to use our new identities, after I brought you in. And I would not have been allowed to see you if we weren't married."

"Where am I?" I struggled to keep my eyes open. "What happened to me?"

"You don't know?" Worry deepened his voice.

"No." Exhaustion dragged me down before I heard his answer.

When I awoke later, I did not know how much time had passed. Sunlight sifted through drawn curtains. I pushed myself into a sitting position. My head ached, but this time it felt clear.

Lars sat in a chair next to my bed, watching. "Better, Spatz?"

"Lars," I answered, so he would know that I remembered our names. "How long have you been watching me sleep?"

"Approximately eighteen hours."

I winced. "You did not need to."

He rose and held a glass of water to my lips. "It is a small thing."

I drained it. It felt good on my parched throat. "What day is it?"

"Thursday." He glanced at his wristwatch. "Around ten."

Something important was scheduled to happen today, but what? I thought of asking him, but I was not certain that I would have told him. Hopefully it would come to me on its own.

He reached across me and rang the bell for the nurse. "Let's get you some food. You haven't eaten a spoonful since it happened."

"What happened?"

He pulled his chair next to my bed and took my hand. "Lars?"

"Schmidt." He gave a small smile. "Remember?"

"My husband. That much I do remember. But before."

"We went snooping around the university."

I remembered a room with dark tables, a glass box. "The flask broke."

He squeezed my hand. "You dropped like a stone and went into convulsions."

I stared at him.

He drew a ragged breath. "I thought you would die on that floor."

I thought of Peter. "Why did I live?"

"Andreas gave you a shot of some kind of antidote. Then he wiped you off so you wouldn't poison someone else."

Andreas. Had he reported us?

"We carried you to the street." Lars's gaze was far away. "I gave

them false names so I could see you if—" He drew another shuddering breath. "—if you came to."

We sat in silence. The nurse bustled in. "Awake again?"

"Do you think you could find some broth, Sister Matilda?" He gave
her a charming smile. I stared in astonishment.

She blushed. "For you, Herr Schmidt, of course."

She hurried out.

"You have an admirer," I told him.

"Always the wrong ones, isn't it?" He smiled, but his eyes were sad.

I squeezed his hand. I had nothing to say to that.

"Your American hero won another gold," he said. "In the two
hundred meter."

"Did he?" What a lovely thumb in the eye for Goebbels. A Negro
kept trouncing his Aryan champions.

When Lars opened the curtains, the light stung my eyes. I covered
them with my hand.

"Forgive me." He pulled them closed again.

I wiped my eyes on the sheet. The poison was not completely out
of my body. "What happened after I came to the hospital?"

He cleared his throat. "When they let me see you again, you were
unconscious. The doctors feared that you had hit your head when you
fell, causing the convulsions, and perhaps damaged your brain enough
that you might never wake again."

I massaged my temples, shaken. "Yet here I am," I said with forced
cheer. I tried to change the subject. "Did Andreas inform on us?"

"Not yet."

"Will he?"

"I'm not certain. He doesn't know the names I used to check into
the hospital, but he could find us easily enough if he chose."

"Did you say today is Thursday?"

"I did."

"We have to leave." I remembered. Peter's will was to be read at
three. I needed to attend it, to see what he had left for me.

"Let's wait for the doctor, shall we? A few more minutes will make no difference."

"How did Andreas make the connection between Peter Weill and me?"

"That is an interesting conundrum, isn't it?"

My head throbbed. "He knew about the antidote. Perhaps he even developed the poison that almost killed me."

"Perhaps."

I struggled to sit upright. "I must talk to him."

"He said very explicitly that he hoped never to see either of us again." Lars positioned a pillow behind my back.

"We must leave now."

"You are still ill."

"The worst is behind me. After the doctor leaves, let's—"

Sister Matilda returned with a bowl of steaming broth. My stomach rumbled.

"I'll let you help Frau Schmidt eat," she said. "Your doctor should be by soon."

She tossed Lars another flirtatious glance before leaving.

I tried to feed myself, but my hands shook so that I could not hold the bowl. I let Lars hold it to my lips while I drank, as humiliating as that was.

The broth tasted wonderful, rich and salty, and I could have drunk ten bowls. My strength returned with each swallow.

When I drained the last drop, he wiped my chin and swiped the napkin across my nose for good measure. I glared at him.

"You must have been a charming baby," he said. "Easy to feed."

"As soon as I am up and around," I said, "you will regret that comment."

He chuckled. "I look forward to it."

My head pounded, and I felt dizzy. Aftereffects of the poison? "I wish to leave now."

"Not until you are cleared by the doctor," he said.

"You are not responsible for me," I said. "I choose where I go and what I do. And I choose to leave."

"Spatz." His voice was angry and dangerous. "If you think, even for a moment, that I am going to let you—"

"Let?" I swung my legs off the side of the bed. The room spun. I grabbed the basin, but the broth stayed down. I was curiously reminded of the time Lars had interrogated me after my brother's death. Then, too, I had been sick and in the hospital. Then, too, he thought he had ultimate power over me. "You are in no position to *let* me do anything. Do you understand?" I knew I yelled, and I did not care.

He stepped back, surprised. He had never seen me this angry. Dimly, I realized that he was not the true cause of my anger. If only I did not feel so dizzy, I was certain I could have sorted it out.

Sister Matilda bustled in, cap pinned to her head at a sprightly angle, probably for Lars's benefit. I wished I had a lock for that door. I certainly would not give her a key. Keys and locks. Something flitted by the edge of my mind.

Sister Matilda plunked a tray on the stand next to my bed. On the tray rested a bowl of soup, a piece of bread, and a glass of what smelled like old apple juice.

"Please take it away," I said.

"Enough of that." She plumped my pillow as if I had not spoken.

Lars looked at me as if he expected an explosion.

"You must keep calm," said Sister Matilda. "And quiet."

I stood, almost knocking her over. "I am ready to depart this hospital."

"Yelling will get you nowhere." She pushed me back onto the bed with more force than necessary. "First you must eat. Tomorrow morning you can go. I'm certain that Herr Schmidt will take excellent care of you. He's been such an attentive husband."

Lars winced.

She thrust a paper cup of pills into my hand. "Take these."

"What are they?" he asked.

"Pain medication, mostly. Nothing too strong. Everything that is broken has been fixed."

"Then I may leave."

"You must ask the doctor. And your husband."

I stared at her, dumbfounded. "My husband?"

"Of course. He is in charge of you." She put her hands on her hips and glared at me. "If you saw the women I take care of in here. Some of them beaten, too. I bind them up and send them back on the street alone. That's all I can do for them. But you have somewhere to go and someone who loves you. Don't you dare yell at him. Do you have any idea what he has been through?"

He gaped at her. I had never seen him so flummoxed before.

"I—," I started, but she had obviously been saving this, and she would not be stopped.

"You should have seen him when he brought you in. He—"

Lars recovered. He took her arm and marched her out. "Thank you, Sister Matilda, but I believe you've said more than enough."

"I've said no more than my piece. And it needed saying," she called over her shoulder.

I stood shakily. My leg felt much stronger than it had yesterday. It was the only part of my body that did. I lurched over to my suitcase. It rested on a chair mere steps away. I kept one hand out to touch the wall, and though I felt light-headed, I made it.

He closed the door and hurried over. "What are you doing, Spatz?"

"Clothes," I said, slightly out of breath. "Everything that is broken can be fixed. But not without leaving a mark."

"What are you talking about?" He opened the suitcase. He stood next to it, one arm out and ready to catch me. "May I help you?"

"Thank you." I pulled out a dress and undergarments. "I can manage."

The walk back to the bathroom stretched in front of me. I regretted my decision to turn down his help. Foolish pride had its price.

Once there, I washed and dressed. When I opened the door, he stood on the other side.

"Spatz," he said. "Is this wise?"

"First"—I leaned against the wall—"I am sorry for yelling at you."

"No apology is necessary." He put one hand on my lower back, apparently as unconvinced as I that I was not about to pitch forward and collapse. "Please, go back to bed."

I shook my head. "Could you drive me somewhere?"

"You are in no condition to argue." He steered me out of the bathroom.

"Then do not bother." I made my shaky way to the bed and downed the food on the tray. I needed to rebuild my strength. The pills I left untouched. I remembered too well my actions under Frau Doktor Spiegel's opium. I needed to keep my head clear.

He watched. "But, Spatz —"

"Lars," I said. "Don't. Please."

A hard silence rose between us. Finally, he gathered my suitcase, argued us out of the hospital, and brought around the car.

Once in the car, he did not start the engine. "I promised Andreas one thing in exchange for his silence."

Compromise, from Lars? "And?"

"I promised him that we would leave as soon as you were well enough to travel."

"Do you think I am well enough to travel?"

"No."

"Then I do not need to leave."

He stifled a smile. "I gave him my word."

His fingers curled around the steering wheel, and I dropped my hand over them. His hand felt much warmer than mine.

"I must talk to Andreas," I said. "Then I wish to look at a car and say good-bye to someone. After that: Switzerland."

"That's all?" he asked with a smile.

A few minutes later, Lars parked in front of the university and together we hurried across the empty square to Andreas's office. I tried not to think about the last time I had crossed this square, just yesterday, unconscious on a stretcher and not expected to live. Instead, I thought of Andreas. I hoped he was at work. I had thought of calling in advance, but did not want him to bolt.

We encountered no one, which was not surprising since, the university was on holiday. Everyone who could be must be at the Games. What was I missing today? Saber fencing. Yachting and cycle racing. I knew I distracted myself from thinking about my collapse by running through the event schedule, but I did not care. It got me to the office.

Lars knocked on the frosted glass in Andreas's door.

"Come in!" called Andreas. He looked up from between stacks of papers and journals on his desktop, and when he saw us, he seemed to regret his easy welcome.

"Andreas." I nodded to him.

He stood and hurried around his oak desk. He put a warm hand on my forehead. "You are up and around already? How do you feel? Is there any residual dizziness? Pain?"

I could almost see him taking notes. He wanted to know for his research. He probably had never had the chance to talk to a human subject.

"I am fine," I lied. I did not want to help him develop poison.

"Are your eyes more sensitive to light?" His curious brown eyes peered into mine. "There is some redness there. Do you have any muscle soreness?"

"I did not come here to be a research rabbit." I tried to keep distaste from my voice. "I wish to speak with you."

Andreas turned to Lars. "You promised you would not come back—"

"It was my idea," I interrupted.

He kept his eyes on Lars. "Regardless. You both present a risk to me."

"I will answer your questions, if you answer mine," I said. Andreas hesitated. I knew the scientist in him could not resist the chance to talk to someone who had proved his antidote worked. "You can even do an examination."

Andreas's eyes gleamed. "Fine. But only if I can see you alone."

"Under no circumstances," Lars said.

"Of course," I said. "Lars, could you please wait outside?"

His gaze flitted from Andreas to me and back.

"I am not in any danger," I said softly. "Please."

Lars hesitated.

"He saved my life," I reminded him.

Lars nodded once, stiffly. "I will be on the other side of the door. If I knock once, someone is coming. If you need me, call out."

"Thank you," I said.

After the door closed behind him and I could no longer see the dark gray outline of his form through the frosted glass, I turned to Andreas.

He gestured to the chair in front of his desk. "Please, sit."

The old swivel chair squeaked loudly when I sat in it.

"Please describe your experiences since you were exposed." He held his fountain pen poised.

I quickly listed off my reactions and let him examine my eyes and mouth. He took copious notes.

"You were working with Peter Weill," I said when he had finished and returned to the other side of the desk. It would be easier for him to confirm things he thought I already knew.

He studied his hands as they creased and uncreased the corner of a piece of paper. "Yes."

"You supplied him with information about a chemical weapon." I struggled to keep my voice calm and expressionless.

He placed both palms flat on his desk blotter. "I did."

I stifled my sigh of relief. I had been correct. "Was that what poisoned me?"

"If you had not been meddling with things you did not understand—"

"I know," I interrupted. "Thank you for saving my life."

"I wasn't certain the antidote would work." Animation crept into his voice. "It's never worked on the rabbits."

I thought of the crosses in the vacant lot.

"But your exposure was slighter than theirs. The liquid in the flask was impure." His voice rose with his excitement. "And you are a considerably larger organism, so—"

I would provide him no more information to help his research. "Did Peter give you a package for me?"

He raked one hand through his short brown hair. "He did not."

I glanced around at walls lined with bookshelves, volumes stuffed in so tightly, it seemed as if the bookcases might explode. Another stack of papers on the floor next to his desk reached almost to the surface of the desk itself. Finding a particular file might prove impossible without his help.

But I did not think I was searching for something as small as a file. Peter had other sources to smuggle out something a simple as a sheaf of papers. What could I take out that he could not entrust to Bella?

I studied Andreas's nervous face. I could tell that he did not trust me. But once he had. In the stadium, Peter had said that Andreas fancied me. And trust, of course, was the answer. "Are you the package?"

His hands jerked on the blotter.

I waited. I knew he was. I just needed the details.

"Andreas?" I said softly.

He glanced at the closed door before whispering, "I was."

"Why?" That was why he tried to get me alone and away from Lars. It was not about attraction at all. I felt a fool.

He gestured around the office, and the pride in his voice was unmistakable. "What I am doing is amazing. We have leapfrogged all existing battlefield gases in terms of potency and effectiveness."

I kept my face neutral. Now was not the time to lecture him on scientific responsibility. "But?"

"But we shouldn't be developing it. It's against the Treaty of Versailles, against international law."

"Yet you continue to do it?" I asked.

"They'd kill me if I stopped. My only recourse is to leak information about it and get it stopped. I cannot stop it on my own." Andreas leaned forward, his voice urgent. "But the British can, and that's what Peter Weill promised to help me with."

"How did you meet Peter?" I had been puzzling over this since Peter mentioned, back in the stadium, that he knew Andreas.

"I did a series of interviews with him about poisoning," he said. "A sensational trial about ten years ago. Back then he was strongly anti-Nazi. I was pro-Nazi, then."

"Now?"

"Now everyone is pro-Nazi, or pretends to be. The alternative is a camp."

I nodded. "Go on."

"When I realized the significance of my work, I knew that the international community had to be alerted. I hoped that Peter would still be anti-Nazi. If so, I thought he would know someone who could help me get this information out."

"I gather that he also wanted to help you leave Germany. Perhaps during the Games?"

"I have d-decided to stay." His hands clenched and unclenched. He pulled them off the surface of the desk.

"Why?"

"Because I, too, watched Peter die."

I stared at him.

"I was a few steps behind Lars. I was not trying to hide, but it was too noisy to tell him I was there, luckily. After I saw you and Peter on the floor, I ducked behind a pillar until Lars dragged you away."

"Why did you not help Peter?"

"It was only later that I realized what he must have died from. Even if I had known, I had no antidote with me. I did not expect to run into a poison victim. But when I saw him die, I realized that he had been poisoned by my gas. If they killed him, then the Gestapo must also know that Peter had a source that supplied him information about the gas. It's a fairly large team, but if I bolt, they will know that source was me. I doubt I can leave Germany safely, but even if I could, they would hunt me down."

"The British—" I broke off. Could they keep him safe? Would they?

"My colleague, a fellow Project Zephyr scientist, was tortured to death a few days ago. He was suspected of having unpatriotic motives." His eyes remained fixed on his lap, where he had hidden his hands. "I know too much for them to let me go."

"You know too much to stay."

He took a deep breath. I could tell that his decision had already been made. "I will stay."

"But you will do great evil. Your work will be used to kill people. You know people will die, as I almost died." I gestured toward the door. "Not three meters from this chair."

"I also love my country," he said. "I am a German and I will stay in Germany. I know things are wrong here, but I cannot just abandon my country."

"But you are also a human. Surely that transcends nationality."

"Does it?" he asked. "Have you been watching the Games? Every member of that audience belongs to a nation first and humanity second."

I thought of the screaming crowds. Most wore their national costumes and strongly identified with their own athletes. Every day, the stadium contained tens of thousands of people who identified with their nation first and humanity second. "This is more important than athletes on a field."

"Perhaps." His eyes looked over my head at the wall.

"I can get you out," I said. "I have a friend who is very adept at such things." Bella.

"Is it the Jew Peter wanted to use?" His voice crawled over the word *Jew* with disgust.

"A human being, the same as you." I remembered how Peter had referred to me as an Aryan prize in the stadium. Someone Aryan enough for Andreas to trust.

"I won't trust a Jew," Andreas said.

Live a Nazi, die a Nazi. "But I—"

"I don't trust you anymore either."

I looked at the closed door. "Do you trust Lars?"

"Him least of all. How long has he been betraying his country for you?"

We stared at each other. I did not point out that Andreas had betrayed his country, too. Although true, it would only hinder my efforts to get more information.

He would not budge. I sighed. "Can you help me? Can you give me enough to show the British?"

"That," he said, "is what I have been trying to do."

He pulled a simple gray folder from his middle desk drawer. "I am going to leave this on my desk and talk to Lars. When I come back, I expect it to be intact."

"I want a sample, too," I said.

"Too dangerous. You saw what happened to the glass flask you tried to . . . abscond with before."

I pulled my perfume atomizer from my purse, not without a pang. Joy was advertised as the most expensive perfume in the world, and the atomizer was a connection to my happy days with Boris. Andreas would have to pour the perfume down the drain, just as I had done with the relationship. I sighed. "It does not leak. It is difficult to break. And it will arouse no suspicion."

He took the mother-of-pearl cylinder and left. I closed the door behind him and clicked the lock.

I pulled out my camera and carefully photographed each page in the file. So, this was what Peter had been murdered for. I felt a deep sense of satisfaction that I could now write his final story.

I stopped when I reached a page listing the original project scientists. Frau Professor Müller's name was listed. I photographed that page and moved on to the next.

All the pages rested safely in the folder when Andreas knocked.

I opened the door and he stepped in, closing it between us and a very irritated-looking Lars. Andreas brought with him the complicated floral fragrance of Joy, so he had at least opened the atomizer.

He slipped the cool cylinder into my palm. "Be very careful with that. It is terribly dangerous."

"I know." I stuck it into my satchel with the camera. "Believe me, I know."

Had he really put a sample in the atomizer? Or would whoever examined it find only very expensive perfume? I had no way to test without exposing myself to death. I had no choice but to trust him. And I did not.

"Thank you," I said.

In his hands he held a syringe full of a clear liquid.

I stepped back. "What is in there?"

"Saline," he said. He depressed the plunger, and liquid squirted into the air and landed in a thin trail on the floor. "If Lars asks, please tell him that I went to the lab to mix you another shot of the antidote."

"I will."

"Get what I have given you out safely." He put down the syringe and took my hand in both of his. "If the British see it and understand it, they can stop it. They know that this kind of work is forbidden by the Treaty of Versailles. The British are the only ones who can step in. They can fix this and set Germany on the right track again."

I wondered if he tried to persuade me or himself. "It would be more convincing if you delivered it yourself," I said.

He dropped my hands. "That I cannot do. My mind is set. I have done what I can to help change Germany's direction."

"Then I thank you for all that you have given me, and we will have to hope that it is enough." Pressing my point would only anger him, and I might have need of him in the future.

He put one hand on my shoulder. I smelled his tar soap. "Do not trust Lars," he said.

A chill ran down my spine. Too late. I had already trusted Lars.

"I do not know all the places where his allegiance lies, but he is more complicated and dangerous than you know."

I swallowed, wondering what other dangerous secrets Lars kept. I answered slowly, "I will take care."

"I hope so."

He returned to his desk and sat down. We said our good-byes and I joined Lars in the hall.

Lars waited until we were safely out of the building and in the middle of the square, where we could not be overheard, before speaking. "Well?"

"He questioned me about the effects of the gas," I said.

"That should not have taken that long, plus a trip to the laboratory."

"He had to get a second dose of the antidote."

"You needed another one?"

I shrugged. "Andreas felt I did, and he knows more about what I was exposed to than anyone."

I felt guilty lying to him, but I also had to keep Andreas's confidences. "We have only one more stop. And then I will follow your long-standing advice and go to Switzerland." I relaxed as I said it. I was almost ready to go home.

"Your carriage awaits."

I gave him von Eulenhaus's address and rested my head against the back of the seat while he drove. I felt exhausted, but I sat up to watch a trio of Chinese women in brightly colored cheongsams cross in front of our car. In front of them walked Chinese men in well-tailored Western-style suits.

Lars parked in front of a grand office building. Here, too, Nazi flags hung from the roof. Weariness weighed on my heart at the sight. "We are here, Spatz."

I shifted to look at him. Soon, I could leave.

"Why are we here?" Lars gestured to the stone building.

I hesitated before I answered. But he already knew everything. It was too late to hold things back. "I am attending the reading of Peter Weill's will as Hannah Vogel." And to check a car.

"Who knows you will be there?" Lars turned off the ignition and studied me.

"Only the lawyer, and if Peter trusted him, I trust him."

Lars looked like he was trying to marshal a convincing argument.

"Lars, I know it is dangerous, but if Peter left me some kind of message, this might be the only way I will ever know. I have been through a great deal to find this out. In an hour, I will be finished."

Lars drummed his fingers against the steering wheel. "I don't like it."

"I can meet you somewhere after. There is no reason for you to go with me."

"There are many reasons," he said. "If you go in there, I will as well."

"I intend to attend the reading. You may make your own decision."

"How kind of you," he said. "To grant me free will."

I smiled at him. "After this, we will leave."

"No matter what the lawyer has to say? We leave for Switzerland?"

"Yes."

"Your word?" He held out his hand.

I shook it. "I promise."

He hurried to help me out of the car. I stopped in front of the office building and looked up at the arched windows. Hopefully someone up there knew more about Peter's secret than I.

Lars held the office door open and pressed the button to call the ancient elevator. We rode the creaky lift to the third floor. When it lurched upward, I fell against Lars. I felt stronger than I had in the hospital, but my legs wobbled.

The lift doors opened directly into a room with a grand desk next to a large arched window. Tall oak doors on both sides of the room were closed. The lawyers must have owned the entire floor. A handsome secretary opened one of the doors, led us down a dark-paneled hall, and ushered us into a room at the end: Herr Doktor von Eulenhaus's office.

Herr Doktor von Eulenhaus himself sat behind an old rococo desk. His gray hair was carefully parted in the middle; his high collar had been the height of fashion thirty years before. In precise High German, he introduced himself. I felt uneducated before I even opened my mouth, probably a reaction he strove to cultivate. He gestured to the chairs and we perched in the first two of a row of six. I sipped the strong, sweet tea his secretary had provided and waited for others to arrive.

Panzer was first. He looked shocked to see me. "Sisterlein!"

I rose, and we embraced stiffly. "Panzer."

Lars cleared his throat. I introduced them, omitting Lars's SS title.

Still, Panzer eyed him suspiciously before sitting. He leaned over. "Are you well?"

"It is nothing contagious." I lifted my hand to push my hair behind my ears. Panzer's eyes lingered on my wedding ring. I had forgotten I wore it. His gaze dropped to Lars's hand.

His eyes widened. "Hannah—"

Bella entered, a lanky aristocrat trailing her. He wore an oyster gray three-piece suit and a monocle.

"Hannah!" When she wrapped her perfumed arms around me, she whispered in my ear. "You look terrible."

She sat and introductions were performed all around. Her escort was named von something, nobility, but I forgot his name instantly.

The lawyer brought more tea and petits fours. I ate two, plus two from Lars's plate. I had to get something in my body to get through this.

The lawyer nattered on about the will, and my attention wandered. I drifted off to sleep.

"To my dear friend and colleague," von Eulenhaus said loudly. I jerked awake and ignored Lars's nervous look. "Fräulein Hannah Vogel." The lawyer enunciated each syllable as carefully as if he were auditioning for a movie role. "I leave my fedora and my antique fountain pen. May she use them both to find good stories. Also ten marks to buy red roses. She'll know why."

Red roses, as clichéd as they were, were Peter's favorite flower. I wiped my eyes with my handkerchief. The lawyer pushed a box toward me.

I opened it and took out the pen and fedora. I stroked the soft brim, remembering the way Peter always mashed it on his head as if he did not care how he looked, but how it always sat at exactly the right jaunty angle. I wondered if he had practiced it in front of a mirror as young man. I put it into my satchel and dropped the pen in after, thinking of the words it had written. The words it might still write.

The lawyer continued in his precise voice, "To my son, Peter Weill Jr., I leave my two-cent Hawaiian missionary stamp. A representative of my lawyer's office can take him to the appropriate bank to fetch it when he so desires."

So, the stamp was never in Peter's apartment. Had the killer come in, found the empty box, and tried to force Theresa to tell him the location?

Panzer pulled a silver flask from his inside pocket, held it up to me as if in a toast, and drank a large slug. I recognized the flask, of course. With its geometric design and monogramming, it was hard to mistake. I had last seen it on the floor at the stadium, next to his father's body. It had been listed in Peter's personal effects, but it disappeared before I arrived at Theresa's apartment. I remembered Panzer telling me that he had not been there for a long time when I met him on the afternoon of Theresa's death.

A lie.

He must have taken the flask from his aunt's apartment. He had a key, after all. He had unlocked the door when I was there. Only the chain had kept him out. He must have been there the morning Theresa was murdered and taken the flask. Probably smashed the stamp box while searching for it, little knowing that it would soon be his.

Blood pounded in my ears. I did not look at him. I did not need to. My mind filled the outline of his burly form into the driver's seat of the car that struck me.

I had to see his car. Now. Perhaps it had evidence that Panzer had tried to run me down.

"Excuse me." I stood abruptly and limped to the door. "I feel unwell."

Lars followed.

"Stay," I whispered. "Keep an eye on Panzer. Do not let him leave."

Lars gave me a baffled look but turned back.

I closed the door, hurried down the hall, and nodded to the curious receptionist. There were many Peter Weills in the newspaper business, but only two in real life. I had not used Panzer's given name in so many years, I had forgotten that he carried the same name as his father. It had been his name on the gambling debts at Jack Ford's.

I took the elevator to the first floor, slightly dizzy, but faring better than I expected. Parked a few meters from Lars's car was a wine red Opel Olympia. I ran my hand over the chrome metal hood ornament. The zeppelin looked new, and a dimple and scratch in the paint next to it seemed to confirm my suspicions. Did the scratch show where the zeppelin had been wrenched off by my satchel?

I looked in the window. On the passenger seat rested a pile of blue composition books, ready for correction. On the front of each was written HERR PROFESSOR P WEILL. I froze, remembering the Olympia full of composition books I had almost walked into as I left Theresa's apartment the morning I met Panzer. That had been Panzer's car.

Had he killed his father because Peter would not give him the stamp? Had Panzer poisoned his father with something in the flask from which he himself now drank? Had he used whatever was in the vial that I broke in front of the laboratory? A new poison would probably be undetectable in a blood test. His onetime girlfriend, Frau Professor Müller, had once worked on the project. It was not much of a leap to imagine that she still had a key to the laboratory. But his own father?

They had a falling out, but I could not, did not want to, believe he would murder his father. And what of Theresa? Had he strangled her and lifted his father's silver flask from the box of personal effects? Panzer? Why kill Theresa? Had he thought she was next in line to inherit the stamp?

If he had done all that, running me down would have been easy. But why kill me? Perhaps he thought that Peter had left me the stamp.

Or perhaps he thought his father suspected Panzer might do just such a thing and had told me so before he died? Perhaps Panzer had always hated me. It was all supposition. The scratch could have come from anything. But its presence was at least a giant coincidence, and Peter had always told me not to believe in coincidences. Panzer had run me down and left me to die. My Brüderchen.

I would see to it that he did not profit from Peter and Theresa's deaths, that he paid his debts. All of them. I rose stiffly and returned to the lawyer's office. The elevator operator pressed the button for my floor with the same stolid expression he had worn a minute before. Only my world had shifted. My "brother" had tried to kill me.

The handsome secretary allowed me to place a call from the telephone on his desk. I rattled off the number from memory. I turned my back on the secretary and instead stared out the window, down at the street below. From here, I could not see the scratch in Panzer's hood.

"Ford's," said a husky female voice.

"Agnes. Peter."

The secretary picked up a handful of folders and left the room. Discretion. A valuable trait. But so was eavesdropping. I would need to keep my voice down.

"Darling," Agnes said. "Whatever can I do for you?"

"When last we spoke, we discussed a certain person." Agnes would not need a name.

"Yes?"

"I believe that the person you are interested in is the son, not the father."

"I had gathered that myself. We are searching for him."

"He is with me. We are only blocks away. I believe he has come into money and can settle his accounts." I gave her the address of the lawyer's office. What Panzer had sown, he would reap.

"Stall," she said. "I will send men right round."

"I have a package for you as well."

"How much?"

Down on the street, a large black car parked in front of Lars's. Out stepped Bauer.

I drew back from the window, heart pounding.

"Peter, are you there?"

"Only just," I said. "Something has come up. You must also stop by in person for your package. And now it is on the house."

I hung up on her protest. I looked into my satchel, wishing I had Ernst Röhm's old Luger in it. But I had not dared to bring it from Switzerland. I took out the passports Herr Silbert had made, and my purse-sized atomizer. The atomizer I slipped into my pocket. It was the closest thing to a weapon that I had. But it was as likely to kill me as someone else.

I picked an envelope off the desk and dropped in all three pass-ports. If Lars and I managed to escape the Gestapo interrogation alive, we would need these identities to remain secret. I wrote Agnes a quick note and tucked it into her passport.

The secretary returned as I sealed it.

I handed him the envelope and my satchel. "Please give both of these items to a dwarf named Agnes Johansson. She should be here shortly."

"As you wish." He took the envelope and shut it in his drawer as if he received similar instructions every day. Perhaps he did.

"It is most urgent."

"Of course." His expression was bland.

I ran back to the door to the lawyer's office.

"Lars," I called from the doorway, not concerned with etiquette. Everyone's head whipped around.

He rushed over. Behind him, Bella watched.

"We must go," I told him in a low voice.

But when we stepped into the hall, I saw Bauer and Sturmbann-führer Hahn through the open door near the secretary's room. I stepped back inside von Eulenhaus's office and closed the door, but not before Lars saw them, too.

We sprinted to the window. Bella stared curiously, well-bred reticence no match for our strange behavior.

The window opened onto a three-story drop.

We were well and truly trapped. I read it in his face, and he in mine.

He pulled me into an embrace.

"I am sorry," I said into his chest.

He shook his head. "Not your fault."

Bauer must have known about the reading of the will. He had known that Hannah Vogel was Peter Weill and gambled that he would find me here. I cursed my need to know the truth, and my need to have revenge on Panzer.

"Ahem," the lawyer said. "May I finish?"

We stepped apart. The door banged open. Lars and I alone did not jump.

"Hauptsturmführer Lang, Fräulein Vogel, you must come with me." Hahn's smooth voice was insistent. I wished I had slapped him good and hard on the dance floor when I had the chance. Although he would have paid me back in full now.

Lars watched Hahn with calculating eyes. I suspected Lars would attack him.

Hahn must have thought so, too. He drew a Luger and pointed it at my chest. "Care to try your chances on getting to me before a bullet goes through her heart?"

Bella gasped. Hahn and Lars ignored her.

"Lace your hands behind your head," Hahn said. "You both know the procedure. Then stay still."

Lars and I raised our hands. In his eyes, I saw his mind working furiously. I hoped he was thinking up a way for us to get out of this alive. Unfortunately, my mind seemed to be detaching itself from everything in the room. I swayed on my injured leg, but kept my balance.

Bauer pushed into the room. In the split second that Hahn's eyes shifted to him, Lars stepped between us and sprang at Hahn.

Hahn's arm arced through the air. He brought the Luger down on Lars's head with a thud.

Bella screamed.

I ignored Hahn's orders to stay still and dropped to my knees next to Lars. I touched the back of his head. My fingers came back covered in blood. When I rolled him over, his eyes were closed. I felt for his pulse. Still there. That was something.

Bauer hauled me up, handcuffing both hands in front of me. Hahn handcuffed Lars, and Bauer slung his limp body over his shoulder like a sack. We stepped into the hall, walked down to the reception area, and crossed the room to the lift.

The lift doors slid open. Four hired muscles towered over Agnes. She wore a white dress that draped in the style of a toga.

Her copper-colored eyes flicked past with no sign of recognition. No point in starting a fight she was uncertain she could win. I knew it. I understood it, and I did not turn my head. I had caused enough trouble for Lars. I had no desire to add Agnes to my list of victims.

She and her men marched off the elevator and toward the open office door. Panzer ducked back into von Eulenhaus's office. I did not think that would fool her, and I hoped it would not slow her down.

We crowded into the elevator. The operator acted exactly as if we were ordinary clients, not an unconscious bleeding man, a hulking thug, an angry-looking SS officer, and a strangely calm small blonde.

Two more men waited at the car, probably left there to intercept me if I had tried to run before Hahn reached me. One hurled Lars into the backseat. He landed hard, and I winced. They stuffed me in next to him. One thug climbed into the back, with me smashed between him and an unconscious Lars. It reminded me of when Ernst Röhm's flunkies had kidnapped me two years before. But then I had been with Anton. As bad as this situation was, it was definitely better than that. My son was safe in Switzerland. Bella might find a way to tell him what had happened to me, so that he would not have to wonder.

Hahn, Bauer, and the other thug took the front seat.

I flexed my fingers. The handcuffs bit into my wrists, my hands already asleep, but I knew better than to complain.

We drove away from the lawyer's office, but not toward the Gestapo headquarters on Prinz-Albrecht-Strasse. I had suspected that Hahn would take us elsewhere.

"Where are we going?" I asked Bauer. He gave me a guilty look but no answer. "Not what you expected, Sergeant Bauer?"

His head jerked to the side, but he said nothing. Buildings flashed by too quickly. I smiled bitterly at the Olympic flags and decorations on the street. Life in Berlin was not a game.

"Sturmbannführer Hahn, would you be so kind as to inform me of our destination?"

He turned to face me with an amused smile. "Why?"

"When I saw the Gestapo badges, I assumed that we were going to your office, although for reasons I cannot fathom. Unless it is because you did not care for my behavior on the dance floor." I smiled back.

He slid the back of one finger along the pink dueling scar on his cheek. "Your spirited performance was charming. It has nothing to do with the reasons you are in this car."

"Indeed? Then where are we going?" The automobile careened forward at an unsafe speed. Perhaps a fatal accident would save me a great deal of pain and suffering.

I suspected the answer before I asked the question, but I wanted to see his reaction. "Prinz-Albrecht-Strasse?"

"Not quite yet," he said. "We have a stop to make first. If it's necessary after, you may enjoy SS hospitality."

The way he said it told me that our stop, wherever it was, was more unpleasant than SS headquarters. I should be terrified, but felt nothing. Like opium, but without euphoria.

"You wish to keep our arrests secret?" I asked.

"Why would I do that?"

"Because," I said, "you do not wish anyone to know what you think we will reveal."

He chuckled. "Always too smart for your own good, weren't you, Fräulein Vogel?"

"It is no help to me in this instance, is it?"

"Indeed not."

He drew a silver flask from his pocket. An elaborate art nouveau design and the initials *PW* were engraved on the side. I fought to keep my face expressionless. Peter's flask. Hahn had switched flasks in the stadium. Hahn had murdered Peter.

I had turned Panzer in to Agnes for a crime he had not committed.

"Familiar?" Hahn asked.

I shook my head. Had he killed Theresa as well?

"I'm confident that you will remember." He ran his eyes from the crown of my head down to my breasts and he shifted in his seat, excited. "After suitable persuasion has been applied."

I closed my eyes. He intended to torture us, then kill us, without an arrest. He did not want it revealed that his own subordinate had betrayed him, as he must suspect Lars had done. He would tidy up this unfortunate mess in his own way.

I did not think we would enjoy it.

23

The car rolled to a stop next to an empty warehouse. Far from houses. Far from anyone who might hear us scream. Not that anyone in the Third Reich was curious enough about screams to act on them anymore.

I brushed the fingers of my cuffed hands across the back of Lars's head. It must have hurt, but he lay inert. The bleeding had slowed. Blood matted his hair. Was there also internal bleeding? I could not tell. I hoped his skull was not broken. Though, if he was lucky, Hahn had done him enough damage to spare him the ordeal ahead.

The thugs hauled us out. I concealed my limp as best I could. No point in revealing yet another weakness to Hahn. When we reached the door, I stumbled sideways, smearing my bloody hands across a nearby glass window. I had marked it, just as Moses told the Hebrews to mark their doors in blood. Perhaps I, too, would be saved.

Bauer half carried me over the threshold and inside. Two battered wooden chairs faced each other in the middle of the otherwise empty warehouse. Bauer sat me in one with surprising gentleness. One of his companions slung Lars into the other and held him there. His head drooped sideways. He looked dead.

"I think he is the weaker of the two." Hahn pointed to Lars. "Fetch me water."

I took in our surroundings. Dirty windows in the front of the building opened onto brown grass and nettles. The room stretched out on either side of us. On the concrete floor, I noticed overlapping red brown stains that I suspected were old blood. Judging by the size of the stains, the unfortunates who had bled there had not left the building alive.

Bauer returned with a rusty bucket of water. Hahn sluiced it over Lars's head. Lars sputtered and sat up on his own. I groaned inwardly. He had awoken after all.

Lars raised his head to glare at Hahn.

Hahn stood between us. Lars did not look at me. He had eyes only for Hahn.

"You know what I used to like about you, Lang?" Hahn stroked the back of his finger across the dueling scar again.

"You are a fool, Dirk," Lars said. "But I expect you are accustomed to hearing that."

"You had no vices."

Bauer stood on one side of Lars, Hahn on the other. The other two men stood on either side of me.

I glanced out the windows that ran along the sides of the warehouse. No sign of life outside, not even a cat. We would die alone. Hahn would make certain we did not leave this room alive, no matter what we said or did.

"And yet," Hahn's voice dripped venom, "like all good men, you found yourself one." He turned sideways and pointed at me. "Her."

Lars did not look at me. Good. This would be easier for him if he did not.

Hahn stepped forward and struck Lars's face. A sound like the breaking of a wet stick cracked across the room. Lars's nose. I bowed my head toward my lap, swallowing nausea.

The man next to me used a fistful of hair to yank my head upright. Bauer flinched, obviously not yet used to Gestapo techniques. "Watch," growled the man with his fist in my hair.

Blood spilled down Lars's face.

I closed my eyes. I did not see the next blows land, but I heard them. Lars groaned. I opened my eyes again.

"I didn't hit your eyes," Hahn said, "because you'll need those."

Lars spat blood onto Hahn's highly polished boot. "You will regret this, Dirk."

Hahn stared at his boot with distaste. "I will need names. And dates of everyone involved. What you did. Why you did it."

"You won't like it—"

"You are an interrogator, you know how this goes." Hahn spoke low and pleasant. "One of the best, in fact. Especially with women."

Fear flickered across Lars's face. Hahn saw it, too. We were lost. Hahn smiled and watched Lars, savoring the moment.

Hahn stepped behind me and yanked me up by my hair. I concentrated on not yelping. He would enjoy that too much. I wished I could get to the atomizer without being seen, but with my numbed hands cuffed together, I did not think I could operate it.

Hahn's grip on my scalp held me so high that I balanced on tiptoes.

"You know how this goes, don't you, Lang?"

Lars would not look at him. He kept his eyes on mine, and every second was an apology. As if this were his fault.

"Usually," Hahn said easily. "Usually, I rape her first, then you get the information for me."

Lars sucked in a deep breath.

Bauer paled. Good. Whatever happened, I hoped he remembered it forever. I gave him a pleading look. He looked away. He could not help us without risking his own life. We all knew that.

"Shall we skip that first step?" Hahn ran the Luger's barrel from my throat across my breasts, down my stomach, and stopped it on my crotch. The metal felt cold, even through my dress. "It's my favorite part."

Lars raised his head and nodded to Hahn. "You think you have won, of course. But you have lost."

My voice returned. "He will do what he wants to us after you tell him, Lars. You will save nothing."

His eyes met mine. "I know."

Hahn released my hair. I sprawled facefirst on the floor, bringing my cuffed hands up at the last second to protect my face. My forearms scraped painfully against the concrete.

Hahn knelt and undid my handcuffs. I stared in surprise.

He whispered in my ear. "I'm not letting you go, my dear. I like to let the men hold your arms. It makes them feel as if they're participating."

I rolled onto my side and rubbed my wrists. Blood rushed painfully back into my hands. I pretended I had not heard him, but I was so frightened that I feared to try standing.

"Uncuff me, Dirk," Lars said. "Contact Obersturmbannführer Richter. She is mine. And you are not to touch her."

Hahn put one boot on my back as if I were a hunting trophy. And I suppose, to him, I was.

"I am tired of cleaning up your messes, so I'll explain this only once," Lars's voice sounded more angry than worried.

Hahn laughed. "Names. Or first me, then Bauer." He gestured to the two men near my chair. "You two can flip a coin for the third spot."

"Technically," Lars said, "I was there first, wasn't I? So you would be second."

I jerked my head up. Lars ignored me.

"I will give you names," Lars continued. "You won't like them."

I wriggled out from under Hahn's boot and painfully hauled myself to a sitting position. *Do not shake,* I told myself. *Count. Breathe. Think about Switzerland.*

Lake Zürich. Silver water sliding by the wooden hull.

I remembered my last sailing trip. June. Boris and I sat in the prow. He'd taken off his shirt, and his skin was already browning.

"Ahoy!" shouted Anton from the back of the boat. He had the tiller. I did not turn to look at him, afraid to bring him into the warehouse.

Boris pulled me over against him. "Straight on!" he called back to Anton.

I melted against Boris's sun-warmed chest.

Lars's voice broke into my recollection. "Everything you force me to divulge in front of civilians will weigh heavily against you with Obersturmbannführer Richter."

I was back in the warehouse, sitting on the bloodstained concrete. Mercifully, Anton and Boris were far away. That life was gone, and soon they would be alone. I shook my head. *Do not think about Anton watching the path you will never walk down*, I told myself. *You must keep him out of this room. That alone is what remains.*

Lars leaned his head toward the man next to him. "Send him to a telephone to call Obersturmbannführer Richter, unless you want to die in worse pain than you have planned for me."

Hahn glanced over at the thug next to Lars. "What should he verify?"

I slipped one hand into my pocket. My fingertips stroked the silver mother-of-pearl.

"It's on your head, Dirk. You have left me no choice." Lars looked down at me. His dark eyes were cold, the eyes I remembered from his office five years before, when he was a policeman disparaging Jews. I looked down at my lap.

"I have been running a misinformation campaign for the past two years," Lars said. "In 1934, I was ordered to recruit Adhelheid Zinsli, Swiss reporter, when we had her in custody. I was to use her to bring false intelligence to the British. I had informed Obersturmbannführer Richter of her identity as Hannah Vogel, and her ability to elude us before. As you may recall, Dirk, he was my commanding officer at that time."

"I knew nothing of this," Hahn said. I sensed that he was beginning to worry. And he was not the only one. I remembered Richter, the pudgy man from the party who had said he had been waiting for years to meet me.

"Of course not," Lars sneered. "You can't run an operation. Especially not with women involved. I, however, as you so kindly said, can get them to do what I need."

I hung my head, hoping he would not see my fear. If he told the truth, I had been the worst kind of fool. I had done everything he wanted. If he had used me all this time, he might know enough to find Boris. To find Anton.

Hahn nodded to the man next to Lars. "Go check out his story."

The man saluted and left the warehouse. That left us three to two, assuming Lars was lying and was still on my side. Otherwise, it was four to one. Wilhelm, Herr Silbert, and even his friend Andreas had warned me not to trust Lars.

I heard a thud by the door. Lars spoke loudly, as if to cover the sound. "Uncuff me, Dirk. You are in more than enough difficulty already."

Surprisingly, Hahn did.

"We'll wait for confirmation," Hahn said. "And please try nothing that would cause me to use force on you."

"Hardly," Lars said. "I know how you enjoy it. That's your problem, Dirk. You lose perspective."

"Tell me what she knows about Project Zephyr."

"Little," Lars said. "I have kept very close to her since she started to investigate it. Like a guard dog. But it was useful to see what she could find and how she could find it. A loyalty test of the men on the project."

I scraped my palm hard against the rough floor to keep myself from slipping away. I had to stay alert. Had Lars really shown me Peter's file to see what I could dig up? To see who might betray the Reich for me? Poor Andreas. Lars did not see what he gave me, but he knew that I had visited him, sat in his office unchaperoned. More than enough to sign his death warrant. Andreas had told me to question where Lars's loyalties lay. And I had not. Andreas would die because of my mistake. Herr Silbert as well, and possibly Agnes. Remorse, thicker than fear, gagged me.

"If she had uncovered anything significant, I would have had to terminate her, as I imagine you did with the crazy old man and his criminal sister." Lars's matter-of-fact voice frightened me more than his words.

Out of the corner of my eye, I saw Hahn nod. "They knew details," he said. "That could not be tolerated."

Hahn had murdered them.

So Panzer must have come while Theresa was alive, taken the flask, and left. He had probably ransacked the apartment and broken the stamp box. When he heard that Theresa had died, perhaps been murdered, he had probably lied to distance himself from the scene of the crime. But he had killed no one. And I had turned him in to Agnes, perhaps to his death from Jack Ford's thugs. At least I would not have to live with my guilt for long.

But who had hit me with the car? Had that been Panzer, drunk and angry that I was his father's favorite, or Hahn? I thought of the scratch in Panzer's hood. But still, I did not know for certain. Lars, too, drove a dark-colored Opel Olympia, and he had just said that he had no compunctions about killing me.

"There can be no loose ends," Lars said. "That must be perfectly clear."

A shadow flicked across the window behind his head.

"What about her?" Hahn pointed his empty hand at me.

"You've made certain that she is useless to me now, haven't you?" Lars massaged his wrists savagely. "I will finish up with her and turn her over to Obersturmbannführer Richter. I imagine he'll send what's left of her to the camps."

I turned the atomizer top one quarter turn counterclockwise in my pocket. The piston opened.

"If she is useless to you," Hahn said. "Why can't I do what I wish with her?"

Hahn knelt next to me.

"I think we could be great friends," he said, echoing his words on the dance floor. The Luger's cold barrel brushed my cheek. "For a time."

I summoned the last drops of saliva in my mouth and spat on him.

Hahn slammed his body forward on top of mine. The back of my head struck the concrete so hard, I saw flashes of white light. Hahn was so heavy that I could scarcely breathe.

Lars jumped from his seat. The guns in the room swiveled toward him, including Hahn's.

We were dead now. I brought the atomizer to within a centimeter of Hahn's face and pumped. Liquid shot into his eyes. He yelped and yanked himself away from me. I darted to the side, hoping that not a single drop fell on me.

Hahn convulsed on the floor, already hit by the effects of the liquid. Andreas had filled it with poison after all.

The room erupted in gunfire. Lars threw his body across mine, flattening me on the hard floor again. He wrapped his arms tightly around my head. Warm blood trickled down the back of my neck.

After what felt like an eternity, but was only a minute later, a husky voice called, "Stop!"

I inhaled the smell of sulfur. Gunpowder. I struggled to move.

Hands pulled Lars off my back and turned me over. I stared into an unfamiliar lumpy face. "Paycheck's alive," it said.

The face belonged to a man who lifted me like a doll and set me on my feet. Lars stood on shaky legs. Alive. Relief flooded through me. But should I be relieved or terrified?

I turned slowly.

The third man lay on his stomach. Blood pooling under him told me that he was not going anywhere, but one of the standing men walked to him, patted him down for weapons, and checked for his pulse.

Bauer lay spread-eagled. His surprised eyes stared at the ceiling. I guessed he would not remember the events of today as long as I had thought. He had not seemed a bad sort. I wondered who waited at home for him. Did he have a wife? Children? I turned away, trying not to feel anything.

Hahn lay motionless on the floor, face as red as Peter's had been, body torn by bullet holes. I had killed him. Even if a bullet had ended his life, he was dead the minute I sprayed him. Should I not feel satisfaction at having killed such a monster? Mostly I felt sadness, and guilt.

Without taking my eyes off Hahn, I saw Lars bend to retrieve my atomizer. Touching it only with a handkerchief, he carefully closed it. He wiped down the mother-of-pearl and dropped the handkerchief on the floor. Then he slipped the atomizer into his pocket.

Lars turned to the man who had helped me up. "The one who left?"

"Taken care of," he grunted.

Lars took my shoulders and turned me from Hahn's corpse.

Fashionable heels crunched across broken glass. Our rescuer. A small hand held the note I had left for her. I remembered each word: *Please follow. Name your price. Bring the car. Put the satchel in the backseat.*

"Hello, my dear," she said.

My brain felt smothered in cotton wool. "Thank you, Agnes," I finally managed.

"You haven't heard the price yet," she said.

Lars looked between us. "You had a plan?"

"I had a hope," I said. "But it sounded as if you were never in any danger."

He shrugged and winced. "I was trying to talk us out of here."

I must have looked unconvinced, because he said, "I'd break more than your arm to save your life."

I remembered him threatening to break my arm when he yanked me away from Peter at the stadium. He had saved my life with his actions then. But he had also saved his own.

Agnes raised one hand, and her men hurried over. "Enough fun. Even here, that much gunplay might arouse suspicion."

"Agnes," I said. "What did you do with Panzer?"

"Panzer?"

"Peter Weill, Jr.?"

"He gave me an item valuable enough to cancel his debt, and I let him go."

At least he, too, had not been harmed because of my actions.

Lars turned his back on me and brought both hands to his face. A wet crack, a loud curse, and more blood spattered onto the floor.

My stomach heaved. One of Agnes's men gave Lars a look of grudging respect.

"Straighter?" Lars asked him. The man studied Lars's nose before nodding.

He turned to me. "What do you think, Spatz?"

"You look terrible."

His smile revealed blood on his teeth. "How odd. You have never looked better."

Agnes hurried us out of the warehouse. Lars's car was parked behind a lorry.

She nodded to the lumpy-faced man. He sat in the front of Lars's car. We got in the back. Agnes and the other three men got into the lorry.

I stared straight ahead. I knew I should watch where we were going, but my eyes could not focus. All they saw was Hahn's face. Even when I closed them.

24

The car rolled to a stop in front of a dilapidated apartment building near the Spree River. Scaffolding covered the front, but no workmen hammered there this late afternoon. Had they been let go to attend the Games, or had Agnes made calls of her own? My satchel rested on the floor of the backseat. I opened it and checked that the camera containing the pictures of Andreas's file was there. As were our passports.

Agnes's lorry pulled in behind. Two of her men walked us up the stairs, carrying our suitcases and my satchel. The interior reminded me of my old Berlin apartment: a kitchen, a door that probably led to a bedroom, and, hopefully, a bath. The kitchen was bare of furniture.

Agnes spread a piece of paper against the wall. She wrote on it with a stub of yellow pencil and handed it to me.

I stared at the list of numbers.

"The first is for my account at Credit Suisse Bank. I imagine you are familiar with the bank."

"I am."

"The second is our fee."

I would have to sell more of my brother's jewelry. "Understood."

She dropped Lars's keys into my hand. "You can stay here through the end of the Games."

"Thank you," I said fervently. "I owe you."

"Don't thank me. Just pay me." But her eyes twinkled as she turned toward the door. She crooked a finger, and the large men lumbered after her.

I crossed to the window and watched them drive away. My leg throbbed. So much evil had been done today. If I had been more cautious, the men in the warehouse would be alive.

"Spatz?" said Lars.

I jumped.

"I'm sorry to have startled you. Is it safe here?"

"Safe for you or safe for me?" I tried to make myself think.

"Nothing I said to Hahn was true." His voice was matter-of-fact. "But nothing I can say to you now will convince you of that."

I turned and looked at him. Had he saved my life countless times only because he thought I would be a valuable tool against the British? Or because he was not a Nazi?

His lips turned down. "You are afraid of me."

"Yes." Although, in fact, I was not afraid of him. And that trust frightened me. Because I knew I should be terrified.

"I have done many things I am not proud of," he said quietly, "but I have never betrayed you."

Simple and to the point. But true? Just as he had told Hahn, he recruited me from that Gestapo meeting in 1934. I myself had told him that I did not read the documents he photographed. Even if I had, I had no way to know if the documents were real or fake. His story of a misinformation campaign made a horrible kind of sense. But of course, it would have to, to convince Hahn.

His dark eyes studied me. I yearned to trust him. But I heard the careless tone of his voice when he had talked of sending me to the camps.

I crossed the room and picked up my satchel.

"In the end, you must decide for yourself." He smiled. The cut on his lip opened again. "As you always do."

I stared at him, torn. I did not know what to do. I pulled out his Lars Schmidt passport and handed it to him. He took it.

"Then—" He cleared his throat. "—perhaps it is time for Hannah and Lars Schmidt to go their separate ways. Can you get yourself back to Switzerland?"

"Of course." I took a deep breath and kept my face calm. "You?"

"I intend to go to Saratova, once I look a bit more presentable. I would like to put together the final pieces of the Project Zephyr puzzle." He took a deep breath and winced. "Could you see if my ribs are broken?"

He, of course, knew that I'd had nursing training in the War. He had compiled my files. He had watched me for years. I hesitated.

"Never mind," he said. "I can manage."

He dropped onto the floor next to his suitcase and jerked out a clean shirt.

I lowered myself next to him. "Lars—"

He turned his battered face to me. "Since we won't be seeing each other again, cards on the table."

I froze.

"I love you, Spatz." He looked utterly miserable. "I have for a very, very long time. I don't expect you to reciprocate it, but I would appreciate it if you could at least recognize it."

He knew more about me than anyone, even Boris. But what did I know about him? "I don't know what to say."

"No answer is an answer, too, isn't it?" He handed me two rolls of film, probably filled with photos of the documents I had come to Berlin to pick up and courier to Switzerland, and my atomizer. "Please be careful with this."

Then he stood and walked through the door that led to the bedroom.

I thought of gathering my belongings and leaving. If I did not trust him, that was what I must do. But I had trusted him for so long, and so deeply. Had I been wrong? I had been proved wrong about so many people I loved, from Boris to Bettina. I hated the thought of losing someone else.

I tried to think about what he had done, not just what he said in the warehouse. He had given me the atomizer to smuggle out, and he knew what it contained. Lars had attacked Hahn the minute he tried to hurt me, even though he must have known it was a suicidal act. Once the shooting started, he had thrown himself over me without a thought of the flying bullets, and he had protected my head instead of his own. His cold words in the warehouse did not match his actions.

What about since we met? After Anton and I fled in 1931, he had not turned me in to the Gestapo, even though he knew where I was during those years. It was unlikely that he'd had plans to use me to run a misinformation campaign at that time. I'd had no plans of ever returning to Germany. And when I was forced back into Germany in 1934, he had warned me off instead of arresting me, as he should have done. Since then, he had never pushed to meet my British contacts, although they were more valuable than I. His story to Hahn made sense only if one knew as much as Hahn had known. But I knew more. Everything I knew seemed to show that Lars had taken great risks to protect me, that he had always been honest with me even when lying would have been easier.

I hauled myself to my feet and rummaged in my satchel for the bottle from Frau Doktor Spiegel. Her words rang in my ears as I limped toward the door. "I have never known you to trust a man, not fully."

The bedroom contained only a single mattress tossed carelessly on the floor with a folded blanket on the end, but it did have a door that hopefully led to a bathroom.

Lars stood with his head leaned against the doorframe. He looked like he was listening, probably to hear the front door close behind me.

I watched him. My heart pounded and my palms felt clammy. Instead of running out the front door and not stopping until I was in Switzerland, I cleared my throat.

He turned to face me, eyes wary.

"Let's take a look at that rib," I said in a false hearty voice. I sounded like Sister Matilda.

He smiled.

I stepped past him. He followed me into the bathroom. He spared a quick glance at his reflection in the mirror, grimaced, and faced the window. Clear afternoon light shone through naked panes, illuminating his wrecked face.

I winced. "Let's start at the top."

I fingered the bump on his head, checked his pupils to make certain they were evenly dilated, as he had done for me two days before. "Have you felt nauseated at any time since you were hit?"

"Not counting when Hahn ran his gun all over you?"

I swallowed. "Not counting that."

"No."

I pulled the bottle of opium pills from my pocket. "Do you want one for the pain?"

He shook his head, lips pressed tight.

"Why not?"

"I might need to think."

"I can do the thinking for both of us," I said. "At least for the next few hours."

"I prefer to do my own."

I hardly blamed him. As I put the bottle back in my pocket I wondered if I was thinking or trying not to.

Lars bent his head into the sink and turned on the tap.

I stepped behind him and stroked my fingers gently through his wet hair to wash the blood out, directing the stream of water until it ran clear. A few seconds later, I realized that the blood was gone, but I still stood with my hands buried in his hair.

I wiped my hands on my skirt. "Do you want me to help you wash your face?"

He shook his head and ran his palms down his face, rinsed out his mouth, and spat into the sink. Blood. He poked his finger along the inside of his mouth, rinsed, and spat again. The water was mostly clear.

He stood and pushed wet hair out of his face. Water trickled down the front and back of his ruined shirt. "Better?"

Better than what? His nose was clearly broken, bruises had formed around both eyes, and he had a split lip. Blood spatters covered the front and back of his shirt. I feared once I got his shirt off, I would find at least one broken rib. I hesitated.

"You should see your face," he said gently. "I can't imagine you looked at patients so when you were a nurse."

"I did not bring about *their* wounds." I studied the white floor tiles. "If it were not for me, you would not have been in that warehouse."

"If it weren't for you, I wouldn't be here and safe, either."

"You seemed to be doing fairly well on your own." My eyes traced the thin gray lines between the floor tiles.

He tilted my chin with one hand so I had to meet his eyes. "I was floundering. I wanted to get as many of his men out of the warehouse as possible, and to get his guard down." He sighed. "But I lost control when he got on top of you. Which was exactly the kind of error he wished to provoke. If your friends hadn't arrived, Hahn's men would have shot us both."

I suppressed a shudder. It had been very close.

"I knew better." His voice was soft. "But where you are concerned, I cannot always stop myself from behaving irrationally."

My heart sped up. I knew what he meant.

"Hahn was correct about my feelings for you being my greatest weakness. But they are also, I think, my greatest strength." He stroked the corner of my mouth with one fingertip. An electric shock zinged from my lips down my spine.

I stepped away. "I th-think you have a broken rib."

He took a deep breath with a hitch at the end. "Or two."

"Stand still." I undid the buttons of his shirt with trembling fingers. I had to get myself under control. I slipped his shirt off, then carefully pulled his bloodstained undershirt over his head, holding it away from his swollen nose.

First I examined his back. Smooth and unblemished except for several scars that ran down the left side. Old wounds. I traced my fingers over them to see if any fragments lodged there.

"Shrapnel. From the War." Gooseflesh chased up his back. His voice grew husky. "But you can leave your hand there as long as you like."

I drew my hand back as if I had burned it.

He pivoted to face me. His chest was more muscular than I had expected. In all the years I had known him, I had never seen him with his shirt off. I ducked my head to hide my blush. I was no twelve-year-old schoolgirl. I had examined plenty of men wearing less when I was a nurse.

I pulled myself together and examined the bruise that darkened most of his left side. I gently felt his ribs. He inhaled sharply. Two ribs involved? "Hurts?"

"Yes."

I pressed my fingers more firmly against his injured ribs, trying to concentrate on my examination. "Breathe in."

His chest rose and fell, and his ribs moved together. Probably fractured, but in only one place. I did not think they had broken loose.

I put both palms against his chest, then placed my ear against his bare skin to listen, too distracted by the warmth of his skin under my cheek to hear anything but my own heartbeat. His breathing was uneven, but so was mine. I forced myself to listen carefully. His lungs sounded clear. I let out a breath I had not known I held.

"Good news?" he whispered, dropping his hands to the crown of my head.

I took my ear off his bare chest, but did not move my hands. "It will be painful for a while, and you must keep breathing deeply to avoid a lung infection."

With a voice less steady than I would have liked, I kept going. "I do not think the ribs are broken enough to puncture any organs."

"That makes me a lucky man."

I gave him an incredulous look.

"It's all about perspective," he said in a low voice. "Without your help, I could just as easily be dead on that warehouse floor."

The room spun. The red face on the concrete flashed through my head. I had killed Hahn. I knew he had been evil, that my action had saved my own life and the lives of others. But I had still taken a human life.

I stepped away, back bumping against the wall. Four men dead on the floor. Hahn. Bauer. The others. "All of it was because of me."

Lars looked startled. "No."

I shook my head. "If I were not here, they would not have been there either."

"They are Gestapo. They would have been in another room beating another person to death." His voice was angry.

"Not Bauer." My knees gave out. I slid down to the cold floor. "He was just a policeman. The only reason he is dead is because he recognized me at the stadium."

Lars knelt in front of me. "Recognized you and turned you in to the Gestapo."

I crossed my arms in front of my chest. I started to shake. I clenched my jaw, trying to bring it under control. "I did that."

Lars picked me up and carried me the few steps to the mattress.

My teeth chattered. I had murdered Hahn. Indirectly, I had killed the other men in the warehouse, too. All their days were gone. And mine were not. That was the trade I had made.

"Spatz." Lars folded me in his warm arms and rocked. "I am so sorry it had to come to that."

Much later, I stopped crying and shaking.

"Better?" he asked.

I shook my head. "Does it get better?"

"A little." He wiped tears off my cheeks with his palm. "Over a long time."

I hiccupped. "That is the most reassuring answer you have?"

"No. But it is the true one."

"How long?" I could not stand to feel like this for even another second. Four men dead because of me. I looked up at him. "How long?"

He kissed me with immense gentleness. I kissed him back. I had no room for anything but the feeling of his lips on mine. I sank into it and let everything else go.

When he pulled away, I whimpered. "Come back."

He lowered his head again, and I saw his split lip.

"Wait," I said. "Your lip—"

"Trust me, Spatz," he whispered, "this is exactly what my lips want to be doing."

He kissed me again. His hands explored my body as lightly as if I were made of glass, more tender than I had ever expected. I ran my hands down his scarred back. From far away, I heard him moan.

I pulled him closer. He felt warm and alive. I fit myself against him and fumbled with the buttons of his trousers.

"Spatz," he said with a catch in his voice. "Are you certain?"

"Please," I said. "Please don't stop."

As long as one of us was moving, I felt only passion. If one of us stopped, I thought of Hahn. I did not know if Lars knew what I thought, but he did not stop. Not for a long, long time. And when he did, I thought of nothing at all.

I awoke the next morning entwined with Lars. At some point, he must have thrown the blanket over us, although I did not remember it. Lying there felt warm and safe and simple. But, of course, it was not.

I tried to shift away from him, but his arms tightened around me. "Lars," I whispered.

He released me, and I propped myself up on my elbow to look at him. His face looked worse than ever, nose swollen, eyes bruised. But they certainly had not slowed him down the night before. My body still felt drugged.

Lars opened his eyes and smiled. "Good morning, Frau Schmidt."

So said my passport, my ring, and my wedding certificate, but I was not certain I was ready for that just yet, passionate night or no. "Good morning."

"One step at a time?" he said. He had, of course, noticed the missing *Herr Schmidt* in my reply.

"I think we have taken some fairly large steps recently." I traced my fingertips along his cheek, and he turned to kiss my palm. A shiver arced straight through me.

Much later, I dressed and fetched us food. Lars wanted to go in my stead, but finally admitted that his face might attract unwanted attention.

My limbs felt deliciously heavy as I smeared honey on a roll and handed it to him. We sat side by side on the wooden kitchen floor, backs against the wall. The room had no table or chairs, but I found I did not miss them as I leaned against him.

Lars Lang. I never would have thought of such a thing.

"Spatz? Your eyes are a million miles away."

"Just reviewing very recent events."

He smiled and leaned over to kiss me. "I could refresh your memory."

I kissed him back, surprised at how easy it was to let myself go and relax into him. Perhaps Frau Doktor Spiegel was correct about trust.

Lars pulled back and took a bite of his roll. "What's next?"

"I must call Bella and tell her we survived, plus arrange with her to keep reporting for Adelheid so that I do not lose my position at the paper. And so that Anton knows I am still alive."

He wiped his fingers on a dish towel I had purchased. "When do you go back to Switzerland?"

I could go back now, but I wanted to stay until he had healed enough to cross the border without attracting too much attention. And, selfishly, I wanted to have time alone with him. I took a deep breath, frightened of what I was about to say. "We go back to Switzerland after the Games."

He pulled me against his chest and held me there. "Not exactly," he said.

I sat up. "Lars?"

"I think I should go to Saratova first."

A weight settled in my stomach.

"I do not want to go either." His words came out fast, anticipating my dissent. "But I want to know more, enough to show the British how far along the Germans are in the manufacturing process. Perhaps that will frighten them enough to act."

Logically, his words made sense. But my heart did not want him to go. It was dangerous, and he might never come back. Now I knew how Boris felt. I swallowed it down and said only, "How long?"

He took my chin in his hand, and I stared into his worried dark eyes. "One month. No more. If I cannot find anything, I will leave regardless."

"I see." It was not my place to stop him any more than it was Boris's place to stop me. Like everything else, it was harder from this side.

He smiled at the expression on my face. "I promise."

I pulled my chin out his hand. What promises did I want from him? "I must go call Bella."

He cleared his throat. "I would like to accompany you."

"You still look like someone who has been through a Gestapo interrogation."

"The mere fact that I am outside and walking gives lie to your statement."

"But, Lars—"

"I cannot stay in here forever, especially if you are not here to . . . occupy me."

I would not have wanted to be shut up in the apartment either. I pulled Peter Weill's fedora out of my satchel and placed it on Lars's head. When I tilted it forward, it hid his bruised eyes. There was nothing to be done about his swollen nose.

We walked down the stairs hand in hand.

At the side of the car, Lars held out his hand for the car keys, but I kept them. "I will drive."

"I am perfectly capable—"

"Of driving with a concussion?"

"I can do many things with a concussion," he said. "You may recall."

I blushed. "One thing you can do is be passenger in a car."

I opened his door. He hesitated, then got in.

We drove to a phone booth, where I called Bella. Lars stayed in the front seat, fedora pulled so low, it looked like he was napping.

I fed my pfennigs into the slot and made my connection.

"Hello?" asked a cultured male voice. Friend or manservant?

"This is . . . Petra Weill. I wish to speak to Bella Fromm."

"I will ascertain whether she is available." His voice gave away no hint one way or the other.

I waited in the booth. Lars fidgeted with his hat, adjusting the brim up and down by millimeters, more nervous about being seen than he wanted to admit.

Men walked by on the sidewalk in light summer shirts, women in colorful dresses holding their hands. A young boy with a brown mutt passed the booth. A sunny late-summer afternoon scene unscrolled before me. All felt peaceful and soothing, yet yesterday I had almost died on a warehouse floor.

"It is I," said Bella.

"Petra." I pictured her in an elegant parlor, although I had never been to her house.

"Last time I saw you, you had rather too many dance partners." Her voice sounded calm, as if the last time she saw me, I had been on the dance floor, not being dragged off by four thugs.

"I discarded that dance card," I said. "I am now with the partner I had at the beginning of the event."

"Such a lucky girl."

"Indeed." I thought about the bullet-ridden bodies. Today I felt guilt for having killed Hahn, but also relief that he was dead. As Lars had pointed out, killing Hahn had saved many other women from torture. But, as Lars had also pointed out, I also wished that it had not been necessary.

"I am pleased to hear it, of course, but is that the reason for your call?"

"I am calling about my homework," I said, leaning against the side of the telephone booth. "You offered to help me."

"The fencing article?" She sounded relieved to start talking about something concrete.

"Please." I pulled out my notebook and held my fountain pen at the ready.

Bella recited off statistics for the day, including a few amusing anecdotes, and mentioned that the Negroes on the American team were wreaking havoc on Hitler's ideology. Archibald Williams won a gold medal for the four hundred meter, Jesse Owens, the hero of the event, had three gold medals to his credit, and there was speculation that he might be included in the hundred-meter relay team, which would give him the chance to win a fourth. The basketball elimination matches had also happened, although they were not well attended, as it was a new sport this Olympics. The Americans seemed likely to win that, too.

Bella and I fixed a time to call back on the following day. By then, Lars had climbed out of the car and was feeding the sparrows crumbs he must have secreted away during breakfast.

"Thank you, Bella," I said. "Tomorrow."

"I enjoy our conversations, Petra," she answered. "And I have one more message for you."

"Yes?" I kept the surprise out of my voice.

"A Panzer gave me a letter for you."

No last names. "Indeed?"

"Shall I open it?"

"Of course." As if he heard the tension in my voice through the glass, Lars turned to face me. I smiled and waved. He raised his hand in return, but I could not see if he smiled under the brim of his hat.

Paper crackled on Bella's end of the telephone, and then there were several seconds of silence. I imagined her pursing her perfectly formed lips, reading and trying to figure out how to pass the message on without revealing anything.

"Panzer begs your forgiveness. . . ." Her voice trailed off.

"He does?"

"He does. He mentions an incident on Unter den Linden."

So Panzer had tried to run me over, after all. "Does he explain why?"

She sighed irritably. This was clearly complicated enough without me asking questions. I waited.

"He says," she continued, "that he was drunk and upset and did not really know what he was doing. And that he regrets it deeply. And that is all."

"I appreciate his apology." I was relieved to know who that enemy had been, but it still hurt to know that my Brüderchen had tried to kill me.

"I imagine it's better not to have anything to apologize for," Bella said.

We said our good-byes.

I broke the connection and joined Lars.

"What happened?" Lars asked.

He wrapped his arm around my waist and I leaned against him, enjoying the peace and the sun.

"Spatz?"

There was no need for any more secrets between us. "Peter Weill, the son, hit me with the car."

His arm tightened. "Isn't it bad enough that you have political enemies without creating personal ones?"

"I did not make him an enemy. He did that himself, the same as Hahn." I stepped away from him. "I need to find another telephone booth to call in my story."

Lars took a deep breath and let it go.

And so it went over the rest of the week. Every day, I called Bella, wrote down the details, and called my happy editor in Switzerland to file my stories. Finding a pair of new booths every day became a game to distract us from our inevitable parting.

Germany had, predictably, dominated the Games. It won a total of eighty-nine medals: thirty-three gold, twenty-six silver, and thirty bronze. The Americans came in second with twenty-four gold, twenty silver, and twelve bronze medals. Switzerland came in sixteenth, with fifteen medals: one gold, nine silver, and five bronze. Nine of the Swiss victories were from its celebrated gymnastics team. I wished I had actually seen them.

I also met with Wilhelm and he agreed to look up my file, and Lars's, to see what Hahn had recorded there. A few days later we discovered that Hahn had not recorded anything at all, probably too worried to admit that Lars had fooled him and thinking that killing him would solve the problem more easily.

That week, Lars was lighthearted and witty and an incredible lover. But I knew that we had one stolen week and after that, everything would change again.

Lars had been so many men since I met him: anti-Semite and proper police kommissar, spy against the SS for the British, witness to women being tortured, and finally, caring and charming lover. Who would Lars be in Switzerland? How would Anton react to him? How would Boris?

What would our lives be like if we tried to create a normal relationship? What would life be like if we did not? I tried to push these worries from my thoughts so that I could enjoy our few uncomplicated days. With luck, we would have time to sort things out in Switzerland.

Lars healed quickly. Shortly before I left Berlin, he took a train to Saratova, Russia, to investigate Project Zephyr. He again promised to join me in Zürich in a month's time, but I worried that he might change his mind, or something might happen to him in Saratova.

So I stood alone next to two customs officers in a train car on the Swiss border, hoping that Adelheid's passport would pass muster one more time. Herr Silbert's work had always been impeccable, but my mouth grew dry as they read the document.

"Excuse me," asked the first customs officer. His bristling mustache looked like a caterpillar on his face. "Did you buy this in Germany?"

In his hand he held my Le Kid, still full of poison.

"This is old. I paid those duties long ago."

He held it to the light, studying the silver mother-of-pearl.

Panic flashed across my stomach. "A gift from my husband," I lied.

His fellow officer, an older man who walked with a pronounced limp, said, "Your wife would love it."

I took out my wallet. "I am more than happy to pay the dues again. How much might they be?"

The younger one named an amount triple what the dues should have been. A bribe. I carefully counted out all the money I had.

It was not enough.

I showed him my empty wallet. "Please," I said. "Just this once."

He studied me for a moment, then folded the money I had given him and stuck it in his pocket. "Just this once," he said. He handed me the atomizer.

I breathed a sigh of relief. I had enough information now to carry out Peter's news. I could write this last story for him.

I tucked the silver cylinder back into my satchel. It had cost so much more than money already.

Glossary

Alexanderplatz. Central police station for Berlin through World War II. Also called "the Alex."

Delmer, Sefton. British journalist for the *Daily Express*. He was bureau chief in Berlin (1928 to 1933) and later worked all over Europe. He eventually became a spy for the British government and sent black propaganda radio broadcasts into Germany.

Fromm, Bella. A German Jewish aristocrat who worked as a reporter in Berlin in the 1920s and 1930s. Her fascinating diaries have been published as *Blood and Banquets: A Berlin Social Diary*.

Führer, Der. "The leader." Term used to refer to Adolf Hitler, leader of the National Socialist Party.

Garmisch-Partenkirchen. German towns that hosted the 1936 Winter Olympic Games. The cities (along with Munich) have recently put in a bid to host the 2018 Winter Olympics.

Hall of the Unnamed Dead. Hall in the Alexanderplatz police station that showed framed photographs of unidentified bodies found by the police.

Hauptmann. Rank in the German army equivalent to captain.

Hauptsturmführer. Rank in the German Sonderstaffel (SS) equivalent to captain.

"Horst Wessel Song." Anthem of the Nazi party. The lyrics were written by Horst Wessel, a Sturmabteilung (SA) commander in Berlin.

He was killed by Communists in 1930, and the song later became the official anthem. Since the end of World War II, the music and lyrics have been illegal in Germany and Austria.

Hotel Adlon. Expensive hotel in Berlin, built in 1907. It quickly became known for its vast wine cellars and well-heeled clientele. On May 2, 1945, the main building was burned to the ground, either accidentally or deliberately, by Russian soldiers. The East German government opened a surviving wing as a hotel, but demolished it in 1961 to create the no-man's-land around the Berlin Wall. A new Hotel Adlon was rebuilt on the original location and opened on August 23, 1997.

Kommissar. Rank in the police department similar to a lieutenant.

Korn schnapps. Strong German alcoholic drink.

National Socialist German Workers party (Nazi party). Party led by Adolf Hitler that assumed control of Germany in 1933.

Obersturmbannführer. Rank in the SS equivalent to lieutenant colonel.

Paragraph 175. Paragraph of the German penal code that made homosexuality a crime. Paragraph 175 was in place from 1871 to 1994. Under the Nazis, people convicted of Paragraph 175 offenses, which did not need to include physical contact, were sent to concentration camps, where many died.

Pfennigs. Similar to pennies. There were one hundred pfennigs in a Reichsmark.

Reichsmark. Currency used by Germany from 1924 to 1948. The previous currency, the Papiermark, became worthless in 1923 due to hyperinflation. On January 1, 1923, one American dollar was worth nine thousand Papiermarks. By November 1923, one American dollar was worth 4.2 trillion Papiermarks. Fortunes were wiped out overnight. In 1924, the currency was revalued and remained fairly stable until the Wall Street crash in the United States in 1929. When the novel takes place, one American dollar was worth approximately 2.48 Reichsmarks.

Riefenstahl, Leni. Dancer, actress, film director, and photographer. Among other films, she made the famous Nazi propaganda films *Tri-*

umph of the Will and *The Olympiad* (about the 1936 Berlin Olympics). After World War II, she was discredited because of her links to Hitler and the Nazi party. In the 1970s, she wrote an award-winning series of photography books about the Nuba people in Africa. Her final film was an underwater documentary completed when she was one hundred years old.

Röhm, Ernst. Early member of the National Socialist party and close friend to Adolf Hitler, often credited with being the man most responsible for bringing Hitler to power in the early days. Openly gay.

Schrader, Gerhard. German chemist sometimes called "the father of nerve gas" because he invented both tabun and sarin.

Schutzstaffel (SS or blackshirts). Nazi paramilitary organization founded as an elite force to be used as Hitler's personal bodyguards. Led by Heinrich Himmler.

Spatz. Sparrow. A German term of endearment.

Sturmabteilung (SA, brownshirts, or storm troopers). Nazi paramilitary organization that helped intimidate Hitler's opponents. Led by Ernst Röhm.

Sturmbannführer. Rank in the SS equivalent to major.

Tabun. The first nerve gas. It was created in Germany in late 1936 by Gerhard Schrader, who was researching insecticides.

Tiergarten. Park in central Berlin.

Treaty of Versailles. A peace treaty that negotiated the end of World War I between Germany and the Allied powers.

UFA (Universum Film AG). Principal film studio in Germany during the Weimar Republic and World War II. UFA went out of business after World War II, but now produces movies and TV shows.

Winnetou. The Apache brave hero in a series of bestselling books written by German author Karl May. Originally published in the late 1800s, the novels are still very popular today.

Author's Note

A Game of Lies is set in the 1936 Berlin Olympic Games. Most characters in the book are fictional, and I took great liberties with those
who weren't (Sefton Delmer, Bella Fromm, and Leni Riefenstahl). For
a list of real people who appear in the book, just skim the glossary.

The novel does deal with real events, including the discovery of the
first-ever nerve agent, tabun, by a German scientist. Tabun was not
discovered until December 1936, but I moved it up a few months so
that Hannah could investigate it during the Olympics. No actual bunnies were harmed in the writing of this book. For that matter, I don't
know if tabun was ever tested on rabbits. But according to Sefton
Delmer's autobiography, *Trail Sinister*, the Germans did develop and
test chemical weapons at the Russian town of Saratov beginning in
1927.

The 1936 Olympics were indeed held in Berlin, and the big story
of the Games was not Aryan supremacy, but rather the exploits of a
young black man from Ohio: Jesse Owens. He and the other black
athletes did exceptionally well in the Games. The eighteen black athletes who competed for Team USA won fourteen medals. In further
defiance of the Nazi ideology, Jewish athletes from Hungary, the
USA, Canada, Belgium, Austria, Germany (Helene Mayer, female
fencer and the only Jewish athlete to compete for Germany), and Poland won thirteen medals.

I used the flower names as resistance fighters to pay tribute to the White Rose, a nonviolent resistance group in Munich whose members were caught and executed at Stadelheim Prison in 1943.

On a lighter note, I struggled with the zipper in the back of Hannah's dress just as much as she did. That scene is much better with a zipper than buttons, but most women's dresses did not have zippers in 1936. I finally found that Elsa Schiaparelli used zippers in her avant-garde gowns in the early 1930s, so I had Hannah rent one of those.

When Hannah says, "I can do the thinking for both of us," she paraphrases Ilsa from *Casablanca,* except in *A Game of Lies,* both she and Lars Lang insisted on doing the thinking for themselves.